Passi

Awareness doused Maggie like a pail of cold water. Her eyes snapped open . . .

"Where are we?"

He tightened his arms around her. "In the ruins. I found you asleep." Shifting positions, he covered her with his full length.

A tidal wave of sensations flooded Maggie. And needs. Needs she couldn't define or identify. Needs as primitive as the shelter over her head. The quivering in her stomach reached lower until it settled in the private place between her legs. She groaned, and he caught the sound with his mouth. His lips moved against hers with practiced ease.

She took his kiss, her tongue welcoming his with the hunger of a woman too long denied . . .

DIAMOND WILDFLOWER ROMANCE

A breathtaking line of searing romance novels . . . where destiny meets desire in the untamed fury of the American West.

Lightning Strikes

Jean Wilson

DIAMOND BOOKS, NEW YORK

This book is a Diamond original edition,
and has never been previously published.

LIGHTNING STRIKES

A Diamond Book / published by arrangement with
the author

PRINTING HISTORY
Diamond edition / August 1994

ISBN: 0-7865-0024-7

Diamond Books are published by The Berkley Publishing Group,
200 Madison Avenue, New York, NY 10016.
DIAMOND and the "D" design
are trademarks belonging to Charter Communications, Inc.

PRINTED IN THE UNITED STATES OF AMERICA

10 9 8 7 6 5 4 3 2 1

To Don,
my husband,
who loves me in spite of;

To Jeanne, Carl, and Debi,
my children,
who love me because of;

To Kyle and Karissa,
my grandchildren,
who love me anyway;

And to Metsy, Erica, Terry, Karen,
and all the "Renegades"
for their support, encouragement, and love.

Lightning Strikes

Chapter One

"Don't move and don't make a sound."

The voice behind Maggie Callahan was barely audible, a raspy growl at her ear. But the cold hard steel pressed against the base of her skull and the click of the hammer spoke loud and clear.

Maggie's heart slammed against her ribs. Her gaze dropped to the rifle at her side; but before she had time to think, a gloved hand snatched it out of her reach. She bit her lower lip to keep the cry muzzled in her throat.

Too late she remembered Aunt Olivia's warning about the dangers on the Western frontier, of desperate men committing unspeakable deeds. Was this one of the marauding outlaws she'd heard about?

All warmth drained from her body. Not daring to move or glance over her shoulder, Maggie stared into the darkness beyond the glowing campfire. A burning log snapped and shot white sparks into the air.

"What do you want?" She squeezed the words around the lump in her throat.

"Food . . . and a horse."

Hands trembling, she emptied the leftover stew into a tin dish, knowing her best chance of survival was to do as the man ordered. Lord, she prayed, don't let Tim or Sarah wake up. A man without a conscience would think nothing of raping a woman, and killing two youngsters as well.

When their guide, Grady, had gone into town for supplies, Maggie thought she'd be safe in this isolated valley. He promised to be back in one day, and she wanted to stay behind to print the negatives she'd made during the past week. Would Grady return to find three bodies rotting in the sun?

"Coffee," the man added in a low, hesitant tone. "Set it down and don't turn around."

From the corner of her eye she spotted the shadowed movement behind her. She filled a mug with hot, strong coffee, and a hand took it from her.

"Thank you," he whispered.

A polite desperado? Maggie didn't dare hope the man would leave without harming her or her brother and sister. A rope of fear tightened around her chest.

Maggie shrugged deeper into Papa's woolen jacket against the chill of the dark night. Even in July the Rocky Mountains grew cold after sunset. Low-hanging clouds blotted out the moon and stars. The mournful call of an owl and the occasional wail of a coyote tore through the bleak silence. While the world slept the creatures of the night prowled the lonely hills.

Beyond the blazing campfire, she could pick out nothing—not the canvas tent, the white-topped covered wagon, or the photographic wagon containing the cameras and load of equipment necessary for a working picture taker. The sky was as black as the inside of her darkroom where she developed the glass plates for her photographs.

She should have gone to bed hours ago, but some instinct, some premonition, had made her too nervous for sleep. The fire repelled the predatory animals, and the only men she'd seen for days were the cowboys she'd photographed while hidden in a stand of trees. They hadn't seen her and Tim, and by now they were miles away with their herd of cattle. Maggie had only her wits to deal with this human predator.

Behind her, the man's gasping breath and the clink of the

spoon told her he was still there. "The only horses we have are for our wagons. I don't have a saddle." Her voice grated in the grim silence.

"Don't need one."

He coughed, and for the first time Maggie identified the odor she'd tried for weeks to forget—dried blood. Before finally giving in to consumption, Papa had choked up what looked like gallons of life-giving blood.

"I'll leave mon . . ." His words faded. The clang of metal striking a stone and the thud of an object hitting the ground brought Maggie to her feet.

Heedless of the consequences, she spun around. Her battered felt hat flew off, and her braid escaped down her back.

A large figure lay crumbled on the ground, a revolver inches from his hand. Snatching the gun, she pointed it in the vicinity of the man's chest. She would teach him not to threaten Mary Margaret Callahan.

"Get up," she ordered, the gun giving her a certain amount of bravado. He didn't move, and his breath came in shallow gasps. "I said get up." This time she nudged him with the toe of her boot. He remained as still as death.

Straining to see into the night, she searched for another figure possibly lurking in the shadows. For several heart-stopping moments she waited, listening, watching. A red-hot log cracked in the fire, and her heart pounded in her ears. As far as she could tell, she was alone with this dark, ominous stranger.

Was he pretending and would he pounce on her if she got too close? Her finger closed on the trigger of his gun. Although she'd had little experience with firearms before leaving St. Louis three months before, Grady had given her basic instructions. A big man was an easy target.

"I've got your gun and I'm not afraid to use it." Still no answer. Had he struck his head and knocked himself unconscious?

Keeping the gun on him, she stuck a twig into the fire for a makeshift torch. Cautiously she moved closer, holding the dim flame in front of her. His hat had fallen off, and black hair tumbled across his forehead.

He lifted his head and started to move. "Don't point—"

His head dropped back to the ground, and his eyes closed.

"Oh, no," she moaned. "He's dead." A rusty, brown stain spread across his buckskin jacket.

His raspy breathing sounded much like Papa's death rattle. Leaning over, she eased her fingers into his shirt and searched for a heartbeat. Under blood-matted hair, his skin was icy. Several seconds passed before she felt the beat— weak but steady. He was alive, but not for long if he didn't get some help.

She looked at her fingers, sticky with his blood, and struggled with her conscience. A strange affinity for him curled through her heart. Even an outlaw didn't deserve to die on the cold hard ground. She shoved the gun into the waistband of her canvas breeches, hoping she would not regret her decision.

"Sarah . . . Tim," she called. Her voice ricocheted across the lonely hills.

As much as she hated involving the youngsters with this bandit, she needed their help—and Sarah's skill.

While she waited for her brother and sister to respond, she studied the man further. His buckskin jacket was new and soft, of fine quality, and his broadcloth shirt was stiff with dried blood. A new wetness began to spread across his right shoulder near a hole in the material. His skin was gray, the color of ashes. Even with the dark stubble on his square jaw, he didn't look like her idea of an outlaw.

But how would she know what a murderer or a thief looked like? Until Papa had returned to St. Louis five years ago, she'd lived a quiet, sheltered life with her aunt Olivia. The only bandits she'd encountered were in the newspaper stories about the James brothers and in books like *Robin Hood*.

"Maggie, what's wrong?" Sarah's youthful voice pulled her out of her reverie.

Tim shoved his sister aside and knelt beside Maggie. "Holy cow! What happened?"

Sarah hesitated while she tightened the belt of her flannel wrapper. "Who is he?"

Maggie shrugged. "I don't know."

"Did you shoot him?" Tim asked.

"No, but somebody did." There was no use alarming

them with the fact that the man would have killed all of them if given the chance.

"Is he dead?"

"He's not far from it. He's lost a lot of blood and needs our help." *And if he's fortunate enough to live, he'll probably be facing a hangman's noose.*

Sarah stared at the man, alarm in her green eyes. "Maggie, this isn't a dog with a lame leg, or a bird with a broken wing. I've never tended a gunshot wound."

Maggie draped her arm across her half sister's slender shoulder. "We don't have a choice. Since we can't get him to a doctor, we've got to stop the bleeding and try to prevent infection. His life is in our hands."

She swallowed her own trepidation and put on a brave front. After all, Papa had trusted Maggie with his two younger children. He expected her to make the right decisions for all of them. Something deep inside told her helping this stranger was both right and proper—what Papa would have wanted.

"Just do your best. Remember what you learned in all those hours you spent volunteering at the hospital and following Dr. Henderson around."

Sarah fingered the medallion that hung from the chain around her neck. The gold disk had been given to Sarah by her Indian mother and was the girl's most prized possession. At times Maggie suspected the emblem had mystical powers. The strange markings were of some ancient people, and had been almost worn off. Sarah touched it often, as if to gain wisdom and strength from the talisman.

The expression in Sarah's eyes changed. Determination replaced uncertainty. "Do you think we can carry him to the wagon?" She pressed her delicate hand to the stranger's forehead. "He's freezing and it's getting colder."

"He's pretty big, and I doubt we can lift him. We'll get him closer to the fire while you get the bag of medicine."

Careful not to jostle the man unnecessarily, they worked together to move him. Sarah spread a blanket on the ground, and Maggie and Tim rolled him onto it.

Tim held the coal-oil lamp and the revolver while Maggie removed the man's jacket and blood-soaked shirt. His wide

chest rose and fell with every strangled breath. A steady
trickle of blood seeped from the life-threatening injury.

Helping this man was a tall order for Sarah, but the girl
was more than capable.

After Maggie's mother had died, her father, Michael, had
married a Shoshone princess, Rising Sun. The beautiful
young woman had given him two children, Sarah and Tim.
As the daughter of a great shaman, Rising Sun had been
skilled in the healing arts of her people. She'd passed her
gift and her knowledge to Sarah.

With slow, trembling hands, Maggie cut away his under-
shirt and studied the injury. A bullet had passed through the
man's right shoulder, and he'd lost a lot of blood. So far
there was no infection, but without care he might not
survive.

Maggie shivered at the thought. In her short twenty-three
years, she had witnessed too much death—first her mother,
then Rising Sun, and most recently her father. Now she was
working to save the life of a stranger who had threatened to
kill her.

Tim put a pot of water on the fire to boil. Maggie wrung
out a clean cloth to wash away the dried blood. Hands
shaking, she touched the man's bare skin and found the
varying textures of his skin intriguing. His chest was wide,
and springy black curls covered taut muscles. She'd never
touched a man this intimately before, and to her surprise she
found the experience not at all unpleasant.

He flinched when she touched the area around the wound.
Warning herself to be careful, Maggie worked as gently as
possible. When she finished, Sarah took out the bag of roots
and herbs she'd collected in the mountains and mixed a
strange-smelling potion.

Using the knowledge and skill learned from generations
of her mother's people, Sarah worked through the night to
save the stranger's life. With a competence that surprised
even Maggie, the girl cleaned the damaged flesh with
ointments and cauterized the wound. Maggie held the man
down to keep him quiet during the operation.

Once the man opened his eyes and tried to sit up. Maggie
forced him to drink some of the medicine. His struggles
stopped, and she wasn't sure if he was asleep or if he'd

fainted, but he didn't make a sound until Sarah began to close the wound. A low moan came from deep inside him, and Maggie's heart constricted at the mournful sound.

Sarah prepared a poultice, and Maggie placed her hands on his chest and shoulder while Sarah dressed the wound. His heartbeat was strong and steady under her palm.

The sun was spreading its first golden rays across the eastern sky when Sarah finally pressed a piece of white linen to his shoulder and Maggie bound his arm to keep him from tearing it open in his sleep. She wrapped another blanket around him.

When they'd done all they could, Sarah added a Christian prayer, learned from their Irish father, to the skills learned from her Shoshone mother. Sarah placed her hand over his heart and looked up at Maggie. "This man is in a great deal of pain."

"I know. But you've done your best. No doctor could have done better."

"That isn't what I mean. It isn't physical pain. Something in his life has made him very sad. There's a shadow over his heart."

"Sarah, he's probably an outlaw on the run. We've done all we can to help him. If he gets a fever or an infection, we'll have to take him to a doctor."

Her limbs stiff from kneeling on the ground, Maggie stood and stretched. "Try to get some sleep. I'll watch him."

"You have to rest, too." Tim turned down the lamp and tossed another log on the fire. His thoughtfulness made Maggie smile. Since their father's death, Tim had proudly stepped into the role of man of the family—much too big a load for a twelve-year-old boy.

She shoved him and Sarah toward the covered wagon and tent that were their temporary homes. In another month, when the photographic assignment was finished, they would settle in Denver and open the gallery. And sleep in real beds for the first time in months.

"You've both done your share and you need your rest. I'll watch in case he wakes up. I'll call if I need help."

Tim returned seconds later with a thick quilt and draped it over Maggie's shoulders. She whispered her thanks and

sat on the ground with her back propped against a spruce.
Carefully she wrapped her fingers around the revolver.

She studied the man again. His ebony hair glistened in the
pale morning light. Although he was darkly tanned, his skin
lacked the leathery texture of a man who spent his life in the
sunshine, and his clothes seemed out of character for an
outlaw. His buckskin jacket and Wellington boots were very
expensive, and his black canvas trousers hugged long,
powerful legs.

He tossed his head and turned his face toward Maggie.
Under the thick stubble of beard, a long white scar marred
the sculptured line of his cheek.

A strange fluttering twisted deep inside Maggie. How had
he gotten the scar? she wondered. In a fight or a duel? The
mark didn't at all deter from his looks, only made him more
interesting and mysterious. More than anything, she wanted
to know how he had gotten a bullet hole in his shoulder.

Since none of her questions would be answered until he
regained consciousness, Maggie closed her eyes. What
seemed like only seconds later, the loud squawk of a blue
jay jolted her awake. She hadn't meant to fall asleep, but the
long night must have caught up with her. Rubbing her eyes,
she looked around.

Proudly displaying his sapphire plumage, the bird darted
from one branch to another, and a gray squirrel scurried up
the trunk of a towering pine. Warmed by the sunshine
filtering through the canopy of leaves overhead, she
shrugged off the quilt and heavy coat. Thankful for another
bright cloudless day, she sat up with a start. How could she
waste the valuable sunlight needed for printing her photographs?

Once she scrambled to her feet, she spotted the stranger
lying on a blanket. Her heart constricted. She'd promised to
watch over the man, but instead she'd fallen asleep. He
opened his eyes, groaned, and blinked. Maggie gazed into
eyes as blue as the Colorado sky above. The contrast
between his dark coloring and bright eyes was as startling as
a flash of lightning in the midnight sky.

He squinted into the glaring sunshine and tried to
remember. Who was he? Where was he? What had hap-

pened? He took a deep breath and gasped at the pain. That was all he remembered. Pain and walking. Then nothing.

Squeezing his eyes shut, he struggled to clear the cobwebs from his brain. From a mist as thick as the fog on the Thames River came his father's voice. "Geoffrey Andrew Wexford, you killed your mother, and your carelessness killed your brother. One day you'll kill yourself, too."

He had almost succeeded this time, that much was certain. Unless he was already dead and this was hell. Using all his limited strength, he opened his eyes. Relief surged through him. Hell didn't have blue skies and green trees. He focused his gaze on the figure next to him. Or women who looked like angels.

"Where am I?" He choked the words from his parched throat.

"In my camp," replied a soft, female voice.

"What happened?" He tried to lift his head, but it fell back. Pain throbbed in his shoulder, though not as tormenting as the previous night.

"Don't you remember?" The woman squatted beside him and pressed the back of her hand to his forehead. Her gentle fingers were warm on his skin. "You threatened to kill me before you passed out. I suppose I should have left you to bleed to death, but we did our best to patch you up."

A vague memory crowded into his consciousness. After stumbling through the wilderness for two days, he'd come upon a camp. But she had to be mistaken; he would never threaten a woman. "Water, please."

She reached into the bucket next to the campfire and pulled out a ladle. She slid her hand under his head and held the cup to his dry, parched lips. He choked on the first swallow, but continued until he drank his fill. The cool, fresh water eased his thirst and chased the haze from his mind. His gaze locked on the woman.

Wisps of auburn hair escaped the braid that brushed her shoulder. She was pretty, not beautiful, but more than attractive in spite of the frown that pulled her lips to a thin line. Long dark lashes shaded incredible green eyes, eyes that showed every emotion. He read uneasiness in her look. Not fear, or anxiety, merely confusion, as if she didn't know what to do about him.

"Are you in a lot of pain?" she asked.

The blanket slipped, and for the first time he noticed his bandaged right shoulder. Surely she wasn't part of the outlaw gang. They would have hastened his death, not tried to prevent it.

"Yes." He reached for the bandage, but his arm wouldn't move. Alarm slashed through him. The nightmare wasn't over—he was paralyzed. "Can't move my arm."

She sat back on her heels, and without touching him, she drew the blanket to his chin. "We tied your arm to your side so you wouldn't tear open the wound. It was for your protection as well as ours. I have your gun, so don't try anything funny."

He wiggled his fingers. He was her prisoner, but he was all in one piece. "Madam, are you threatening me with an empty gun?"

"Empty?" She picked up the Colt Peacemaker he'd purchased in Cheyenne and weighed it in her hand. The costly .45-caliber revolver boasted fine engraving and a smooth black grip. She swung open the barrel and glared at him through narrowed eyes. "That's no excuse for pointing it at me."

"I wasn't going to hurt you." Since she'd been dressed in men's breeches and a heavy coat, he hadn't known she was a woman. Now, in the daylight, he wondered how he could have made the mistake. The buttons of the shirt strained against her breasts, and her hips filled out the trousers like no man he'd ever seen. He forced his thoughts back to the situation at hand. "Did you treat my injury?"

She moved to the fire and began to build it up for cooking. "We did our best, but you need a doctor. We'll turn you over to the sheriff when we get to town."

"I am not an outlaw."

Hands on her hips, she turned and narrowed her eyes. "Could have fooled me. You asked for food and tried to steal my horses."

He paused for a moment, gathering strength. Who could blame her for being suspicious? Hadn't he come out of the darkness and stuck his gun in her back? "I was prepared to pay for what I took."

"Sure. And the next thing you're going to tell me is that you accidentally shot yourself with your empty gun."

"Dear lady," he whispered, his strength waning, "I am too weak to argue with you. I'll be happy to continue when I'm stronger."

"Just tell me your name."

"Wexford."

"British?"

He grunted and managed to release his hand from his bonds. The numbness eased as he flexed his fingers. "Yes, I suppose my accent gave me away."

A tiny smile curved her lips and transformed the pretty woman into a real beauty. "No Westerner I've ever met speaks with that proper King's English." She set a pot on the fire. "I'll fix some coffee, and when you're stronger you can tell me why you were sneaking around my camp in the dark of night."

Maggie felt his gaze on her while she worked. From time to time she slanted a glance at him. In spite of his pain, his blue eyes were alert and intelligent. Before long, she had coffee made and a pot of oatmeal on the fire. She spooned the food into a bowl and returned to his side.

"Would you like to try some of this?" she offered.

He frowned, but nodded his assent.

"Mr. Ford. This isn't London. We're in the middle of the Rockies. There aren't any inns nearby, and my kitchen staff has deserted me. It's either gruel, or you go hungry. Your choice."

"I am not complaining. Thank you for sharing your hospitality." His haughty tone irritated Maggie, but she refused to let him know.

"My aunt taught me to help those less fortunate," she said in a vain attempt to put the stranger in his place. "If you had asked last night, I would gladly have fed you."

"I really am sorry." He stumbled on the words, as if unaccustomed to any type of apology. Arrogance glittered in his eyes.

Just like a Brit, she thought, her temper rising. Papa had told her about the English lord who owned the estates in Ireland where he'd lived before coming to America. Although the tenants were starving because of the potato famine, the lord cared more for his horses than the people. Well, this Englishman was in no position to act so high-and-mighty. He owed his life to the children of an Irish immigrant.

Maggie knelt beside him, thankful she was wearing her breeches instead of a cumbersome skirt. "I'll have to feed you. I don't think you can handle a bowl with one hand."

"Especially since it's tied at my side."

"I'll untie you later. Meanwhile, I'll fold a quilt under your head so you can eat."

He swallowed the first spoonful of food. "Are you going to tell me your name?"

She gave him a sip of coffee. "Maggie Callahan." With one finger she dabbed a drop from the corner of his mouth. Maggie resisted the urge to swipe her fingers across his full lower lip and along the long white scar under his growth of beard.

"A lovely Irish lady with green eyes and red hair."

Self-conscious, Maggie turned away from his penetrating gaze. The smile in his eyes meant to disarm her only raised her hackles. "My father was an Irish immigrant, but I'm an American from St. Louis."

"Forgive me. I didn't mean to offend you."

She tilted her chin. "I'm not offended. It might be fair to warn you that like most Irish I have little love for Englishmen." She tilted her chin at a proud angle. "You might be interested in knowing Papa left Ireland because he killed an English lord."

The man choked, and Maggie gave him a drink of water to clear his throat. "How interesting."

"The great landowner was letting his tenants starve while his horses grew fat. When Papa caught the man attacking a young woman, his temper exploded. Of course, Papa didn't intend to kill the man." She shrugged. "Accidents happen. He stowed away on a ship to America and changed his name." She narrowed her eyes in a sign of warning. Not that she would ever hurt another human being, but it didn't hurt to put a little fear into her uninvited guest.

Further conversation was cut off when she slid another spoonful of oatmeal into his mouth. She watched his lips move as he savored the food, not that it was very good.

Maggie had never bothered to learn to cook; photography was her life, her love, her occupation. She was thankful Sarah had taken over the cooking and "household" chores.

The man swallowed slowly, then swiped at his mouth with his tongue. He widened his eyes in a silent plea for more.

Maggie's heart tripped, and her breath caught in her throat. Inwardly she cursed herself for the way the man affected her. An outlaw—and an Englishman to boot. She looked down and found him studying her through thick dark lashes.

"Where is your husband?" He nodded to the tents and wagons across the campsite.

Although Maggie abhorred deceit of any kind, self-preservation took priority over honesty. For all their sakes, it would be safer to let him think a man was nearby. She hoped her guarded response would satisfy his curiosity. "Grady will be back anytime now."

His eyes widened. "He left you alone without a man to protect you?" By now the bowl was empty, and he'd finished the coffee.

His typically male attitude irritated her. Her former fiancé, Harry, had talked about protecting her, too, until she'd learned he was more interested in her inheritance than in her. She tilted her chin. "I can take care of myself."

Before he could respond, Sarah ran toward them, her skirt lifted above her ankles. "Is he awake? Why didn't you call me?"

"You needed your sleep, and I can feed him." Maggie set the bowl and cup aside. "I fixed breakfast."

Sarah wrinkled her nose; her green eyes sparkled with mischief. "Maggie, you know that's my job. I hope you don't poison us."

Maggie laughed and tugged at her younger sister's long braid. "We'll find out soon enough. I fed some to our guest. He cleaned his bowl."

The man turned pale, but didn't respond to her barb.

"How are you feeling?" Sarah brushed her fingertips across his forehead.

"Like h . . . the dickens." He drew his brows together. "Did you help? I woke up last night and saw two beautiful angels hovering over me. I thought you had come to carry me away. Not that I ever thought I would make heaven."

"We aren't angels," Maggie said, forcing the unbidden smile from her face. "This is my sister, Sarah. She did the doctoring. I helped."

A puzzled expression crossed his features. "My eyes must be failing. You're much too young to be a doctor."

A frown pulled at Sarah's pert mouth. "I used the remedies my mother taught me. She had the powers. I know little. But I know how to clean a wound and prevent infection. When we get to town, we'll take you to a real doctor."

"And a real sheriff," he whispered. His guileless blue eyes locked with Maggie's suspicious green ones.

Tim approached slowly, tugging his suspenders over his shoulders as he walked. "What's going on? Is he an outlaw? Do you think there's a reward for his capture, dead or alive?" Tim's questions came out in a rush.

"No." The man swung his gaze toward the youngster. "I am not a bandit."

"Tim, quit asking questions. His name is Mr. Wex Ford, and I'm sure he'll tell you all about himself when he's stronger. Let him rest." His explanations had better be satisfactory, Maggie thought. It would be a shame to see such a good-looking man rot in jail—or worse.

Maggie helped Sarah check his bandaged shoulder. His skin was warm to the touch and the muscles hard. She centered her attention on the injury, not on his wide chest or the luxurious mat of curly dark hair. Maggie swallowed hard. She'd never been this close to a partially naked man before and found it a strangely exciting experience.

Sarah lifted the bandage and probed gently with her fingers. "There's no fresh blood, and I don't see any infection." She pressed a clean cloth to the wound. "You're a strong man. You should mend quickly."

Satisfied with the progress of her patient, Sarah sat back and glared at her brother. "For your information, Tim, Mr. Ford isn't an outlaw."

"Oh, yeah?" Tim took a long sip of his coffee. "How do you know?"

"I just know, that's how."

Maggie met Sarah's fervent green eyes. Age-old wisdom lurked behind her long black lashes, wisdom of a people who had inhabited this land long before the white man came to settle it. Maggie learned Sarah was different from other girls when Papa had first brought her, Rising Sun, and Tim back to St. Louis to live. Sarah always seemed much too serious and wise beyond her years.

Although Maggie didn't understand it, she respected Sarah's intuition. Sarah's instinct about Maggie's faithless fiancé had been right on target. She hoped Sarah was right about this man, too.

Chapter
Two

While Mr. Wex Ford slept Maggie took advantage of the bright sunlight to make prints from the negatives she'd developed. With Tim's help, she carried the glass plates from the photographic wagon to a table in the middle of the clearing. They worked as a team to secure the negatives in the wooden frames with the albumen-coated paper and set the frames to catch the light. For Maggie the hardest part was finding the patience to wait as the sun transferred the images to the treated paper.

She knew the pictures were good, some of her best work. The sharp clear photographs of the cattle drive would make the New York publisher stand up and take notice. He would see that Maggie Callahan had the talent to continue Callahan Photographic Gallery even without Papa. Michael Callahan had been a true artist, and Maggie was proud to have been his apprentice.

But Papa was gone, and he'd left Maggie and Tim to fulfill his contract. The idea of hiding behind her father's name cut like a knife to her heart. Her photographs were as good as any man's, or better. Fury overwhelmed her whenever she thought about the prejudice women faced in this so-called modern society.

What made people think a woman couldn't do anything a man could? In St. Louis she and Aunt Olivia had worked for the suffrage movement to win voting rights for women. Papa understood, but Harry never had. As a condition for marriage, the obnoxious man had expected Maggie to give up working in the gallery and abandon the fight for social justice. Fortunately she'd learned of Harry's scheme before she married him. Breaking off the engagement had been the best thing she'd ever done. Maggie Callahan didn't need a domineering man running her life. And she certainly didn't have time to deal with a mysterious Englishman.

From time to time she glanced at the stranger lying in the shade of a tree. Sarah had given him a dose of one of her medicines, and he appeared to be asleep.

Sarah stayed close to the fire and kept her patient within sight. She washed his shirt and mended the hole in the shoulder. Then she made a large pot of soup.

By afternoon the medicine wore off, and the man began to stir. Maggie kept her distance and allowed Sarah to feed him and change his bandages.

Without his shirt, his tanned shoulders gleamed like bronze. She remembered how strong and warm his skin had felt under her fingertips the night before. When Sarah moved away, Maggie met his steady blue stare. His eyes locked with hers, and her heart lurched. Maggie wasn't sure what was happening to her. She'd never had this kind of reaction to a man before.

Even when she'd fantasized about being married to Harry, she'd never felt this kind of fluttering in her stomach. And she couldn't begin to imagine Harry without his shirt—or trousers.

After she'd safely stored her newly mounted pictures in the photographic wagon, Maggie picked up her rifle and some other things and wandered to the nearby stream to freshen up. The afternoon had grown warm, and she needed a few moments alone before further questioning this Mr. Ford.

Imposing mountains surrounded the narrow valley on two sides, with lower hills on the others. A profusion of wildflowers spread out like jewels across the meadow. Small blue butterflies fluttered from one blossom to another like petals floating on the sea of grass. In the distance whitecapped spires kissed the clouds.

At the edge of the stream, cottonwoods and willows closed out the sky like a giant umbrella. Hidden from view of the camp, Maggie gave in to temptation for a full, relaxing bath. She stepped behind a tree and stripped off her breeches and shirt.

Mindful of the moss-covered rocks, she worked her way slowly into the cool, clear water. Goose bumps broke out all over her flesh, and her nipples tightened into tiny buds. A silvery trout slithered between her legs, causing her to jump. Too bad she hadn't brought her fishing pole. He would have made a fine addition to their supper.

Waist-deep in the brook, Maggie sat and let the chilling water flow over her. She closed her eyes, and the stranger's handsome face flashed across her eyelids. Her skin tingled when she thought about his bright eyes and shiny raven hair.

The paintings in the museum and pictures of the Greek gods came to mind. He could have posed for the statues. She wondered what it would be like to photograph him—to pose him in the studio with the sunshine glistening off his strong, masculine body, and herself behind the camera, studying him from all angles. The image in her mind sent delicious tingles to the core of her body.

At the sound of a noise from the shore, she snapped her eyes open. Maggie halfway expected to see him standing at the water's edge watching her. She covered her breasts with her hands and looked around. To her relief, the movement from the bushes was a young deer drinking from the stream. When he spotted Maggie, he bolted and ran.

Would the man bolt and run if he were able? Of course he would, she thought.

Men couldn't be trusted to stay. Hadn't Papa left Mama so he could take his pictures during the war? Then, after Mama died, hadn't he joined the expedition to the West and left Maggie with Aunt Olivia? Hadn't Harry run off when he found out he couldn't get his hands on her inheritance? Hadn't Papa . . . died? Although she knew she was wrong to blame her father for something he couldn't help, Maggie still felt rejection like a knife to her heart.

Angry at the way her thoughts made her feel, Maggie grabbed the perfumed soap, the one luxury she allowed herself in the wilderness. She scrubbed her skin until it glowed, and washed the grime from her hair.

A few minutes later she slipped on a simple calico gown. She wasn't sure why she'd chosen the dress rather than the trousers she usually wore. It wasn't because of Mr. Ford, she told herself. Maggie had never gone out of her way to please a man. Leaving her waist-length hair loose to dry, she made her way back to the campsite.

At the edge of the clearing, she stopped in her tracks. Propped up against a rock, the man held a cup in one hand, while his injured arm rested neatly in a sling. He'd washed his face, and his straight dark hair shone like blue-black raven's wings. He wore his clean shirt. Tim laughed at something he said, and Sarah gazed adoringly into his eyes.

What had he done to her brother and sister?

Wex glanced up and spotted Maggie, her rifle pointed directly at his head. His heart leaped into his throat. On general principle, he didn't like guns pointed at him, but a weapon in a woman's hands was even more dangerous.

"What's going on?" Anger flashed in Maggie's eyes. "How did he get loose?"

Tim sobered and jumped to his feet. "Mr. Ford needed to . . . to . . ."

With a deep steadying breath, Wex finished, "Relieve myself. Your brother was kind enough to help me into the woods. I washed up in the stream." He leveled his gaze at Maggie's face and tried to forget the glimpse he'd gotten of her in the woods.

He'd spotted her through the trees, but she hadn't seen him. Unable to keep his gaze off her, he'd watched as she stepped naked into the water. Not wanting to be called a Peeping Tom, he'd done the gentlemanly thing and turned his back. Not that he'd ever been accused of being a gentleman where women were concerned. Even now, the memory of her creamy white flesh came creeping into his thoughts. His hands itched to touch her, and his body ached to know her. He took a sip of the coffee to control his carnal urge.

Since his survival depended on their good graces, it wouldn't do to incur either Maggie's wrath or her husband's.

A tinge of pink surfaced on her cheeks. "You've made a miraculous recovery, Mr. Ford."

"Thanks to your sister and her magic potions, I may live. I'm afraid it will be quite some time before I'm strong enough to get into the nearest town and to that constable, however."

Slowly Maggie moved closer, suspicion etched across her lovely face. "Now perhaps you can answer a few questions."

"Forgive me for not standing, Mrs. Callahan." He gestured to a folding camp stool. "If you would be so kind as to sit down, I will be delighted to satisfy your curiosity."

"I love the way he talks, don't you, Maggie?" A wide smile of youthful enthusiasm danced across Sarah's face.

Maggie frowned at her younger sister and shifted her attention to him. "Tell me, Mr. Ford, why is an Englishman like you wandering the Rocky Mountains with a bullet hole in your shoulder?" She sat with the rifle across her lap.

"You believe in getting to the point, don't you?" With one long finger he shoved the barrel of the rifle away from his chest. "First, my name is Wexford, Geoffrey Andrew Wexford. Please call me Wex."

She lifted a brow. "Sorry I misunderstood, Mr. *Wexford*. Please go on."

Wex smiled at her attempt at formality. Since he'd been in America, he'd been called Wex, while his friends in England knew him as Drew. "I was just telling Tim and Sarah how Her Royal Highness, Queen Victoria, rides through London in her carriage. It's truly a sight to behold."

"Yeah," Tim piped in. "She's surrounded by a whole bunch of soldiers decked out in fancy uniforms every time she goes out."

Judging by the scowl on her face, he knew she was unhappy about the way he'd impressed the youngsters. Somehow he had to convince her to trust him and let him remain with them. In his present condition, he needed their assistance. And for some odd reason he wanted to learn more about the lovely redheaded woman.

"That doesn't explain why you're here."

"You could say I was in the wrong place at the wrong

time." He fingered the scar on his cheek, a vivid reminder of his sordid past. "It's a bad habit of mine."

"Please explain."

"I'm a . . . writer, and I am on a tour through your beautiful country." He shifted his gaze to the tall mountain capped with snow and considered how much to tell. That part was true enough. His New York agent had found a ready market for his Western adventures.

The conditions under which he'd left England, however, were less than honorable. Shooting one's lover's husband was a criminal offense in any part of the world. Fortunately Baron Whitehall had survived, but it had cost a small fortune to convince the wronged husband not to press charges. To Wex, a year in exile on the Western frontier was preferable to years in jail. Soon the scandal would blow over, and he could return home to his rightful place in society.

Maggie lifted an eyebrow, waiting for him to continue. He decided to state the facts as simply as possible. "A week ago I hooked up with a band of cowboys driving a small herd of cattle to a buyer in a mining camp."

"Maggie, maybe that's the herd we took pictures of the other day," Tim said, his eyes wide.

Excitement surged through Wex. He ignored the pain in his shoulder. "You photographed us? I didn't see you."

"We can't be sure they were the same herd. We were in a stand of trees where we wouldn't spook the cattle. You wouldn't have noticed us." She dropped her gaze to his shoulder. "How did you get shot?"

His mouth turned down at the corners. He still couldn't believe he'd been caught in an ambush. "We were waylaid by a band of highwaymen."

Tim wrinkled his brow. "Highwaymen?"

"Ambushed by cattle rustlers. They killed the cowboys, took the cattle, our horses, and gear, and left me for dead." Thinking about the confrontation made his blood boil. He touched his injured shoulder. As soon as he was back in commission, he would find a way to make the rustlers pay.

Maggie's eyes darkened. "How did you escape?"

"I grabbed my saddlebags and crawled into the bushes.

The rustlers were in a hurry and didn't notice me. Then I started to walk. Last night I came upon your camp."

He winced when he remembered stumbling through the mountain wilderness, a fire in his shoulder, his life's blood oozing from his body. For a while he'd thought he'd used the last of the nine lives he'd been accused of having. Was this retribution for all the wrongs he'd committed during his degenerate life?

In his thirty years he'd gotten out of more scrapes, compromising situations, and escapades than he could count. But this time his father's money, influence, and name were of no significance. He'd had to depend on his own wits and determination for survival.

For a long moment Maggie stared at him, her green eyes dark and questioning. He knew it sounded implausible. Would she believe a stranger who'd come up on her out of the shadows and held a gun to her back?

"Then why did you sneak up on me like you did?"

"It's simple. When I saw a lone figure silhouetted by the fire, I didn't know if you were friend or foe. For all I knew, you could have been part of the gang. The way you were dressed, I thought you were a man. I would never pull a gun on a woman."

He squeezed his eyes shut for a moment before continuing. The despair of the past night washed over him. His luck had held out and brought him to the Callahans' camp. "I was desperately in need of food, water, and a horse." His gaze locked with Maggie's and issued a challenge. "I can pay for my medical care and any assistance you can give me."

"That won't be necessary, Mr. Wexford. We'll share our hospitality with you until we're able to get you to Sherman." She tossed her head and ran her fingers through the long strands of damp, burnished hair. "Then you can be on your own way."

His gaze lingered on the shiny tresses. The breeze caught a stray wisp, and the lock of hair kissed her cheek. He clutched the tin mug to keep from brushing the hair from her face.

"Very generous. Now that you know about me, tell me about yourself. I haven't met many female photographers, although I've seen some of Julia Margaret Cameron's portraits in London. Her work is rather interesting."

"I'm sure you'll meet quite a few more in the coming years. More and more women are entering fields once reserved for men. In America women are becoming lawyers and doctors, so why not photographers?"

"It seems strange, that's all."

She narrowed her eyes. "In St. Louis I had to hide behind my father's name to sell my portraits. Even now, I send my photographs out under the name of M. Callahan." Her hands tightened on the rifle. "Are you one of those men who think women are only good for keeping house and bearing children?"

He bit his lip to hide his smile. A woman as full of fire and passion as Maggie Callahan could undoubtedly do anything she set her mind to. He pitied her husband if he tried to tame her spirit. "Not at all. Females have been given a great deal of privileges in the past few years."

An angry flush crept across her cheeks. "Except the right to vote and handle their own affairs. Even a woman's inheritance goes to her husband if she marries."

Wex set his empty cup aside. Clearly he'd touched a sensitive subject. "Dear lady, I hope you can control your temper when you're carrying that rifle."

"I only kill for necessity, Mr. Wexford. Just don't make it necessary."

"Touché. I'll be certain to remember the warning. Why don't you show me those photographs? I'd like to know if you saw the same herd I was riding with." He didn't dare hope for help in identifying the outlaws.

"I'll get them." Tim jumped up and ran to the wagon.

"I'm sure it's a different herd," she said. "Tim, bring the magnifying glass."

Wex shifted on the hard ground and groaned.

"Are you in pain?" Sarah rushed to his side.

"Some. I suppose I'm not as strong as I'd like to be." An understatement to say the least. With the amount of blood he'd lost he felt fortunate to be able to sit up at all.

"Here are the pictures, Mr. Wexford." Tim handed him a stack of photographs. "Do you see yourself?"

Carefully he spread them on the ground in front of him

and checked each with the glass. "Of all the bully luck.
These are the rustlers, the men who shot me."

He couldn't believe the way his luck was improving. The
pictures were a godsend, as were the Callahans, who'd
surely saved his life. A Wexford never forgot to reward
those who helped him, and never failed to punish those who
opposed him.

Maggie leaned closer, setting her rifle on the ground.
"How can you recognize them? Their faces are hidden by
their hats."

"I recognize the brands of the cattle. See here." Passing
the magnifier to her, he pointed to the cattle. "This is the
brand of the outfit I was riding with—the Double H. The
others are different, mostly Lazy E."

"That still doesn't prove anything. Sometimes herds get
mixed up together, or get sold."

"Or stolen." With his one free hand, Wex pointed to
another photograph—amazingly sharp and clear, one of the
best he'd ever seen. Maggie Callahan was a talented
photographer. "This is my horse and gear. I'd recognize that
black stallion anywhere."

"Wow!" Tim stared wide-eyed at the pictures. "That's
your horse?"

"Yes. He's a Thoroughbred and cost me a pretty penny
from a horse dealer in Cheyenne. A despicable horse thief
has him now. But I'm going to get him back." Wex leaned
against the rock he was using as a backrest, careful not to
hurt his damaged shoulder. Thanks to Sarah, the pain had
subsided to a dull ache.

"If you should be lucky enough to find him, it'll be only
your word against his," Maggie said.

As Maggie handed the picture back to him her fingers
brushed his hand. She smelled as fresh as the wildflowers in
an Irish meadow—and she was every bit as wild and
untamed. He inhaled deeply, trying to remember how long
it had been since he'd enjoyed a beautiful woman's company. Too long. The girls in the mining camps and cattle
towns didn't interest him. A woman like Maggie Callahan
did. Moments ago he'd pitied her husband; now he envied
the unseen man.

Shoving his wayward thoughts aside, he returned his attention to the problem at hand. "I have papers detailing his markings. It should hold up in any court in the land."

"England, you mean." In one graceful movement, Maggie stood and reached into the bucket for a cup of water. "The law isn't quite the same out here."

"Surely there's some form of law and order. Most towns have a local constable or marshal, don't they?"

When she shrugged, the front of her blue calico frock tightened across her breasts. The air grew suddenly warmer.

"Sure. But this is a big country, and the thieves could be miles away by now."

What she said was true, but nobody had ever crossed a Wexford without paying for his mistake. The British code of honor had been bred into him for his whole life, and he vowed not to rest until he avenged the deaths of his companions and brought the killers to justice. But mentioning this to Maggie would serve no purpose. He doubted a woman would understand.

He studied her while she drank, holding the tin cup in her long, slender hands as delicately as if it were of the finest porcelain. The late-afternoon sunshine turned her long hair to burnished copper, and her green eyes sparkled with intelligence. The common dress didn't do her justice, but even in the canvas breeches and mannish shirt she'd worn earlier, she made a man stand up and take notice.

Too bad there was a husband lurking somewhere in the background, although he couldn't understand how any man could have gone off and left his wife and the youngsters alone in the wilds. Maggie's man was either very trusting or very stupid. For her sake, Wex hoped it was the former.

"You promised to take me to the nearest lawman." He caught her rifle by the barrel and held it out to her, stock end first.

Her eyes widened as if she'd forgotten to protect herself from the man she believed to be a dangerous desperado. She snatched the rifle and rested it over her arm.

Sarah laughed, the delightful sound of a young girl on the brink of womanhood. "You see, Maggie. I told you Mr. Wexford wasn't an outlaw. He isn't going to hurt us."

Sarah's eyes locked with Wex's as if she needed to confirm her belief in him. A band tightened in his chest. Not since Arthur had anyone put this kind of trust in him. He'd failed then; he prayed he was now worthy of her faith.

"Never." He smiled at the girl and noted the rush of crimson to her cheeks. "You've saved my life. I would never repay you with any unkindness."

"Just to be sure, Mr. Wexford," Maggie said. "I have your gun, and I'll keep my rifle handy."

"Mrs. Callahan, I'm not in any position to argue, but I've found that firearms in a woman's hands can be quite—how do I put this—risky."

She lifted the rifle and held it to her shoulder, the barrel trained on him. "Are you implying I don't know how to handle firearms?"

Without flinching, he ran his gaze up the shiny barrel, past the sight, and met her eye. "Do you?"

"Quit messing around, Maggie." Tim took the gun from his older sister's hands. "Grady taught us how to shoot. Maggie can kill a bird in flight and a rabbit on the run."

Wex released the breath he'd been holding. That revelation wasn't the best news he'd ever heard. The last woman who had pointed a gun at him had come close to sending him to St. Peter's pearly gates. A year ago he'd tried to break off with a mistress who didn't take kindly to rejection. Fortunately her aim was off, and the bullet missed his head by inches.

"Very admirable," he murmured. "I don't care to be used for target practice, however."

Maggie planted her hands firmly on her hips. "Just don't give me cause, Mr. Wexford." She gathered up her photographs. "If it will help you to recover your horse, we can show these to the sheriff when we get to Sherman."

He couldn't resist smiling. "Then you believe me?"

"We'll decide when Grady gets back." She leveled her gaze on him. "How are you going to prove it's your horse?"

"The bill of sale is safe in my saddlebags, with all my other valuables. Everything I have left in the world." It was partially true. In this wild country, the only thing a man could count on was what he had at the moment. Who knew when he would reach a bank and wire New York for more funds? "Did you find them in the bushes?"

"I did," Sarah said. She picked up the brown leather bags and handed them to him.

Maggie snatched them from her hands. "I'll take a look first."

He frowned at her apparent lack of trust. "What do you think I'm hiding in there, Mrs. Callahan? A weapon?"

"Could be," she said. "A woman can't be too cautious."

She dug through the contents of the bags, her mouth pulled into a determined frown. Seconds later she handed them to him.

"Are you satisfied I'm not hiding anything sinister in the bags?" Wex flipped open a leather pouch and reached inside. His fingers closed on his gold pocket watch. Relief flooded him. He rubbed his thumb over the engraved cover and felt his grandfather's initials before shoving it back into a protective corner of the bag. "Actually, I was concerned about my journals." He pulled out a leather-bound volume. "These represent weeks of work, most of it irreplaceable."

The beginning of a smile sneaked across Maggie's face. It lent her a youthful, vulnerable look.

An overwhelming desire to protect and help the Callahans surfaced within Wex. It had been years since he'd felt this solicitous about anybody. After half a lifetime of self-indulgence and pleasure seeking, the idea of accepting responsibility for another human being was at the same time exhilarating and frightening. He owed them his life and if he could repay by taking care of them until they reached civilization, then by George he would. With or without Grady's approval.

Maggie seemed unaware of the danger the photographs could cause for her and her family. If the rustlers knew she'd taken pictures of them, they would stop at nothing to hide their identities. Wex vowed to protect the people who had saved his life.

"How do you know you can trust us?" she asked.

He grinned up at her. "If you wanted to do me in, or rob me, you had ample opportunity last night and this morning."

Sarah touched his arm. "We would never hurt anybody. I

want to be a doctor, and Maggie and Tim only shoot enough to eat."

"Thank you, I appreciate your faith in me." He hoped her trust wasn't misplaced.

More color surfaced to the younger girl's cheeks. She stroked the medallion lying on the white yoke of her dress. The gold sparkled in the sunlight.

"That's an unusual piece of jewelry, Miss Sarah. Is it an heirloom?"

Sarah leaned closer and held the gold disk away from her chest. "It was my mother's, and she gave it to me before she died. A strange medicine man entered the village moments after she was born and gave this to my mother. No one had ever seen him before or after. Maggie gave me the chain for Christmas."

He fingered the engraved markings, surprised at the design. He thought it looked familiar. "Do the markings have a meaning?"

"The only thing he said was that the medallion comes with a blessing and a curse. If given in love, it will bring great good fortune, but if taken by force, it places a curse on the wearer."

The gold grew warm under his fingertips. "The design resembles the hieroglyphics I saw in Egypt at the pyramids."

Maggie leaned closer, her eyes wide. "We believe it's very old. Probably an amulet from one of the ancient tribes."

"It should be quite valuable." He let the medallion fall.

"To me it is," said Sarah. "I feel as if it's a link to my mother and my heritage. You see, my mother was a Shoshone princess and the daughter of a great shaman. She was trained to be a medicine woman."

Wex smiled. "You Callahan women are certainly an unusual crew. A lady photographer and an Indian princess. I feel privileged to be in your presence."

Sarah lowered her eyelids and turned away. "Are you hungry? The soup is ready."

"It smells delicious. You're quite an accomplished young lady, Miss Sarah. You'll make some lucky man a wonderful wife."

Sarah ladled the soup into a bowl. "I'll never get married. I'm going to be a doctor and devote my life to helping others. Aunt Olivia and Maggie said a woman should learn to take care of herself. They're both spinsters, and I'll be one, too."

Spinster? Sarah's innocent revelation startled him. "Who's Grady?" he asked.

"Our guide," Sarah answered without a pause.

Maggie groaned and turned away. "Sarah, you talk too much."

Wex suppressed his laughter. It hurt too much to jiggle his injured shoulder. Maggie's cryptic responses were falling into place. So she wasn't married—a ploy to keep him in line until this elusive Grady returned. If the man returned at all.

Wex smiled at Sarah. "Your sister is hardly old enough to be called a spinster." And he'd never seen a spinster as appealing as she. Yet he suspected she wasn't aware of her beauty or the natural sensuality of her fiery hair and emerald eyes. He wished they had met under better circumstances.

Tim took a bowl of steaming soup from his sister and sat cross-legged on the ground next to Wex. "She's pretty old. She'll be twenty-four on her next birthday."

Color surfaced on Maggie's cheeks. How could the woman manage to look both seductive and innocent at the same time?

She frowned at her brother. "That's twice as old as you, Timothy Michael Callahan. So you had better learn to respect your elders."

Maggie set Wex's bowl where he could reach it. She clearly had no intention of helping him as she had that morning. Somehow he regretted not feeling again the touch of her hands and the closeness when she'd fed him.

Shoving aside his wayward thoughts once more, he took a large spoonful of the thick soup. Tender game mixed with herbs and vegetables to make a rich blend. "Delicious, Miss Sarah. I've dined in the finest restaurants on the Continent, but I've never tasted better."

The compliment brought a shy smile to Sarah's lips. She was a pretty girl and with her clear fair skin, raven hair, and green eyes she would grow into a stunning woman.

With the right clothes and under his tutelage, she and Maggie could take London by storm. He switched his gaze to Maggie, picturing her in emerald silk with her bare shoulders gleaming in the candlelight. Men would swarm around her like honeybees after a single perfect rose. He blinked away the image and the twinge of jealousy that jabbed at his chest.

Maggie settled back on the camp stool with a bowl in her hand. "Have you traveled a great deal, Mr. Wexford?"

Her soft voice brought him back to the present. "Some."

"How long have you been in America?" Maggie's subtle attempt at interrogation brought a smile to his lips.

"Close to six months—long enough to fall in love with your beautiful country. I like the wide-open spaces, the freedom of a land where a man can be himself, regardless of his name, background, or what his father had done. A place where a man is judged by his own deeds and accomplishments."

Maggie's eyes widened, and he realized he'd said more than he'd intended. "A place where a man can hide?" she asked.

He shrugged, and pain shot up his shoulder. "If need be. But that's enough about me. What are you doing out in this wilderness all alone?" He glanced around the small clearing hidden in the shadow of light-colored aspens, dark evergreens, and spruce. Purple, yellow, and white wildflowers danced in the breeze. A single bumblebee darted past his head and landed on a daisy.

Tall mountains guarded the narrow valley, cutting them off from the world. Beyond were settlements, towns, mines, ranches, and farms. Plus unscrupulous men capable of theft and murder without a second thought. This rough country was hardly a place for two young women and a boy.

"We aren't alone," Tim piped in. "We have each other and Grady. When Papa died, Maggie promised to finish his assignment, and then we're going to Denver to live."

"Then Denver is your ultimate destination?"

"Yes. Right now Grady is guiding us to some Indian ruins he and Papa discovered during their expedition after the war." Maggie set a cup of coffee in front of him.

"Do you have family in Denver?"

"No. My aunt Olivia is my only relative, and she lives in St. Louis." Maggie lowered her lashes, hiding the pain in her eyes. As hard as she tried to be strong, her vulnerability came out whenever she talked about her family. "About a year ago we learned Papa had consumption. His doctors advised him to go to a drier climate. A New York publisher gave him an assignment to furnish photographs of the Rocky Mountains. He died a few weeks ago, and I want to complete the assignment before we open the studio in Denver."

Something tightened in his chest, a new and pleasant sensation. "You have my deepest condolences, Miss Callahan. Where is your mother?"

"My mother died when I was five, so my aunt Olivia raised me. Papa joined a geological expedition, and a few years later he came home with a beautiful Shoshone princess for a wife and these two pups."

"Pups?" Indignant, Sarah stretched to her full height, certainly not an inch over five feet. "Mary Margaret Callahan, Tim may be a pup, but I am a woman." She tossed her head like a proud young filly. "In my mother's tribe, I would already be married."

Maggie laughed. "I beg your pardon, Miss Sarah Maureen Callahan, fourteen-year-old spinster."

In spite of his pain and his precarious situation, Wex felt more at ease than he had in years. Sarah's smile was infectious, and Maggie's laughter was clear and seductive. He relaxed and sipped the coffee from the tin cup. Quite a change from the Sevres china and Ceylonese tea in his London town house.

From somewhere, a different sound filtered into the back of his brain. He stiffened and glanced around, expecting to see a deer or rabbit. It wasn't the noise of a foraging animal, however, but the clop of a horse and the jingle of reins.

In one quick motion he snatched Maggie's rifle and gestured toward the path. "Somebody's coming. Get out of sight."

Before they could react, a shrill whistle and the cackle of a crow rent the air. "It's only Grady. He gives the signal so we won't be scared," Maggie said.

"How can you be sure it's him?"

"Trust me."

He balanced the rifle on his left arm and tightened his finger on the trigger. Being left-handed had its advantages. From out of the forest ambled a dappled horse—without a rider. A pack mule trailed behind.

"I'd drop that rifle if I was you, young fella." The voice was as cold as the metal nudging his back. The man meant business.

Maggie covered his hand with hers. "It's Grady," she repeated, firmly.

With a sigh of relief, he lowered the rifle and allowed Maggie to take it from him. He had no desire to be a dead hero.

"Everything's all right, Grady. He won't hurt us," Sarah said.

A buckskin-clad man moved around Wex, keeping a shotgun pointed at his chest. "Damn and thunderation! I go off for one day, and you whippersnappers pick up a stray mongrel. Can't trust any of you to behave. Your papa warned me about you."

Maggie stepped forward and flashed a smile that would defuse a loaded cannon. "I'm glad you're back. Come get some hot soup. Sarah just made it."

Grady glanced around the campsite. With the man's sense of devotion to the Callahans, he wouldn't hesitate to pull the trigger if he thought his charges were in danger. A Colt revolver and a bowie knife hung from the belt at his waist.

"Where'd you find this scalawag?" he asked, his eyes narrow and filled with suspicion.

Employing all his strength, Wex eased to his feet and saluted with his left hand. "Geoffrey Andrew Wexford at your service, sir."

The old scout stopped and looked him up and down. "A Brit, huh?" When his eyes met Wex's, he finally nodded. "Grady Clinton." Grady's shrewd gaze settled on Wex's bandaged shoulder. "Did Maggie shoot you?"

Maggie laughed. "I'm one heck of a better shot than that. If I had fired, it would have been straight through his heart or between the eyes."

Wex slanted a glance at Maggie. "Thank you for the warning, Miss Callahan. I'll keep it in mind." He turned his attention back to the guide. "Actually, it was cattle rustlers."

Grady nodded and signaled toward Tim. "Tim, unload that mule while Sarah gets me some soup and coffee. Maggie can fill in the details." The old scout shoved the brim of his hat back with his rifle. "And if I don't like this young fellow's story, he's buzzard bait."

Chapter
Three

Four hours later, Maggie watched in awe as nature's sensuous display exploded across the sky. Every evening for the past three months, she'd gazed in wonder at the magnificence of the sunset that was no less glorious than the sunrise. She only regretted that she couldn't capture the brilliant colors with her cameras. The azure sky faded into a sea of pearl, and the crimson glow from the west overspread the heavens. The coming of twilight signaled the end of one of the most eventful days in her life.

Anyone who saw the little troop around the campfire would have thought that Mr. Geoffrey Andrew Wexford and Grady Clinton were old and close friends. Grady, who was normally suspicious of even his own shadow, accepted the stranger's story without reservation.

Grady agreed to help Wex. On the return trip from the Indian ruins, they would present the photographs to the sheriff in Sherman, Colorado.

Rarely did Grady welcome people so easily, Maggie thought. Without halfway trying, this stranger had won the trust of her entire family. Was she the only one skeptical of the man and his motives? His good looks didn't make him trustworthy. A rattler was pretty, and deadly.

She frowned and studied the stranger from across the small circle. Like Sarah and Tim, the craggy-faced old scout hung on to every word the Englishman said. And he said plenty.

Yet, in all his stories about his travels in Europe, he'd revealed little about himself and his mission in America. Maggie wondered if he was hiding something, like being something other than what he professed to be. An outlaw, perhaps?

From time to time Maggie's gaze met his over the blazing fire. A smile curved his lips, a crooked grin that tilted only one corner of his mouth. The result made Maggie's insides quiver. She suspected it was the way he'd looked at many women over flickering candles in intimate rooms—his eyes smoldering with hidden promises. The thought deepened the scowl on her face.

"Is something wrong, Miss Callahan?" he asked. "Have I done something to offend you?" In spite of the humor in his blue eyes, his face was pale and drawn. "If I have, I humbly beg your forgiveness."

In spite of his mild words, Maggie knew there was nothing humble about the man or his manners. Arrogance was as much a part of him as his sable-colored hair and aristocratic bearing. Well educated and widely traveled, Mr. Wexford didn't fit into the American West any more than Rising Sun had fit into St. Louis society. The man would be much more at home in a London salon than around a campfire with a grizzled scout and the children of an Irish immigrant.

"Of course not, Mr. Wexford. It's getting late, and I was wondering if you weren't overtiring yourself. After all, you have a nasty wound to your shoulder."

Although the others had moved to a given-name basis, a veil of formality hovered between them. Maggie needed the barrier against his charm, a means of keeping aloof from a man who had no place in her life. She was much too busy with her photography and taking care of Sarah and Tim to let a charming Englishman distract her from her goals.

"I appreciate your concern, but I'm not at all fatigued." The hint of pain at the corners of his eyes belied his brave words. His skin had paled, and his scar stood out in the shadow of his face.

Sarah brushed her fingers across his forehead. "I don't believe you're running a fever."

"I greatly appreciate your tender care, Miss Sarah. You will make a wonderful doctor." He caught her fingers and kissed her knuckles. Sarah's cheeks turned crimson.

This was the first time a man—a mysterious foreigner at that—had paid so much attention to Sarah. A smidgen of jealousy shot through Maggie. As quickly as it came, she shook the feeling and directed her anger at Wex. He had no business tampering with the emotions of an innocent young woman.

When he released her hand, Sarah brushed the back of her fingers across her lips. "I'll fix you a potion to help you sleep," she said, her voice wistful and her eyes bright.

The urge to jerk her sister away from Wex brought Maggie abruptly to her feet. The rickety camp stool tilted over with the movement. "It's time we all turned in. I'd like to start out early tomorrow and reach the ruins by the end of the week."

"But, Maggie." Sarah stood and stretched out her hands. "Wex isn't well enough to travel. Maybe we should go into Sherman and get him to a doctor."

"I don't need a doctor, and although I doubt I can stay on a horse for any length of time, I'm able to ride in one of your wagons." His jaw tightened, and his eyes flashed with determination. "I promise not to hold you back or cause any trouble."

Renewed apprehension rose up in Maggie. Was it her imagination, or was he reluctant to go into town? If he was the victim rather than the villain, wouldn't he be eager to get into town and present his case to the sheriff? Maggie didn't understand him at all.

"He looks like a pretty strong chap, Maggie. After all he's gone through already, I expect he'll survive a wagon ride." Grady rubbed his bearded jaw. "And if he don't, we'll just feed him to the bears."

Wex let out a roar of laughter and attempted to rise. Off balance, he staggered to one side. At that moment Maggie sprang to him and caught him around the waist. Her hands tightened on his waist to steady him. His arm fell across her shoulders.

His breath caught in his throat. She was all soft and womanly under his touch. He struggled for composure. "I suppose Sarah's right," he said, his mouth at Maggie's temple. The reaction of his body was expected, if unwelcome. "I'm not as strong as I had thought."

His lips touched her silky cheek. The feathery strands of her long hair caught in his whiskers. A wave of her flowery fragrance wafted around them. He rested heavily on her, and a tremor surged through him.

"Thank you, Miss Callahan." He breathed her name as softly as a caress.

Under his arm her shoulders trembled slightly. "You can share the tent with Tim."

Sarah moved to his other side to help. "I'll bring you the elixir."

"Add a shot of your papa's Irish whiskey, and he'll be a new man in the morning." Slowly Grady came to his feet. "So would I if you gave me a drink now and then."

Sarah glared at the guide with laughter in her eyes. "Grady, you know we're in the Temperance League, and we don't believe in drinking alcohol. Papa only used it for medicinal purposes."

The lighthearted banter brought a smile to Wex's face. He couldn't believe the stroke of good fortune that had led him to the Callahans. But who was he to question fate? A woman like Mary Margaret Callahan didn't come along every day.

Truth to tell, only a truly fortunate man met a woman like Maggie once in a lifetime. Wex didn't deserve either good luck or Maggie, but only a fool would reject either.

"Thank you." This time Wex's teeth touched the tip of her earlobe. She tasted as delicious as she smelled. "You're very kind to a poor, wayfaring stranger."

Judging by her sharp intake of breath, he knew she wasn't as unaffected as she pretended. And if Wex knew one thing, he knew women and their responses to a touch, a kiss, or a word.

"I think you can make it the rest of the way," she said, and slipped free of his grip. "Tim will wake you up in the morning."

But morning was a long way off. Maggie and Sarah climbed into the covered wagon where they shared a mattress while the men crawled into a tent a dozen feet away.

In spite of the tiring day and little rest the night before, sleep eluded Maggie. Through the canvas shelter she listened to the men getting ready for bed.

Tim was still wound up and continued questioning Wex about his travels. The Englishman's voice drifted across the space. In the dead of night, his rich, sensuous tones brought immodest thoughts to Maggie's mind. Thoughts of lying next to him, kissing his cheek, touching his strong, wide shoulders, feeling the textures of the hair on his chest.

The memory of the springy curls that tickled her palms when she'd bandaged his shoulder made her skin tingle. She punched the pillow and tugged it over her ears. She had no business entertaining such dangerous thoughts.

Sleep continued to evade her. The cramped quarters were uncomfortable and offered no privacy. At times she longed for the big, white house in St. Louis and her soft feather bed. She was certain Aunt Olivia kept the rooms aired and ready for their return. But they weren't going back. Their future lay ahead in Denver or beyond.

Sarah touched Maggie's arm. "Are you still awake?" she whispered.

"I'm trying to sleep, if those men ever settle down and be quiet."

On a long sigh, Sarah snuggled her petite form into Maggie's side. "Don't you think Wex is the handsomest, most wonderful man you've ever met?"

Maggie's heart beat faster. "Not particularly," she whispered in an effort to sound nonchalant.

"You thought Harry was handsome, but Wex is better looking and much nicer."

Reluctantly Maggie had to admit her younger sister was right. Whereas Wex treated Sarah and Tim as equals, Harry had merely tolerated their presence. Sarah had sensed his deceit long before Maggie.

Sarah laughed softly. "That scar on his cheek makes him

look so dashing. I can't believe we've met such a fascinating Englishman clear out here."

"How do you know he isn't an outlaw planning to murder all of us in our sleep?"

"Even if he is an outlaw, I know he won't hurt us. After all, Robin Hood was a wonderful hero, robbing from the rich to give to the poor."

The wistful sound of her sister's voice annoyed Maggie. "Sarah, that's just a foolish romantic notion."

Sarah only giggled and ignored Maggie's admonition. "In fact, he looks like the drawings of Robin Hood in that book you gave me for my birthday." She yawned and rolled onto her back. "Same dark hair, beautiful blue eyes, except Robin Hood has a beard. I hope Wex lets his grow. . . ." Her voice trailed off, and her breathing became deep and even.

Robin Hood, of all the preposterous ideas. He was a witch, or a warlock, someone who had cast a spell over an impressionable young girl. An older and much wiser Maggie would never let a handsome man turn her head. One mistake a lifetime was enough.

For what seemed like forever, Maggie tossed and turned. The men had grown silent, and the breeze whispered a song in the trees. Crickets chirped, and insects buzzed in the night. The night grew cool, but the cramped insides of the wagon became stifling.

Not wanting to wake Sarah, Maggie picked up her flannel wrapper and slipped on a pair of leather moccasins. Carefully she found Wex's gun, now loaded, and shoved it into her pocket before she leaped from the back of the wagon.

A thin sliver of moon lit the path that led to the stream. Rarely did Maggie have trouble sleeping. Tonight was different. Tension sizzled in the air like electricity before a storm. Only now the storm wasn't one of nature, but of the emotions within Maggie. Much more dangerous and much more exciting. Maggie's heart pounded in anticipation.

Beds of dried pine needles cushioned her footsteps as she walked across the rocky ground. She paused at the edge of the stream and listened to the roar of the water as it tumbled and rolled over mossy rocks. The steady rumble of the current brought with it a thrill of excitement. Maggie relaxed and let the sound wash the turmoil from her mind.

Sitting on a boulder, she stared up into the inky sky. Millions of stars glittered above, like diamonds strewn by a giant hand over a velvet canopy. She'd never seen a sky like this. The stars were so close, she thought she could reach up and touch them. The fragrance of fresh, clean pine balsam filled the night. Every nerve in her body was heightened, alert to something happening inside her.

Nearby an owl sent its mournful message into the night. In the short time she'd been in Colorado, Maggie had grown to love the wild mountain state. The sight of the white-capped peaks, the sound of the animals, and the fresh aroma in the air were beyond description. Maggie was glad she could share a portion of the beauty through her photography. Her pictures were the closest some people would ever get to the magnificence of nature.

The snap of a dry twig drew Maggie out of her reverie. Automatically her fingers closed on the gun.

"Couldn't sleep, Mary Margaret?" came the now familiar voice from behind her.

This time it wasn't fear but something else that made her heart slam against her ribs. "Do you make a habit of sneaking up on women in the night, Mr. Wexford? This is your second time. You're lucky I didn't fire at you."

"That's why I put a tree between us." He stepped from behind a fir tree, whose trunk offered little protection. "I wanted to make sure you're all right. You never know what you'll meet in the darkness. Anything can happen to a woman alone in the night." He joined her on the rock.

Maggie was all too aware of what happened every time he came near her. He was warm and strong at her side. "Shouldn't you be getting some rest? You almost fainted earlier."

"I'm much better since I took that magic potion your sister mixed for me."

"Just don't faint again. I can't pick you up by myself." She hugged her arms to keep from touching him. "I'll just leave you here for the wolves."

His enticing laughter flowed over her like a warm summer breeze. "I wanted to talk to you."

She turned her head and found him staring at her. "About what?"

He smiled. His even white teeth glittered in the moon-light. "I would like to make you a proposition."

Maggie curled her fingers into fists. The soft, seductive tone of his voice sent rivers of desire up her spine. She stiffened and strove to repress the longings he aroused in her.

"What are you talking about?"

He brushed gentle strokes along her arm. "I mean we should form a union, a relationship of sorts."

The moon slid behind a cloud, and a sudden breeze off the mountains made her shiver. His nearness confused her, giving provocative connotations to his words. The night often revealed more than it concealed.

"Cold, Mary Margaret?" He began to slip his arm across her shoulder.

Maggie regained her lost composure and brushed his arm aside. "I'm fine." She inched away from the warmth of his body, too close to hers. "What kind of . . . of union do you have in mind?"

"You don't have to be afraid of me." He sighed. "With one arm I'm hardly a threat to you. Besides, I'm wary of a woman with a gun in her hands."

Embarrassment turned her cheeks to fire. He was right. All she had to do was pull the trigger or yell, and Grady would come running with his shotgun cocked. It wasn't her safety that bothered her; it was the way her heart lurched whenever he touched her or spoke in that rich, cultured-sounding King's English.

She laughed to quell the pounding in her chest. "I'm not afraid of you. With your sore shoulder, you're as harmless as a kitten."

He let out a deep rumble of laughter. "Please, Mary Margaret, no man wants a lady to think he's a milksop."

Maggie swallowed hard. Even in his weakened condition, Wex was more dangerous than a coiled rattler. "Wex . . ." His name rolled off her tongue as if it belonged. "My friends call me Maggie."

"Ah, fair lady." He sighed. "I don't know if we can be friends. Lovers, perhaps. Adversaries, I hope not. But friends? It's difficult for a man and woman to be friends. Especially when they're attracted to each other."

The tremble in her stomach turned to an earthquake. "Attracted? I'm certainly not attracted to you."

His gaze slid over her. In the darkness she felt more than saw his bright eyes. "Perhaps not. But I'm attracted to you, and that will get in the way of our friendship."

The beguiling words fired her imagination. She was certain many women had fallen under his spell and moved into his arms and his bed without a second thought. But some women were stupid when it came to men. Not Maggie Callahan. She'd learned her lesson well. Harry had taught her not to trust men or their motives.

She cleared her throat and struggled against her needs. "What kind of offer did you have in mind?"

"I believe it would be quite profitable to both of us if we formed a kind of partnership. People in Europe as well as in the East are hungry for information about the frontier. You're a brilliant photographer, and I'm a fair writer. We can combine our efforts and submit our work together. I'll write about this beautiful country, and we'll illustrate with your photographs."

Maggie thought for a minute, letting his words sink in. He was offering a chance to exhibit her work under her own name without deferring to her father's reputation. "I still have Papa's contract to fulfill, but after that I'd hoped to get an agreement of my own."

He covered her hand with his. "I have an agent in New York who'll make all the arrangements for us. He's handling my business. He'll be delighted to get hold of your pictures."

The warmth from his fingers worked its way to her heart. An agent would save her months of letter writing, searching for a publisher—time better spent on her work. She glanced at him from the corner of her eye. Could she trust him to be telling the truth?

"Then you really are a writer?"

"Yes. Although I'll never rival Dickens or your own Mark Twain, I make a living." He lifted her hand and brushed his lips across her fingers. "Do we have a bargain?"

Her breathing became labored in the thin mountain air. Harry's advances had never so much as quickened her pulse, yet this stranger's every touch sizzled through her like a branding iron.

The quiet night was broken by the cracking of a footstep on the dried leaves and the loud screech of an owl. Maggie swung her head, but saw nothing.

"What was that?" she whispered.

Wex dropped her hand and groaned. "I think that was Grady's way of letting you know he's keeping an eye out for your safety."

She wanted to laugh, but moaned instead. "In St. Louis I had Aunt Olivia looking out for me. Now I have Grady." Lifting her voice, she said, "I have his revolver, Grady. I'm fine. Go back to sleep."

The only response was a growl like a wounded grizzly, then silence.

"Were there many beaux for Aunt Olivia to keep an eye on, Mary Margaret?" With one long finger, he brushed a stray tendril of hair from her cheek and stroked it between his fingers.

The tender gesture stole her breath away. He was right about not being friends. A friend had never affected her like this, not even Harry when she'd thought herself in love with him. Maggie picked a daisy from the clump growing at the base of her rock. Absently she plucked at the petals.

"A few." She paused, not ready to reveal her relationship with Harry and the broken engagement. Only Sarah knew the details, many of which she'd guessed. Maggie wasn't about to tell this stranger how her fiancé had loved her money more than he loved her. After all, she didn't know anything about the mysterious man who'd come to her out of the shadows.

"Was she as protective as Grady?"

Maggie dropped the flower, now nothing more than a stem. As suddenly as it had disappeared, the moon reappeared, lighting the night with its glory. In one bold move, Wex slid his arm across her shoulder and pulled her close to his side. The gesture was so natural and felt so right, Maggie didn't want to move or spoil the tender moment. After all she'd been through, it was good to lean on someone else for a few brief moments.

"Grady promised Papa he'd stay with us until we settle in

Denver or return to St. Louis." Since her father's death, Maggie hadn't allowed herself the luxury of grief and did not let her uncertainties show. For Sarah and Tim she had to retain her composure and show nothing but strength. Here in the darkness she needed to be comforted, in spite of her own misgivings about Wex's motives.

"Are you going back to St. Louis?"

"No. We've decided to make Denver our home."

Warmth from his body penetrated her robe and gown. He smelled of leather and the strong fresh soap. His abrasive jaw brushed her soft cheek. Needs she didn't understand and couldn't put a name to vibrated through her. But this wasn't the time or the place to identify those feelings. And Geoffrey Andrew Wexford, rogue or gentleman, wasn't the person to share her desires.

She slipped out of his grip and stood. "About your offer to work together, Mr. Wexford." Using the surname, she resurrected the barrier his kindness had broken down. "I'll do so, on two conditions."

By the light of the moon, she caught the roguish gleam in his eyes. "I'm your obedient servant, Miss Callahan."

She lifted her brows. A man with his aristocratic bearing would never be obedient, and he certainly was nobody's servant.

"First, I want full credit for my work. When Papa photographed the battles during the war, Mr. Brady took credit for all the work of his team. Toward the end, Papa scratched 'Callahan' onto the plates to get the recognition he deserved."

"I wouldn't dream of plagiarizing your work. What else can I offer to consummate our relationship?"

Maggie hugged her robe against the impact of his stare. His blue eyes turned smoky, warm, intimate. She forced herself not to tremble. "Our arrangement is strictly business. A working relationship is all I have to offer."

A sly smile curved his lips. "I accept your terms. I see this as the beginning of a most profitable association."

"Thank you." In the distance, the howl of a wolf echoed across the hills. Maggie shivered again. "We had better get back to bed. I'd like to get an early start in the morning."

Wex cupped her elbow with his free hand. "Or Tim will be joining Grady behind that boulder."

Maggie followed his line of vision, but saw nothing. "Grady went to bed long ago."

He inclined his head to hers so only she heard his whisper. "If I'd made the same promise as Grady, I wouldn't let you out of my sight, either—especially with a stranger I neither know nor trust."

"I'm quite able to take care of myself," she said loud enough for anyone stalking in the bushes to hear. Maggie turned toward the narrow path through the high grass. "Next thing you know, Sarah will be out here looking for me, too."

Wex kept his grip on her elbow until they reached the clearing and the covered wagon. "Good night, Mary Margaret," he said. "Tomorrow we can begin our collaboration." He brushed a gentle kiss on her cheek, then slipped away into the shadows.

Maggie covered her heated cheek with her fingers. He'd done it again—gotten under her guard and made her vulnerable. As many times as she'd warned herself about men, she'd let him get to her.

Hadn't she learned her lesson with Harry? At least she'd known what her former fiancé was after. He'd wanted control over her inheritance and control over Maggie. Andrew Wexford remained a mystery. And Maggie didn't like secrets or being kept in the dark.

She heard the whisper of canvas as he slipped into the tent. Until she knew who he was and what he wanted, she would have to fortify her defenses and keep her distance.

An inner voice warned Maggie that might not be as easy as it sounded.

Chapter
Four

For the next week Grady led the small caravan along trails that were no more than animal paths. Although the bouncing wagon was a far cry from the carriages Wex had been accustomed to in England, he endured the trip without complaint.

During the journey Maggie seemed determined to keep a distance from him. Since the night they'd met in the moonlight, he hadn't had a minute alone with her. She made sure Sarah rode with her while he rode with Tim. Grady kept an eye on all.

When they reached Durango, in the high canyon country, they left the wagons and loaded the equipment on pack mules and horses. Wex also took the opportunity to visit the local general store and purchased several shirts and canvas trousers.

The sight of a Wexford wearing the common ready-made apparel would have made his friends in London howl with laughter. Yet Wex was becoming accustomed to the clothes—and the anonymity offered by the simple garb.

Maggie suggested he stay in town rather than endure the rigorous horseback ride up the rim of the canyons, but her words fell on deaf ears. He had no intention of being left behind. This opportunity to view the ancient Indian ruins was the chance of a lifetime. He'd never before heard of the cliff dwellings, and as Grady told them, few white men knew of their existence. In addition, he wanted to be with the Callahans, to protect them, or so he tried to tell himself.

In truth, the lovely redheaded photographer fascinated him more than any woman he'd ever met. A strong, dedicated woman, she worked hard at her profession and would accept nothing but the best in her photographs. He was proud to be associated with Mary Margaret Callahan.

He was lucky Grady couldn't read his thoughts, for the guide would surely pump Wex full of buckshot. Every time Wex looked at Maggie, he mentally stripped the mannish shirt and trousers from her slender, firm body and thought of the figure he'd spotted that first day at the stream. The memory haunted him day and night. Especially at night, when he slept only yards away from her. For all the good it did him, she might as well be on the other side of the Atlantic.

He hadn't lied to her about not being friends. The man–woman physical needs, as primitive as the surrounding hills, hovered between them whenever their gazes locked. Sooner or later they would be forced to deal with these feelings. For now, all Wex could do was bide his time. And he wasn't a particularly patient man.

Thanks to Sarah's ministrations, he'd recovered enough to sit on a horse, although he wouldn't be playing polo for some time. And the old mare was hardly comparable to the stallion the rustlers had stolen.

Sarah insisted he keep his arm in a sling to protect the wound from tearing open. Fortunately, being left-handed, he was able to continue his entries in his journal. His excitement grew with every mile closer to the ruins. With his accounts and Maggie's photographs, his editor would be forced to sit up and take notice. As a team, they should make quite a name for themselves.

How Grady found the paths, he had no idea. The man had the instincts of a mountain goat as he led them through the canyon-sliced mesa country. The surefooted mules and horses traveled east on the rimrock of the mesa on no trail at all. Perpendicular cliffs of green basaltic rocks rose hundreds of feet. A river, like a silver ribbon, snaked along the valley far below. The magnificence of the scenery took his breath away.

By late afternoon Grady called for a halt and set up camp. While Maggie, Tim, and Sarah unloaded the mules Wex and Grady went in search of water. A short distance from the camp, they spotted a small grove of willows in a ravine. They began to dig and found a small spring, adequate water for the camp and the photographic needs. Wex took a moment and used his handkerchief to wash some of the trail dust from his face and arms.

When they arrived back at the camp with buckets of water, Sarah had a fire going and supper started. Maggie and Tim were readying the cameras for the next day. The amount of equipment was staggering—developing and washing tray, chemicals, glass plates, and tripods for the cameras. The remainder of the supplies were stored in the wagon in Durango.

Maggie met his gaze then glanced away. She took off her bandanna and wiped her face. Wex set a bucket in front of her. "I thought you might want to freshen up, Mary Margaret."

A small, reluctant smile touched her lips. Her gaze dropped to the clear, cool water. "Thank you. It would be nice." She removed her hat and dunked the red bandanna into the bucket, then wrung it out above her head.

Wex watched, aware he should turn away and give the lady a few moments of privacy. But he couldn't. Sheer pleasure glowed on her upturned face as drops of water trickled over her chin and down her long slender throat.

Mesmerized, his gaze followed a single shimmering drop as it rolled lazily down her chest, then disappeared into the valley between her breasts. He fought the longing to catch the moisture on his tongue and linger in the secret place where it had gone. The tightening in his body became painful. He wished he had the strength to step away. She looked up and caught him staring. Her cheeks pinked. He reached out and took the cloth from her. With a gentle touch, he wiped a long smudge of dirt from her warm face. The expected protest didn't come; instead she remained stock-still and allowed him to perform the intimate task.

A bird squawked in the trees, the horses whinnied, and

the others went about their business. For a long moment they were the only two people in the world. Her breath came in harsh gasps, and her chest rose and fell with the sounds. His own pulse accelerated, and his heart pounded.

As gently as patting a baby, he wiped the handkerchief across her forehead, her cheeks, and jaw. Her green eyes turned smoky. He brushed his thumb across her lips, damp and soft. She parted her lips and leaned slightly toward him.

Wex held his breath. The desire—no, the need to kiss her overrode common sense. He tilted her chin and moved his face toward hers. Warmth radiated from her, and Wex's control was melting in her heat. An instant before their mouths touched, Tim's voice penetrated his passion-dazed brain.

"Wex . . . Maggie! Didn't you hear me calling?"

Wex bit back a groan. Damn. A man of his experience should have better sense than to get carried away like a schoolboy having his first encounter with a woman.

Maggie snatched the bandanna from his hands and buried her face in the damp cloth. How had she let a man take such liberties with her? In those few moments she'd forgotten who she was, where she was. He'd wanted to kiss her, and she'd waited to feel the firm, hard touch of his lips on hers. Slanting a peek at Wex over the handkerchief, she saw her own frustration mirrored in his eyes.

She hoped against hope that Sarah, Tim, and Grady hadn't witnessed her scandalous behavior. "What's wrong?" She turned to her brother.

"Grady told me there's a bunch of cliff-top dwellings on the other side of those woods. Let's go take a look while Sarah is fixing supper."

Taking a deep breath to calm her racing heart, she glanced at Sarah. A wide smile burst across Sarah's mouth, and she winked at Maggie. So much for that wish, she thought.

"Go on, Maggie," Sarah said. "I don't need any help."

The scout settled on the ground and wiped his brow with a red bandanna. "Go through those trees, but don't get lost."

Maggie shoved her hat back onto her head, grateful for the chance to get away from Wex and clear her cloudy brain. No man had ever had this kind of effect on her. From now on she'd have to keep all her wits about her and avoid being near him.

"I'll go with you and mark the path," Wex offered, moving to stand beside her. "I have an excellent sense of direction."

She eyed him warily. "I'm sure finding your way through the streets of London is no experience for a mesa top."

Wex stroked his chin, his beard now grown to a shaggy mess. Her sarcasm wasn't unexpected—a defense for letting down her guard moments ago. "Miss Callahan, I'm aware this rough country is a far cry from the parks and forests of England. More than once, however, I've found my way out of the thicket after bagging my game. Besides, I can't have adventures worth writing about by sitting in camp."

"Are you sure you're strong enough to trudge through the forest?"

He smiled at what he knew he was strong enough to do. Erotic things that concerned a certain red-haired woman. "I'll keep up. Lead the way."

She shoved his Colt into the waistband of her canvas breeches and started toward the forest.

Tim took the lead and tramped through the pine forest with ragged limbs and dusky green foliage. Shoving tree branches aside, they stepped over dead logs and rocks. After about a quarter hour they caught a glimpse of a white crumbling structure. Brambles and bushes overran the mesa-top dwelling.

They paused and took in the eerie sight. Deserted buildings, several stories high, hugged a cliff. Tiny yellow wildflowers grew in cracks of the stone walls.

"This is truly amazing," Wex said, awed. "How could such primitive people construct something like this?"

Maggie shoved back her hat and waited at his side. "Sometimes we think we're so intelligent. But these people probably built this before Columbus discovered America."

"*My* people." Tim lifted his chin in pride. With his straight black hair, dark eyes, and high cheekbones, he carried more of his Indian heritage than Sarah. "Grady told us about the ancient ones who lived here over a thousand years ago. They had cities built into the cliffs and were a great nation."

Wex studied the empty, lonely buildings. The last glimmer of twilight cast an eerie glow over the scene. A shiver ran up his spine as if some ghost of the past stood at his side, watching, listening. "What happened to them?"

The youngster shrugged his shoulders that strained against his plaid shirt. "No one knows for sure. Perhaps it was drought or warring tribes that drove the people away. Some say their spirits remain behind."

"That's ridiculous," Maggie said. "Grady said it's only superstition."

Tim lifted his gaze to the sky, a faraway look in his green eyes. "There are many things in this world we don't understand. Things we were not meant to know. Let's go inside."

"Wait," Maggie cautioned. "It's getting late. Let's wait until tomorrow when we can set up the cameras and photograph the site."

The boy planted his hands on his narrow hips. "What's the matter, Maggie, scared of ghosts?" He proceeded into the dark interior, stepping over crumbled stones and broken masonry.

"I'm not afraid of anything," she replied, her fingers on the butt of the revolver—Wex's revolver.

Wex caught her elbow. "Let's go with him. We can take the pictures tomorrow."

She allowed Wex to usher her into the darkened building. Through her cotton shirt, her arm felt small and soft. Again his protective instincts took over. For a woman who professed not to fear anything, her arm was trembling.

In the first room, broken pottery littered the floor, and strange markings covered one wall. They stepped over broken stones that were once part of the roof. With only one small window, the room was shadowed and dark. A dank odor hung in the air.

Tim ventured ahead and slipped through a narrow opening into an inner room. The instant his shoulders cleared a doorway, a loud succession of hisses and squawks tore into the deadly silence. The boy leaped backward, his face pale.

"It's a ghost," he said, backing to his sister's side.

Maggie stiffened. "Don't be silly, there's no such thing as ghosts." In spite of her bravado, she remained rooted to the spot.

The loud hisses continued, an eerie sound in the house long abandoned by the inhabitants. For a moment Wex, too, began to believe the place was haunted by specters from the grave. Then common sense took over. "Tim, run outside and get a pine knot for a torch. We'll light it and find out what all the commotion is."

Seconds later the boy returned, and Wex lit the makeshift torch. Leading the way, he ducked his head and slipped through the narrow opening. Maggie followed on his heels with Tim bringing up the rear.

Holding the torch over his head, Wex scanned the large open room. Maggie pressed against his back, her body warm and real in the mysterious surroundings. His eyes adjusted to the gloom, and he spotted the debris from decades of vacancy that littered the floor.

"Look." Maggie expelled a breathless gasp.

He glanced around and spotted Tim, eyes wide, well behind his sister. Maggie pulled out the revolver and pointed it toward the fuss in a far corner. Bright, brilliant eyes glittered in the yellow glow from the torch.

As much as he dreaded seeing a gun in a woman's hand, for once he was glad she'd taken the revolver along. Since the creatures didn't come forth, he ventured on, his heart in his throat.

The commotion grew louder in the stillness of the room and echoed off the walls. Wex held the torch above his head until the light fell on the darkest corner. A thrashing white mass of arms and bright eyes met his gaze. Whatever the beast, he was certain it wasn't human.

"They're eagles," Tim said. Moving forward, he approached the disturbance. "They must be six or eight weeks old, maybe more. Come see."

Wex released the breath he'd been holding, cursing himself for being such a coward.

Maggie laughed and returned the gun to her trousers. "Look at us, afraid of two birds."

Tim swung his gaze to his sister. "It's a good thing the

parents aren't here. They could rip us up pretty good with their talons."

In the nest, the two eagles were flapping their wings, their eyes wide with terror at the invasion of their home.

"Don't touch them," Tim admonished. "The parent birds don't like the nest disturbed. Let's get out of here and leave them alone."

"I wish we had the cameras," Maggie said. "They would make a wonderful picture."

With his hand at the small of her back, Wex urged her ahead of him. "We can come back tomorrow. Let's get back to camp."

Together they squeezed through the narrow opening, their bodies brushing in intimate contact. He bit his lip at the unexpected surge of heat. Although the touch lasted only seconds, desire struck him like a fist to his stomach.

She gasped, and he suspected she was as shocked as he at the contact. In the dim glow of the torch, her cheeks pinked, and he knew she wasn't entirely unaffected by his touch.

Following a few paces behind, he stepped into the late-afternoon sunshine. He snuffed out the torch and blinked to adjust his eyes to the light. His gaze settled on Maggie, rushing toward the thicket. Instead of concealing her feminine allure, the tight men's breeches enhanced her rounded hips and slim waist. He tugged the collar of his shirt and prayed for control.

Tim followed on his sister's heels, and then Wex noticed they were both going in the wrong direction.

"Hold up," Wex called. "That isn't the way back to the campsite."

Maggie stopped and turned toward him. "Yes, it is. We came from the east. This is the right way."

"No, it isn't. I marked the trail over here." He gestured toward a fallen log and a broken branch from a tall bush.

She propped her hands on her hips and glanced around. "You're wrong, Mr. Wexford. I know my directions."

He set his jaw in a stubborn line. "No, Miss Callahan, *you're* about to make a grave mistake."

"My only mistake was when I allowed you to accompany us."

"If you wish to get lost, have your own way. I intend to

return to camp before it gets dark." Without a backward glance he trudged toward the barely discernible path. Let the obstinate woman have her own way. He'd had all he was going to take of her imperious attitude. Since he'd been with them, she'd ruled her brother and sister with more haughtiness than Queen Victoria ran her empire. Only Grady dared question her authority.

Taking orders went totally against his nature. In his lifetime, only his father dared exert any authority over him. Even then, Wex rarely obeyed. He certainly had never taken commands from a woman.

When he reached the thicket, he paused to allow them a chance to follow. Behind him, he heard Tim's voice. "Maggie, Wex is right. Camp is that way."

At the rustle of the bushes, Wex sighed with relief. Making sure they could follow his lead, he broke more limbs and continued toward the clearing where Sarah and Grady awaited their return.

With the glow of the fire in sight, he stopped and waited for Maggie and Tim to catch up. Tim ran through the trees and began to recount their adventures to Grady. The second Maggie reached him, Wex caught her arm and hauled her up short.

"If a man can find his way through the jungle of streets in London, Miss Callahan," he whispered, "this forest is less confusing than a garden maze."

"I'm quite certain I could have found my way back without your assistance." Her gaze dropped to his hand. "Mr. Wexford, please let go of me before I shoot you."

He tightened his grip and pulled her closer. "If you intend to shoot me, I would appreciate your doing so now to put me out of my misery." Smiling, he gently stroked her arm with his thumb. "I hate for a woman to make threats."

For a long moment she glared at him as if unable to form a response. Her fingers closed on the grip of the gun. "This isn't a threat, it's a promise."

"Even worse is a woman who taunts a man with promises she has no intention of keeping."

Color rose in her cheeks, and her lips puckered in anger. "I always keep my promises."

His gaze dropped to those soft, pink lips. The woman

needed a man to kiss away that stubbornness and uncover
the passion that lurked behind those fiery green eyes. "Mary
Margaret, your words belie what your body and eyes are
promising. It will be interesting to see which will win the
battle you're waging with yourself."

With a quick nod, he released her and strode into the
clearing to the campfire. Only when he settled on the ground
across from Grady did he dare slant a glance at Maggie. She
hadn't moved; her back was stiff, and her fingers were
locked on the revolver.

He still didn't trust a woman with a gun, but he knew she
wouldn't shoot him. As much as she wanted to, she couldn't.
Although he had no doubt she wouldn't hesitate to kill to
protect her brother or sister, they were in no danger from
him, and she knew it.

"Wex? Wex?"

Sarah's insistent tone made him realize she'd spoken to
him, but he hadn't heard a word she'd said. "I beg your
pardon, Sarah. My thoughts were elsewhere."

Sarah slanted a glance at Maggie, who was slowly
approaching the fire. "I asked if you wanted some coffee."

"Thank you, I would love some."

Sarah filled the tin cup and handed it to him. As he
reached for the cup Maggie took it from her sister. "Let his
nibs get his own."

"Maggie, that's terribly rude," Sarah said. "Aunt Olivia
would be horrified at your behavior toward our guest."

With a shrug, Maggie sat cross-legged on the ground.
"This isn't London, and we don't have imported tea or fine
china. Besides, Aunt Olivia is hundreds of miles away."

Sarah shot an angry glance at her sister. Wex sat back and
watched the clash of the two pairs of green eyes. He
wondered which of the stubborn women would win the
battle of wills.

"Good manners bring civilization even into the wilderness." Sarah proceeded to fill another cup and pressed it into
Wex's hand.

Silence fell over the small gathering while Grady
struggled to keep a smile from his face. Even Tim stopped
talking and stared at his sisters.

"Wex hasn't complained one minute, in spite of being wounded," Sarah said.

"I don't mind roughing it, Miss Callahan. The safaris in Africa are much more primitive than this."

Maggie eyed him over the rim of her cup. "Mr. Wexford, is there someplace you've never been, something you've never done?"

He'd never made love to a redheaded Irish wildcat in the Colorado Rockies. But all good things were worth waiting for. He smiled and considered his words carefully. "Many, many things, Miss Callahan. I'll admit I've traveled a great deal, but there's so much of the world left to see, so much to explore. Life is too short to waste time on triviality."

"So I gather you're an adventurer."

"A writer in search of adventure." He hoped the simple statement satisfied her, although he was certain she would press for more information.

It wouldn't do any good to tell her why he'd left England, or the reason his father had exiled him to America. But time healed all wounds, even gunshot ones, and before long he would be allowed to resume his previous life. Though at times he wondered if he would miss the freedom he'd enjoyed in the West.

Sarah looked at him adoringly. What had he done to inspire such confidence from the girl? Trust he, of all people, didn't deserve.

"Wex," she said, "have you ever been to Sherwood Forest?"

"Funny you should ask," he replied, grateful for the change of subjects. "When I was a boy, I pretended the woods around our home in Allenshire were Sherwood Forest. My brother was the Sheriff of Nottingham, and of course I was Robin Hood."

Maggie choked on her coffee. "You? Robin Hood?"

"Of course, Maggie," Sarah said. "I told you he looked like the illustrations of the bandit in the storybooks."

Grady laughed in great howls. "You young'uns sure got some imagination. Next thing Maggie'll be his Maid Marian and the rest of us his Merry Men."

Maggie's cheeks reddened, and Wex swallowed his own

laughter. "If Mary Margaret has her way, she'll turn me over to the sheriff and see me hung."

"Don't tempt me, Mr. Wexford." A tiny smile curved her lips.

"Tempt you? Miss Callahan, I wouldn't dream of it." He flashed a smile over the rim of his tin mug.

Her cheeks reddened, and she turned toward her sister. "Let's eat supper. I want to catch those ruins with the first light of morning."

Chapter Five

The morning dawned in a glorious burst of golden sunshine and blue skies. Anticipation made Maggie's heart flutter like a flag in a stiff breeze. The first photographs of the ancient ruins were her golden opportunity to earn her reputation as a photographer of note. The thought of receiving credit for her work made her as excited as a child at a birthday party.

With the vast amount of equipment needed for shooting and developing the glass plates, Maggie enlisted the services of the entire troop to carry the needed supplies to the site.

Even Wex. Being the tallest and strongest, he volunteered to carry the largest camera. Maggie watched him struggle to lift the heavy piece of equipment with one arm. She swore under her breath.

After trying all morning to avoid him, now she hurried to his side. The valuable camera was more important than her petty annoyance. "Let me help you with that," she offered. "I don't want you to break my camera before we even reach the site."

He glanced at her over his shoulder, his blue eyes flashing with exasperation. A frown pulled his dark brows together. "Just slip those straps over my shoulder, and the burden will balance itself."

She heaved the bundle while he slipped his left arm through the wide leather straps. Carefully adjusting the buckles, she brushed her hands along the taut muscles of his back. A quiver of excitement shuddered through her.

Every time she made the slightest contact with him, that strange fluttering ruffled through her insides. Again she cursed her decision to allow him to accompany them. If she'd had any sense at all, she would have turned him over to the sheriff in Sherman, or at least left him behind in Durango.

A slow seductive smile tugged at the corners of his lips. It reminded her of a cat cornering a fat, tasty mouse. A niggling voice warned Maggie to beware. It was only a matter of time before the cat caught the mouse in his velvet claws.

Aware that her fingers continued to rest on his shoulder, she jerked her hand away. "Be careful, that's my best camera."

"Yes, Mary Margaret," he said in a slightly agitated tone. "I'm aware of the importance. These photographs will be as valuable to me as to you."

She turned and lifted her own burden. A strong hand reached out to assist her. Wex lifted the heavy glass plates with one hand and supported the weight long enough for her to slip her arms through the straps.

"Thank you," she said, reluctant to admit she'd needed help.

"Are you positive you can handle this?" His hand rested lightly on her shoulder.

Her breath caught in her throat. No, she thought, she couldn't handle the way he made her feel—vulnerable, dependent. For her own and her siblings' sakes, she needed to be strong and self-reliant. "I can handle anything."

He stepped away. "I'm quite certain you can, Mary Margaret."

Able to breathe again, she spotted Sarah studying her with an all-knowing look in her sparkling eyes. The expression said Sarah understood exactly what was happening between Maggie and the Englishman. Heat rushed to Maggie's cheeks. Whatever was happening, Maggie didn't like it or want it. She spun on her heel and tramped toward the thick bramble separating the campsite from the ancient dwellings.

Grady waited at the path they'd taken the night before. As soon as the others reached him, he took the lead through the woods. Sarah followed close at his heels with Tim next. Maggie and Wex brought up the rear.

The heavy burdens made the going much slower than the day before. By the time they reached the cluster of ruins on the mesa top, they were sweaty and winded. Maggie dropped to the ground and freed herself of her burden. She pulled off her hat and fanned her damp face with the wide brim.

Wex settled beside her. "Mary Margaret, would you be so kind as to assist me with these straps? I certainly wouldn't want to damage your camera."

Embarrassed she hadn't offered to help him, she knelt and reached for the buckles on the thick leather thongs. At first the catch refused to release, and she braced her hand against his back. Under his coarse cotton shirt, his skin was damp and warm.

Maggie bit her lip to concentrate on relieving him of his burden rather than on the heat sizzling from the hard flesh under her fingertips. Frustrated with her ineptness, she groaned aloud and jerked hard on the catch. This time it gave. The boxed camera slipped to the ground, but her hand lingered on the indentation the thick strap had left across his shoulder.

Unable to stop herself, she brushed her fingers along the mark. He removed his hat, and drops of perspiration trickled down the strong column of his neck. His hand covered hers, and he gazed at her from the corner of his eyes. The heat in those intense blue eyes made her heart beat faster.

"Thank you," he whispered.

For a long moment she couldn't move. Without taking his gaze from hers, he bent his head and brushed his lips across her fingertips. Maggie swallowed down the moan that threatened to slip from her lips.

A long shadow fell across them. "How about a drink to cool you'uns down?"

Jerking her hand from Wex's shoulder, Maggie looked up at Grady and the canteen he'd thrust toward her. She needed more than a single canteen to douse the fire raging through her veins—she needed a dunk in a cold, clear mountain stream. Or an ocean between her and the Englishman.

"Thanks," she said. Hands trembling, she took a long drink from the canteen.

"Pass it to Wex while I look around. There's usually a good spring back behind the rooms." Grady stalked away, and Maggie jumped to her feet. She shoved the canteen toward Wex and moved over to where Sarah and Tim were waiting.

Sarah was staring wide-eyed at the buildings. "This is wonderful," she said. "I thought Papa was exaggerating when he told us about the ruins."

Tim moved toward the opening in the first room and called over his shoulder, "Come with me. I'll show you the eagles."

"Be careful," Maggie called. "Stay out of trouble."

A soft chuckle came from the man beside her. "Quite the little mother, aren't you, Mary Margaret?"

With a determined tilt of her chin, she gazed into his amused blue eyes. "I promised Papa I would look after them, and as I told you, I always keep my promises."

"I remember."

A trickle of perspiration rolled down her throat. His gaze dropped and followed the rivulet between the swell of her breasts. Aware of how her damp shirt clung to her body, she felt the touch as strongly as if his hands rested on her heated flesh. A look of pure male pleasure fluttered across his face, and the day grew decidedly warmer. Where was the cooling mountain breeze when she needed one?

Not wanting Wex to know her heart was galloping like a runaway team of horses, she stuck the old hat back onto her head. Only a complete idiot would let a man turn her knees to jelly and her mind to mush, she told herself. And Mary Margaret Callahan was anything but stupid. Though one wouldn't think so, the way Wex made her act whenever she got within ten feet of him.

For sanity's sake, she had better stay well outside that tomcat's grasp.

As she reached to unlatch the mahogany box containing

her five-by-seven-camera, Sarah and Tim came running out
of the ancient house.

"The eagles are gone," Tim said, disappointed.

Maggie looked up. "Are you sure you were in the right
room?"

"Of course. You think I'm dumb or something? The nest
is there, but the eagles aren't."

"Look." Wex had come up to stand beside her. He pointed
into the sky.

A hundred feet above their heads, two magnificent eagles
circled in a spiral flight. Two smaller birds glided in the
wind beneath their wings. The eaglets from the nest now
soared with their parents.

The grace and power of their wide wings mesmerized
Maggie. She felt a pressure on her shoulder and knew
without looking that Wex had rested his hand there. This
time she didn't move or rebuke him. They were sharing a
special moment—she, Sarah, Tim, and Wex.

The parent eagles swooped lower, almost as if saluting
the spectators on the mesa top. With a mighty swish of their
wings, they sailed to the far side of the mesa, their children
in pursuit, and were hidden from view. Only when they
were certain the eagles weren't going to return did anyone
dare speak.

"Now I know why they called my grandfather Mighty
Eagle," Sarah said, her voice quiet and awed. Her fingers
clutched the medallion lying on the yoke of her calico dress.
"He was a great man, loved and respected by his people. As
mighty as an eagle."

A tiny tear trickled down Maggie's cheek, and Wex
tightened his fingers.

"'They shall mount up with wings of eagles. . . .'" His
voice trailed off.

Tim glanced at Maggie, then scanned the skies. "I wish I
could fly high above the clouds like an eagle. It would be
wonderful to feel so much freedom."

Wex stroked her shoulder with his strong fingers. "Someday man will conquer the skies. It may be within your
lifetime."

Maggie sighed. "At the rate things are moving back east,
it's only a matter of time. For myself, I'm more interested in

getting some photographs of these ancient ruins and any artifacts we can find." She shrugged away from Wex. "Let's get the cameras set up while we still have the strong morning light. I want to set up a darkroom inside."

By afternoon Maggie had selected one of the inner rooms for her darkroom and had arranged the various trays to develop and wash the glass plates. Grady had found a good source of water behind the buildings. Wex felt privileged to assist her and study the way she worked.

Sarah and Grady returned to the campsite to tend the animals and prepare the evening meal, leaving Wex alone with Tim and Maggie.

Besides carrying the heavy equipment, the most difficult part was finding the proper location to set up the cameras for the best views of the ruins.

With quiet determination, she studied the site from under the dark tent of her viewfinder, adjusting the lens and instinctively knowing the correct shutter speed. Tim handed her the double-plate book holders, then carried the exposed gelatin plates to the building's cool interior to be processed that night.

Wex did his best to help, carrying the tripods and the boxes of glass plates, but mostly he admired Maggie's methods. And the woman herself.

The longer he was with her, the more fascinated he found the woman with the fiery hair and emerald eyes. Even the mannish clothes couldn't hide her feminine curves and natural sensuality. If anything, the rough clothes only enhanced her earthy beauty. She was like the wild roses that grew in the valleys—beautiful and untamed, inviting and fragrant. But there couldn't be a rose without a thorn. Wex had already been pricked by the lovely flower.

He settled on the ground and wiped his face with a large handkerchief. In spite of the breeze, he'd been uncommonly hot all day—since the moment Maggie had brushed her hands across his back and shoulder.

In England, he'd been appalled at the sight of women in men's clothing or wearing the trousers that Mrs. Amelia Bloomer had deemed the latest fashions. Fortunately the ladies of his acquaintance had rejected the style and remained true to the enticing lace-and-silk gowns.

He narrowed his eyes and tried to picture Maggie in emerald satin. The image failed to materialize. Instead he saw her in a clear mountain stream, water cascading over her shoulders and off the dusky tips of her firm, white breasts. He shifted to ease his growing discomfort.

At that moment something must have gone wrong, because she slammed her hat onto the ground and mumbled unintelligible words under her breath. The image faded, but the heat in his veins didn't. This spitfire would be fetching no matter what she wore—or didn't wear.

She glanced at Wex, and he couldn't refrain from smiling. Color surfaced on her cheeks at her unladylike outburst. Wex wet his lips with his tongue. He couldn't wait to turn that temper to passion. The idea held arresting possibilities.

"Something wrong, Mary Margaret?" he asked. "May I help?"

"No." She picked up the hat and beat it against her thigh. "The light shifted, and I probably ruined one of the plates. I don't have any to spare."

He looked up at the sky. With his absorption in Maggie, he hadn't noticed the sun slipping toward the horizon. Shades of lavender and purple streaked across the sky. Every sunset shot different hues across the heavens. He wished he were an artist to capture the colors that changed hourly.

"Perhaps we should return to the camp. The light may soon be too dim for the photographs."

She opened her mouth as if to argue. Instead she slammed the hat on her head and stalked toward the buildings. "I'll get Tim, then I'll come back tonight to develop the plates."

His smile widened. For once she had accepted a suggestion without a debate. Now, if only she would be as acquiescent when they were alone. The need to have her grew stronger every day. He'd been celibate too long, and the temptation of a woman like Maggie was more than a healthy male could resist.

After moving the cameras into the shelter of the houses, they returned through the thicket to the campsite. This time, he was happy to note, Maggie followed docilely behind. Yet, as they sat around the fire and shared their meal, she continued to keep her distance from him. Wex wondered what it would take to win her trust.

The instant she finished eating, Maggie insisted on returning to the ruins. When Wex slipped into his jacket to return with her, Maggie set her hands on her hips and glowered at him.

"Where do you think you're going?" she asked, a determined set to her jaw.

After her earlier compliance, her renewed stubbornness caught him off guard. "To help you, of course."

She tilted her chin. "Tim and I can handle the job. We don't need your interference. You'll only get in the way."

He gritted his teeth to keep his temper in check. Mary Margaret Callahan exasperated him far beyond any woman he'd ever encountered. No man should be expected to endure so much from a woman. "As long as I don't jar my shoulder, I can use my hand." He flexed his fingers to show the use of his hand. "Being left-handed, I can carry water, and I'm eager to see how the negatives come out."

"That's great, Wex." Tim shoved his arms into the sleeves of his jacket. Although the afternoon was warm, an evening chill began to seep across the mesa top. "We can use all the help we can get."

"Tim, we can get along without him." Maggie nudged the revolver in the pocket of her jacket. She lifted her gaze and shot a warning glance at Wex.

"Take him with you." Grady's softly issued order came from his position near the fire where he was sipping a cup of coffee. "I'll stay with Sarah. If you need me, fire two shots into the air."

Maggie opened her mouth to protest. After one glance at the scout's stern look, she changed her mind. "Oh, all right."

"She'll be safe," Wex said. "I stake my life on it."

"She'd better be, Wexford. I gave her daddy my word, and I intend to see she reaches Denver safe and sound." Under his floppy hat, his eyes narrowed dangerously. "Tim, take the rifle. Never know what kind of varmint is prowling the darkness."

"Yes, sir." Tim squared his shoulders with manly pride. Already as tall as Maggie, he would probably reach well over six feet when fully grown.

Sarah pressed a package into Wex's hands. "Take this with you. It's biscuits and dried beef in case you get hungry."

"Thank you, Sarah." He smiled at the young woman who clearly was the only person in camp who truly trusted him.

Without further argument, Maggie led the way to the path that Grady had widened and clearly marked for the return trip after dark.

Wex slipped Sarah's food rations onto his shoulder and kept his eyes on Maggie, hastening through the thicket. When they reached the clearing, he was surprised to find Maggie waiting for him. Tim ran ahead into the ruins.

She folded her arms over her chest. "Just because Grady sent you with me doesn't mean you're wanted. Stay out of my way while I work."

Tired of her constant taunts, he faced her, the toes of his boots touching hers. "Mary Margaret, you don't have to be afraid of me."

For a moment uncertainty glittered in her green eyes. "Don't flatter yourself. I'm not afraid of you."

He brushed his fingers through his rough beard. "Then what are you afraid of? Yourself?"

"Myself? Ha!" She threw back her head in a burst of haughty laughter. "Why should I be afraid of myself?"

His gaze moved down the slender line of her neck into the open collar of her shirt. If she could read the lust in his thoughts, she wouldn't be so quick to dismiss her concerns. Not that he would ever hurt her. Just the opposite. No woman had ever complained about his lovemaking. Neither would the haughty Miss Callahan.

With one finger he touched the hollow at the center of her throat. "It's the passion, Mary Margaret. When the pressure gets too great, a volcano erupts and spews hot lava." The pulse began to throb under his fingertip. "How long can you control the inferno bubbling inside you?"

She opened her mouth, but no sound came out. His gaze moved to her lips, and he tilted his head to taste the sweetness of her kiss. The instant he touched her mouth she jerked away, a shocked expression on her face.

"I . . . I . . ." She rushed toward the ruins. "I have work to do."

Wex inhaled the thin mountain air and struggled to control his lust. It wouldn't do to run after her and frighten her into using the gun on him. He moved toward the opening in the house. Patience, he told himself. With a little patience and gentle wooing, Mary Margaret Callahan would give up her struggle, and the banked fires would ignite into a raging holocaust.

Ducking his head, he stepped into the dark interior. Nightfall rapidly approached, and he lifted the coal-oil lamp he'd left inside the opening earlier that day. He struck a match, and in the pale yellow light he spotted Maggie slipping through the next doorway.

She held a similar lamp and led the way to the inner room where Tim was waiting.

For the next few hours Wex carried water, mixed chemicals, and assisted in developing the glass negatives. Working in darkness, he felt more like an owl than a man. Somehow Maggie was able to handle the plates with the dimmest of light.

When half of the negatives had been developed, Wex noticed Tim was beginning to sag. The boy clearly needed his sleep. "Tim," he said, "why don't you lie down and rest. I'll help Mary Margaret."

"No, it's my job," he protested.

Maggie set the plates aside and turned up the lantern. "He's right, Tim. I'll probably be working most of the night. You and Wex can go back to the camp. Tell Grady I'll be all right, and you can come back in the morning."

Tim yawned and picked up the rifle. Not wanting the boy to face the woods alone, and also afraid to leave Maggie in the ruins, Wex was torn with indecision. "Mary Margaret, I think it would be best if you come with us."

"Why? There's nobody here but a few ghosts. They won't hurt me."

The stubborn woman refused to take even a gentle suggestion. "Then at least rest and eat some of this food Sarah packed for us."

"I know how to take care of myself, thank you. I'll decide when I need to rest."

Wex threw up his hand in submission. "Have your way."

As he slipped through the narrow door he spotted Maggie folding her legs and settling on the ground.

He worked his way through the thick woods and stopped when the camp was in sight. "Go ahead," he told Tim. "Tell Grady I'm staying with Maggie, and we'll see you in the morning."

Tim handed the rifle to Wex. "Here. Take care of my sister."

His heart lurched at the trust shown by the youngster. "I won't let anything happen to Mary Margaret." Taking the rifle, he retraced his steps to the ruins.

The moon was high in the sky, glittering off the white sandstone buildings when he returned. The Winchester lay loose in his arm, offering a certain amount of security. In the distance he heard the howl of a coyote, but no animals came near the mesa dwellings.

A shiver raced up his spine. In the darkness he felt eyes on him, something hovering beyond human sight, out of human understanding. Could it be true that spirits guarded the dwellings? Yet he knew no fear. Living beings were far more dangerous than ghosts.

The lantern held high, he made his way through the maze of rooms to the one nearest the center. "Mary Margaret," he called, not wanting to startle her into using the Colt on him.

No answer. His heart began to pound. She should be there in the room, alone. Fear leaped into his throat. He knew better than to leave a woman alone in this wilderness. A thousand ominous thoughts flashed through his mind. If anything had happened to her . . . He snuffed out the lamp.

Careful not to make a sound, he slid along the wall, ready to fire the rifle if necessary. At the entrance to the inner room, he strove to see into the near darkness. The pale glow of the lamp in a far corner did little to penetrate the deep shadows. He paused, waiting, listening. In the unnatural stillness, his own breathing sounded abnormally loud.

He picked up a stone and tossed it into the darkness away from the lamp. It thudded on the ground . . . then unearthly silence. Pressed to the wall, he entered the room and strained to make out even the slightest movement.

The washing trays and plates were where Maggie had left

them, and nothing appeared to be out of place. At the edge of the circle of light he saw a form. It was Maggie—slumped against a wall, her chin resting on her chest.

His stomach plunged to his feet. Heedless of the consequences, he rushed to her side and brushed his knuckles across her cheek. Her skin was warm, her breathing even and deep. She moaned and turned her head.

He let out the breath he'd been holding. She was sound asleep.

With her father's old jacket draped over her shoulders, she looked small and vulnerable. Tenderness roiled up in him. Wex set the rifle against the wall and slipped out of his buckskin jacket. Laying it on the ground, he sat beside her. Without disturbing her, he slipped his unfettered arm across her shoulders and cuddled her to his chest.

She shifted and snuggled her head into the curve of his neck. Holding this woman felt both natural and right. For a man who'd spent his entire life in selfish pursuits, this newly found sensitivity was both satisfying and scary. He hoped he could live up to the responsibilities that came with the caring.

Once before he'd been given the responsibility of caring for someone weaker than himself. That time he'd been distracted, and disaster struck. The tragedy had devastated all those close to Wex. He wouldn't let it happen again.

Shifting his position, he dropped to the floor and cradled her in his embrace. Her soft breasts pressed against his chest, and his body responded in turn. She smelled of lavender soap, and wispy strands of copper hair tickled his nose. He pressed a gentle kiss to the top of her head.

She groaned and stretched her arm across his chest. He pulled the heavy coat over both of them like a blanket. The hard ground and ancient ruin was quite a change from the luxurious boudoirs he'd become accustomed to in England. But no woman had stirred him more than the spitfire in his arms. He wondered what her reaction would be if she awoke and found his hand resting lightly on the soft curve of her breast.

If he handled her with his usual finesse, her initial response would soon turn into unbridled passion. He hoped.

When she moved again, her leg covered his, and he

pressed his thigh between hers. He bit back a groan and prayed for strength.

A small cry tore from her lips. "No, don't, Harry." She shoved against his chest and went stiff in his arms.

He tightened his grip. *Harry?* Who in hell was Harry? What had this Harry done to bring the cry of distress in her sleep?

"Hush, love," he whispered. "Everything's all right. I'll take care of you."

Chapter
Six

Why doesn't Harry leave me alone? Maggie shoved at the hand that was teasing her body. Wave after wave of sensation washed over her. Her fingers collided with the hard body crushed to hers. When had Harry gotten so big, so muscular? And why did the touch she'd once dreaded suddenly feel so delightful?

In the netherworld between sleep and wakefulness, Maggie moaned and snuggled closer. Aunt Olivia would be furious if she knew Maggie was lying with a man.

He kissed her hair, her forehead, her cheeks. Maggie didn't care what anybody thought; the flutters in her stomach were all that mattered. She reached up and brushed her fingers across his face. When did Harry grow a beard?

The kisses continued until he began to tease her mouth and nibble at her lower lip.

"Are you waking up, love?"

His voice had gotten deeper, richer, with a crisp British accent. Harry had never called her "love" before.

With a sigh, she struggled to open her eyes. Rough-tipped fingers brushed her hair from her cheek. It was dark, with only a tiny glow of light from several feet away. Her gaze fell on blue eyes and dark hair. She was sprawled on the hard ground, crushed against a man with a lean, muscular body, a British accent, and—

Awareness doused Maggie like a pail of cold water. Her eyes snapped open, and her numbed brain jolted to attention.

Wex! The man stirring her senses wasn't Harry. Worse, he was the Englishman she'd sworn to avoid.

She clutched his shirt in her fingers. "Where are we?"

He tightened his arms around her. "In the ruins. I found you asleep." Shifting positions, he covered her with his full length.

A tidal wave of sensations flooded Maggie. And needs. Needs she couldn't define or identify. Needs as primitive as the shelter over her head. The quivering in her stomach reached lower until it settled in the private place between her legs. She groaned, and he caught the sound with his mouth. His lips moved against hers with practiced ease.

His tongue stroked across her teeth, until Maggie couldn't help opening her mouth and welcoming his invasion. Rational thought warred with desire. She took his kiss, her tongue welcoming his with the hunger of a woman too long denied.

Desire was winning. The slow thrusting of his tongue matched the undulating of his pelvis into hers. The full, thick ridge of his maleness met the softness of her femininity. Her heart opened to him as surely as her body. She'd never known this kind of longing, this need to be filled.

With one hand, he pulled her shirt from her breeches. He stroked her bare skin and Maggie suspected she'd lost the battle.

He ended the kiss and nuzzled her ear. "Mary Margaret," he whispered, his voice a seductive invitation in the shadows. His fingers closed on her breast, stroking the tip until it tightened into a hard bud.

She sighed. Nothing in her past had prepared her for this. One thought and only one filled her foggy mind—they were about to make love. More than anything, she wanted it, wanted to know him in the most intimate ways of male and female. It was new and exciting, the blossoming of womanhood. Her virginal body cried out, but a voice somewhere in the back of her mind whispered "caution."

Taking a deep breath, she struggled to get some air into her lungs, to quiet the confusion that was building within her. He wanted her, she wanted him. That should be enough. The here, the now, was all that mattered. Tomorrow would take care of itself.

He would leave, and Maggie would be alone—like Mama.

His lips continued their sensuous foray, unaware of the battle waging within Maggie. She shoved at his chest. "No, Wex. Please stop."

He paused with his hand cupped on her breast. The delicious feeling thrilled but at the same time alarmed her. Control was rapidly slipping away.

"Why, love? I won't hurt you. We can soar to the heavens like the eagles."

She shoved harder at his shoulders. He fell away with a loud groan. Horrified that she'd hurt his injury, Maggie leaped to her feet. The walls were closing in on her. She had to escape, to get away—to think, to breathe. Grabbing the lantern, she darted through the narrow opening into the maze of rooms that led out of the ruins.

The first red glow of sunrise turned the morning sky to pink. Maggie sucked in gulp after gulp of the fresh, crisp morning air to clear the musty odor from her nose and calm her racing pulse. Her actions shocked her. Never had she panicked like that. She'd also never come so close to losing herself. The few times Harry had pressed her to make love, she'd merely speared him with a scathing glance and a few stinging words. The additional threat of losing Maggie's inheritance had stopped him in his tracks.

Why hadn't she employed the same tactics with Wex? Perhaps it was the claustrophobic ruins with their dank odors—the darkness—the ghosts of the past.

Or the overwhelming desire to make love to him.

She cupped her heated cheeks with her cold hands. It was as if her very survival depended on her escape. Yet she knew Wex wouldn't hurt her, not physically. But he was capable of inflicting a much deeper pain and leaving her alone to cope. Like Mama when Papa went off to the war. Like Maggie when Papa had died.

"Maggie!"

A quick glance over her shoulder told her Wex would be on her within seconds. She wasn't ready to face him. He would demand to know why she'd run out, and she had no rational explanation for her behavior. She'd acted strictly on instinct, the primal need for survival.

Her best course of action was to return to the camp. With Grady and the others nearby, she could be safe from his questions and disturbing advances. In the pale dawn, she scanned the woods for the path and plunged headlong toward safety.

"Maggie, wait." His voice grew louder.

Tree limbs and brambles scratched her face and arms. The narrow path disappeared, and Maggie was faced with an impregnable thicket in front of her and Wex behind. Dark and silent, the forest loomed like a menacing foe. Heart pounding, she veered to the right, and had only taken a few steps when her feet flew from under her. The ground slipped away, and she skidded downward.

A scream tore from her throat. Arms flailing, she grasped the nearest handhold—a prickly bush. Her fingers tightened on the fragile stem, and her legs dangled in the air.

"Oh, God. Maggie, hold on. I'll get you." Wex's voice seemed to come from far away.

Not daring to look down, she looked up and saw the real terror in his eyes. The yards separating them looked as wide as an ocean. Her fingers slipped, and she shifted her hand for a stronger grip. A cracking noise shot fear through her. The bush, rooted in the shallow soil between boulders, could not hold her weight.

With nothing else to do, she waited to meet her destiny. She'd always heard that at the brink of death, a person's entire life flashed in front of her eyes. Maggie saw nothing except the side of a mountain and a few straggly shrubs. Again she found herself coursing through the air. This time she came to an abrupt halt flat on her back. Her breath had been knocked out of her, but she was still alive.

Wex watched in horror as Maggie slid out of his sight. Her voice bounced off the canyon walls and sounded like a death knell in his ears. Oh, God, not again, he prayed. His heart leaped into his throat, cutting off his breath.

He stared at the spot where she'd been only seconds ago. The first shrub that had broken her fall tumbled to the canyon floor. Time stood still as he watched her hurtle downward. His heart stopped beating. About twenty feet below, she lay crumbled on a narrow ledge. Below her precarious perch, the canyon was a vertical stone face.

It's all your fault, you should have been watching. The words from long ago rang in his ears. *Your fault, your fault.* Wex shook off the fear that had immobilized him. Maggie had to be alive, she had to be all right.

"Don't move. I'm coming," he called.

Without a second thought, he started down to her. The ground sloped at a steep angle, but he'd learned mountain climbing in the Alps. Loosing his arm from the confining sling, he managed to grasp a bush and lower himself over the edge. He found a foothold and slowly began to work his way toward her. Pain shot through his still-sore shoulder, but he ignored it. Maggie needed him, and he couldn't fail her. Not the way he'd failed his brother.

"No, go back," Maggie called, her voice choked and shaky. "Get Grady. He'll know what to do."

Relief surged through him. Fortunately she was alive and conscious. "Be quiet and don't move." His foot slipped when the brush tore loose from its shallow roots. Frantically he dug his toe into the hillside and continued toward Maggie.

Time stood still as he continued his slow descent. A rock slipped, and he prayed it wouldn't hit Maggie. Finally he dropped the last few feet and landed next to her on the ledge. A small boulder broke off and tumbled toward the canyon floor. That could have been Maggie. His heart constricted at the thought.

"Are you hurt?" He cupped her face in his hands. Her skin was icy, and her pulse pounded in her neck.

"I don't think so." She tried to stand, but he stopped her with his hand on her shoulder.

"Don't move. I want to check you for broken bones."

At his commanding tone, she did as he ordered. Kneeling beside her, Wex started at her ankle, tenderly pressing above her boots and running his fingers up her shin, around her knee, and along her thigh.

"This leg seems all right." Shifting his position, he repeated the procedure with her other leg.

"I'm not hurt," she said, shoving his hands away when he

started to pull her shirt from her breeches. "And I don't want you touching me like . . . like that."

"Relax, Mary Margaret. Your legs and arms aren't broken. I want to check for broken ribs."

Ignoring her protests, he shoved the shirt above her breasts. With gentle fingers he probed her smooth skin, along her side and under her breasts. His gaze dropped to her bare breasts. Her nipples puckered into tiny buds as his thumb brushed the sensitive flesh. She trembled and drew a sharp intake of breath.

He swallowed a groan. He tightened the muscles in his jaw to keep his mind on the task at hand. Maggie may be hurt, she needed help. Abruptly he lowered her shirt and pulled it to below her waist.

He cleared his throat before speaking. "You'll probably be muscle sore, but nothing is broken." Sitting back on his heels, he took a long slow drink of the dry air.

"Running away was very foolhardy, Mary Margaret. You could have been killed." He gestured to the floor of the canyon far below them. Near the river half a dozen buzzards circled a carcass. He shivered.

"You're right," she said, contrite for the first time. "But you could have been killed, too. Are you a hero or an idiot?"

"Neither. Why were you running away from me?"

"I wasn't running away from you. Can't you simply believe there's a woman in this world who doesn't find you irresistible?"

He ignored her sharp rebuke. "Were you running away from Harry?"

She gasped aloud. "How did you find out about Harry?"

He gripped her arm. "You mentioned his name in your sleep, and you seemed upset. What did the bastard do to you?"

"That's none of your business. I haven't asked you how many women you've . . . known." She tore her gaze from his and shook off his hand. "Ow . . ." She bent her arm, and he spotted the torn sleeve. A trickle of blood ran down her elbow.

He swore under his breath, colorful phrases he'd picked up on the waterfronts of several European cities. "We have to get you back to Sarah. She will have something to doctor your injuries. Let me help you up."

Slipping his hands under her arms, he eased her to her feet. "Can you stand?"

"Yes. How are we going to get out of here? If you'd done the sensible thing and gotten Grady and a rope, he could have pulled me up."

His eyes narrowed, and the muscles twitched in his jaw. She was probably right. But when had he ever done the sensible thing? "Be quiet and let me think." He took one step to the edge of the ledge while holding Maggie away with his arm. "If we follow this ridge, we may come to a place where we can climb back to the top of the mesa." After studying the ledge, he turned back to Maggie. "Can you walk?"

"Yes." She rubbed her bruised backside and stretched out her legs.

Although she would never admit it, he was certain she was stiff, and there was no telling how many black-and-blue marks would probably appear by the next day. Getting back to safety was their major concern.

For what seemed like forever, they followed the narrow ledge, at times no wider than their feet. On one side the canyon wall was too steep to climb, and the other too dangerous to go down. Scrub pine and piñons grew in thick profusion, with numerous bushes and shrubs crowding the canyon floor below. The morning grew warm, and he was getting thirsty.

For a change, Maggie obeyed orders and followed in his steps without complaint. He didn't realize they'd been climbing until he shoved aside a prickly shrub and found himself on the top of the mesa.

Wex collapsed on the ground and pulled Maggie down beside him. He took off his hat and ran his fingers through his hair. "Looks like we made it."

For the first time since she'd fallen down the cliff, Maggie dared to take a deep breath. "I guess I owe you," she said. She glanced at him and noted the tiny smile on his face. Her skin grew warmer.

"We're even. You saved my life, and I helped you out of a dilemma."

She cringed. If she hadn't been so reckless and run away, she never would have been in danger. And she wouldn't be in debt to him. "How are we going to get back to camp? We must be a far piece away."

Nothing around them looked familiar, yet it all seemed the same. The trees and bushes looked like thousands of others. Birds fluttered from tree to tree, and an occasional butterfly landed on a wildflower.

Wex reclined on one elbow, an arrogant grin on his face. He picked a yellow dandelion and twirled it between his fingers. "If I can find my way through the confusion of London streets, I can assure you I'll return you safely to your sister and brother."

She brushed the loose hair from her face. "They're probably worried about me . . . us. They expected us to return for breakfast."

Wry laughter came from the man lying next to her. "If we hadn't neglected to pick up a gun, we could fire those shots and alert Grady to our location."

"Or kill a rabbit to cook."

He stretched to his feet. "Come." Reaching for her hand, he pulled her to her feet. "I think I hear water. At least we don't have to go thirsty."

With her hand locked in his, Wex guided Maggie into the trees. His touch was warm and reassuring. She had no choice but to trust him. Within seconds she heard the gurgling of the water over the rocks. The narrow stream was a welcome relief to her growing thirst.

They drank their fill and drenched their heads with the cool water. Wex dipped a large handkerchief in the water and wrung it out. "Come here."

Perplexed, Maggie looked at him. "What . . ."

"I want to wash some of the dirt from your scratches. You don't want an infection."

Maggie remained still as he gently wiped the grime from the scratches on her hands and elbows. She refused to show the bruises on her backside. His gentle touch made her heart race in double time. When he was through, he lifted his gaze to hers. His blue eyes darkened, and for a moment Maggie thought he would try to kiss her again. The idea was both frightening and thrilling.

Instead he combed his fingers through his shiny black hair and stretched to his feet. "Come. Let's get back to camp."

Shocked at his abrupt change in mood, Maggie hurried to her feet. "Which way?"

He gestured to the north and started through the thicket. Maggie followed close at his heels.

Leaving the stream behind, he started through the wild undergrowth and the thicket. Their progress was slow as they trudged over fallen trees and shoved aside branches.

Once more they stopped when they came to a tiny trickle of water oozing between some rocks. The sun was higher, and her stomach protested the lack of food. She looked at the wilderness surrounding them.

"Are you sure we're going in the right direction? We could get lost and never be found."

"I'm quite certain. If we don't reach camp by noon, I'll start a fire and hope Grady sees the smoke."

He pulled his watch from his pocket and flipped it open. Maggie noticed the picture of two young boys in the lid. Abruptly he snapped it shut and shoved the watch into the tight pocket of his denims. "It's eleven o'clock."

With the corner of his big handkerchief, he wiped a smudge from her face.

"Mary Margaret." His voice softened as if he were speaking to a petulant child. "I know you're tired and hungry. I promise I'll make this all up to you when we reach Denver. I'll take you to the finest restaurant and treat you to the most elegant meal in the city. You'll wear a beautiful green gown, and I'll be in evening dress. Think about how lovely you'll be."

Maggie squeezed her eyes shut and tried to envision the scene—candlelight, a handsome man, wine, roast beef . . . Her stomach growled and broke the spell. "It only makes me hungrier. Let's go."

A short time later they came out of the trees to the edge of a cliff. Maggie stopped, and Wex came up short behind her.

"Holy cow," she whispered. "Am I seeing things? Is that a fairy castle?"

Moving beside her, he shaded his eyes and gazed across

the canyon. "It's the most remarkable sight I've ever seen."
His voice dropped to a husky whisper. "I've been to
Buckingham Palace, Versailles, and the Taj Mahal, but
this . . . this is like something from another world."

"Have we stepped into another world?" Maggie held her
breath, almost afraid to breathe. The enchanting sight
couldn't be real. A huge cliff extended from the top of the
mesa, forming the crescent shape of an amphitheater.
Beneath the shelter lay a city of numerous buildings, several
stories high, with turrets and terraces. The crumbling houses
had been built by another people, living in another age.

She reached for Wex, needing to feel something real and
of this world. His arm was hard and warm under her
fingertips. "It's amazing," she whispered, almost afraid to
speak aloud.

If she stared long enough, Maggie was certain she would
see men walking across the walkways, or women sitting in
the courtyards with their children.

"I've never seen anything like this," Wex said. He slid his
arm across her shoulder, and Maggie didn't move. She
needed the touch to keep a sense of reality.

Maggie could only nod. The morning sun glittered on the
houses and towers, castles from the past, giving the white
sandstone the illusion of marble. The fairy city was nestled
in a huge cave above the canyon, an almost impregnable
fortress. Above the cliff, the mesa was covered with a dark
forest of piñons and cedars.

Automatically Maggie slid her arm around Wex's waist,
glad she had somebody to share this magical moment with
her. Surely nobody would believe some ancient people had
achieved this remarkable feat.

"I hope I can capture this with my camera, although I'm
sure photographs won't do justice to this beautiful city."

He pulled her closer. "Words certainly won't be able to
describe this sight. It's like seeing the pyramids or the
Sphinx for the first time."

"This must be the place Grady was going to show us. He
said few white men know of this site."

"Then we're doubly fortunate to see this together."

His voice was dreamlike, soft, seductive. This entire
experience, being with him on the mesa top and viewing the

magic city, was a moment lost in time. Maggie turned to face him. Her gaze dropped to his lips, full and sensuous under his newly formed mustache.

Maggie's heart began to pound. She wasn't sure if it was because of the charged atmosphere or Wex's closeness. Whatever the reason, she only knew she needed to be held, touched, to know she was whole and alive. All thoughts of being lost from her family, of being hungry, disappeared.

As if he read her thoughts, Wex inclined his head. Slowly, with infinite care, his lips brushed hers. The kiss was light and gentle, like the brush of butterfly wings. Maggie's mind went numb, and longing surged through her body.

Wex dropped his hand to the center of her back and pulled her hard against him. Her breath caught in her throat as he increased the pressure of his lips on hers. She circled his waist with both her arms, her hands pressed against the hard flesh of his sides. Needs she'd never known cried for satisfaction.

Something melted inside Maggie, and she felt as unreal as the ancient city across the canyon. She tightened her hold and opened her lips, offering the fullness of her kiss. With a single bold thrust of his tongue, he parted her teeth and stroked the inner recesses of her mouth.

Maggie returned his kiss, reveling in the delicious sensations from the closeness. His hard body pressed against her, and bursts of desire exploded deep inside. The kiss ended, and Maggie drew in a long shuddering breath.

Wex bent his head and trailed rows of tiny kisses along her jaw to the side of her neck. His hand brushed gently against her breast. She relaxed and let the tingles flow through her. Something was happening—something new, something wonderful, something . . . forbidden.

With his lips he nuzzled her collar aside and touched the warm flesh at her throat. "Mary Margaret." Her name sounded as precious as a prayer from his mouth.

Excitement stirred inside her. She knew she was stepping beyond the bounds of propriety. But at this moment, in this place, all that was real was the way this man made her feel. She was totally female, hot and needy.

She clawed at his shirt, eager for the feel of his flesh under her hands. He groaned deep in his throat and cupped her breast in his palm. Nothing in her past had prepared Maggie for the tremors that ran through her.

His mouth captured hers once again in a bruising kiss, demanding, promising. She ached for more, the completion that turned a lady into a woman. Time stood still as she met his kiss with equal fervor.

Lost in her passion, Maggie was shut away in a world of her own. "Mary Margaret," Wex whispered, putting an abrupt end to the kiss. "Somebody's coming."

"No, we're alone." She clutched his sides, now bare under her touch. They were the only people that existed in the world.

A long sigh racked his body. "It's Tim. He's calling."

She opened her eyes and glanced beyond his shoulder to the forest. Surely he was wrong. They were lost, and the camp was far away. Then she heard the voices.

"Maggie . . . Wex . . . are you here?" It was Sarah, her voice getting louder with every word.

Suddenly realizing that she was still in his arms, Maggie tried to step away. Only then did she notice how weak her knees had gotten. Wex caught her elbow to steady her. She covered her lips with her fingers to muffle a frustrated cry. What had she done? What had she been thinking? But she hadn't been thinking; feelings were all that had mattered.

"Over here," Wex called out.

Maggie gazed at the marble city and wondered if she'd been transfixed by the timelessness of the place. Against her better judgment, she'd fallen into his arms twice in one day. But goodness knows it had felt more than good—it had been heavenly. Exactly as he'd promised it would be.

"Are you all right?" he asked, still holding her arm.

She stepped away, struggling to regain her composure. "Of course I am. We've been found. It's what we wanted." Hands trembling, she tucked her shirt back into her breeches.

Confusion warred with anger. How had she let herself get carried away like that? She'd almost made love to a man she neither knew nor trusted. She touched her heated cheeks.

At that moment Sarah and Tim burst through the undergrowth into the opening near them.

Sarah rushed to her sister's side. "Maggie, are you all

right? Did you get hurt in the fall?" She reached for Maggie's hand and began to examine her arms.

"No, I'm fine, thanks to Wex."

"How did you know she fell?" Wex asked, his eyes wide with astonishment.

As if noticing him for the first time, Sarah turned her gaze to Wex. "This morning I had a dream. I saw Maggie running and tumbling downward. I prayed she wouldn't be hurt." Reaching into a small sack, she removed a jar and began to smooth the ointment on Maggie's scraped elbow.

Maggie winced at the burning on her skin. "Ow. The treatment is worse than the injury."

Wex shook his head. "Amazing. How did you know where to find us?"

Tim lifted his rifle and fired two shots into the air. The sound echoed across the treetops. "We went to the ruins looking for you. When you weren't there, we started to search. Sarah said you would be near a white city. Grady led us to this canyon." He swung his gaze to the ruins. "Wow. She was right. Look at that."

Maggie touched Wex's arm. "Wex, Sarah is very special. She has certain powers. It's a gift."

A pink tinge stained Sarah's cheeks. "Be quiet, Maggie. Sit down and let me check your other injuries."

Although Maggie had become accustomed to Sarah's unusual abilities, Sarah was embarrassed to let others know. Maggie changed the subject. "You don't happen to have something to eat in that sack, do you?" She settled on the ground.

"Just some biscuits and dried beef. I knew you would be hungry."

Tim shoved a bundle at Maggie and turned toward the edge of the cliff. "Look at that. It's a magic city like in the storybooks about the knights and dragons and stuff."

Maggie had to agree. She slanted a glance at Wex. Sunlight glittered on his hair, and he stood as tall and stalwart as a mythical god.

But he was human, very real and overwhelmingly masculine. He sat next to her on the ground and picked up a biscuit. "This isn't the meal I promised, but it's probably the best I've ever had."

Maggie shoved a biscuit into her mouth and smiled at him over the bottle of water. "This doesn't get you off the hook, you know. I expect you to keep your promise."

His wide smile stole her breath away. "Mary Margaret." He brushed a crumb from her lips with his fingertip. "I always keep my promises."

Chapter
Seven

"Jumping Jehoshaphat!" Tim pulled hard on the lines, and the wagon jerked to a stop. "What the heck is going on?"

Wex gripped the side to keep his seat. The road leading into Sherman, Colorado, bustled with activity. Wagons and riders moved in a long procession toward the far edge of town. Laughing children shouted from the boardwalk and ran to and fro between the adults.

"I think that answers your question." Wex pointed to a banner strung from one side of the road to the other. FOUNDER'S DAY CELEBRATION—EVERYBODY WELCOME. The sign fluttered in the breeze.

"Looks like we're in time for a celebration." Wex shoved his hat back and wiped his face with his handkerchief. A break from the tedium of travel was long overdue for all of them, especially Maggie, who never took a moment to relax.

"This is great." Tim turned to Maggie when she pulled her wagon next to theirs. "Maggie, can we join in the fun? It's been a long time since we've been to town."

She frowned, and for a second Wex thought she would refuse. Her gaze darted to Grady.

The scout dismounted and tied the mare to the hitching post in front of the hotel. "Reckon it won't hurt none. We can all use the break, and it's about time I get a bath and shave."

"All right," came Maggie's reluctant consent. "Let's get the horses to a livery stable and check into the hotel. I could use a real bed for a change."

Wex smiled. He'd been looking forward to reaching the town since they'd left the Indian ruins a week before. Maggie had taken all the photos she needed, and they'd boxed the developed plates for shipping. The package of negatives and stories waited at the freight station for shipment to the railroad twenty miles way. In a few hours the negatives and stories would be on their way to the agent in New York.

Maggie's photographs captured perfectly the haunting beauty of the ruins. Wex knew that the agent would be able to find a market for the pictures of something few people had seen or knew existed. His words paled next to Maggie's pictures.

Most of all he was looking forward to a hot bath, a shave, and clean clothes. Plus a visit to the sheriff. He hoped the photos of the rustlers would prove useful in identifying the men responsible for the deaths of his companions.

After they stabled the horses, they checked into the hotel. Wex shared a room with Grady and Tim, while Maggie and Sarah took a room on another floor. They agreed to meet in the hotel lobby to join the festivities at the edge of town.

Two hours later Wex descended the stairs. At the mercantile he'd purchased some new clean clothes. The bath and shave made him feel like a new man. He looked like one, too. With the leather vest, rough denims, and cotton shirt, he could blend right in with the locals. All in black, of course. Since Arthur's death, he rarely wore anything but black and an occasional white shirt.

He settled on a burgundy velvet couch to wait for the others. The hotel's attempt at elegance brought a smile to his lips. A kerosene chandelier, with smoke-coated chimneys, hung in the center of the small lobby. The ornate furniture had obviously seen better days and was covered with a veneer of dust. Any respectable hosteler in London would be appalled at the conditions that were customary in the West.

A lady dressed in a silk-and-lace afternoon dress descended the stairs. A man wearing a tailored dark suit pulled her close at his side and whispered something that brought a light feminine giggle. Except for the man's wide-brimmed hat and high-heeled boots, the couple would have been fashionable in any Eastern city. The woman, clearly half the man's age, flashed Wex a smile over her shoulder. Wex tipped his black Stetson and smiled back. As pretty as she was, he had no interest in her. Her blond paleness faded next to Maggie's vibrant coloring.

His gaze was still on the lady when a voice came from the stairway. "Tim, I ordered a picnic basket from the dining room. Will you go see if it's ready?"

Wex swung his head and spotted Maggie and Sarah on the landing. In one swift movement, he jumped to his feet, his eyes locked on Maggie.

In a simple cotton dress printed with tiny pink flowers, Maggie was as elegant as if she wore a silk gown decorated with yards and yards of frills. Her coppery hair was hidden under a straw bonnet, and a tiny smile curved her lips. He swallowed to moisten his mouth, now gone dry.

Since their encounter in the ruins, they'd had no time alone. He was certain Maggie had arranged it that way. He was also certain she planned to leave him behind in Sherman when she proceeded to Denver.

This was one time Miss Callahan wasn't going to have her way. The memory of her kisses, wild as the canyon country they'd been exploring, had him yearning for more. Wex wasn't going to leave the passionate woman until he drank his fill of her sweetness.

Sarah hurried past her sister and bounded to Wex's side. He pulled his gaze from Maggie to the younger girl. There was no doubt Sarah was on the verge of becoming a real beauty. Her dark hair hung in soft waves to her waist, and under the blue calico dress her body was blossoming into womanhood. A protective and unexpectedly paternal sensation surfaced within him. Much as he'd felt about Arthur. His heart constricted. He'd failed with his brother. This time he would succeed, or die trying.

"Wex." Sarah paused with her hands on her hips. "You shaved off your beard." She laughed, a sparkling sound that warmed his heart. "Now you don't look so much like Robin Hood."

He shook his head and glanced at Maggie from the corner of his eye. "Your sister thinks I more closely resemble the Big Bad Wolf."

Maggie ignored the remark and continued down the stairs.

"There's a dance tonight." Sarah gazed up at Wex. "Are you a wonderful dancer, Wex?"

"I've attended a ball or two," he said, understating the facts.

More times than he wanted to admit, he'd attended two or more balls in one evening before finding the right lady with whom to spend the remainder of the night. It would never do to mention his past indiscretions to Sarah. "I'll teach you some of the latest steps from London, although they're probably out of vogue by now."

Tim entered the lobby, swinging the basket in his hand. "Ready? I want to get there in time for the horse race."

Wex stuck out his arm. "May I escort you to the festivities, Miss Callahan?" With a broad wink at Maggie, he turned to Sarah. The glow in the young woman's cheeks turned crimson.

She curtsied, then took his arm. "I would be honored, Mr. Wexford."

Maggie opened her mouth then snapped it shut. She'd been positive Wex would insist on escorting her to the picnic. Turning his attention to Sarah was a kind gesture, and Maggie's twinge of jealousy made her mad at herself.

"Well, Tim," Maggie said, offering her arm to her brother, "looks like you're stuck with your old spinster sister."

Wex turned and smiled. Under his black Stetson, humor glittered in his azure eyes. As hard as she'd tried to avoid him, every time she looked at him she was reminded of the kisses they'd shared and the way she'd responded to his caresses. If Sarah and Tim hadn't found them on the mesa top when they did, she would have violated all the rules of propriety. Her reaction to him shocked her.

In a way she was looking forward to the dance that night. Dancing would give her an excuse to feel Wex's arms around her and enjoy the closeness of his body, all within the confines of polite society.

She and Tim followed Wex and Sarah out of the hotel. As they stepped onto the wooden walkway a troop of rowdy cowboys staggered out of the saloon across the street and headed toward the picnic grounds.

Sarah stopped abruptly, and Wex stumbled. Her face turned pale. "Let's . . . let's not go. We can stay at the hotel and rest."

Maggie touched her sister's cheek, suddenly grown cold. "What's wrong, Sarah? Are you ill?"

A distant look darkened Sarah's emerald eyes; she clutched her medallion. Then, as quickly as it came, the expression in her eyes changed. "Nothing's wrong. I'm just being silly."

The smile disappeared from Wex's face. "We don't have to go if you don't feel well."

"No, truly, I'm fine." Sarah tightened her grip on Wex's arm. "I like picnics and celebrations."

His gaze clashed with Maggie's. She shrugged. "Let's go."

"I'm glad we got here today," Tim said. "You know why they call this town Sherman, don't you?"

Maggie shrugged, her gaze on Wex's wide back. Her eyes dropped to his narrow hips and strong, muscular thighs. His bold masculinity sent a quiver to the pit of her stomach. Aware that Tim had spoken, she pulled her attention to her brother. "No, why?"

"A man named Elliott started the town. He served in the war with General Sherman and named the town for him." He glanced at his sister. "Maggie, did Papa know General Sherman?"

"I suppose he took his picture a time or two. Papa met most of the generals. He even took President Lincoln's picture at Gettysburg."

"Wow!" He let go of Maggie's arm and ran ahead to Wex. "You heard that, Wex? Papa knew the president."

Maggie watched from behind as Wex clapped his hand on Tim's shoulder. The gesture was natural, full of the warmth and spontaneity of a big brother Tim never had. "Maggie told me that your papa was a famous photographer during the War between the States."

"Yes, he was," added Sarah. "But Wex knows the Queen of England."

"I've met Her Majesty. I don't know her." Wex glanced back at Maggie, a sly grin on his face.

Something about the way he said it made Maggie wonder about his background. Judging by his speech and manners, he was well-bred, probably from an aristocratic family. Yet he never mentioned his family or his upbringing. Of course, there were many impoverished noblemen in England. Maybe he was embarrassed to admit he wasn't as wealthy as his family once was. She shook her head. The man continued to be a mystery. And Maggie hated a puzzle she couldn't solve.

At the edge of town, they entered a wide mowed field with areas set aside for footraces and games. Families gathered in groups under shade trees, their picnic lunches spread on tablecloths and blankets. Shouting and laughing children frolicked with friends they probably hadn't seen in weeks. Everyone had come for a good time. Maggie determined to shake off the uneasy feeling that had settled on her.

Since they were late arrivals, the only remaining shade trees were in the woods and away from the others. Wex spotted a large oak and spread a blanket under the sheltering limbs. Thin streams of sunshine filtered through the trees. The smell of freshly mowed grass mingled with the aroma of fried chicken, roast beef, and a variety of delicacies.

After finishing their lunch, Sarah and Tim excused themselves to join some youngsters their own age. Several people passed and nodded politely, but since they were strangers, Maggie and Wex remained aloof from the others.

Wex stretched out on the blanket and pulled his hat over his eyes. Propped against a tree, Maggie studied the man who'd turned her emotions upside down. He evoked feelings she'd never known existed. Her stomach fluttered every time she looked at him.

Her gaze drifted down the long length of him. Still in the sling, his right arm rested on his wide chest. Her eyes moved lower. His stomach was flat and his hips narrow. She flushed at the memory of the hard bulge she'd felt when he'd pressed against her. Heat surged down from her stomach to her toes.

She twisted her fingers together to keep from touching him and returned her gaze to his face. How would his kisses feel now that he was clean-shaven? she wondered. She doubted they could get any more delicious or thrilling. Her mouth went dry. Would she get a chance to find out?

Surely now that they'd reached town and his wounds were healing, he would be on his way. He wasn't under any obligation, and his stay with them was only temporary. The thought brought an unwanted twinge of sadness.

Maggie removed her straw hat and fanned her heated face. She should be glad to see him leave. After all, she didn't need another responsibility. Her photography and taking care of Tim and Sarah were enough for any woman. The last thing she needed was his disturbing presence in her life. She was better off without him.

Wex contained the smile that tugged at his mouth. From under the brim of the hat, he watched the play of emotions that danced in Maggie's eyes. Her expression wavered between longing and restraint. He would love to learn which part would win the battle waging within her. Tonight he would use the dance to nudge her a little closer to the edge.

He relaxed and let his mind wander. With the clear blue sky and gentle breeze to welcome them, he supposed everybody from the county must have gathered in the meadow. His gaze wandered over the crowd. Were any of the men laughing and playing the ones who'd murdered the cowboys and stolen the cattle and horses? He hated being suspicious of these people. It seemed unlikely that the rustlers would be nearby. They were probably miles away by now. Regardless, he would contact the sheriff the next day and show him the photographs.

Lulled by the warmth and peace of the day, he felt his eyelids grow heavy. He didn't realize he'd fallen asleep until something tickled his nose. With one hand he swatted at the elusive object and opened one eye. To his surprise it wasn't a pesky insect, but a blade of grass suspended between Maggie's fingers. At some point he'd moved to rest his head on her soft, warm thigh.

She smiled and brushed the blade across his bare upper lip. "Going to sleep all afternoon? You'll miss the race."

Heat from her legs penetrated through her skirt and petticoats and warmed the back of his neck. The effect was like throwing kerosene on a brushfire. He opened both eyes and gazed past her breasts into her laughing face. A garden of pink flowers grew inches from his eyes. When she moved, her breasts jiggled gently, and Wex swallowed down a groan. In one quick movement, he snatched her wrist and pulled her hand to his lips. "This is much more interesting than any horse race."

Her hand trembled. "I thought you Brits were fond of racing and all sorts of competition."

He dropped his gaze to her hand. The temptation to touch her, revel in her femininity, was too much for his already heated body. A bead of perspiration broke out on his upper lip. "We are. But Englishmen enjoy a variety of interests," he said, his voice a husky growl. "Both indoors and out." He stroked his tongue across her palm.

She gave a quick intake of breath but didn't move. The warm summer breeze ruffled her loosened hair and her lashes lowered provocatively. He wanted nothing more than to reach up and pull her head to his. Tightening his grip on her fingers, he felt the beating of her pulse at her wrist, strong and rapid.

Lost in his desires, Wex didn't hear anyone approach until Tim said, "What are you guys waiting for?" The youth stood over them, his eyes wide with astonishment. "You're going to miss the race."

Wex squeezed his eyes shut. Not again. Tim had an uncanny sense of timing. Were he and Maggie ever going to get a chance to be alone? He struggled to control his needs. Judging from the heated look in her eyes, he figured Maggie was as disappointed as he. Her brother had no idea what he'd interrupted. Wex rolled onto his stomach so as not to embarrass himself.

"We're on our way." He took a deep breath and rose to his feet. Catching her hand, he pulled Maggie up next to him.

With Tim's help, they folded the blanket and shoved it into the empty basket. Tim grabbed the basket and ran ahead. Wex tangled his fingers in Maggie's and started toward the edge of town, where the finish line had been marked across the main street. As they neared the already gathering crowd Sarah's voice caught his attention.

"I said no," came her strangled cry.

Wex's blood ran cold. He spotted the girl trapped against a tree by a tall, slender young man. Sarah shoved at the youth's chest.

"Come on, pretty girl. All I want is your blue ribbon to wear on my arm, like the knights used to wear their lady's scarf."

"I'm not your lady, so leave me alone."

Pure rage surged through Wex. In a few long strides he was at her side. "You heard the lady." He gripped the boy's shoulder and jerked him away from Sarah.

A few inches shorter than Wex, the young man glared at him, a shocked expression on his face. "I wasn't hurting her. All I wanted was her ribbon. All the guys are wearing their girls' ribbons."

"She's not your girl," Maggie interjected, her face as pale as Sarah's.

The young man threw off Wex's hold. "Okay, sweetheart." He sneered. "I can get any girl in town. I don't want a half-breed bitch, anyway."

Unable to control his temper, Wex grabbed the front of the boy's shirt. "Sarah Callahan is a lady. Apologize." He shook the boy. "Now."

Fear and hatred glittered in the boy's steely-gray eyes. "I don't have to do nothing."

By then a crowd had gathered, and several brawny men were elbowing their way toward them. Maggie laid her hand on his shoulder. "Wex, let him go. We don't want to start a riot."

"What's going on?" The well-dressed man Wex had seen earlier in the hotel interposed himself between them. "Let go of my son." The words rang with the authority of a man accustomed to giving orders.

Far outnumbered, Wex released the boy and stepped back. "Your son insulted a lady." Around them, the murmur of the crowd grew loud.

"Something wrong, Mr. Elliott?" Another man, this one

wearing a silver badge on his shirt, inserted himself between them.

"No, Sheriff. I have everything under control. We don't want to ruin the picnic for these people, do we?" Elliott narrowed is eyes on his son. "Cole, apologize." The man would brook no argument, and his son knew it.

Cole ran his fingers through his tousled blond hair and glared back at his father. "I'm sorry."

Elliott turned to the people gathered around them. "Let's start the race. Cole has a new horse that looks like a winner. I'm taking all bets."

With excited voices, the sea of faces drifted away. With an angry backward glance, Cole plopped his hat on his head and stalked past.

Elliott remained a few steps behind. He stopped, turned, and took a cigar out of his pocket. "Stay out of my way, Brit." After biting off the end, he shoved the cigar between his thin lips. With a steady hand, he struck a match to the end, took a long draw, and blew the gray smoke into the air. "If you know what's good for you, you'll get out of my town."

With slow nonchalance, the man turned on his heel and faded into the waiting crowd.

Wex clutched his hands into fists, struggling to control his rage. He glanced at Sarah. Her face was pale, but she was calmer than Maggie, who was cursing under her breath.

"You made an enemy, mister," the sheriff said. "I know Cole is a little wild, but it doesn't pay to rile Ross Elliott." His gaze dropped to Wex's arm, still in the sling. "Looks like you've already had your share of trouble. You'd best get out of town while you're still in one piece."

The threats added fuel to Wex's determination. "I have business to take care of first, Sheriff. Will you be in your office later?"

The lawman took out a cigarette and lit it. "Reckon I will. What kind of business you got?"

Maggie placed her hand on his arm. "Wex, you can talk to the sheriff tomorrow. Let's go watch the race."

Aware he wasn't going to get anywhere with the antagonistic lawman, Wex shrugged. "Look for me."

The sheriff tipped his hat to Maggie and Sarah and

sauntered toward the crowd now lining the main street of the town.

Wex glanced at Sarah. "Are you all right, Sarah? Did he hurt you?"

She shook her head. "No, he was just becoming a pest."

"Forget him," Maggie said. "You'll never see him again. We're leaving in a few days."

With Sarah safely between them, they moved to join the others, although a horse race was the last thing on Wex's mind. Tim located a spot on the boardwalk in front of the feed-and-grain store where they had an unrestricted view of the race. At the far end of town, the riders had lined up their horses. The race would end at the carriage where Ross Elliott waited with his lady.

Wex studied the couple. Considering the cut of his clothes and the ornate carriage, the man was clearly well-off. The sheriff had deferred to him, so Elliott must wield a great deal of power. Not unlike Wex's own father, who ruled his estates like a feudal lord. Wex had been the only rebel among his subjects.

His gaze dropped to the woman. Although she was young enough to be Elliott's daughter, Wex was certain she wasn't. He'd seen too many powerful men with their mistresses not to recognize the relationship. Once he'd even spotted his father with his mistress. To this day, he doubted that the duke was aware his son knew about his clandestine liaisons. Wex often wondered if his stepmother was aware of the situation. She had her house, her servants, her charity work, children, and grandchildren. As far as Wex knew, she was happy.

Shaded by a lacy parasol, the woman glanced in his direction. She smiled, proving his assessment was correct. With her blond curls and pixie face, the woman possessed a certain sensuality that said she knew all about men and how to please them.

"She's very pretty," Maggie whispered tersely, "if you like the type."

Wex swung his gaze to Maggie, surprised at her curt remark. She sounded almost jealous. "What type is that?"

Maggie continued to stare unabashedly at the woman. "You know the type. A woman who's caught the biggest fish in the pond, but she keeps her hook in the water to see how many others she can add to her collection." Her eyes glittered with amusement. "That one probably has a stringer a foot long."

He chuckled softly. "Mary Margaret, where did you learn about women like that?"

"I'm not as naive as you think I am. I know all about scheming women . . . and men." She pointed toward the far end of town. "The race is about to start."

The loud boom of a gunshot rent the air, and the horses broke into a burst of speed. The crowd hooted and shouted, each cheering for his favorite. A huge palomino took the lead, pounding its hooves into the dusty street, the rider leaning forward to gain the optimum speed.

Then, from out of the pack, a black stallion surged forward. Cole Elliott struck the horse on the flank and gouged his spurs into the Thoroughbred's sides. Renewed outrage threatened to choke Wex. The boy treated horses worse than he treated women.

The cheering spectators grew louder as the race neared the finish line. As they approached, Wex got a better look at the horse. A white diamond on his face was his only distinguishing feature—the same characteristic of the horse the rustlers had taken from Wex. He held his breath as the dust from the horses swirled around them.

In a startling spurt of speed, the stallion broke from the pack and crossed the finish line a full length in front of the palomino. Cole Elliott took off his hat and swung it over his head in victory. The crowd began to swell around him, and his father stood up and cheered.

Wex took one step into the street, stopped by the press of spectators. His jaw set, he elbowed his way to the carriage, where Elliott was holding court. A hand on his arm stopped him.

"Wex, where are you going?" Maggie asked, shouting to be heard above the roar of the crowd.

"That's my horse. I'm going to claim him."

Chapter
Eight

Maggie clutched Wex's sleeve. "What are you talking about? It can't be. A lot of horses look alike."

Wex gazed into her eyes, bright with anxiety. "I'm going to take a closer look and find out for myself."

"You can't accuse that boy of being a horse thief. They'll never believe a stranger. Wait until you talk to the sheriff."

He curled his fingers into fists; the nails bit into his palms. As much as he hated to admit it, what she said made sense. Half a dozen cowboys surrounded Elliott—hands familiar with the guns slung low on their hips. Wex wouldn't stand a chance against this crew. He hated asking for help, but he needed the law if he expected to stand up against Elliott and his allies.

"You're right. I'm going to find the sheriff."

Shaking off her grip, he shoved his way through the milling throng. Above the din of the crowd, Ross Elliott called for a victory celebration at the Fool's Gold Saloon. Wex had only taken a few steps when Maggie again tugged on his shirt.

"I'm going with you."

He spun around and glared at her through narrowed eyes. "Mary Margaret, this is my battle. There could be trouble, and I don't want you involved."

She lifted her chin and met his gaze without flinching. "I

got involved when I took those photographs. Get the pictures and your ownership papers to show the sheriff. I'll confirm anything you say."

A huge knot twisted in his stomach. The last thing he wanted was to get her mixed up in his problems and subject her to danger. "This could get ugly. I doubt that Ross Elliott will take this lightly."

"Wex, it probably isn't your horse." She brushed her fingers along his arm, her touch warm and comforting. "He could have had that stallion for ages."

Wex clenched his jaw to hold back the string of profanities that formed on his tongue. If he knew anything, it was horses. After a lifetime of training and breeding horseflesh, he could identify his own mount in any herd of Thoroughbreds. He squeezed her fingers lightly to reassure her he knew what he was doing. "We'll soon find out."

Five minutes later, the photographs and ownership papers in hand, Wex and Maggie entered the jail house. He'd all but begged her to remain at the hotel, but the stubborn woman had dogged his heels every step of the way. Inside the doorway they paused to let their eyes adjust to the dim interior. A low railing divided the room in half. Two desks stood on one side, while a row of iron-barred cells filled the far wall. The men lying on the bare cots shoved back the hats covering their faces when they heard the thud of boots on the dusty, plank floor.

Wex spotted the sheriff seated behind his scarred wooden desk with his feet propped on the top.

The lawman jumped to his feet, his hand on the six-shooter at his side. "Thought you were coming in tomorrow." His cold brown eyes were devoid of welcome.

"Something came up, and I couldn't wait." Remembering his manners, Wex stuck out his hand. "My name is Wexford, and this is Miss Callahan."

"Wade Steward," he said, taking the offered hand in a strong grip. "Ma'am." He nodded to Maggie. With pleasantries out of the way, he settled back onto his seat and shoved his brown hat back off his forehead. He drew his thick dark brows together and studied the situation. "You're a Brit, ain't ya? What are you doing in these parts?"

Wex gestured to a chair and held it for Maggie. He chose to stand, liking the advantage of his height. "I'm a writer and I'm spending a few months in the West to gather material."

The sheriff stroked the two days' growth of whiskers on his jaw. "So what did you want to see me about?" Steward folded his hands across his stomach. "Planning to write a story about a lawman?"

"Maybe." In a concise report, Wex told the sheriff how he and the cowboys had been ambushed by the rustlers. He'd been wounded, and thanks to Miss Callahan he was alive to tell the story.

The sheriff listened, his only reaction the narrowing of his eyes. He revealed that the bodies had been found and brought to town. Unfortunately there was no trace of the bandits.

"Not only did they take the cattle, they also took my horse." Wex reached into the inner pocket of his vest and pulled out a document. "Here's the bill of sale with the description." He handed it to the sheriff. "Does it look familiar?"

After a few moments of studying the papers, the sheriff shoved them back. "I've seen a lot of horses like this."

Maggie gasped and leaned forward. "A black Thorough-bred stallion with a white diamond on his forehead? I've only seen one."

The sheriff swung his gaze to Maggie, his thin lips drawn into a scowl. "Tell me about it, ma'am."

Her eyes flashed with green fire. She opened her mouth, but Wex held up his hand to silence her. He'd fought his own battles for too many years to allow a woman to defend his actions. "Did you happen to notice the horse the Elliott boy was riding when he won the race?"

Steward shrugged. "Nice Thoroughbred. Sort of re-sembles this horse, but that doesn't mean it's the same one."

Wex snatched up the papers. "That's my horse. But I have other proof." Taking the photograph from Maggie, he held it out for the sheriff's inspection.

"Miss Callahan is a photographer. The day after the horse was stolen, she took this picture. If you'll look closely, you'll see the same horse and the cattle bearing the Double H brand, mixed with some from the Lazy E." A thought dawned, and the blood drained from his face. "That's Elliott's brand, isn't it?"

A shadow fell over the sheriff's face as if a cloud had blotted the sunshine. "Could be. A big outfit like Elliott's loses cattle all the time. Reckon they hit the Lazy E before they robbed the Double H."

With a gigantic effort, Wex controlled the tone of his voice. "I know you can't see the faces of the cowboys, but do you recognize any of their horses?"

After only a cursory glance, Steward shoved the pictures away. "No. They're probably miles away by now. Unless"— he rocked back on the rear legs of the chair—"you were part of the gang, and they left you behind. Now you're trying to get even."

The accusation hit Wex like a fist to the pit of his stomach. "What? That's ridiculous. I'm a British citizen and I've only been in America for six months."

Maggie shot to her feet. "He's right, Sheriff. Mr. Wexford couldn't have been involved."

Fixing his hard gaze on Maggie, the sheriff said, "And how would you know, Miss Callahan? You could be part of his scheme, too."

Maggie's cheeks turned crimson. She leaned over the desk, her knuckles on the pictures. "Sheriff, I'm a traveling photographer. It was by chance that I met Mr. Wexford. You may have heard of Grady Clinton. He's my guide. He'll tell you the truth."

The legs of his chair hit the floor with a loud thud. "I'll talk to Grady. In the meantime, don't go around making accusations against Mr. Elliott. His men won't be as tolerant as he was earlier."

Wex gritted his teeth to resist the urge to slam his fists into the sheriff's smug face. "That's my horse. Get the Elliott boy in here so we can settle this once and for all."

The sheriff rubbed his jaw, then appeared to come to a decision. "Okay, Wexford, I'll talk to Ross. You and the lady wait here." He heaved himself to his feet and sauntered out the door.

"Hey, greenhorn." The voice came from one of the cells across the room.

Wex looked at the man dangling his arms through the bars. Every prisoner was standing, alert to the performance in the office. He lifted his brow in question.

"Take a word of advice." The man had dark bruises on his face and an ugly cut above his eye. "Elliott don't take kindly to greenhorns interferin' in his business. Ya oughta git out of town while the gittin's good."

A new surge of determination flooded Wex. Six months ago he'd left England rather than stand up and accept the consequences for his deeds. He'd be damned if he would run again. "I'll leave when I'm damn good and ready."

The man shrugged. "Suit yerself. Don't say I didn't warn ya."

Wex folded his arms across his chest and set his jaw. He was staring at the prisoner when the door opened and slammed against the wall. At first Wex didn't recognize the man—clean-shaven and wearing a brown suit and bowler hat. But the shotgun resting like an extension of his arm was vintage Grady Clinton.

Maggie jumped up and ran into the scout's open arms. "Grady, I'm so glad you're here."

"Came as soon as I heard you and the Brit were in the hoosegow. Can't you young'uns stay out of trouble? Sarah and Tim are worried sick about you."

Maggie sighed. "We didn't do anything wrong. Wex is trying to convince the sheriff that Cole Elliott has his horse."

"I heard you've already had one confrontation with Elliott. You got a hankerin' to get yourself killed?"

A chill raced up Wex's spine. How many times had he heard those exact words from his father? "No. But I want to see justice done."

With a loud guffaw, Grady propped his hip against the desk. "Elliott owns this town, and he has the biggest spread in this part of the state. Nobody, including the sheriff, is going to buck him."

"That's my horse," Wex said between his teeth.

"Remains to be seen." Grady picked up the photograph and studied the images of the horses and cattle.

Seconds later the sheriff returned, followed by a very unhappy Ross Elliott and his son. Wex moved to Maggie's side, his protective instincts on alert.

"This had better be important, Wade," Elliott said as he stepped into the office. "I have plans for the rest of the evening."

Cole Elliott stopped in his tracks. "What are they doing here? I didn't hurt that b—girl."

"Shut up, Cole," his father ordered. "What's this about, Wade?"

The sheriff cleared his throat. "I'll get right to the point. Wexford lost his horse a while back, and he thinks it's the same one Cole was riding today."

"Lost?" Wex clenched his fist and struggled to control his voice. "My horse was stolen along with a herd of cattle from the Double H. I have photographs that show your cattle and my horse with the rustlers."

Ross Elliott narrowed his eyes to cold steely slits. "Are you calling my son a cattle rustler and a horse thief? In this country we hang horse thieves."

Wex shifted his gaze to Cole. The young man turned pale and glared back with hatred in his gray eyes. "I didn't steal nothing."

The sheriff stepped between the combatants. "Nobody's accusing Cole of anything. Just tell Wexford where you got the horse, and I'll send him packing."

"I bought it."

"From whom?" Wex asked.

"I don't have to tell you nothing, greenhorn." He turned on his heel and started for the doorway. "My girl's waiting for me to take her to the dance."

"Cole." His father's voice brought the younger man to an abrupt halt. "I don't want any trouble, especially today. Where did you get the horse?"

Cole's back stiffened, and his hand dropped to the gun at his hip. "I bought him from a . . . from a man over in . . . Colorado Springs." He tilted his chin defiantly.

"When?" Wex asked, ready to stake his life on the fact Cole was lying.

"I don't remember. A couple of months ago, I guess."

Cole shifted his gaze from his father and glanced around the jail.

The sheriff threw up his hands. "You see? It can't be your horse, Wexford. I'd advise you to keep your mouth shut from now on."

"You're wrong, Steward," Grady said.

The scout's soft voice drew every eye in the place. Even the prisoners stopped mumbling among themselves and listened. Grady shoved the photograph toward Elliott's chest. "I examined that stallion and these ownership papers. It's the same horse."

"Clinton," Ross said, glowering at the scout, "what stake do you have in this?"

Grady propped one foot on a chair, his shotgun draped across his knee. "I promised this gal's daddy I'd take care of her and all the Callahans, along with their friends."

"I don't give a good goddamn what you or anybody else says." Ross Elliott glanced at the picture and tore it into pieces. "This is what I think of your proof. Nobody accuses an Elliott of being a low-down horse thief."

Maggie gasped as her photograph dropped to the floor. "That won't do any good, Mr. Elliott. I have the glass negatives. I can make as many as I want."

Damn. Wex speared Maggie with an angry glance. He wished she hadn't mentioned the negatives. It put her and her family in further jeopardy. "All I want is my horse," he said.

"You'll get that stallion when hell freezes over." Ross Elliott spun on his heel and headed toward the door. "I'll shoot the bastard first."

At that moment the woman he'd been with earlier stepped into the office. "Ross," she purred, "I'm tired of waiting. You promised to take me to dinner before the dance."

Her gaze shifted from Ross to Wex. Interest glittered in her golden eyes, and she smiled an invitation. Wex ignored her blatant flirtation.

"You haven't heard the last of this, Elliott," Wex said.

The man stopped, his face mottled with anger. "Wexford, in one day you've accosted my son twice. Take my advice and get your whore and your two half-breeds out of my town."

Wex took one step forward, but was stopped by Grady's shotgun across his chest. "We don't want no trouble, Elliott," Grady growled, "but we can give as good as we get."

Raw fury threatened to choke Wex. He glimpsed Maggie from the corner of his eye. Her face was blanched, and her hands clenched into fists. "We'll leave when we get damn good and ready, and not a minute sooner."

The sheriff spoke up. "Go on with Laura, Mr. Elliott. I'll take care of these troublemakers."

Cole Elliott tipped his hat and flashed a cocky grin at Maggie. "I'll see you at the dance, *sweetheart*."

Wex growled, a deep primal sound, as he sprang to attack. Grady used his full strength to stop Wex from tearing the boy's head off his shoulders.

Maggie clutched his arm. "Let's go pack, Wex. We can't fight the whole town. I'm in a hurry to get to Denver, anyway."

Wex eyed the boy swaggering out the door, his cronies at his heels. Fury fired tenacity. Nobody was going to run him out of town with his tail between his legs. Forcing a smile, he covered Maggie's hand with his.

"I promised to take you to that dance tonight." His gaze shifted to the crowd gathered on the boardwalk. "And I always keep my promises."

"Maggie, will you please hurry?" Sarah took one last look at herself in the tiny mirror over the washstand. "Wex will be here any minute." She lifted the skirt of her royal-blue gown and danced around the small hotel room.

"If he's that impatient, he can go without me," Maggie said, adjusting the scooped neckline of her lavender dress, which bared her shoulders and arms.

After the confrontation in the sheriff's office, she'd talked until she was blue trying to persuade Wex not to attend the dance. She'd told him he was only borrowing trouble by showing his face in public. The stubborn Englishman refused to listen to reason, however. Maggie was forced to go if only to keep him from doing something foolish—like getting himself killed.

She picked up Wex's loaded revolver and stared at the large heavy weapon. For a long moment she wondered how she could carry it to the dance. Quickly she dug into her carpetbag and pulled out her largest reticule. The gun barely fit inside, and it weighed heavily on her arm, but Maggie liked the security of having the weapon at hand. Who knew when it would come in handy?

Sarah stopped dancing. "Do you think you're going to need that gun?"

Maggie flinched; she'd hoped Sarah hadn't noticed. "Probably not. I'm only being cautious."

"Be careful, will you, sis?"

Maggie smiled. "You aren't having any premonitions about tonight, are you?"

On a long sigh, Sarah shrugged. She clutched the gold pendant that lay against her chest. "Not really. I've tried to keep my mind blank. I want to go to the dance."

"Well, I'm certain you're going to be the belle of the ball."

She adjusted the blue ribbon that held Sarah's hair off her face. Every time she looked at the younger girl, she was struck by her beauty. Shorter and more delicate than Maggie, the girl possessed a beauty that went much deeper than her pretty face. Sarah had a pure and loving heart. Maggie renewed the vow she'd made to their father to protect her sister and to see that Sarah received the education to become a doctor. It had been Papa's dream as well as Sarah's.

Sarah stepped around the large box camera shoved against the wall. "I wish you'd let me fix your hair. I know Wex would like it better long and flowing like molten copper."

With an embarrassed laugh, Maggie brushed a stray tendril of hair that had escaped the bun twisted on top of her head. "I'm not in the habit of primping for Wex or any man. It's cooler like this." She turned away so Sarah wouldn't note the flush on her cheeks.

Reaching out, Sarah pulled a few more strands loose, softening the look around Maggie's face. "That's better. Too bad we left the trunks with our good clothes in Denver. Wex would really like you in that green silk you wore to the engagement party."

Groaning, Maggie said, "Please don't remind me of that disaster. This lavender is good enough. Besides, Wex doesn't care what I wear."

A shrewd look glittered in Sarah's green eyes. "I love the way he says 'Mary Margaret' and the way he looks at you when he thinks nobody's watching. Then you look right back at him. It's the way Tim looks at a great big piece of chocolate cake."

Maggie let out a roar of laughter. "From Robin Hood to chocolate cake. Sarah, you read too many books."

The younger girl shot a haughty glance over her shoulder. "Maggie, you know you like him, so you can quit pretending with me. You never did tell me what happened that day at the ruins. How you slipped down that ravine, and why you both looked so . . . so guilty when we found you."

"Sarah . . ." A loud knock on the door saved further explanation. Not that Maggie would tell the truth. Her love for Wex was too new and fragile to share even with her sister.

Love? She stopped with her hand on the latch. When had love come into the picture? No, she didn't love him. She couldn't. Only a fool would waste her time on things like love and marriage and demanding men.

"Who—" Her voice cracked, and she began again. "Who is it?"

"It's us, Wex and Tim."

Her heart fluttered at the sound of that broad British accent. This feeling wasn't love. Any healthy, normal woman would have the same reaction to a handsome man.

She slipped off the bolt and opened the door. Tim rushed into the room, but Wex stood in the hallway and waited. Her gaze collided with his, his eyes warm and yearning. He wore a black silky shirt that stretched across his wide chest and tucked into black wool trousers. In his hands he held a new black Stetson, and his Wellington boots were so highly polished she could see her reflection in them. He looked even more dangerous than the night he'd come to her out of the shadows.

For a long moment they looked at each other. A wide smile curved his lips, and his eyes glittered with pleasure. His gaze moved over her like a caress, touching, stroking, loving.

She had never seen a more handsome, appealing man. The white scar on his cheek only added to his roguish appearance. Her mouth went dry, and she flicked her tongue across her lips to moisten them. Surely he could hear her heart pounding against her ribs.

He broke the silence when he said, "You look lovely, Miss Callahan." With one finger he toyed with a stray wisp of hair at her cheek. His touch was as gentle as the brush of a feather.

Maggie wiped her damp palms on the sides of her lavender dress. At the look of appreciation in his eyes, a shiver of pleasure washed over her.

"Thank you, Mr. Wexford." She looked him over once more, giving in to the sheer pleasure of seeing him. Then she noticed something different. "Where's your sling? Is your shoulder better?"

A short burst of laughter came from inside the room. "Maggie, while you and Tim were hauling your cameras into the room, Wex and I went to see the doctor."

Wex nodded. "He said I must have had a wonderful physician taking care of me, because I'll have a very small scar. In a few weeks I should be as good as new."

And on your way back to England. Maggie's heart ached at the thought. She drew a deep steadying breath as she stepped into the hallway.

"Are you sure you want to go to the dance?" she asked for the hundredth time.

Wex smiled and offered his arm. "Tim and I will be escorting the two prettiest girls there. We want to show you off to the world." In spite of the bravado of his words, Maggie spotted a flash of anxiety in his eyes.

She shifted the reticule to her other hand and placed her arm in his. "Promise you'll behave—that you won't start any trouble."

He pulled her closer to his side. The muscles in his arm were hard under her fingers. "On my word as a gentleman, I will not start any trouble. I only want to dance with you."

Maggie swallowed down her trepidation. If only the Elliotts and their cohorts had the same intention, she thought. The weight of the reticule bumped her leg. She was grateful she had the gun . . . just in case.

Chapter Nine

Wex tucked Maggie's arm close to his side as they approached the large barn at the edge of town. A waltz melody flowed from the orchestra, and boisterous laughter welcomed them to the festivities.

Kerosene lamps and candles sent a stream of pale yellow light through the open doors. The air was fragrant with the sweet aroma of freshly baled hay. Wex smiled at the contrast between this dance and the balls he'd frequented in London and on the Continent—as different as Maggie from the women in his past.

This was real—the farmers, the ranchers, the wide sky above, the woman on his arm. Maggie was genuine, sincere and honest. Her earthy beauty excited him far more than any woman he'd ever known. She was as natural as the wild roses that grew in the valleys of the Emerald Isle. He suspected that if she ever let go, her passion would erupt with the intensity of a tidal wave, sweeping them both away in its force. A quiver of anticipation shot through him. He hoped he would not have to wait too long to ignite that passion.

As they walked through the town, he'd boldly pulled Maggie close, needing to feel the warmth of her. For a change she'd been amicable and didn't complain when he'd stopped in a shadow and stolen a quick kiss. He prayed the remainder of the evening went as well—for all of them.

The sheriff held up his hand to stop them as they stepped into the dim interior of the barn. "I'm checking all the guns, Wexford. Got one?"

He lifted his arm and shrugged. Maggie had taken his holster and pistol that first night and hadn't given either back. "Completely defenseless, Sheriff." Wex knew he was walking unarmed into a hornet's nest. But at least his adversaries were equally unarmed.

Through narrow eyes, the sheriff studied him. "Okay, just don't cause any trouble."

Before he could answer, two rambunctious boys shoved at them, eager to be free of their parents' supervision. Maggie's reticule bumped against the door with a loud thump. Wex suppressed a smile. He'd wondered why she'd become attached to her handbag, and why it looked so heavy. He might not have a gun, but he'd bet every penny of his inheritance that she did. Mary Margaret Callahan apparently did not like to take chances.

Moving past the sheriff, they stepped across the hard-packed dirt floor, swept clean of the debris that normally littered a barn. Long tables laden with punch and cake lined the walls. A group of teenage boys hovered around the dessert table.

Tim broke away from Sarah, his dark eyes wide with delight. "Maggie, I'm going to get some of that chocolate cake. Want some?"

Maggie grinned, and Sarah started to laugh. The sisters looked at each other as if sharing a secret. Wex couldn't begin to guess what the women found so amusing.

"I see a girl I met today," Sarah said. "See you around." Tim and Sarah disappeared in the crowd near the tables.

Wex smiled down at Maggie. "I thought we'd never be alone."

She gestured to the people milling around the fringes of the dance floor. "I hardly call this being alone."

"Close your eyes and pretend we're in an elegant ballroom. Crystal chandeliers are glittering like stars on the gilded ceiling, and we're the only dancers on the shiny marble floor."

Her hand trembled slightly on his arm. "Where is this elegant ballroom, Mr. Wexford?"

"Buckingham Palace."

With a smile she turned into his arms. "When did you attend a ball at the palace?"

"A very long time ago, Miss Callahan." He bowed over her hand. "May I have this dance, my lady?"

"I would be honored, sir."

He swept her into his embrace and twirled her in time to the energetic waltz music. Her reticule bumped against his back, but he refrained from mentioning the bruises he was bound to sustain.

The orchestra was fourth rate at best, but Wex had never enjoyed a dance more. Unable to contain his needs, he pulled Maggie tight against him, closer than was socially acceptable. Her soft, warm body had his blood pounding through his veins. "Mary Margaret," he whispered, "you smell like an Irish meadow in May."

She tilted her head, and the look in her eyes was enough to melt an iceberg. "Thank you, Wex. And I must say, you look very smart tonight. Where did you get the duds?"

With a soft chuckle he spun her around several times. "I got the 'duds' from a local tailor. Unfortunately he didn't have a jacket to fit." These ready-mades didn't even compare with the fashionable wardrobe stored in his trunks at the hotel in Cheyenne. But he fit in perfectly with the other men, many of whom wore denims with chambray work shirts. Noticeably absent were the guns strapped to their hips. The sheriff clearly didn't want trouble.

One dance blended into two, and soon the clearing filled with more dancers. Sarah waltzed by with a young man she was keeping at arm's length. Wex studied the throng over Maggie's shoulders. Laughter from a group of youngsters blended with the music, and in one corner a group of young women gossiped among themselves. From time to time a wife grabbed her husband and hustled him into the circle of dancers. Most of the men looked as if they'd rather be hog-tied and branded than endure the torture of dancing with their wives.

When the orchestra announced it was taking a break, Wex led Maggie to the table that held a large punch bowl.

"Champagne, my lady?" he asked, twining his fingers in hers.

"It looks more like fruit punch. But I can use something cool." A gray-haired matron handed them tin cups of the drink.

Wex touched his cup to hers in a toast. "To the loveliest lady present." Their eyes met and held. She sipped her drink, and he dropped his gaze.

A thin sheen of perspiration glistened on her bare shoulders, giving them the glow of fine porcelain. Wex resisted the temptation to brush his tongue across the silky flesh. Wouldn't the good ladies of Sherman be shocked at such inappropriate behavior? Later, he promised himself. Later he would take her outside for a breath of fresh air and let nature take its course.

A soft murmur coursed through the crowd. Wex looked up to see that Ross Elliott and his lady had made their grand entrance. The woman wore an even fancier gown than earlier in the day, and the man's arm was hooked possessively in hers. The sea of people parted as Elliott strutted to the raised platform where the band had been performing.

"Friends." Elliott held up his hands to silence the crowd. "I'm glad to see you're all having a good time here tonight."

"Sure are, Ross," a man yelled. "Thanks to you."

A smattering of applause rippled through the group. Next to Wex, Maggie had stiffened and clutched her handbag to her chest. Lord, he prayed, don't let her do anything foolish. He tightened his grip on her fingers.

Elliott waited until the applause ended. "Forty years ago, when my parents came to this valley, there was nothing but a few redskins and stray horses. We built the Lazy E from blood, sweat, and tears. Then more people came, and the town was born. We decided to name our little city after one of the greatest men I've ever known, the man I served with in the war. A great general who rousted the rebels in Georgia and chased the savage Indians from our land."

Wex glanced at Tim who stood a few feet away. The boy's bronze skin turned white. Wex reached out and squeezed his shoulder in encouragement.

Somebody shoved a cup into Elliott's hand. "A man I respect so much, I named my oldest son for him. Too bad

W.T. can't be with us tonight to honor his namesake. Without further ado, let's drink to General William T. Sherman."

Maggie squeezed Wex's fingers so hard she was afraid she would break them. "The man is an ignorant bastard," she whispered, her voice shaking with suppressed anger. "He chased the Indians from land that had been theirs both by tradition and by treaty."

Wex leaned closer, his breath warm on her cheek. "Calm down, Mary Margaret. Don't get yourself upset."

Upset didn't half describe her emotions. "I can't help it. Rising Sun was the most loving, kind woman I've ever met. Her people were more civilized than men who steal horses and insult innocent people."

"The band is starting to play. Let's dance."

Maggie jerked her hand from his. "As angry as I am, I'll probably step all over your feet. I'll sit this one out." She moved into the shadows to a large bale of hay. "I would appreciate another cup of punch, though."

As Wex nodded and moved away Tim settled next to Maggie. "Maggie, why does everybody hate my people? I know there are a few bad Indians, but there are a lot of bad white men, too."

Touched by the despondency in his voice, Maggie draped her arm across his shoulder. Her heart ached for her brother. "It's ignorance, mostly. I remember when you first came to St. Louis, even Aunt Olivia had trouble accepting you, Sarah, and your mother. But as soon as she got to know all of you, she insisted you call her 'Aunt,' and she told all her friends you were her family."

"I know, but it's different here. I almost got in a fight with a kid who called me a half-breed."

Maggie tightened her grip on his narrow shoulders. How much could a young boy be expected to bear? He'd lost his mother and father, and only Maggie remained to protect him from the harsh realities of life. "Fighting doesn't prove anything, Tim. You'll only give Sarah more injuries to nurse."

She glanced around and realized she hadn't seen Sarah for quite a while, not since Elliott's grand entrance. "Speaking of Sarah, where is she?"

Tim shrugged. "Last time I saw her, she said she was going outside for a breath of fresh air."

A wave of fear ran through Maggie. It wasn't like Sarah to be gone for long. "I'm going to look for her."

"Want me to come with you?"

She glanced up and saw Wex talking to Ross Elliott's woman. The pretty blonde had her head tilted toward him and her hand resting on his arm. Jealousy rippled through Maggie. "No, I need some fresh air. Wait here for Wex." *If he ever unhooks himself from that woman's line.*

Seconds later Maggie stepped outside and took a deep breath of fresh air. A gentle breeze ruffled the leaves on the limbs of the spreading oaks. The lanterns from inside cast dancing shadows on the ground. In the dark of the moon, only a sprinkling of stars lit the trees and shrubs. She stepped away from the building and spotted a figure behind a tree.

"Sarah?" she called.

With a loud gasp, a red-faced girl followed by an equally embarrassed young man came into view. The boy tugged on his collar as he trailed at the girl's heels into the barn. How many others would she find if she ventured farther into the grove? Maggie wondered with a grin.

She was forced to admit it was a perfect night for lovers. While dancing with Wex, she'd imagined him walking with her into the yard, holding her, kissing her. A delightful tremor settled in the center of her heart. Maybe later, she thought, after she located Sarah.

Slowly her eyes adjusted to the darkness. "Sarah," she called louder. Perhaps her sister had gone back inside. She started to return to the dance when she heard a noise. It sounded like two animals thrashing in the brush. Her heart stopped beating. What if a bear or wildcat had attacked Sarah?

Heedless of any danger to herself, Maggie pulled her gun from her bag. "Sarah? Is that you?"

"Help!"

"Sarah?" Fear choked Maggie, and the word came out as little more than a grunt.

"Ow." A harsh male voice from the bushes. "Bitch." The sound of flesh hitting flesh tore through Maggie.

She turned in time to see a shadow lift from the ground and begin to run. Taking aim, she fired the revolver. The figure leaped behind a tree. Maggie fired again.

"Maggie . . ." Sarah had sobbed her name.

In the near darkness, Maggie almost stumbled over her sister. Sarah lay sprawled on the ground, her dress bunched around her waist. She stretched out her arms like a drowning sailor reaching for a life preserver.

Pain pierced Maggie's chest like a sharp knife. Somebody had attacked her sister, had tried to rape her. She caught Sarah by the shoulders, hugging her to share her body warmth. Sarah was trembling, her skin icy. "Sarah, are you hurt? Did he . . ."

"No," she sobbed. "I fought him, Maggie. I really tried."

Maggie was torn between chasing the sorry animal who would attack a girl and consoling her sister. Sarah buried her face in Maggie's chest.

Voices and the sound of running feet came out of the darkness. Maggie lifted her gun, ready to kill anybody who dared touch her sister again.

"What's going on here?" someone yelled. "Who's doing all the shooting?"

"Maggie, where are you?"

Wex. Maggie lifted her head. "Over here. With Sarah."

What sounded like an army of feet stomped through the bushes. Wex was the first to reach her.

"God, what happened?" He knelt on the ground.

Relief flooded Maggie. For the first time she realized she was trembling. "Somebody . . . a man tried to . . . attack Sarah."

"Are you shot?" She recognized the sheriff's voice.

"No. I fired at him, but he got away."

"It's all right, sweetheart. I'm here now." Wex eased the gun from her stiff fingers and glanced up at the sheriff. "Why the hell are you standing here? Go after the bastard."

The sheriff hunkered down. "Which way did he go?"

Maggie lifted her head and noted the male faces leaning over them. Quickly she smoothed Sarah's skirt over her legs. All they want is a show, she thought. They don't care about us.

"Behind those trees, that way." She gestured with her

head while hugging Sarah close to let her own warmth continue to penetrate her sister's chilled body.

Several men took off in the direction she'd indicated, followed a few seconds later by the sheriff. Wex brushed his hand gently over the back of Sarah's head. Grass and leaves clung to her hair, and dirt smudged her dress. Somebody held a lantern up, and for the first time Maggie saw the bruise on her sister's flawless cheek.

"Maggie," Sarah whispered, her voice breaking. "He took my medallion."

A long raw scrape marred her neck. "Hush, sweetheart, we'll catch him." Maggie heard a deep angry growl, and she wasn't sure if it came from herself or Wex.

It had happened again, Wex thought. Again he'd been careless and allowed someone he cared for to get hurt. The burning started in his stomach and worked its way to his throat. First his brother, now Sarah.

He looked at the men gathered around them. The bastard could have been any one of them. But who would be so brutal to an innocent girl? He tightened his grip on the gun.

"What was she doing out here, anyway?" someone asked.

Another voice came from above him. "A girl ain't got no business out here alone."

"Guess she was asking for it."

Something exploded in Wex with the force of a volcano. He leaped to his feet and grabbed the first man he saw. "No woman deserves to be treated like this," he growled. "Whoever did this should be strung from the nearest tree."

"Hold it, Wexford." The sheriff shoved the barrel of his gun into Wex's gut. "I'm the law here."

Releasing his grip, Wex glared into the lawman's face. "I suppose you didn't find anything."

"No, I didn't. I'll take a statement from the girl and see what I can do."

Wex glanced down at Maggie, rocking Sarah like a mother with a baby. Pain slashed across his heart. He softened his tone. "Did either of you recognize the man?"

Maggie shook her head, and Sarah could only hiccup between sobs. Wex looked over the men crowding around. At the back of the group he spotted Ross Elliott with his woman. By the dim light streaming from the barn, he caught an annoyed expression on the man's face. Later, Wex thought, he would deal with the bastard and see that he got his due reward. Now he needed to get Sarah back to the hotel and safety.

He jerked away from the sheriff. Hell, let him pull the trigger if he had a mind to. "Maggie," he said softly, "let's get Sarah out of here. We'll take her to the hotel, and you can talk to her there." He shoved his gun into his belt.

Squatting down, he whispered, "Sarah, love, I'm going to pick you up. Relax. I won't let anything happen to you." He slid an arm under Sarah's knees and another behind her back. She wrapped her arms around his neck and buried her face in his shirt.

"Move out," the sheriff roared, parting the crowd. "The show's over. Wexford, I'll come to the hotel and get a statement."

"You'll deal with me, Wade." Grady stepped out of the shadows, his shotgun cocked and ready. "First we'll talk to some of these young fellows, see if they saw or heard anything. Nobody is going to bother Miss Callahan as long as I have old Minnie here on my arm."

Wade Steward's face turned crimson. "Okay, Clinton. Not that it'll do any good." Together they moved back into the barn.

Tim caught Wex's arm. "I'll get my rifle, and he won't get away."

"No, Tim." Maggie draped her arm across her brother's shoulders. "Sarah needs us. Come back to the hotel."

With every step he took, fury swelled within Wex's chest. Anger at himself, anger at the others. How had he let this happen? Was he destined to fail everyone for whom he cared? He cursed himself for his shortcomings.

The girl was such a tiny thing, sweet, loving, pure. Like Arthur, his frail brother, who'd died because of Wex's carelessness.

As clear as if it were yesterday, he saw Arthur clinging to the pommel, trying to keep his seat on the wild stallion. Wex felt the leather reins slip and burn his palms, the pain when the hoof slashed across his cheek. But he couldn't control the animal.

In his mind's eye he saw his brother fly from the saddle and hit the ground. Arthur's twisted body lying in the dirt—the horse snorting and bucking—the screams of the girl he'd been with only moments before.

Worse was the grating of his father's frigid voice. "Andrew, why was that wild stallion in the paddock? How could you let your brother try to ride the animal? You were supposed to be looking after him. You're responsible. It's your fault he's dead."

His fault. He cuddled Sarah closer into his embrace. He should have been watching her instead of trying to make love to Maggie. He should have been watching Arthur instead of trying to make love to that girl, whatever her name was. Twenty years had erased her face from his memory, but nothing could wipe out the grotesque stillness of his twin brother's face in death.

Chapter Ten

Wex paced the hallway outside Maggie's hotel room— the sound of his boot heels on the worn carpet his solitary companion. Icy fingers clutched his chest. He should be out looking for Sarah's assailant; it was his responsibility, his duty. But somebody had to stay and make sure no further harm befell the women. After a fierce argument with Grady, he'd agreed to act as sentry. Grady reasoned he knew the territory, and Wex had already made too many enemies.

He studied the closed door as if he could see through the solid wood. By the time they'd reached the hotel, Sarah had calmed down enough to relay what had happened. Someone had grabbed her from behind, so she hadn't seen her attacker. One good thing, though—if anything about the incident could be called good—the girl hadn't been raped. Only because Maggie had reached her in time.

Maggie, not him. Like before, he'd been caught up in his own selfish pursuits. He rubbed his forehead and tried to understand how he'd become so distracted. After he'd fetched Maggie's punch, a gentle hand on his arm had stopped him. The pretty blonde, Ross Elliott's woman, had taken the punch from him and rewarded him with an inviting smile. What demon had made him engage in a conversation with her, he had no idea. Perhaps because she belonged to Elliott, he hadn't been able to resist the temptation to rile the man a bit. Or had he been trying to make Maggie jealous?

From the corner of his eye he'd spotted Maggie leave the barn. As politely as possible, he'd excused himself from the woman and set to follow her. He'd been waiting all evening for the chance to get her alone outdoors.

Before he'd reached the door, the blast of a gunshot shattered the night. At the memory of the ominous sound, his stomach lurched, and he broke out in a cold sweat. He'd fully expected to find Maggie's body crumpled on the ground. Instead the victim of the attack had been Sarah.

He slammed one fist into the other, wishing it were the face of the assailant—the man who had hurt a girl who wanted nothing more than to heal the sick and help others.

"Mr. Wexford," called a woman's soft voice from the stairway.

Spinning around, he saw the hotel proprietor's wife carrying a tray. He tipped his hat and stretched is arms protectively against the door. "Yes, madam?"

"I made some hot tea. I thought the ladies could use some."

"Thank you. I'm sure Miss Callahan will appreciate your kindness." He took the tray from her hands.

The plump matron wiped her hands on her sparkling white apron. "It's a shame about the little one. I'll never understand how a man can be so cruel to a woman. Why, she's little more than a child." A flush rose in her puffy cheeks. "This is a hard country, Mr. Wexford, not at all civilized like your England."

"We have our problems, too, Mrs. Klein. Men are the same everywhere." Balancing the tray on one hand, he tapped lightly on the door.

"If there's anything I can do . . ." The woman hovered in the hallway as if eager for a glimpse inside the room.

"Thank you, madam. I'll relay your offer to Miss Callahan."

At the dismissal in his voice, the woman retreated down the stairs.

Maggie pulled open the door and peeked out. Her face was blanched and her cheeks damp. "Oh, it's you, Wex."

Wex forced a calmness he didn't feel. Neither Maggie nor

Sarah deserved the harsh treatment they'd received since coming to Sherman. In a few short hours, they'd been called a whore and a half-breed, and Sarah had been attacked. How much more could they endure?

"Mrs. Klein brought some tea. It may calm Sarah down some."

"She's sleeping, but I could use a cup." She moved back and held the door open. "Please come in. I don't want to leave my sister."

"How is she?" he asked.

"She says she's fine, but I'm not so sure." She took the tray and set it on the dresser.

He glanced at the bed where Sarah lay huddled under the quilt, her face buried in the pillow. His heart constricted. She'd lost her mother and her father, but he sensed a strength inside the girl that would carry her through this.

"She's fortunate to have you and Tim to support her." He hung his hat on a peg next to the door.

"Where is Tim?" she asked.

"In the next room, asleep. He wanted to stay up, but he was dead on his feet. I told him I'd call him if you needed him."

"The next room? I thought you were on the second floor."

"I had the innkeeper move our things. We wanted to be nearby in case"—he stumbled on the words—"something happened."

Maggie poured two cups and handed one to Wex. "I don't think we're in any danger. Surely the man wouldn't be stupid enough to try something again?"

"Nobody with all his faculties would have tried what he did in the dance with hundreds of people around, either." He set his mouth in a determined line. "I don't want to take any more chances."

"Please sit down." Maggie gestured to the two chairs near the window. "I don't think we'll wake Sarah if we talk. It would do her good to know you're nearby. She'll feel safer."

A painful knot twisted in his chest. He didn't deserve Maggie's trust. Carrying his cup to the window, he looked out on the nearly deserted street. Thin beams of light streaked from the batwing doors of the saloons. Since the dance had been cut short, the cowboys were taking their pleasure with the music and girls available for the price of a drink. Their hard-earned wages wouldn't last long tonight.

On the boardwalk directly across from the hotel, he spotted a movement in the shadow. A match flared at the end of a cigarette and glowed momentarily on the barrel of a shotgun. With Grady watching outside and Wex in the next room, nobody would be able to get near them tonight.

Finally able to face Maggie and his own inadequacies, he lowered himself to the chair. "I'm so very sorry. It was my fault," he said, his voice flat.

Her eyes grew wide. "Your fault? How?"

He rested his elbows on his thighs, clutching the china cup with both hands. Unable to meet her gaze, he stared out the window into the dark sky. "I shouldn't have insisted on attending the dance. I failed you as I failed Arthur." The words came out in a rush, unintentional and raw.

She gasped, and the cup clinked on her saucer. "Arthur? Who's Arthur?"

For a long moment he debated telling Maggie about his past sins. He chanced a glance at her and noted the empathy in her eyes. "My brother. My twin brother." He drained the tea and set the cup on the floor.

Maggie leaned forward and covered his hand with hers. Her warm touch offered encouragement. "You've never mentioned your family or your brother. Tell me about them."

"It's a long dreary story. I should leave and let you sleep."

"I want to stay awake in case Sarah needs me. Something tells me you need to share the story."

He clutched her fingers, needing her warmth, feeling her strength, wanting her love. Love? No, not love. Never love. He didn't deserve love.

"I have an older brother, Richard. His mother died when he was a child, and my father remarried. His second wife gave birth to twins, Arthur and me. We were opposites. He was blond, small, and frail. I was dark, large, and strong. Our mother died in childbirth." The pain he'd carried for so many years sliced at his heart. "I killed her."

She gasped and shivered slightly. "How can you blame yourself?"

He stared ahead, seeing the past unfold before his eyes. How could he tell Maggie about the rumors and whispers among the servants? How even his father blamed him for his mother's death?

"My mother was too small and weak to deliver two children, and I was twice the size of my brother. The doctors said I drained all the strength in the womb and left my brother frail and with a lame leg."

"Wex, that's foolish superstition. How can you blame a child for being born? Were you and your brother close?"

"Very close. I loved my brother more than I loved myself. Arthur was sickly and spent his time with his books and music. But I enjoyed the outdoors—horses, hunting, sports." He swallowed the lump in his throat. "I often entertained him with stories of the hunts and my escapades with the other boys." Moisture formed behind his eyelids. Outside his family, few people knew about his relationship with Arthur. And this was the first time he'd mentioned his family to a woman. Somehow telling Maggie felt right, necessary, a way to exorcise the ghost that had been haunting him for so long.

"It sounds as though you were a devoted brother. Why did you say you failed him?"

By the light of the dim lamp, he glimpsed the understanding in her eyes. An unseen bond had begun to form between them.

"We were about Sarah's age when a group of my friends came to our home. I'd been training a stallion, a wild, unbroken Thoroughbred. They'd gathered in the paddock to cheer me on. We'd planned a picnic, and I went into the woods and became distracted by a girl. Arthur grew tired of living in my shadow and tried to mount the stallion." He squeezed his eyes shut, but couldn't squeeze out the despair at the memory. "The horse threw him, and my brother . . ." Taking a quick gulp of air, he continued, "Died."

A long anxious silence hung in the room. The emptiness and despair lodged in his chest. He'd thought he could redeem himself by taking care of the Callahans, but again he'd failed. How unworthy of trust could one man be?

Almost afraid of what he would see, Wex opened his eyes

to find Maggie kneeling in front of him, clasping both his hands in hers. Tears trickled down her cheeks. "You blame yourself, don't you?"

He nodded. "I'd always looked after Arthur. I grabbed the reins and tried to control the horse." Without realizing, he brushed his fingers along the scar on his cheek. "I tried to save him, but Arthur fell, and his foot caught in the stirrup. He broke his neck." After all these years the pain, the anguish, were still there along with the guilt.

Maggie covered his hand with hers, her fingers soft and comforting on his face. "No. It was an accident." She shook her head. "What happened to Sarah wasn't your fault either."

"I should have been watching out for Sarah. If I had been alert, none of this would have happened."

"If we're going to place blame, blame me. I accepted the responsibility for Tim and Sarah when our father died. If I had gone back to St. Louis . . ." Her words trailed away in remorse and pain.

"You did your best, Mary Margaret." Their hands still entwined, he swiped a tear from her cheek with the pad of his thumb. "You couldn't watch Sarah every minute. If I hadn't started that ruckus today, nothing would have happened."

She pressed her lips to his knuckles. "Not true. We're both beating ourselves up when we both know the fault lies elsewhere."

The warmth of her touch melted some of the ice from his heart. Lord, he needed this woman. If only he were worthy.

"Did Grady find out anything?"

"Nothing. Nobody saw anything, heard anything, knew anything."

"I figured as much."

"Who did you think it was?"

"Cole Elliott. If he has her medallion, we'll have him dead to rights."

He stood and pulled her to her feet. "Grady went looking for the boy, but he couldn't find him. Several of the Lazy E wranglers said they'd been talking to him when they heard the gunshots. Then they lost track of him in the crowd."

"Dang! I don't know how I missed. I should have filled him with lead."

"I have to admit it was clever of you to sneak a gun into the dance, but foolhardy. The sheriff was furious." He pulled the pistol from his belt and handed it to her.

She shoved it back. "You keep it, Wex. Never know when you'll need it. The Elliotts could be gunning for you next."

He weighed the Colt in his hand, glad to have the weapon, especially since it meant that Maggie was beginning to trust him. "Thank you," he said around the lump in his throat. "I won't let you down again."

A half smile curved her lips. "You didn't let me down."

"Maggie's right, Wex."

He swung his gaze to the bed. Sarah was sitting up, the quilt clutched to her neck. The candle on the table cast a tiny beam of light across her face. The bruise stood out like a beacon.

"Sarah." Maggie rushed to her sister's side. "You're supposed to be sleeping."

"I woke up when I heard you talking. This wasn't either of your faults. I should have listened to my feelings. But when Mr. Elliott started talking about the Indians, I got really upset. All I wanted was some fresh air. I didn't expect trouble."

Maggie sat on the edge of the bed and brushed Sarah's hair from her face. "Sarah, you have a special gift. As you grow older, you'll gain the wisdom and knowledge necessary to use it. Nobody blames you for what happened. Wex and I have enough guilt for all of us."

"Wex, I'm sorry about your brother. From the first I sensed you were carrying a heavy burden. Someday you'll have a son to take his place."

Wex walked over to the bed and stared down at the young girl. Was this another of her visions, or was she simply guessing? He decided to let it pass without comment. "Thank you, Sarah." He leaned down and brushed a gentle kiss across her forehead. "Get some sleep. It's been a long day." He glanced at Maggie, whose eyelids were drooping. "You, too, Mary Margaret."

She yawned. "I didn't realize how tired I am. You'd better try to sleep, too."

He walked to the door and retrieved his hat. "Lock up after me. Remember, I'll be right next door, and I'm a light sleeper."

"Wait a second." She moved away and reached into a carpetbag. When she turned, she handed him his heavy cartridge belt and holster. "This is yours, too." She followed him into the hallway.

His eyes locked with hers. The confidence in her gaze humbled him. Unable to help himself, Wex cupped her face in his hands and lowered his head. In the seconds before his mouth met hers, he gave her the chance to stop him, to turn away. Instead she leaned closer and parted her lips.

With a light, tentative touch he grazed her mouth. He didn't want to frighten her or pressure her, but he needed to feel her, know her, and let her warmth penetrate his frozen soul.

She clutched his arms and pressed against him. Moaning, he deepened the kiss, wanting nothing more than to become one with her. Sweetness and need, innocence and fire came together in the kiss. He dropped his hands and crushed her to him.

Reality surfaced hard and fast when he felt the pressure of the pistol between them. The timing was all wrong. He was unsuitable for her. He ended the kiss and pulled away. She staggered, and he caught her arms to keep her from falling.

"Good night, Maggie." He dropped his hands.

"Good night, Wex." She took a step back and shut the door.

"Maggie, open up." Tim's voice sliced through the closed door the next morning. "I have breakfast for you and Sarah."

She stopped brushing Sarah's long hair and moved to let her brother into the hotel room. Her sister was amazingly calm, considering the trauma she'd experienced last night. She'd risen early, and after her usual time of meditation, she'd washed and dressed.

Except for the bruise on her face and burn on her neck where the assailant had ripped off her chain, she seemed perfectly normal. But Maggie knew the pain deep inside her heart, and only love and tender care would cure her sister. If she could get her hands on Cole Elliott, she'd gladly skin him alive. She'd spent half the night dreaming up ways to torture the impudent young buck.

The other half of the night she'd spent thinking about Wex. His story about his brother made him more human, more vulnerable than before. And his kiss had left her breathless. She could no longer deny she loved him. But what she was going to do about it was a problem she wasn't ready to face.

She opened the door and took the tray from Tim. Expecting to see Wex standing there, she felt a tinge of disappointment when he wasn't in the empty hallway.

"Come on in. We're starved."

Tentatively Tim moved across the room to Sarah. "You okay, sis?" he asked, a tremor in his youthful voice.

Sarah's smile didn't reach her eyes. The light had gone out of her spirit. "I'll be fine. He didn't hurt me. But I hate losing Mother's medallion and the gold chain Maggie gave me for Christmas." She fingered the scrape on her neck.

Her hand trembling with anger, Maggie splashed the tea on the tray when she tried to fill a cup. The gold amulet was Sarah's most prized possession. "I'll have another one made for you. I'm sure we can find a jeweler in Denver who can duplicate the medallion."

"Thanks, Maggie," Sarah said, "but it won't be the same. I'm almost afraid for the man. What if he's cursed because he took it by force?"

Maggie handed Sarah a cup of tea and a biscuit. "He'll deserve whatever bad luck he gets."

Sarah nodded. "I suppose you're right. Tim, where's Wex?"

Tim smeared jelly on a biscuit. "I don't know. He was on his way to get your breakfast when Grady showed up. They told me to get your tray and to stay in here with you until they got back."

"Where did they go?" Maggie asked.

"Didn't say. Grady said something about the livery stable, then Wex strapped on his gun. He was mad as thunder."

Fear twisted in Maggie's gut. Something bad must have happened to take Wex away after the solicitous way he'd behaved last night. She prayed he wouldn't do anything rash and get himself hurt. "Tim, stay with Sarah." She handed him her rifle. "Lock up after me and don't open the door unless you know who knocks."

Tim stood and grabbed her arm. "Maggie, Wex said for you to stay here."

"Since when do I take orders from him?" She shoved her brother back into the chair. "I'll be back as soon as I find out what's going on."

She lifted her skirts and hurried through the doorway and into the hallway. Behind her, Tim clicked the lock. Taking the stairs two at a time, she rushed past Mrs. Klein, who was carrying a bundle of linen to the second floor.

With a barely managed apology, Maggie hurried into the lobby and out into the bright sunlight. She blinked to get her bearings. Heedless of her unladylike behavior, she lifted her skirt and ran toward the livery where they'd stabled the horses.

The wide door of the barn had been flung open, and a dozen or so men stared at a commotion. As she'd expected, Wex stood tall and stalwart, smack in the middle of the furor.

"Hell, Wexford, it could have been anybody." Sheriff Steward's voice carried above the murmur of the bystanders. "You and the woman made a lot of enemies in one short day."

A lump rose in Maggie's throat. She shoved past a boy with a pitchfork full of hay and stepped into the dark interior.

"Only a few people knew about the negatives. Start with Elliott or his son. They're the only ones who stood to gain by this." Wex stood toe to toe with the sheriff.

"What's going on?" she asked.

The men swung their gazes toward her. Grady stepped toward her, his shotgun cocked. "What are you doing here, Maggie? We told Tim to keep you in your room."

She ignored him and turned to Wex. "What about the negatives?"

Wex caught her arm and steered her to the door. "Leave it to us, Mary Margaret. We'll take care of everything."

"I don't need you to protect me." She shook off his hand and glared at the sheriff. "I asked what's going on?"

"Vandals broke into your wagons last night."

Maggie's heart sank. She moved to the boxlike darkroom wagon and peeked inside. She bit her lip to keep from crying out. Papa had spent days building the shelves, fitting the boxes, and equipping the wagon with chemicals and equipment. Now nothing remained but splintered wood and broken glass. The boxes of gelatin plates were shattered, and the odor of the chemicals was repulsive. Maggie covered her mouth to keep from being sick. All their hard work gone, wasted by vandals.

A warm arm fell across her shoulder. "I'm sorry, Mary Margaret. We should have expected something like this." Wex's voice was tight with barely controlled anger. "At least your cameras were safe."

Speechless, she could only nod. She swung her gaze to the covered wagon that had carried their everyday supplies. It, too, had been thoroughly ransacked. Everything, from the pots and pans to the bedding, had been turned upside down. But the major damage was to the photographic wagon.

Maggie took a deep breath and turned to the sheriff. "I don't suppose anyone knows who did this, either?"

The sheriff shrugged. "Like I told Clinton and Wexford, could have been anybody."

"Does that mean you aren't going to investigate?"

"Miss Callahan." He spoke slowly, as if explaining a simple problem to a slow child. "If you'd taken my advice and left town, none of this would have happened."

Wex tightened his fingers on her shoulder. "We'll leave when we finish our business." His glacial eyes glittered with barely contained fury. "I'll hold you personally responsible if anything else happens."

"Look, Wexford, you don't have any right to talk to me like that. You've been asking for trouble since you got here."

Grady shoved his shotgun between the hostile men. Maggie was certain it was only a matter of seconds before Wex took a swing at the sheriff. "Calm down, boys. You're forgetting one thing. Those were unexposed plates.

The ones with the pictures of the rustlers are on their way to New York."

Although he was right, that didn't stop Maggie from feeling violated by the invasion of her property. "And I can buy new chemicals when I get to Denver." She tilted her chin defiantly. "So you see, Sheriff, the vandals did all this for nothing."

A smug smile snaked across Wex's face. "Like I said, we'll leave when we get damned good and ready, and not a minute sooner."

"I'll get some boys to clean up this mess," Grady offered.

Maggie sighed. "Thanks, Grady." With nothing left to do, she walked slowly toward the door with Wex at her side. After everything that had happened since they'd entered the town, she couldn't wait to get away. "I'm ready to leave now."

Wex remained silent as they continued to the hotel. At the entrance he caught her by the shoulders and turned her to face him. "Mary Margaret, I want you to go upstairs and stay in your room."

She looked into the face of a man she'd never seen before. Gone was the cultured Englishman. This man was as hard as steel—uncivilized and primitive. She shivered slightly. The defiant response died on her lips.

"Where are you going?"

His fingers tightened on her arms. "I have some business to take care of."

"Please don't go after Elliott alone. I'll go with you, or you can take Grady."

"Love, I've no penchant for getting myself killed. This isn't about Elliott, not directly. I'm going to the Double H, to offer my condolences."

Relief flooded Maggie. "I can go with you."

"Sarah may need you. Stay with her. I'll be back as soon as possible."

"Be careful."

He brushed his thumbs along the soft flesh of her inner arms. "I will." Bending his head, he touched his lips to hers. Not caring that they stood in the doorway of the hotel in broad daylight, Maggie pressed closer and opened her mouth in invitation.

The kiss was hard, and deep, but far too short. Wex pulled away, his breathing ragged. Maggie's heart pounded against her ribs. "I'll be back before you can miss me." He spun on his heel and marched back toward the livery stable.

Maggie covered her lips with her fingertips. The warmth, the taste of him, lingered long after he disappeared around the corner and out of sight.

Chapter
Eleven

The road to the Double H Ranch twisted around the base of a mountain and followed a narrow creek. After about an hour's hard riding, Wex spotted a barbed-wire gate and a sign across the entrance to the Hillcroft place.

He dug his heels into the horse's flanks, eager to complete his unpleasant task and return to Maggie. As he approached a small copse of trees the unexpected crack of a rifle shattered the quiet afternoon.

Instinctively he leaped from the saddle and rolled behind a small boulder, the only protection on the dusty road.

He drew the Colt from its holster and took aim. "Damn," he cursed under his breath. He should have been watching, alert for an ambush. Instead he'd been lost in his anger, despondent over his inability to protect Maggie and Sarah. He hated the feeling of impotence, of helplessness, and the inadequacies that had plunged him into further danger.

The next bullet struck the boulder, shattering fragments of rock into his face. Who the hell was shooting at him? Most of all, why? Only one man had any reason to attack him, and he wouldn't put it past Ross Elliott to have him murdered.

"I'd drop that six-shooter if I was you," a man's voice shouted. "I don't want to kill you, but I've had all I'm gonna take from Elliott and his henchmen."

If Elliott wasn't behind the attack, who wanted him dead? "I'm not from Elliott," he yelled back. "I came to talk to Mr. Hillcroft."

"I'm Hillcroft. Throw out your gun and stand up with your hands over your head. We've got you covered."

Wex glanced around. Unless he could reach the horse he'd rented from the livery, he had no choice but to comply. The only way out of the valley was through the pass directly behind him. Whispering a prayer that the man wouldn't shoot, he tossed the gun into the middle of the dusty road.

Hands held high, his body a perfect target for attack, he stretched to his full height. A man and a boy about Tim's age stepped from the shelter of the trees. The man held a rifle; the boy brandished a shotgun.

"State your business."

Fury at the continued inhospitality of these people threatened to strangle Wex. First the humiliation he'd endured in the sheriff's office, now the threat by this man. "Is this how you greet your visitors, Mr. Hillcroft?"

"Uninvited ones. I've had too many encounters with Elliott's men to take chances," Hillcroft said in the soft drawl of the southern part of the United States.

Wex took a step closer, facing the man like an opponent in a fighting match. Hillcroft was a few inches shorter than Wex's six feet, but broader in the shoulders. Under the man's faded blue shirt, the muscles in his arms bulged with tension. Although Hillcroft was a few years older, in his mid-to-late thirties, Wex felt they were probably evenly matched—except Hillcroft had a rifle and the boy a shotgun. Neither took their sights off him.

"My name is Wexford. I was with some of your wranglers when they were killed and the cattle were run off. I came to offer my condolences."

"You that Brit who was causing trouble in town yesterday? You accused Cole Elliott of stealing your horse?"

"Word certainly gets around quickly." Slowly Wex lowered his hands, taking the chance that Hillcroft didn't intend to kill him. "I didn't mean to cause trouble for anybody. I suppose trouble follows me."

Hillcroft studied him for several seconds from under a dusty brown hat. Then he nodded. "Reckon you're okay."

He bent down and retrieved the gun from the ground, but tucked it securely into his belt. "Come up to the house. The missus can fix something cool to drink, and you can tell me what happened to my boys and cattle." The boy brought two horses from the trees.

Relieved, Wex mounted his horse and followed the boy through the gate with Hillcroft bringing up the rear. A barbed-wire fence surrounded the property, and the sign over the gate had been riddled with bullet holes. No wonder the man was as skittish as an unbroken colt. Wex guessed that Elliott was responsible.

The road led past a grove of willows flourishing along a bubbling creek. White-faced Herefords grazed along the banks or lazed in the shade. At the end of the road stood a small whitewashed cabin with a front porch containing overflowing pots of red and yellow flowers.

In one swift glance, Wex scanned the barns, corrals, the chicken yard, and a well-tended vegetable garden. The neat arrangement of buildings spoke of a man proud of his homestead. Far in the background, a snowcapped mountain glittered in the sunlight.

As they approached, a woman stepped onto the porch. She wiped her hands on her calico dress and tucked a stray lock of dark blond hair into the bun at the nape of her neck. Two barefoot girls—identical twins—joined her, hiding behind their mother's skirts.

Hillcroft dismounted and handed the reins of his horse to his son. In a few long strides he met his wife on the porch. "Tillie, got anything cool to drink?" He planted a quick kiss on his wife's cheek. "I've brought company."

Wex swung down from the horse and stepped onto the porch. Hillcroft draped his arm across his wife's shoulder. "Tillie, this is Mr. Wexford. My wife, Matilda." She stretched out a hand.

"It's an honor, Mrs. Hillcroft." He took her hand, red and rough from hard work.

A warm smile curved her generous mouth. "You're that English fellow who was dancing with that pretty redheaded woman at the dance, aren't you?"

Nothing escaped the residents of Sherman. "Yes, madam.

She's Miss Callahan." He lifted her fingers to his lips and planted a brief kiss on her knuckles.

Her cheeks pinked, giving her a pretty, youthful look. "I haven't seen such gallantry since before the war." Rich brown eyes scanned him briefly. "I'm awfully sorry about what happened to that young girl. Some men are despicable."

"I'll convey your sympathy."

"Tillie, a drink," Hillcroft said with a hint of impatience.

She hurried into the house, leaving the two little girls behind. They giggled and tugged on Wex's pants leg. "You talk funny," they said in unison.

Wex squatted down, eye to eye with the youngsters. Both had light brown hair and golden eyes. A tiny twinge of longing touched his heart—longing for his own twin, long gone. He shook off the feeling and smiled at the girls. "That's because I'm from England."

"England? Is that close to Texas?" asked one.

Her twin continued, "Mama and Papa and Shane are from Texas."

That accounted for the soft Southern drawl. "Much farther than Texas. England is far across the Atlantic Ocean."

They looked questioningly to their father. "Papa, what's a landic goscen?"

Hillcroft laughed and picked up a girl under each of his brawny arms like two sacks of flour. "The Atlantic Ocean is a great big lake way past Texas." He moved easily to the door. "Come in, Wexford. It's cooler inside."

He led the way into the main room of the cabin, a spotlessly clean combination sitting room and kitchen. An embroidered cloth covered the dining table with two benches at the sides. A davenport and a rocker stood in front of the fireplace. A ladder led to a loft, and beyond an open door he spotted a bedroom.

Hillcroft gestured to the table and took the chair at the head. "Hope you like lemonade."

Wex removed his hat and settled on the bench. "Yes, of course. It's very refreshing on a day like today."

Mrs. Hillcroft handed each man a full glass. "We don't get guests from England very often."

"Often? Never is more like it." With a playful grin, Hillcroft swatted his wife's bottom. "Actually you're our first foreign visitor."

The twins sat on each side of Wex and propped their arms on the table. Wide golden eyes stared at the newcomer.

"Thank you, Mrs. Hillcroft." He lifted the glass in a toast and took a quick sip, the sweet-tart flavor a welcome relief to his parched throat.

One twin tugged on his sleeve. "I'm Elizabeth, and she's Victoria."

"We're six years old and we're going to school this year."

Wex grinned at the girls. He guessed these two were a handful now and would be quite a tribulation to their parents when grown. "You were named after two great queens."

On his left, Elizabeth shook her head. "No, we weren't. We were named after our grandmothers."

Hillcroft tugged on the pigtails of the girl nearest him. "Quit pestering Mr. Wexford. Run out and play."

Victoria tilted her chin like a young monarch. "We like the funny way he talks."

When neither girl moved, Hillcroft shrugged and finished his glass of lemonade. "How did you happen to be with my wranglers when they were killed?" In spite of the hospitality, suspicion glittered in the man's faded blue eyes.

Wex met the man's gaze without blinking. "As a writer, I've been touring the country to find material for my stories. One evening I happened upon their camp. The men invited me to share their supper. I rode with them the next day, and that night we were waylaid by the rustlers."

Hillcroft nodded. "How were the boys killed, and how did you escape?"

He'd wondered the same thing himself. "I was wounded, but I managed to crawl into the brush. In the confusion, with the horses and the stampeding cattle, the rustlers didn't notice me. They stole all the horses and gear. When they were gone, I started walking, but I was bleeding badly." Without thinking, he rubbed his shoulder, still sore from the wound. "I came upon Miss Callahan's camp, and she and her sister saved my life."

The man nodded. "I think you're telling the truth,

Wexford. They tell me you accused Cole Elliott of stealing your horse."

At the sound of the name, Wex's temperature rose a notch. "I didn't exactly accuse the boy. But his horse looked amazingly like my valuable Thoroughbred. Miss Callahan had photographs of the rustlers with my horse and Double H and Lazy E cattle mixed together."

"You got the pictures?"

"We have copies. But somebody smashed all Miss Callahan's photographic equipment last night in retaliation."

"Sounds like something Elliott would do," murmured Mrs. Hillcroft from the stove.

"Tillie," warned her husband.

She turned and shook a large meat cleaver at him. "Hank, you know good and well that man would do anything to get what he wants." Waving the dangerous weapon, the woman swung to Wex. "He wants the Double H. That's why we're having so much trouble."

Although this news came as a revelation, Wex wasn't surprised. "You've been having problems?"

"Problems? Lots of trouble." Tillie Hillcroft emphasized each word with a whack of the cleaver on a large cutting board. "We've had cattle run off, the sign shot up, and now this. I don't know how much longer we can hang on. We needed the money from the cattle to carry us through the winter." She threw up her hands in surrender. "I thought we were finished with that kind of harassment when we left Texas. But it's started all over again here."

"Tillie, we're not giving up." Her husband slammed his fist on the table. "I'll get a second mortgage, enough to last until we get another herd to market."

She returned to the stove. "Markenson said he couldn't lend us any more money."

"Dammit, woman, we'll manage. Nobody is going to run us off our land again." Hillcroft glanced at Wex as if embarrassed that his guest had witnessed something private between him and his wife. "Sorry, Wexford."

"Mr. Hillcroft—" Wex began.

"Hank. Everybody calls me Hank."

Wex took a deep breath. "Hank, why did you leave Texas?"

"I fought for the Confederacy, and after the war I returned to the ranch in Texas and married Tillie. All I wanted was to be left alone, but it seems the carpetbaggers didn't like Rebels. To make a long story short, we were taxed off our land. We packed up and came to Colorado to get a fresh start." His eyes grew hard. "I built this place with my bare hands, put up my fences, and started on a breeding program to raise quality beef."

"Judging from what I've seen, I know you have a fine place."

"Thanks. A while back, Elliott started buying up all the small ranches around here. He offered to buy me out, too. But I wouldn't sell. This is our home, where the girls were born, where Tillie and I will be buried."

Tillie chunked the cleaver across a piece of meat. The sound echoed through the small cabin. "If Elliott has his way, it'll be sooner than we plan."

An idea took root in Wex's mind—a way to help this family and get the upper hand with Elliott at the same time. "Hank, would you mind showing me around your place? I've toured several other operations in Wyoming."

"Why not? Not much to show, though. This place is small compared to some of the Wyoming spreads. But we have good water and grass. And a mountain to boot." Hank rose and moved toward the door. "Be back in a while, Tillie. Behave yourself while I'm gone."

The woman smiled at her husband and slammed the cleaver down once again. "I'm only practicing for when I get hold of Elliott. Can't blame a woman for having a little fun, can you?"

Wex couldn't help laughing. The woman had spirit, like Maggie. He hoped that for once the stubborn Miss Callahan had listened and remained in the hotel.

"Thank you for the lemonade, *madame*," he said in the French pronunciation. "I hope we meet again."

The girls giggled again. *"Madame,"* they mimicked. Pigtails flying, they danced around their mother. *"Madame, madame, madame."*

Their youthful song followed the laughing men onto the porch.

Hillcroft was right. His ranch was far smaller than those in Wyoming. But with the fresh-flowing creek and lots of good grass, he didn't need more acreage. He planned to breed bulls and perhaps horses. That way he could handle the chores with a minimum of help. The efficiency of the place impressed Wex. For a small homestead, the Double H had the potential to turn a nice profit.

After riding several miles of fence, the men returned to the corrals. Pride shone on Hillcroft's face when he showed Wex his champion bull, his hope to replenish his herd by the following spring and make up for the loss of his cattle.

Wex crossed his arms on the upper rail and propped his foot on the lower rung. "I like what I see, Hank. Even my father's most experienced overseer with a number of workers isn't as efficient as you."

The rancher took out a bag of tobacco and rolled a cigarette. Wex refused the offer of the same. "Thanks, Wex. But unless the bank extends my loan, I'm not sure how long we can hold on. Those cattle that were stolen were for my next mortgage payment and winter supplies."

Several horses strutted around the fenced area. Although this country was wilder, untamed, Wex was reminded of his father's estate in Allenshire. The place where Arthur was killed. He pulled his thoughts back to the situation at hand.

The sun was high in the sky and glistened off the rocks of the mountain that guarded the valley. He couldn't blame Hank for not wanting to give up this place. If this were his, he would fight to the death to keep it.

"Hank, have you ever thought of taking on a partner?"

Hillcroft blew out a stream of gray smoke. "Wex, I fought a war to keep my independence. I don't want to have to ask permission every time I want to move a herd or brand a cow." He shook his head. "Nope. I don't need anybody to interfere with the way I run my ranch."

Never one to give up, Wex took a different tack. "What about an investor, somebody to funnel in fresh cash without obstructing your operations?"

Hank laughed and took a long draw on his cigarette.

"Know anybody with a lot of spare cash who wants to risk it on a second-rate ranch?"

"Yes, as a matter of fact I do." Wex shoved back the brim of his hat and met the man's gaze. "Me."

"Come on, Wex." Hank slapped him on the shoulder, seeing a great deal of humor in the offer. "Where does a writer get that kind of money?"

Wex didn't see anything amusing about his financial situation. "I received a substantial inheritance from my grandparents. My father has an investment in a Wyoming ranch, so there's no reason why I can't invest in an enterprise in Colorado."

The man sobered. "You can't be serious."

"Never more serious in my life." He leaned against the rough rail. "I feel partially responsible for you losing your herd. I need to help."

"I don't accept charity from nobody." His voice grew hard.

"I'm not offering charity. It's an investment, and I expect to make a profit." Wex gestured to the cabin where the twins were chasing each other on the porch. "Do you want to move your family again?"

Hank let out a string of curses, and his face turned red. "Hell, no. But I'll find a way on my own."

"Dammit, man." Now Wex's temper heated to the boiling point. "Don't let stubborn pride stand in the way of providing for your family. I'll be leaving for England in a few months. I want to be a silent partner. You run the ranch your way. I won't be here to interfere."

"Sounds like charity to me."

"We'll take it, Mr. Wexford."

Wex swung around in time to see Tillie Hillcroft emerge from the shadows of the barn. He hadn't seen or heard her approach.

"Tillie," her husband said between his teeth, "this is man's business. Go back to the house."

The woman, half a head shorter than her husband, met his angry gaze without flinching. "It's family business. I say we take Mr. Wexford up on his offer. The bank won't lend us any more money. I don't want to sell out and start over again."

Hank's face turned so red that Wex thought he would burst. "Woman, enough."

Wex knew it was time to retreat. He had no desire to get caught in the cross fire between the pair. Taking out his watch, he checked the time. He'd been gone much longer than he'd intended. "I have to get back to town. Let me know what you decide."

"Wex." Hank stretched out his hand and gave Wex back his Colt revolver. "You might need this."

"Thanks." Tipping his hat to Mrs. Hillcroft, Wex sauntered toward the hitching post where he'd left his rented horse. Behind his back the argument was loud and furious. No betting man would be willing to wager on the outcome of this battle. Wex never underestimated the strength of a woman, however. By the time he reached the porch, he heard running feet behind him.

"Okay, Wexford. We'll take your offer." Hands shoved in his pockets, Hank glared at him. "But we're going to the lawyer's office and make it all legal like."

Past the man's shoulder, Wex caught a glimpse of his wife and the self-satisfied smile on her face. Whoever said women were the weaker sex hadn't met Tillie Hillcroft, and certainly not Mary Margaret Callahan.

"Where the devil have you been?" Maggie glowered at Wex, who stood in the hallway outside her room. She'd been pacing for hours, worrying if he would return in one piece. And the fact that she cared made her angry with herself.

With a wide grin, he tipped his hat and bowed low. "Good afternoon to you, too, Mary Margaret." When he stood, he cupped her chin and planted a hard quick kiss on her astonished lips.

Furious at his total arrogance, not to mention his complete disregard for her modesty, Maggie shoved against his chest. "Well, are you going to tell us where you've been and what's going on?"

"Give me a minute to catch my breath." He stepped into the room and moved toward Sarah, who was reading near the window. "How's my favorite girl today?"

"I'm fine." Sarah smiled and closed the book. "But

Maggie has been fit to be tied waiting for you to come back. She was convinced we'd have to patch up a few bullet holes in you."

Maggie folded her arms across her chest and tapped her foot, waiting for them to finish. The audacity of the man—to waltz in here as if nobody had been concerned about his safety. He glanced over his shoulder and winked at her. Patience, never one of her virtues, was pushed beyond her endurance by the Brit.

Wex stretched out his arms, the seams of his black shirt straining with the movement. "See, no bullet holes, no broken bones, and no bruises or scrapes. I spent a very profitable day with Hank Hillcroft."

"We saw you from the window with a man and a woman and some children," Sarah said. "Was that the Hillcroft family?"

"Yes."

"Well, dammit, what's going on?" Maggie's control snapped.

A pleased grin spread across his face. "I've invested in the Double H ranch. I'm Hillcroft's silent partner."

Her mouth gaped open. If he'd told her he'd visited the moon and come back, Maggie couldn't have been more surprised. "You what? Where did you get that kind of money? I thought you were supporting yourself with your stories."

His blue eyes glittered with humor. "I am supporting myself. But I have an inheritance from my grandparents. I felt responsible for what happened to Hillcroft and I thought this was a sound investment of my funds."

She narrowed her eyes. Somehow this didn't all add up. Like two and two equaling five. This man was not what he pretended to be. "How much money are we talking about?"

He shrugged. "Enough to keep Elliott off the man's back, and to keep Hillcroft going until he can get another herd to market."

Sarah stood and took his hands in both of hers. "Wex, that's the nicest thing I've ever heard. Now you won't want to go back to England since you have interests here."

Maggie's heart tripped as she studied his response. She'd known all along it was only a matter of time until he returned to England. But she'd refused to face the possibility until Sarah voiced her own thoughts.

"Sarah, love, England is my home. But it will be months before I'm ready to return." He lifted his gaze to meet Maggie's. "If ever."

Those two little words planted a tiny seed of hope in Maggie's heart. She tried to tell herself she didn't care what he did. But she did care. When he'd been gone longer than she'd anticipated that morning, she knew exactly how much she cared.

"Ladies." Wex swept his hat and bowed in an extravagant, old-fashioned manner. "I've arranged a special dinner for us in the hotel's restaurant. If you would like to change, I'll be back for you at seven."

Sarah curtsied and then took his arm, escorting him to the door. "We'll be ready and waiting, sir."

"Wait a minute," Maggie said, her stubborn streak making her argue with the man. "Do you think you can just waltz in and order us around?"

His blue eyes darkened with exasperation. "When we were lost on the mesa top, I promised you an elegant dinner. And as I told you, I always keep my promises."

He turned on his heel, leaving Maggie feeling as if she'd been rightfully reprimanded. She slammed the door and counted to ten.

When she lifted her gaze, she found Sarah smiling at her. "Maggie, why do you keep arguing with Wex?"

"I don't like the way he keeps giving me orders."

Sarah laughed. "I think it's because you love him and you're afraid to let him know."

"Love? Don't be foolish. You've read too many of those romantic novels." Maggie turned toward the wardrobe so Sarah wouldn't see the flush on her cheeks.

"I saw the way he kissed you last night. You can both quit pretending around me. I know he loves you, too."

As much as she wished it were true, Maggie didn't believe it would ever be possible. "An Englishman and the daughter of an Irish immigrant? No, Sarah. That only happens in novels."

Chapter
Twelve

A few minutes before seven o'clock, someone knocked at the door. "Mary Margaret, Sarah, are you ready for dinner?"

Maggie jumped at the sound of Wex's voice. Her breath caught in her throat. She didn't at all understand why her heart raced like a jackrabbit with a hound on his tail every time she so much as heard his voice.

At first she'd thought of a dozen excuses not to have dinner with him. He was much too arrogant, too sure of himself. She needed to check on the cleanup of her wagon. She needed . . . to quit lying to herself.

Sarah rushed to the door and pulled it open. "Come on in. Maggie, Wex is here."

Maggie swung her gaze and tried in vain to quell the pounding in her chest. In his wool trousers and silky black shirt, he looked dark and mysterious. And tonight his holster and Colt weighed heavily at his hip.

"Good evening, ladies." He entered slowly with his hands behind his back. "Are you prepared for a delightful evening?"

"Yes," Sarah answered. "Maggie kept me cooped up in this room all day. I'm glad for the chance to get out. I'm looking forward to having a special dinner with you in the dining room." Sarah picked up her reticule and eyed him suspiciously. "What are you holding behind your back?"

Wex's mouth curved in a charming smile, and he held out two packages. "Gifts for the ladies."

"For us?" Sarah covered her pink cheeks with her fingers. "I love presents." The sight of her sister's animated response brought a pleasant twinge to Maggie's heart.

By all outward appearances, Sarah looked like a normal young woman. Her green flowered dress was neatly pressed, and every black curl was brushed perfectly in place. Only Maggie sensed the turmoil inside her sister. The ordeal of the past day had cut deep wounds into her sensitive young heart. As hard as she tried, she couldn't hide the pain in her overly expressive eyes.

He handed the smaller package to Sarah and turned to Maggie. "What about you, Mary Margaret? Do you like presents?"

Putting on a mask of indifference, Maggie shrugged. "Depends."

"On whom it's from?" He waved the brown paper parcel under her nose.

She wiped her damp palms on her gray-and-white-striped skirt. "I know you've heard the saying 'Beware of Greeks bearing gifts.'"

Laughter rumbled from deep in his chest, straining the seams of his shirt to capacity. "But I'm not Greek, and this isn't a Trojan horse."

"What is it?" she asked, her patience slipping. As much as she was tempted to snatch the gift from him, she held out her hand and waited. To her surprise, he caught her hand and planted a long, wet kiss on the palm. His tongue swirled in tiny circles, sending tingles up her arm.

Above their hands, their gazes met. Blue eyes challenged green ones. The look was as heated as his breath on her flesh. The trembling that started in her fingers spread like an earthquake to the pit of her stomach.

"Wex!" Sarah's voice brought Maggie out of her stupor. "It's beautiful."

Pulling back her hand, Maggie curled her fingers into her palm to capture his touch a little longer, just as she wanted to catch his heart and never let go. An impossible dream, and the realistic Maggie knew it.

She glanced at her sister. An empty box lay on the dresser, and a gold Celtic cross dangled from the chain in Sarah's fingers. The exquisite piece of jewelry glittered in the lamplight.

"It's too expensive. I can't accept this." A single tear rolled down Sarah's cheek.

Wex took the chain from her fingers. "Of course you can. It's little enough payment for saving my life." He hooked the chain around her neck and let the cross fall against the lacy yoke of her calico dress.

Dumbfounded, Maggie could only stare. The beautiful Irish emblem could have come from the finest New York jeweler. Giving it to Sarah was the kindest thing he could have done. "Where did you ever find something like that here in Sherman?"

With a tiny laugh, he said, "At the local mercantile, of all places. A few months ago a down-on-his-luck Irish miner sold the cross for a grubstake. I was lucky to find it. It's perfect for a beautiful Irish lass like Sarah Maureen Callahan."

Sarah covered the cross with both hands. Her smile chased the shadows from her eyes. "Thank you, Wex. I'll cherish it always." Standing on tiptoes, she planted a light kiss on Wex's cheek. "Open yours, Maggie."

Maggie studied the box as if it were a snake about to strike. It was much too heavy for a piece of jewelry, and it thumped when shaken. Eagerness won out, and she tore off the paper. Nestled in the box lay a small, pearl-handled derringer.

Gingerly she lifted it from the box and balanced the small gun in her palm. "This came from the general store, too?"

"Not exactly. The gunsmith carries a line of weapons to fit inside a man's sleeve or a woman's reticule." He grinned with complete confidence. "Next time you sneak a gun into a dance, it won't bruise your dance partner's shoulder." He rubbed his injured shoulder.

She flushed at the memory of being held in his arms. "Is it loaded?"

"I added a box of shells for your use."

Their hands touched and tangled as they loaded the two chambers. Heat flooded her at his nearness. The gift, although not jewelry or flowers, which most women would prefer, was perfectly suited to Maggie. It was a symbol of her independence, her strength, and his trust in her ability.

"Thank you, Wex," she whispered, slipping the gun into her handbag.

"You're both very welcome. It is little enough for all you've done for me." He stepped back, and she noted a touch of color on his tanned cheeks. "I believe our dinner is waiting." He offered one arm to each woman, and they left the room together.

The reticule bounced against Maggie's dress, but she liked the feel of the weight on her arm. More than that, she liked the feel of Wex's strong arm under her fingertips.

Tim and Grady stood when their three companions entered the private area at the rear of the crowded dining room. Maggie wondered how Wex managed to convince Mr. Klein to partition off part of his restaurant with the screen and potted plants. The how didn't matter; what counted was that he'd tried to make the evening special and to keep the prying eyes off Sarah. The gesture only made Maggie love him more.

A silver candelabrum cast its pale glow on the table; the shadows danced on the walls. Wex held Maggie's chair, and his hands lingered for a moment on her shoulders. His touch was warm and exciting. She stifled the desire to have those big hands stroking her body until . . . Until what? she asked herself. The answer didn't come, but she knew it was only a matter of time until Wex showed her all the wonderful things that could happen between a man and woman.

Sarah showed her gold cross to her brother and Grady. Although it wouldn't make up for the pendant she'd lost, the gift was considerate and wonderful. Maggie thought her heart would burst from loving Wex.

Mr. Klein himself served the meal, which would have done the finest restaurant in St. Louis proud. The roast duck, sweet potatoes, and fresh vegetables were a meal fit for royalty. Wex opened a bottle of champagne and filled crystal glasses with the bubbly wine. Even Sarah and Tim were allowed a small glass.

By the end of the meal, Maggie was giddy from the sparkling wine. In St. Louis, Aunt Olivia had stood staunchly against drinking of any kind, so Maggie had rarely tasted alcohol. She didn't know if the champagne was good or poor; she only knew it made her feel light-headed and lighthearted. Her problems floated away on the bursting bubbles.

They were laughing at one of Wex's many stories when a commotion came from the main dining room. The booming voice was enough to rattle the china and shatter the crystal.

"Where the hell is that goddamn Englishman?"

The din of voices in the restaurant died as Ross Elliott appeared around the screen; two large men hovered behind him.

Elliot's face was almost purple with rage, and Maggie could smell danger. Fear rose in her throat. Below the edge of the tablecloth, she reached into her bag for the derringer.

"Wexford, what the hell kind of trick are you trying to pull?" Elliott's gray eyes pierced like daggers.

Wex hid his fury behind a smile. As casually as if the man were an old friend, he lifted his glass and took a sip of champagne. The slow nonchalance gained him time to control his temper. "I *was* having a pleasant dinner with my friends. Would you care to join us?"

Elliott's face turned even redder. The men at his back set their hands on the guns in their holsters. Maggie turned, and Wex suspected her derringer was pointed at Elliott's stomach. At close range the small-caliber bullet could do a great deal of damage.

"Hell no. What right do you have undermining me in my town?"

Wex feigned innocence. "I'm afraid I have no idea to what you're referring. I haven't accused you of anything in"—he pulled out his watch, checked the time, and returned the timepiece to his pocket—"twenty-four hours. And I haven't found your son." After a pregnant pause, he added, "Yet."

From the corner of his eyes, he spotted Sarah and Tim. Tim was ready to pounce, and Sarah's face was ashen. After what had happened yesterday, none of them needed this kind of confrontation. Grady's hands were under the table, and Wex wouldn't be surprised if "Old Minnie" was cocked and ready.

"You know what the hell I'm talking about. You and Hillcroft and this partnership."

Wex set down his glass and stood. His jaw was set in a hard line, and his throat tightened in his effort to control his voice. He didn't want gunplay in the crowded dining room where innocent bystanders could be hurt. "Oh, that. It was a business arrangement, beneficial to both Hillcroft and myself. I don't see that it's any concern of yours."

As if losing the battle for control, Elliott grasped the lapels of his own tailored black suit. His white shirt contrasted with the high color in his face. "Everything that happens near Sherman is my concern. I offered to buy out Hillcroft at a fair price. I thought he was ready to sell until you started meddling."

"According to Hank, he turned you down more than once. He doesn't want to sell out and move. As for my so-called meddling, I made a business investment in a growing cattle enterprise."

"You threw good money into a deep well, if you ask me."

Every muscle in his body ached with tension. "Well, I didn't ask your advice, but I'm prepared to give you a little of my own."

"I don't need no goddamned advice from a stinking Brit."

Wex balled his hands into fists to keep from striking out at the man. "Elliott, I'm now part owner of the Double H ranch. I'll do anything within or without the law to protect what's mine. If Hillcroft has any trouble, I'll hold you personally responsible."

The man let out a bark of mirthless laughter. He shifted his gaze from one of his henchmen to the other. Both had their hands on their guns. "Your threats don't frighten me."

"It isn't a threat. But if Hillcroft should decide to sell out, he's obligated to give me first refusal. And I've already made arrangements to purchase his property—land, buildings, everything."

Elliott roared deep in his throat. The man hated to be thwarted, and Wex had sidestepped him on every issue. "Get out of my town, Wexford, before you're sorry you ever heard of Sherman."

The twitch in Wex's jaw grew more pronounced. "Elliott, I'm already sorry I stepped foot in this place. In one day I've been accused of lying to the sheriff, Miss Sarah Callahan was attacked by a maniac, and Miss Maggie Callahan's photographic supplies were destroyed. Short of killing us, there isn't much more you can do."

"And I'm here to see that doesn't happen." Grady spoke up for the first time since the confrontation began. When he stood, his shotgun was pointed at Elliott and his men.

Malice and frustration radiated from Elliott. By the looks of him, he would gladly tear Wex limb from limb with his bare hands. But Wex wasn't backing down. He couldn't, and he wouldn't. Too many lives depended on his strength and determination. Not only the Hillcroft family, but also the Callahans, whom he'd pledged to protect.

Wex settled back into his chair. "If you're finished, Mr. Elliott, my friends and I would like to complete our meal." The tone of frosty dismissal in his voice would have done Queen Victoria proud.

With a look of unmitigated hatred, Elliott spun on his heel and marched out of the restaurant. His men retreated more slowly, keeping their gazes on Wex and Grady until they reached the door. Only then did Wex dare to release the breath he'd been holding.

Chairs scraped and voices rumbled in the dining room. Wex had supplied the good citizens of Sherman with enough gossip to last a year. Mr. Klein rushed from table to table trying to appease and comfort his patrons.

Maggie turned to Wex, finally able to breathe again. Judging by the look on his face, she knew he was rapidly losing the battle to retain his control. The hard, primitive gleam in his eyes was almost frightening. Maggie would hate to be the object of his unleashed anger.

Needing to comfort him, offer what support she could, Maggie covered his fingers with hers. His hand trembled, and she squeezed it gently. Silence hung over the table like a shroud.

Maggie was the first to break the silence. "I need some

fresh air." Shoving back her chair, she stood. "Wex, would you mind stepping outside with me?"

As if pulled out of a trance, he shook his head. "What? I'm sorry, Mary Margaret." He glanced around the table, all eyes on him. "I apologize for the interruption. Please forgive me for allowing the rudeness to spoil your dinner."

"It's all right, Wex," Sarah said. "I'm ready to go to my room."

Grady slung his shotgun over his arm. "Take a walk to cool off. I'll stay with Tim and Sarah." He pulled out Sarah's chair and helped her up.

Maggie tightened her fingers and pulled Wex to his feet. "We'll be in the garden if you need us."

Taking the lead, Maggie hooked her arm in his. The customers in the dining room stopped talking and stared at them as if they'd each sprouted an extra head. A hush hung over the room until the rear door closed behind them.

They stepped into the moonlight and followed the narrow stone path lined with neat flower beds. The sweet fragrance of roses filled the cool evening air. Under normal circumstances, a walk in the garden with a handsome man would have been a romantic interlude. In Wex's present state of mind, he didn't need romance; he needed Maggie's cool common sense. Wex pulled free and jammed both hands through his hair.

"Damn, damn, damn," he said, then spit out a string of expletives in at least a dozen foreign languages.

Maggie watched helplessly as he chastised himself. She bit her lip to keep from joining him in a few choice phrases she'd heard on the docks in St. Louis. "Wex, it wasn't your fault."

"If we hadn't come here, if I hadn't been so damn stubborn, so irresponsible, none of this would have happened. I didn't intend to put you and your family in danger."

She moved away from the lighted hotel into the shadows of the rose arbor. The buzz of insects whispered a song from the bushes. She sat and pulled him down beside her.

"Will you please quit pistol-whipping yourself? I'm not blaming you for what happened. You did your best to provide a wonderful meal."

"I'm getting indigestion."

At least he hadn't lost his sense of humor. But Maggie couldn't shake her fear. After all that had happened, she was ready to head for Denver. None of them was safe in Sherman. Especially Wex. With his impulsive nature, he was bound to cross paths with Ross Elliott again, and she wasn't sure he would survive the next encounter with the man.

She couldn't let it happen. Her love for him wouldn't allow it. The only way she could make sure he didn't do anything rash was to keep her eye on him. Once he reached Denver, he would calm down. Then he could go on his way, safe and sound.

His arrogance wouldn't permit him to listen to a woman's suggestions. But with his sense of honor, of wanting to accept responsibility, he would escort her if he thought she needed protection.

"Wex," she said, in a soft, weak voice. "I'm going to tell Grady I want to start for Denver."

He leaned forward, bracing his forearms on his thighs. "That's an excellent idea. Sherman isn't safe for you."

For you either, you hardheaded Englishman, she thought. She brushed a finger along his arm. "Will you come with us?" With a deep breath she rushed on. "Sarah will feel much safer with you along. Grady can't be everywhere at once, and you never know when Elliott or his son will try something."

"What about you, Mary Margaret?" He straightened and met her gaze. In the pale light from the windows of the hotel, his eyes grew dark. His fingers captured hers. "Do *you* want me to go to Denver with you?"

She swallowed down the "yes" that bubbled from her heart, not ready to show her true feelings. "It's Tim and Sarah I'm concerned about. I'm only asking for their sake."

Lightly he stroked his thumb across her palm. The sensation sizzled along her nerve endings. For a long moment he studied her. Then without a word, he leaned closer. Automatically Maggie lifted her head and boldly met his lips. The kiss started out with the quick brush of mouth on mouth. She nipped at his lower lip with her teeth.

He moaned deep in his throat, but remained still. With a brashness that surprised her, she crushed her mouth to his.

Need overtook common sense. Desire conquered misgivings. The tension of the past day pushed Maggie beyond the norms of propriety. Her tongue parted his lips, and he answered with brash thrusts into the warm recesses of her mouth.

She gripped his shirt; his heart pounded against her fingertips. He twisted his fingers into her hair, pulling the curls free from the confines of the pins. His touch was like a hot iron, marking her with his brand for all time.

Too soon he broke the contact, but continued to rain kiss after kiss on her face and throat. He shoved her deeper into the shadows of the arbor until her back touched the trellis.

"Maggie, I want you so badly I can hardly stand it." His words rasped against the pulse in her neck.

Quiver after quiver raced through her and settled somewhere in the region of her private parts. She'd never experienced this excitement before. His hand cupped her breast, and the nipple tightened into a sensitive bud. She needed relief from this exquisite torture, but this public garden and the timing were all wrong.

"Wex, I . . ."

"Hush, love. I know we can't do anything here now. There's always Denver."

She sighed with relief. On a shuddering breath, she moved away. "That means you'll go with us?"

Standing, he caught her hand and pulled her up with him. For a moment she thought her knees would buckle under her. Thanks to his strong hand under her elbow, she managed to stand on her own two feet.

In the pale moonlight she spotted the heated look in is eyes. A sly smile touched his mouth. "Yes. Of course—for Tim and Sarah's sake."

Chapter
Thirteen

A warm blanket of contentment covered Maggie when she entered the three-story brick building on Larimer Street. Papa had purchased the property from an old friend who'd wanted to leave Denver and move to California.

The setting was perfect for the new Callahan Photographic Gallery. Located in the middle of Denver's growing commercial district, near drugstores and other mercantiles, the building had everything Maggie needed for a home and studio. The first floor contained a reception foyer, plus private areas for a parlor, kitchen, and dining room. Three bedrooms occupied the second story, while the studio and darkrooms took up the entire third floor and rooftop—plus a room Papa had chosen for his own.

Maggie spun around slowly and let the ambience of her new home flow through her. Although they'd only spent a week in the residence before setting out on the assignment to photograph the Rockies, Michael Callahan's powerful presence permeated the place, the new home for the Callahan family.

Papa's spirit lingered in the large studio cameras he'd arranged, and in the nearby bedroom, where his trunk waited at the foot of the four-poster bed. Slowly she entered the room that would forever belong to Papa. With a feeling of awe, she traced her finger along the stem of a pipe Papa had left on the mahogany bed stand. She'd never felt closer to him than at that moment.

Lord, she missed the redheaded Irishman with the big heart and booming laughter. Why did he have to be taken away from her? On a long sigh she swiped away a tear and turned to leave. A shadow in the doorway stopped her. Then Wex appeared, silhouetted by the light from the bright studio at his back.

"You have a fine operation, Mary Margaret," he said with a note of reverence in his tone.

She fought down the now familiar flutters in her chest at his unexpected appearance. "I thought you had errands to run."

"I've returned from my expedition. I sent the telegrams and then I helped Grady and Tim with the wagons and horses." His heated gaze swept over her, and the flutters intensified into the pounding of a kettledrum. "I've put your things into your chamber, and Tim is bringing in the cameras."

"Thank you." She turned away to keep him from seeing the longing in her eyes.

The trip from Sherman had taken only two days—forty-eight short hours fraught with anxiety. At first she'd been afraid they would be attacked on the road by Elliott or his henchmen. Then the worry had shifted to wondering if these were the last hours she would spend with Wex. Upon reaching the city, he no longer had any reason for remaining with her.

Here in Denver he could get his own lodgings or take the train in any direction he chose. Even to New York and a ship back to England.

Maggie shoved her hands into the pockets of her gingham skirt to keep from reaching for him. If she touched him, she was afraid she would beg him to stay. But a woman had to maintain some semblance of pride. "I hope I can get enough business to keep up the gallery," she said, bringing her thoughts to the problem at hand.

Together they moved into the studio. "I'm sure when word gets out that Miss Mary Margaret Callahan's Photographic Studio is open for business, the residents of the city will flock to your door."

She laughed at his extravagant words. "Is that a prediction, Mr. Wexford, or wishful thinking?"

He strolled to the north windows into a strong beam of sunshine. His dark hair shone under the bright afternoon light. Powerful emotions surged in Maggie's chest.

"I looked into my crystal ball and saw great things in your future. Look at that, Mary Margaret." From the third-floor studio, he gestured to the panoramic view of the mountains that seemed only a few miles away. "The city is little more than twenty years old, yet it's already a metropolis filled with millionaires. People with money, especially the nouveaux riches, like to have their portraits made. It gives them a feeling of permanence, importance. We'll put an advertisement in the newspapers tomorrow, and they'll be flocking to our door."

We? Our? A tiny seed of hope sprang to life in her heart. "I certainly hope you're correct, Mr. Wexford. It's time for me to settle down and make a name for myself."

"Miss Callahan, as soon as the publisher gets your photographs, your name will be known around the world." He stuck his head under the curtain of the large studio camera. "First we should take some sample photographs of you and Sarah to show how lovely a Callahan portrait can be."

Maggie stretched out on a settee and crossed her feet. The skirt draped across her legs and drifted to the floor. Setting her chin on her fist, she struck an exaggerated theatrical pose. A large canvas painting of a pastoral scene formed a backdrop behind her.

"How's this?" She lowered her eyelids and gave what she hoped was a seductive pose.

With a wide smile, Wex removed his head from under the cloth. "No, no, my lady. Let me show you."

In a few long strides he crossed the Oriental rug and knelt in front of her. Taking her left arm, he draped it along the low back of the settee. One rough finger brushed a flyaway wisp of hair from her cheek and curved it around her ear. Maggie bit back a sigh. When he cupped her chin in his hand, she managed a playful smile. "How's this?" The words slipped out in a breathless invitation.

"Perfect," he whispered. His eyes darkened, and his head dipped closer. Bending down, he brushed his mouth across hers. "Delicious."

"Is this how English photographers pose their clients?" Excitement sizzled through her. With a dark three-day stubble on his jaw and the primal gleam in his eye, he looked as dangerous as he had the night he'd stumbled into her camp.

"Only the beautiful females." His thumb stroked her jaw.

"And the men?" She placed a tiny kiss at the corner of his mouth.

"I specialize in women."

He was clearly experienced on that score, she thought.

The shuffle of feet on the stairs snapped Maggie out of her amorous stupor. Wex jumped back. "Hold that pose," he whispered, struggling slowly to his feet.

She looked up and saw Grady standing in the doorway. In one hand he held his battered felt hat; in the other rested his shotgun. "The wagon's unloaded, Maggie. Guess I'll be on my way."

Smoothing her rumpled skirt, she stood. A new ache centered in her chest—a sensation of abandonment, like when she was a little girl and Papa went away. "So soon? We may need you."

He laughed. "Maggie, twenty years ago when Denver was a muddy mining camp, it was too big for me. I can't take the hustle and bustle of the city. Hell, I near 'bout got run over by one of them horse-drawn streetcars."

"At least stay until tomorrow." She moved to the scout, who'd been friend, mentor, and surrogate father for the past months. Tears burned in the back of her eyes. "We'll have a good-bye dinner tonight." Glancing at Wex, she wondered if this would be his farewell, too. The thought twisted in her heart like a dagger.

"I found an interesting restaurant between here and the telegraph station," Wex said. "It will be my privilege to treat all of you to dinner tonight."

At that instant Sarah bounded into the room, her ankle-length skirt swaying with the movement. "We're going out tonight? I love eating in restaurants."

"Yeah, me, too," came Tim's voice as he entered with a large camera in his hands. "I'm starved."

Maggie laughed. "You're always hungry."

Wex tousled the boy's hair. "Let's get cleaned up, and we'll meet here in about an hour. Is that all right with everybody?"

They nodded in agreement. Maggie glanced at Wex, wondering if it would be their final evening together.

Since it was such a beautiful evening, Wex suggested that they walk the few blocks to the restaurant. Denver was alive with activity, with carriages vying with horse-drawn street-cars for space on the wide avenues. Excitement filled Maggie that this was now her home.

Wex and Sarah led the way, with Maggie, Grady, and Tim following closely behind. Maggie kept her gaze on Wex, admiring the way his linen shirt strained across his back and the proud tilt of his head that made him look as if he owned the world. She almost envied her sister for having such a handsome escort. She wanted to frown at the women on the street who turned to smile at him.

He cast an occasional glance back at her, a heated gleam in his eyes. For this night she'd dug into the trunks and found the emerald silk gown that made her feel elegant and attractive. Of course, Sarah was beautiful in her rose gown with her dark hair hanging in ringlets to her waist. In time Sarah would get over her ordeal of the past week, but Maggie often spotted the pain in her eyes. If she never saw Wex after tonight, she would still be grateful to him for all he'd done to help her sister.

Wex stopped at a small building and held open the door. Sarah squealed with delight. "A Chinese restaurant." She turned to Wex and caught both his big hands in her small ones. "I've never had Chinese food. I understand many Chinese came to work on the transcontinental railroad and stayed to open restaurants. This is wonderful."

At her sister's wide smile, a new surge of warmth swamped Maggie. Somehow Wex knew just how to please, how to make a woman feel special. Nobody deserved such fine treatment more than Sarah.

"How about you, Mary Margaret? Do you enjoy Cantonese?" Wex asked as he held the door.

"Yes, I tasted Chinese cuisine in Philadelphia when Aunt Olivia and I attended the Centennial Exhibition. I found it quite interesting."

Grady grumbled under his breath. "Hope the Chinaman knows how to cook steak."

Laughing at the scout's ill humor, Maggie tugged him into the dimly lit establishment. Crimson paper fans decorated the walls, and yellow umbrellas hung from the ceiling. A small Chinese gentleman, dressed all in black, scuffled toward them. He bowed his head several times, making his pigtail dance around his shoulders.

"Welcome," he said, in broken English. "This way, prease."

The proprietor led them through the crowded restaurant to a round table covered with a bright red cloth.

Wex seated Sarah, then held the chair next to his for Maggie. Wanting to enjoy their last few hours together, she accepted with a smile. The proprietor bustled around them, nodding and saying something she didn't understand. To her surprise, Wex answered in what she supposed was Chinese.

All eyes darted to the Englishman. He spoke a few more words, then the little man hurried away.

"You speak Chinese, too?"

Wex laughed. "Only enough to keep from starving. After that, I'm as lost as a sailor on a foggy sea."

"You see, Maggie," Sarah said. "I told you he was wonderful."

Not wanting to admit she felt the same, Maggie picked up the chopsticks in front of her. "By the way, what did you order for us?"

"I told him to bring us his finest food, that the ladies wanted to try everything." He glanced at Grady. "And a steak for Grady."

Tim laughed. "Guess he got a gander at Old Minnie and figured he'd better bring something besides grass. Me, I can eat anything."

"You always do," Maggie said.

Seconds later, a beautiful black-haired young woman, dressed in a silk tunic appeared with a large tray in her delicate hands. She poured tea into each bowl, then bowed low and retreated. Not sure what to do, everyone except Grady watched Wex and followed his lead. He lifted the bowl with both hands and took a sip. Maggie found the tea different but delicious.

"Wex," Tim asked, making a face over the tea, "have you been all the way to China?"

"Yes, but only for a brief visit. I hope to return someday." He shot a glance at Maggie. "Perhaps on a photographic jaunt. What do you think, Mary Margaret? You could get some interesting photographs."

The thought of his leaving brought a twinge to Maggie's heart. "That's too far away for me. Think I'll stick to Colorado. The United States has enough to keep me busy."

Before long, the table was full of fragrant covered dishes. The young Chinese woman uncovered one after another, each with a distinctive texture and aroma.

Grady shoved his plate aside and folded his arms. "Where the devil is my steak? A man can't live on seaweed and little bits of rice."

Wex signaled for the proprietor and again spoke in Chinese. This time when the man returned, he carried a sizzling platter with a barely seared steak in the center.

"Good," said Grady. "Okay, Chinaman, get me a knife and fork. Can't eat steak with these bamboo twigs."

Seconds later he reappeared with a huge kitchen fork and a cleaver the size of a man's arm. Afraid the man had come to do battle with him, Grady stood and cocked his shotgun.

For a moment everyone in the restaurant froze. Chattering incoherently, the little man placed both implements on the table and gestured to Grady.

Wex began to laugh. "He said to eat up. And he hopes you enjoy your meal."

Maggie couldn't help laughing at the humor in the situation. "I suppose I'd better learn how to use these in a hurry, or he'll bring me an even bigger cleaver."

"I'll teach you my technique," Wex offered. After a few demonstrations, Sarah began eating with relish. Tim crossed the sticks and used them like a shovel, his fingers helping.

Not surprised at Wex's expertise, Maggie tried to imitate his actions. But more food slipped back to the plate than reached her mouth. After several clumsy tries, she almost called for that meat cleaver. "I'll never get the hang of this."

"Sure you will," Wex said. "Let me help."

Reaching over, he covered her right hand with his left. His fingers were warm, and her skin began to tingle at the contact. Maggie didn't understand how the most innocent of touches could affect her so.

"Easy, Mary Margaret, just balance them in your fingers and pick up the food between them. It's quite simple."

Maggie bit her lip trying to master the strange bamboo sticks. She lifted her gaze and found his face inches from hers. As she watched, his blue eyes heated with unspoken promises, unspoken needs. Maggie wished she had more time with him. But she knew the wanderlust was calling, and he would soon be on his way. If not England, he'd probably visit some exotic place like China.

"Maggie, you aren't concentrating." Sarah's voice brought Maggie out of the stupor she'd fallen into.

Maggie dropped her gaze from Wex's and watched the way his long, tanned fingers manipulated the foreign utensils. Was there nothing the man didn't do well?

"Let me try." She shoved his hands away, glad to be free of his devastating touch. This time she managed to get about a teaspoon of food.

Wex smiled with encouragement. "You'll never get full at that rate. Here." He scooped up a piece of tender boneless chicken and lifted it toward her mouth. Without giving her a chance to question, he touched her chin with one finger, and automatically she opened.

"How was that?" Wex asked, his voice deep and intimately soft.

"Wonderful." She glanced past him and found Sarah, Tim, and Grady staring at her. Feeling like a child caught with her hand in the cookie jar, she inched away from him. "I think I can manage."

"Mary Margaret, I believe you can do anything you set your mind to."

Except handle a handsome Englishman who'd turned her world upside down, she thought.

Maggie managed to get through the meal and found that the chopsticks weren't all that difficult once she learned to take small bits of the food. Grady, for his part, had sawed his way through the steak without too many complaints except that he would have preferred beer to the tea. Tim thought it was great fun, and Sarah, as always, enjoyed whatever she did. By the time the meal ended, Maggie was sorry that the evening was coming to a close.

Too soon Grady would leave her, and Wex would follow not far behind.

Purple, gold, and red streaks shot across the Rockies, bringing a glorious sunset to Denver. On the slow walk from the restaurant back to the gallery, Wex racked his brain to find a way to remain with the Callahans.

With Grady leaving in the morning, he had no excuse for staying. They were certainly not in any danger from the Elliotts here in the city. Denver boasted a fine police department, and Maggie would surely be safe. Besides, she always kept her derringer in her handbag.

Maggie walked a few paces ahead of him, her arm locked in Grady's. Her emerald silk dress bared her shoulders, and her skin glowed like porcelain. He hadn't been able to keep his eyes off her all evening. The more he looked at her, the more he wanted her.

All he had to do was get her to need him—not an easy task.

When they reached the front door of the building, he struggled to control his emotions. There was too much left unfinished between Maggie and himself to simply walk away.

"Come into the parlor," offered Sarah. "I'll make some tea, and we can sit and talk."

Wex wanted to reach over and kiss the young girl for giving him time to come up with a scheme. He followed closely behind and crossed over the threshold into the parlor. Maggie settled on the crushed velvet settee and signaled for Grady to join her. Tim flopped on a rocker, and Sarah ran to the kitchen. Wex walked over to the cold fireplace and propped his arm on the mantel. When Maggie glanced up, he spotted the sadness in her green eyes.

Was it Grady's leaving that caused her concern, or did she think he, too, might be going away? He hid his smile. He had no intention of leaving, not when there was so much of Maggie's sweetness to sample.

"Reckon I'm gonna miss you young'uns." Grady patted Maggie gently on the knee.

"Where will you go?" asked Maggie.

"Thought I'd head back toward Sherman. Hillcroft offered me a job, or I might try my hand at mining." He ran a finger under the tight collar of his shirt. Again he wore his black suit, and Wex wondered if his shotgun was an extension of his arm. "Hope you can keep out of trouble and make your papa proud."

Maggie covered his hand with her own. "We'll miss you terribly. But I suppose we'll be too busy to get into trouble. Sarah and Tim will be starting school, and I hope to have enough business to occupy my time." Her gaze shifted to Wex. When their eyes met, she quickly turned her attention back to Grady.

Tim jumped to his feet. "School? I have to help you in the studio. I'm your assistant." A pained look crossed the boy's young face.

Sarah entered with a tray filled with china cups. "And if I go to school, who's going to do the cooking and housework?"

Wex felt like an outsider looking in on a warm family squabble. Had he ever belonged? he wondered. Or had Arthur's death changed it for him?

He and his twin had been like two parts of a whole. Each one's strengths complemented the other's. His father had never been a warm man, and the twins had been raised by servants. Richard, his older brother, had his own interests, and his stepmother was kept busy with her girls. When his twin had died, Wex felt as if half of his heart had been cut out.

Maggie held up her hands to silence her siblings. "Papa wanted both of you to continue school. Sarah, how do you expect to get into medical college without the proper education? I'll hire a housekeeper, and as for you, young man"—she pointed to her brother's narrow chest—"I'll manage alone, and you can assist me in the evenings and on Saturday. When you're not busy with baseball or other sports."

"How about polo?" Wex ventured his own suggestion.

Tim's eyes grew wide. "Wow, I've heard about how they play that in England. Can you teach me?"

"Certainly. We'll get a couple of nice horses, and we'll have a jolly good time."

Maggie's eyes locked with his. "When are you going back to England?" The husky timbre of her voice brought a surge of emotion to his heart.

"Not anytime soon," he said. "If you need an assistant, I'll be happy to fill in." He flashed a smile, content his plans were falling into place. "We did agree to become partners, remember?"

She shrugged, her smooth shoulders glowing like satin in the late dim candlelight. "I just assumed . . ."

Sarah set the tray on a low table and came to him. She flung her arms around his waist. "Oh, Wex, I'm so glad. Why, you can even stay in Papa's room."

Over Sarah's head he glimpsed the shocked look on Maggie's face. "I don't want to impose." Leave it to Sarah to come to his rescue.

Sarah pulled away and looked at him through eyes bright with pleasure. "It won't be any trouble at all. Besides, you're like part of the family."

The young woman's trust and confidence soothed like a healing balm on the withered part of his heart. He looked at Maggie for her reaction.

She opened her mouth, but Grady interrupted before she got the words out.

"Danged if that ain't a good idea. With Wex here I won't worry so much about you." Grady slapped his wide hand on his knee. He narrowed his eyes on Wex, issuing an unspoken warning.

Wex met Grady's gaze without wavering. With a nod he accepted the challenge. His mission wouldn't be complete until the Callahans were safely established in their home. Only then would he consider his return to England.

"Wait a minute." Maggie came to her feet, her hands on her hips. "Don't I have some say in this?"

All eyes fell on her. "No," four voices sang out in harmony.

"N-no?" she sputtered. Angry green eyes flared, and her breasts swelled above the low neckline of her dress.

Wex dropped his gaze to the creamy flesh. The tight collar of his linen shirt cut off his breath. Somehow, the temperature in the parlor rose by at least ten degrees. He stifled the groan in his throat and struggled to control his voice. "Don't be upset, Mary Margaret," he cajoled. "This can be advantageous to all."

She stepped closer. "And how is that, Mr. Wexford?"

The flowery scent of the woman wove an invisible net of longing around him. He wanted her—badly. If Grady could read his thoughts, the scout would fill him so full of buckshot, he'd look like a piece of Chantilly lace.

"I will not be forced to seek lodgings here in Denver, you will have an able and hard-working assistant, your sister and brother can attend school, and I'll pay room and board to cover the salary of a housekeeper."

The hint of a smile touched her all-too-kissable mouth. "It sounds like you have everything worked out." She glanced at the others awaiting her decision. "Since I'm outnumbered, I'll give it a try. You can stay in Papa's room."

He took her hand and lifted it to his lips. "You won't be disappointed, Mary Margaret, I can assure you of that."

"I think we're finally ready for business." Maggie spun around slowly in the middle of the studio. The cameras rested on the tripods, potted ferns hugged the wall, and new dry gelatin plates waited in the dark box.

Wex smiled at her from the doorway of the darkroom. As usual when she looked at him, excitement curled in her heart.

For the past two weeks Wex had been invaluable help in readying the gallery for business. It took all of them working together to set up the cameras, take the sample portraits, place the advertisements in the newspapers, and generally get the studio ready.

"All we need now are customers," he said, his gaze meeting hers across the room.

This was their first day completely alone in the studio. Sarah had enrolled in an exclusive finishing school for young ladies, and Tim was attending a fine academy. Flora, the housekeeper, had taken the day off to care for an ill child.

Maggie sneaked a glance at Wex. Certainly her nervous twitters were caused by the opening of the studio, not from being alone with him. "When the good people of Denver learn about the outstanding Callahan and Company photographs, they'll be beating down our doors." The statement came out with more bravado than she felt. She troubled her lower lip with her teeth. "I hope."

Wex caught her wrists and carried her fingers to his lips. "Have faith, Mary Margaret. It takes time for word of a new business to spread to the populace."

She fought the shivers from his touch. "I suppose you're right." Her gaze shifted to the portraits of herself and Sarah in ornate gilt frames hanging on the wall. She'd known Sarah would take a lovely portrait—the girl was beautiful. What surprised her was how Wex's expertise had made Maggie herself look so . . . so attractive. Maggie knew without a doubt he was also responsible for the brightness in her eyes.

Looking up, she caught the fire in his gaze. Since coming to the city, he'd kept his hair cut and was always clean-shaven. He was so handsome that her heart lurched every time she looked at him. The scar on his cheek made him seem more vulnerable, a reminder of his love for his twin. He'd received his trunk of clothes, but he usually wore black cotton shirts and denim pants. "Let me take your picture." The words slipped out before she knew she'd spoken them aloud.

His wide smile snatched her breath away. "I'm not dressed properly." He continued to brush his mouth across her knuckles.

Heat skittered up her arms and made her breasts swell. The sensation was more than delightful; it was totally erotic. She had to get her mind on something other than begging him to make love to her. Resisting her own needs was growing harder with every passing day.

She pulled her fingers free. "You look fine." Truth was, she wanted the picture of him as a memento. He *would* leave, of that she was as certain as the sun coming up in the morning and setting in the evening.

Maggie held no illusions about his not remaining in Denver. Although he'd never mentioned returning to England, it was only a matter of time before he became bored with America and wished for the culture and ambience of Europe. A strange premonition spread over her. Something was about to happen.

"Where do you want me?" He ran his hands through his hair to smooth it off his forehead.

In my arms. Somehow she kept her thoughts to herself. "By the window, with the sunlight on you."

She loaded the double book holder with a pair of the dry gelatin plates. It was much easier and faster than the old wet-process glass plates that had to be prepared immediately before inserting into the camera. She slid the holder into the back of the camera and looked through the viewfinder at the subject.

Wex stood near the window and smiled into the camera. Maggie's heart began its erratic beat. For weeks she'd fantasized about this moment. He was a magnificent specimen—a primitive male under a thin veneer of civilization. Her fingers trembled as she adjusted the focus. "Almost ready," she said. "I'll count to three. One, two, three." She pulled the black slide from the rear of the camera and removed the brass cover from the lens.

With the bright light and new glass plates, it took only seconds to expose the film. She recapped the lens. Of course, most of the timing was from experience and instinct.

She slid the other plate into position. He started to move, but she held up her hand to stop him. "For this one take off your shirt." She didn't know why she'd said it, but the fantasy wasn't nearly complete.

His blue eyes widened, and a provocative smile slid across his face. "If you insist."

She watched the upside-down image on the focusing screen as he released one button after the other. Her mouth went dry when he reached the last button and pulled the shirt from his trousers. Still facing the camera, he shrugged the cotton fabric off his shoulders and tossed it on the nearby settee.

He reached for his belt. "My trousers, too?"

More heat surged through Maggie. She had to swallow

before she could speak. "No, just the shirt." Unable to help herself, she peeked from under the black tent and stared at him. His broad chest was dusted with dark hair, and the bullet wound had left a red scar on his shoulder. She swiped her tongue across her lips to moisten them.

"How do you want me to pose?" he asked. His gaze locked with hers.

On their own accord, her feet moved toward him as the fantasy turned into reality. Now, if only she had the courage to complete the dream.

Wex waited in eager anticipation to see what Maggie would do next. Her green eyes were wide and needy.

Living under the same roof with her had taxed his endurance far beyond what a man was expected to bear. They were together almost constantly, eating, working, and often spending the evenings playing cards or touring the new city of Denver.

Like a heavy London fog, silence shrouded the room. His blood roared in his ears. He swept his gaze over her. A stiff white shirtwaist hugged her full breasts and disappeared into a navy-and-white-striped skirt. From the few times he'd touched her, he knew Maggie rarely wore a corset. A row of lace fluttered around her throat.

Step-by-step she came until he had only to reach out and touch her. Hands at his side, he waited for her to make the first move.

She stopped a hairsbreadth from him and brushed a tentative finger along the scar on his cheek. Then, with a touch as light as a butterfly's, she continued to the mark on his shoulder. A shock rocketed through him. He swelled hard and heavy.

His patience ran out. He gripped her arms and hauled her into his chest. His mouth found hers in a long, hard kiss, releasing the pent-up hunger from weeks of waiting.

A soft moan bubbled from her throat as she wound her arms around his neck. Her response fueled the fire in his blood. Crushed to his bare chest, she fitted herself in his embrace. Maggie was all woman, soft and yielding under his touch. He cupped his palms under her bottom and hauled her against his pulsating manhood. He couldn't remember ever needing a woman the way he needed Maggie Callahan.

He shifted toward the settee. The low couch hit the back of his legs, and he sat, pulling her down on his lap. He ended the kiss by nibbling gently on her lower lip. The heat in his blood threatened to burn him alive.

One by one, he pulled the pins from her hair, freeing the curly masses. He combed his fingers through the silky tresses until they lay like a heavy veil across her shoulders.

She grazed her hands across his shoulders and found the pulse at the base of his throat. His breathing became labored. He buried his face in her hair and inhaled the feminine warmth of her.

With deft fingers he slipped the tiny buttons of her shirtwaist from their loops. To his delight, she didn't stop him. Instead she continued to stroke her fingers along his collarbone and down his chest. Wave after wave of emotion surged through him. He resisted the urge to tear the garment from her body—to feel her flesh against his.

Maggie couldn't breathe. Never had she felt the overpowering need for a man. Cool air touched her chest with each freed button. Under the thin chemise, her breasts swelled, and her nipples puckered. And he had yet to touch them.

When at last the shirtwaist was open, she dared to look into his eyes. They were midnight dark, with tiny silver sparks flickering in the depths. His gaze lowered, touching her, sending shock waves through her. Ever so slowly, his fingers retraced the path up her ribs. He stopped to graze his hand under her breast, then over the crest to the fullness that overflowed the chemise.

He shoved the shirtwaist open. Wanting to help, she shifted and let it fall from her shoulders. An instant later it lay discarded on the floor.

She buried her face in the crook of his neck and inhaled the clean masculine scent of him. He fell backward, pulling her on top of him. Spreading his thighs, he settled her intimately against him and wrapped his legs around her. The thick pressure against her stomach told her how much he wanted her.

He kissed her again, and this time she met his tongue in a bold quick stroke. His breath came in short, rapid gasps, or was it her own?

A sharp gush of cool air washed over her bare shoulders

like a refreshing mountain breeze. Maggie welcomed the relief from the heat that was burning her alive. She met him, kiss for searing kiss, caress for caress. If only she could rid herself of the cumbersome skirt and truly know him.

Lost in her passion, she almost missed the loud gasp and bang against the floor and the voice that called her name. "Mary Margaret Callahan. What are you doing with this man?"

Like being doused with an icy spray from an arctic sea, Maggie froze. Her hands stilled, and her breathing stopped.

Oh, God, she prayed, it can't be. Please don't let it be. Still pressed against Wex, her breasts flattened on his chest, she dared a peek over her shoulder.

Just as she thought. Her aunt, Olivia Stanton, stood in the doorway brandishing her umbrella like an avenging angel waving a sword of wrath.

Chapter
Fourteen

Maggie buried her face in Wex's chest, hoping the woman
in the doorway was a shadow, a mirage, anything but flesh
and blood.

Anyone but Aunt Olivia.

"Mary Margaret Callahan!" Aunt Olivia repeated her
name in the tone she had often used when Maggie was a
naughty ten-year-old. "How can you compromise your
virtue with this . . . this stranger?"

Shame swamped Maggie like a wave dashing over the
bow of a sinking ship. Humiliation spread from the tips of
her toes to the ends of her tousled hair. Aunt Olivia was real,
too real. Maggie prayed the floor would open up and
swallow her, Wex, and the settee.

Under her hands, Wex stiffened. While Maggie lay
shocked and immobilized in his arms, he shoved her gently
to a sitting position and draped his shirt across her bare
shoulders. Then he stretched to his full height and stood
protectively in front of her.

"Madam." He folded his arms across his wide chest and
braced his legs apart. In a voice that would brook no
argument, he demanded, "What is the meaning of this
interruption? Have you no better manners than to walk into
a room unannounced?"

Shoulders back and chin thrust forward, Olivia lifted her

umbrella, ready for battle. "Hold your impertinent tongue, young man. I am Miss Olivia Stanton, this young lady's aunt. I will not have her reputation impugned by the likes of you."

Maggie hurriedly slipped her arms into Wex's shirt and fastened the buttons. Only then did she dare peer around him and meet her aunt's gaze. Anger flashed in Olivia's pale blue eyes. Any second now, she would surely bash Wex's skull with her parasol.

Undaunted by the glare that was guaranteed to make the employees of the Stanton Bank and Trust cower in fear, Wex bowed gallantly. "Andrew Wexford at your service, madam. It's a pleasure to make your acquaintance. Mary Margaret has spoken often of you."

"Andrew Wexford?" Olivia lowered her umbrella and offered her hand. Wex took her fingers to his lips. A hint of pink touched Olivia's cheeks, and a self-satisfied smile curved her mouth. "Since you've seen fit to compromise my niece, I insist that you marry her. Today. As soon as I can make the arrangements."

Marriage? Arrangements? Too shocked to speak, Maggie could only stare. Two shadows moved through the doorway and halted behind Olivia. Maggie's heart sank farther when she recognized the younger man—Harry Seymour, her former fiancé. And she'd thought things couldn't get worse.

The other man, a stranger dressed in an elegant gray suit, rushed forward. His thin face was flushed, and his mustache twitched. "This is preposterous, Miss Stanton. Lord Geoffrey can't marry this . . . this common American woman," he declared in a haughty British accent.

Olivia switched her attack to the newcomer. "Mr. Appleton," she said in a frosty tone, "this is my niece, Miss Mary Margaret Callahan, and there is nothing common about anyone in *my* family. I don't care if Lord Whoever is the King of England. He's going to marry my niece."

Maggie stood beside Wex and watched as if she were in the audience and this was a scene from a stage play. Wex wore a bemused smile, and Harry hung in the background as if awaiting his cue.

But who was *Lord* Geoffrey?

Mr. Appleton removed his hat and glared right back at

Olivia. "Madam, Lord Geoffrey Andrew Wexford is betrothed to Miss Grace Ferguson."

Pain sliced through Maggie. *Lord* Geoffrey—Wex. Betrothed? Her stomach churned, and she wondered if she would be sick. All the time he'd been trying to make love to her, he'd been betrothed to a woman in England. She stared into his eyes. The amusement was gone, replaced by pure bewilderment.

Wex stepped forward, interjecting himself between Olivia and Appleton. "Appleton, what are you talking about? I am not planning to marry anyone."

At that moment Harry rushed to Maggie's side. He was the last person she wanted to see or hear. "Maggie," he said, reaching for her hand, "I'll be happy to marry you."

Wex swung his gaze to Harry. "Who the hell are you?"

Pulling himself to his full height, at least six inches shorter than Wex, Harry jutted out his chin. "I'm Maggie's fiancé, Harry Seymour."

"Former fiancé," Maggie said. "What are you doing in Denver?"

"I've missed you terribly, Maggie. It was all a horrible mistake. I can't live without you. I hope I can convince you to marry me." Harry took her hands in both of his. His gaze swept from her disheveled hair to the oversized man's shirt. Her own shirtwaist lay in a crumpled heap on the floor.

If Maggie didn't know his deceitful nature, she would have believed him. He seemed sincere enough, and his handsome face was a picture of devotion. But he didn't fool Maggie. She'd seen the man beneath the slick facade. She knew her inheritance attracted him most. Harry was like the false fronts of the buildings in many frontier towns. They looked good but had no substance, and were easily torn down and hauled away.

Wex draped his arm protectively across her shoulder. "Well, she didn't miss you, old chap." A smug grin slid across his mouth.

"I can speak for myself, *Lord* Geoffrey." She pulled away from both him and Harry—her two faithless lovers—and folded her arms across her chest. "Who is this Appleton person?"

He gestured to the tall, thin man in the elegant gray suit.

"Sir Jeremy Appleton is my solicitor in London. He handles my affairs."

"Hmmph!" With Maggie in his shirt and Wex bare-chested, both of them were at a definite disadvantage. "And your engagements?"

"Mary Margaret." He ran his fingers through his black hair, combing the thick locks off his forehead. "I am not betrothed. I do not know any Grace Ferguson. I'll speak to Appleton and find out what is going on."

"Maggie . . ." Again Harry reached for her.

She waved him away. She had too much to deal with without his unwanted attention. "Go back to St. Louis, Harry. I don't want to marry you."

Maggie swung her gaze to her aunt and Appleton. The couple stood toe to toe, like rams locking horns in combat. The ostrich feathers on Olivia's hat touched Appleton's mustache as she leaned into the man who towered over her. She banged the tip of her parasol on the floor, missing the toes of his shiny shoes by a fraction of an inch.

Taking a few long steps, Wex moved to the battling couple. "Appleton, Miss Stanton. Please." His words were soft and spoken with authority. The pair of combatants spun to glare at him. For a moment Maggie was afraid they would join forces against their mediator.

Maggie shifted away from Harry, not wanting his touch. Her attention fixed on the trio in the middle of the studio.

"Miss Stanton," Wex said, "I humbly beg your pardon if my behavior has offended you or Mary Margaret. I'm not sure what you thought we were doing, but it was all quite innocent, I assure you."

Maggie's mouth gaped. She stared at his half-nude body and snuggled deeper into his shirt. They were as innocent as foxes in a henhouse with feathers sticking out of their mouths.

"I know what I saw, young man," Olivia responded, not at all fooled by his paltry explanations.

"Aunt Olivia." Maggie couldn't hold her tongue another second. "We weren't doing anything improper." The flush deepened on Maggie's face.

Olivia merely lifted one eyebrow and let her gaze flow over Maggie. "If so, why are *you* wearing *his* shirt?" Her gloved hands remained folded across the handle of her frilly umbrella.

Maggie felt the way she had at age six, caught drawing in her aunt's ledger book. "I . . . I . . . was photographing Wex—I mean, *Lord* Geoffrey—without his shirt. It's all very artistic and proper."

This time Wex's mouth gaped. Admiration glittered in his bright eyes. Maggie stifled a long groan. In a few short minutes she'd gone from wanton to liar. What would she be next? she wondered.

Olivia wrinkled her brow in total disbelief. Maggie's aunt, a brilliant businesswoman, was rarely fooled and certainly not by her niece half her age. Shorter than Maggie by several inches, Olivia squared her shoulders and opened her arms. "I have no choice but to believe you, Mary Margaret. Come, give me a kiss."

Relieved, Maggie moved to kiss her aunt's cheek. Olivia smelled of fresh lavender, and in spite of the train journey, her hunter-green traveling suit was as stiff as when she'd donned it in St. Louis. Her clothing wouldn't dare wrinkle; Olivia wouldn't allow it.

When Maggie looked into her aunt's still-handsome face, Olivia's pale blue eyes glazed over. "What are you doing in Denver, Aunt Olivia?"

Olivia tilted her chin. "I've come to take you and those children home."

"Home?" The word conjured up myriad memories. But home to Maggie meant the house on Larimer Street where she'd set up her gallery. "Denver is our home."

Olivia touched the corners of her eyes with an embroidered linen handkerchief. "When your father was living, I had to accept his wishes. Now that he is gone . . ." She made the sign of the cross, touching her forehead, her chest, and each shoulder in turn. "God rest his soul. You belong with me in St. Louis."

"Aunt Olivia . . ." Maggie groaned.

"Mary Margaret." Wex's hand on her arm drew her gaze. "I'll leave you with your aunt. Appleton and I are going to check into the Windsor Hotel. I'll collect some of my things and send for the trunk." He spun on his heel and went into the adjourning room.

At that Olivia's eyes grew even wider. "Has this . . . this *man*"—she said the word as if she were talking about some slimy insect—"been living with you?"

Maggie took a deep breath. "He's been staying in Papa's room."

Olivia fanned her flushed face with her handkerchief. "Under the same roof."

By then Maggie's patience had evaporated. "Oh, please. We're surrounded by chaperons."

"Oh?" Her gaze swept over Maggie. "Where are Sarah and Tim?"

"At school, you should be pleased to know. Sarah is attending a fine girls' school, and Tim is enrolled in the academy." She glanced to the side and spied Harry near the doorway, his leather valise at his feet. "What is Harry doing here?" she whispered.

Olivia cast an annoyed glance at the young man. "He overheard me making plans to come find you and showed up on my train. He told me he still loves you."

"He loves my inheritance, you mean."

"At least I know who he is. But who *is* this Lord Geoffrey?"

"He's—" She stopped when Wex returned to the studio. He wore a clean shirt, and his hair was combed neatly.

"Ladies." He bowed over Olivia's hand. "We will take our leave. I hope you will honor us with your presence at dinner this evening. I'll send a cab for you at seven."

Olivia's cheeks pinked at the attention. "Lord Geoffrey, I hope you can teach Mr. Appleton some manners by then."

Appleton frowned at her. "Madam, it's you Americans who need to learn proper etiquette. The English *invented* what you refer to as manners."

"Mr. Appleton," she began when Wex ushered the man to the doorway.

Wex clamped a heavy hand on Harry's shoulder. "Harry, old boy. You will join us at the Windsor, as my guest." Without giving the smaller man a chance to protest, Wex shoved Harry through the doorway and away from Maggie.

Maggie rubbed her throbbing forehead. This had been the most confusing afternoon of her life. First she'd almost made love to Wex, then all this talk about lords and ladies, betrothals and indiscretions, not to mention Harry and his proclamation of love. Now Wex was gone, and here stood her aunt, hovering over her as if she were four, not twenty-four.

"Maggie," Olivia said, "are you missing something?" She picked up her niece's shirtwaist from the settee and waved it in front of her face. Her gaze fell pointedly on the large man's shirt.

Snatching the garment, Maggie clutched it to her chest. "I . . . I was warm."

"I'm certain you were." The censure in her gaze was replaced by empathy. "After you prepare me a cup of tea, you can tell me all about this handsome English lord with whom you've been living."

"Obviously I know little about him, since he never mentioned being a lord of any kind." She eyed her aunt and decided to put the shoe on the other foot. "And maybe you'll tell me how you've become so friendly with Sir Jeremy Appleton."

"Friendly?" Beneath her calm exterior, a tinge of pink crept up Olivia's neck. "The man is an insufferable, arrogant, self-important bore. He argued with me from the moment I boarded the train in St. Louis."

Maggie laughed at her aunt's tirade. Self-righteous to a fault, Olivia hated to be opposed on any subject. "Miss Olivia Stanton, president of the Stanton Bank and Trust, I think you've met your match."

She let out a loud hmmph. "Mary Margaret Callahan. I do believe you've met yours."

Still laughing, Maggie moved toward the rear stairs that led to the kitchen. "I'll get the tea, and we can compare notes on pompous, obnoxious Englishmen."

Wex knocked lightly on the leaded-glass panels of the door. Inside the house, the grandfather clock in the hallway chimed seven times. The hansom cab stood at the front gate, and Appleton and Harry waited at the Windsor.

He tugged at the high tight collar on his stiff shirt. It had been months since he'd had occasion to don the black wool suit with the cutaway jacket. Back in London, he seldom

wore anything else. But that was a lifetime ago. Before
coming to America. Before Maggie.

His heart pounded against his ribs at the memory of her
locked in his embrace. He resisted the urge to curse all of
them for ruining what now appeared to be his last chance
with Maggie.

For weeks he'd waited for the opportunity, and after
the events of this afternoon he doubted the occasion would
arise again. Especially since Appleton had dropped the
explosive news that Wex was betrothed to some heiress in
England. Nobody had been more shocked than he. But how
to explain it to Maggie?

The door flung open, and Sarah stood under the gleam of
the gas chandelier. She curtsied, and when she stood up, her
green eyes widened with pleasure.

"Good evening, Your Lordship," she said, and gestured
him in.

He groaned inwardly. "Sarah, I'm still Wex. Please don't
be so formal."

She shook her head and smiled. "Oh, no, Lord Geoffrey,
it isn't proper."

This time he gritted his teeth in frustration. "Is everyone
ready? I've made reservations in the dining room at the
Windsor."

"I think so. This is all so exciting." Her cheeks pinked,
and she clutched the Celtic cross in her fingers. "Just think,
you're a lord, Aunt Olivia's here, and they told me about Sir
Jeremy. Only I wish Harry would disappear back to St.
Louis."

Wex tossed his top hat onto the hat rack shoved against
the wall. "Do I gather you aren't overly fond of Harry?"

"Oh, I like him all right." She shrugged and dug her
hands into the pockets of her pink dress. The lace collar
framed her youthful face. "But I know he isn't right for
Maggie. He'll only hurt her again."

This was an interesting bit of information. Wex planned
to do a little digging and learn more about this situation.
"Maggie is smart enough not to let that happen," he assured
the girl. "The cab is waiting."

"I'll get Aunt Olivia."

He glanced around the long hallway. To the right was the

parlor, and to the left the reception room for the gallery. He lifted his gaze. Maggie's room was at the head of the stairs.

Heedless of propriety, he took the stairs two at a time. This might be his only chance to speak to her alone. He had to explain, let her know he hadn't lied to her. He'd only withheld certain facts. At the time his reasons had seemed plausible, but now he realized his folly.

At the partially opened door, he knocked lightly before entering. Expecting to see Maggie primping in front of the mirror, he stopped at the edge of the carpet. A royal-blue silk gown lay across the counterpane on the bed, but Maggie was nowhere in sight.

"Mary Margaret," he called softly.

He waited for an answer, but none came. Perhaps she was in the parlor or with her aunt. Slowly he retraced his steps to the front hallway. The parlor was empty, and as he turned toward the kitchen Tim ran into his stomach, almost knocking him over. He steadied the boy with his hands.

"Hold it, young man. Where are you going in such a hurry?"

The boy brushed his dark hair from his eyes. "Wex—I mean Lord Geoffrey. Are you really a lord? Do you live in a castle? Do you have lots of horses and servants?"

"Tim, call me Wex. I am a lord, but I have a town house smaller than this one, and one horse and no servants. Go out to the cab and tell the driver we'll be along shortly."

Tim bounded out the door, his long legs racing to the carriage. At the rate the boy was growing, he would reach six feet in no time. An ache settled in Wex's chest. He wouldn't be around to see Tim mature into manhood.

Being with the young man, teaching him to play polo, was almost like having Arthur back. In a short time he'd grown fond of the Callahans—all of them. Especially Mary Margaret. He would miss her most of all.

Olivia and Sarah met him in the hallway. Wex smiled, knowing Jeremy would be delighted to see the handsome woman. Dressed in a deep purple gown, the neckline modestly high, she was as regal as Queen Victoria and looked as fresh as a young girl on her way to a party.

He'd left Appleton pacing the print off the Oriental rug in their suite, waiting for seven o'clock. Widowed for a number of years, the stodgy barrister had never expressed an interest in any of the widows or spinsters who sought his attention. But whenever Wex mentioned Miss Stanton's name, Jeremy's eyes flashed, and he denied any interest in the "obstinate, self-righteous harpy." The man was clearly smitten.

"Where's Mary Margaret?" Wex asked.

Olivia glided past him, her wide skirt brushing his legs. "Isn't she in her room getting dressed?"

A chill skidded up his spine. "No. I can't find her anywhere. When did you see her last?"

She looked at the watch pinned to her chest. "About a half hour ago. She said she had to do something in the darkroom."

Setting his jaw, Wex ran the two flights of stairs to the third floor at a record pace. He stalked through the studio to the darkroom. He'd halfway expected the stubborn woman to try to avoid him. That's why he'd come himself instead of sending the cab. He knocked on the closed door. "Mary Margaret, are you in there?"

Seconds passed with no answer. He shoved, but the door didn't budge. From inside came the sound of movement.

"Don't you dare open that door. You'll ruin my negatives."

"Mary Margaret." He gritted his teeth to control his temper. "It's seven o'clock, and the cab is waiting."

"Go ahead without me. I have work to do."

"Are you hiding in there to avoid me?"

She laughed. "Don't flatter yourself, Lord Whoever-you-are. I thought you would be on your way to your betrothed by now."

"Mary Margaret, come out and speak to me."

"You had weeks to tell me the truth. It's a little late for talking."

Again he rattled the door. The pleasant evening he'd planned had turned into a confrontation with a headstrong woman. "Have your way. But sooner or later you'll have to face me. The sooner, the better."

"Listen, Your Highness, I don't take threats lightly. I still have that derringer and I'm not afraid to use it."

Fury surged through him like a torch to dry brush. "Good

night, Miss Callahan." Turning on his heel, he marched back to where Sarah and Olivia were waiting. If she thought she was going to get away with this little charade, she had better rethink her actions.

"You ladies go ahead. I'll wait for Mary Margaret. Send the cab back for us." He ushered them into the cab and returned to the house.

Soundlessly he entered the studio and turned down the lamps. Propping a shoulder against the doorjamb, he waited. Seconds later the door to the darkroom opened, the hinges squeaking loudly in the silent house.

Maggie stepped out, a glass plate in her hands. The self-satisfied grin on her face faded when she spotted him. She gasped. "What . . . what are you doing here? You're supposed to be gone."

He forced a smile. "I invited you to dinner, and it would be exceedingly rude to leave without you." Gripping her elbow, he guided her to the doorway.

At the head of the stairs, she pulled free. "I'm not going with you." She tilted her chin and glared at him through furious green eyes.

"Yes, you are." The day had gone downhill from the minute Olivia and Appleton had entered the studio, and his last remnant of patience had long since worn thin. "Go . . . and . . . get . . . dressed." He punctuated each word with a finger to the center of her chest.

Still in the wrinkled shirtwaist and skirt she'd worn earlier in the day, she folded her arms across her chest like an obstinate child. Was this the same woman who'd melted in his embrace only hours ago? The same woman whose kisses had matched his in intensity and fervor? Thinking about it heated the blood in his veins.

"I'm not one of the serfs on your estate that you can order around."

He caught her by the upper arms and shook her. "Mary Margaret, either you come willingly, or I'll throw you over my shoulder and carry you kicking and screaming all the way to the Windsor."

Her eyes grew wide. "You wouldn't dare."

Provoked beyond endurance, he dropped his hands and

jammed his shoulder into her middle. With one quick move he flipped her over his shoulder and gripped her legs.

She yelped in surprise and beat her fists against his back. "You brute, put me down."

"I've never manhandled a woman before, but you deserve it." He swatted her bottom and started down the stairs. At her bedroom, he kicked open the door and strolled across the threshold. When he reached the bed, he tossed her in the middle. Her skirts billowed, revealing shapely legs encased in white stockings.

He leaned forward, trapping her between his arms. A volcano erupted in his veins, and his voice dropped to a husky growl. "If you aren't inclined to dress and go out, we can stay here and make love."

Her tongue swiped across her lower lip, making it damp and inviting. Momentary indecision glittered in her eyes.

"We'll miss dinner," he went on without allowing her a word, "and when your aunt returns, she'll find me in your bed."

If she had that derringer within arm's length, he was certain she would use it on him. She shoved against his chest. "Let me up, you big oaf, so I can get dressed. But I'm only going because my aunt is expecting me. She'll be worried if I don't show up."

Wex's body warred with his principles. For the first time in his life he denied his needs. He planted a quick kiss on her mouth and stood. "I'll be happy to play lady's maid if you are in need of assistance."

She leaped to her feet. "Save it for Miss Ferguson. If you'll be a gentleman and leave my room, I'll be ready in a few minutes."

With a quick glance around the room, he spotted a rocking chair near the fireplace. "My wild Irish rose, be assured I've rarely been accused of being a gentleman. I'll wait here," he said, settling his frame on the plump cushion. "I don't want to take a chance on your locking another door in my face."

Growling under her breath, she grabbed the gown and darted behind a tall Oriental screen. "I should have left you in Sherman at the mercy of the Elliotts."

He chuckled, a soft ironic sound. Sometimes he wished

she had left him behind. That way he wouldn't be facing the ache in his loins that grew stronger every time he looked her way.

He couldn't control his gaze from searching for her. Although he could only envision what the screen was hiding, the swish of fabric peeling from her body fueled his growing need. Her shadow moved back and forth, and then a white cotton stocking landed on top of the screen. Another followed, each in the shape of her leg.

He swallowed to clear the tightening in his throat. The proper thing would be to leave, now, while he was still able. Yet some unseen hand held him captive in the chair.

She peeked around the corner of the screen, only her face in view. "Your Majesty," she said, her voice dripping with sarcasm, "since you chose to remain in my chamber, will you be so kind as to fetch a pair of stockings from the top bureau drawer?"

With a long frustrated groan, he stood. "Mary Margaret," he grunted between his teeth, "I'm still Wex."

"No, you aren't. Wex doesn't even own a suit, much less evening attire."

He bit back a string of curses and stalked to the mahogany highboy. Opening the required drawer, he gazed on a row of neatly folded undergarments. His hands stilled. "Which . . . ?"

"The black silk ones." Her voice dropped to a purr, throwing more fuel on the already raging inferno in his loins.

Holding the sheer, silk stockings by two fingers as if they were twin rattlesnakes out to strike him, he shoved them into her waiting hand.

"Thank you." She disappeared back into her sanctuary.

For a long moment he stood only inches from the screen, unable to force himself away. What kind of fool was he to remain here and torture himself? In a few short minutes he could take her and relieve the pressure in his body. He shoved away the thought as quickly as it came. With Maggie's passionate nature, it would take hours, or even days to fully consummate their lovemaking.

"Hmm . . ." Her soft voice yanked him out of his

reverie. "I just love silk, don't you? It's so delicate, so smooth, so sensuous against my skin."

The woman was a witch, he thought. A green-eyed witch, put on this earth to torture him. He now had two choices. Either take her or run. He remembered Appleton and Olivia waiting for them. And Sarah and Tim. One quick roll with Maggie would never quench the fires burning inside him. He decided to run.

"I'll go tell the driver to wait. Meet me downstairs in five minutes."

This time when she stuck out her head, one porcelain-white and very bare shoulder followed. He curled his fingers into his palms.

"Yes, Your Highness."

Pushed to the limits of his endurance, he spun on his heels and bounded out of the room. Feminine laughter followed him all the way down the stairs and into the night.

Chapter Fifteen

Although the sound held no humor, Maggie couldn't stem the torrent of laughter that erupted from her lips. With all his bold maneuvering, Wex had run from her chamber like a scared fox. Strange how the sly animal knew how to corner a helpless rabbit, but when the hounds began the chase, he turned tail and ran for safety.

"Keep on running, Lord Geoffrey," she called to the empty room. "Run all the way across the Atlantic into your precious Grace's arms." A startling burst of jealousy clashed in her chest.

Her hands stilled on the tiny buttons of the gown. She bit back a dispirited sigh. Too soon he *would* be gone, out of her life, back to his own world. To another woman's arms.

She had no doubts he wanted her—wanted to bed her, that is. Trouble was, she wanted it, too. She wanted to feel his strong fingers freeing the buttons of her bodice, easing the gown from her shoulders, his lips in close pursuit, his body hot and . . . Maggie covered her heated cheeks with her cold palms. What was she thinking? As glorious as their lovemaking would be, it was the impossible dream of a woman who was old enough not to rely on foolish romantic notions.

The tears she'd held at bay all afternoon burned at the

corners of her eyes. She knew if the first one burst free, she wouldn't be able to stem the flood of anguish.

"What's wrong with you, Maggie Callahan?" The words echoed around her. In spite of the number of people she'd loved and lost during her twenty-four years, she had always retained her dignity and strength. Now she'd been reduced to a lump of wet clay by an arrogant Englishman who had no place in her life to begin with.

If this was what love did to a woman, she didn't want any part of the senseless emotion.

Maggie knew only too well it was too late for self-lectures, however. She had already handed her heart to Wex on a sterling-silver platter, and he'd done little more than trample it under the heels of his shiny Wellington boots.

Hurrying to complete her toilette, she bustled about the room, her silk-stockinged feet silent on the worn rug. At the small dressing table, she loosened her braid and passed a brush through the thick coppery masses and frowned at the image in the mirror.

From weeks in the mountain sunshine, her skin had darkened like an overripe peach, and a row of freckles danced across her nose and cheeks. She propped her chin on her hand. Surely his betrothed boasted a flawless alabaster complexion, and her hair was probably golden, soft as corn silk.

With an angry glare at the forlorn face in the mirror, Maggie grabbed a handful of unruly hair, the dreadful color of rusty nails, twisted it into a coil, and pinned it to her head. What did she care what His Highness thought about her looks? She didn't need him or his approval.

Liar, an inner voice whispered. Ignoring the censure, Maggie slipped on her shoes and picked up her handbag. As usual, she checked to make sure the derringer was loaded. She balanced it in her hand before shoving it into the bag. A woman couldn't be too careful, she reminded herself. Especially with a hungry fox lurking in the shadows.

Seconds later, a light shawl around her shoulders, Maggie stepped onto the planked sidewalk. A firm hand caught her elbow as she closed the front door.

"Thank you for hurrying, Mary Margaret."

"Wex's deep, smooth voice came from behind her, and

her heart raced in response. "I would be careful about sneaking up on women, Your Lordship," she said. "Especially one who always carries a loaded gun."

He sighed heavily. "I rue the day I made the mistake of placing a weapon in your hands. I still don't trust a woman to handle a firearm." He tightened his fingers and ushered her to the waiting cab.

The driver held the door as Wex helped Maggie into the elegant vehicle he'd hired, quite unlike the wagons of the past weeks. She settled as far from him as possible on the soft leather seat. Instantly the driver snapped his whip. The carriage lurched, throwing her against the backrest as they started down the street.

Trying to ignore the man next to her, she hugged her shawl tightly across her chest and studied the passing scenery. A lamplighter lifted his torch high and moved from pole to pole, lighting the many gas lamps that illuminated the city at night. In the glowing twilight, the flickering flame reminded her of the fireflies she'd caught as a child in St. Louis and kept in a jar in her room.

They paused at the corner to allow a horse-pulled streetcar to lumber past. From the first Maggie had been impressed with Denver's progress. A young city compared with St. Louis, Denver boasted fine boulevards lined with trees, lighted streets, and many impressive homes.

Yellow lights glittered behind lace curtains in the houses, and people seemed to be everywhere. Yet, inside the carriage, only the clatter of the wheels and the steady tattoo of Maggie's heartbeat pounded in her ears.

"Mary Margaret." Wex finally broke the uncomfortable silence.

She glanced at him from the corner of her eye. In the darkness she saw only his head silhouetted against the window. Since she couldn't move farther away, she tilted her chin and pretended his proximity didn't bother her. Certainly the heat that seared through her came from the close confines of the carriage, not from his large masculine form pressed to her side.

"What . . ." The answer died in her throat as he grazed a finger lightly across her jaw. A tingle skipped along her skin. His touch was such exquisite torture that she was torn between leaning into him and turning away. Unable to help herself, she remained still, and his hand fell away.

She stared at the city outside the window. They had left Larimer Street and were on a dark road that skirted Cherry Creek. "This isn't the way to the Windsor," she said.

"I told the driver to take a longer route." Soft dulcet tones filled the carriage. "We'll reach the hotel when I give the signal."

A dash of excitement skipped up her back. Being alone in the dark with this man had all her senses on alert. Yet Maggie was determined not to let him know how deeply his nearness affected her. "When will that be? My aunt will be worried if I'm late."

He chuckled softly, a wry, humorless sound. "You're already late, Mary Margaret. And I'm sure Jeremy will keep Olivia occupied until we arrive."

The thought of her aunt and the solicitor brought an unbidden smile to her mouth. Over the years the wealthy spinster had been courted by any number of widowers and bachelors, but she'd unceremoniously rejected each and all. Maggie wondered if this time she'd met a man she couldn't run roughshod over, and she found the idea intriguing.

With a sidelong glance at the man beside her, Maggie suspected that was one of the reasons for her devastating attraction to Wex. He was like the wild new polo horse he was training—a strong hand could maneuver the stallion, but the animal's spirit could never be broken. No woman, even a lady like Miss Grace Ferguson, would ever be able to conquer Wex's soul.

"I have to explain the situation to you." At the sadness in his voice, something tightened in her heart.

"That isn't necessary, Your Highness. Everything was made quite clear this afternoon. I'm really not interested in the details of your betrothal, or of your marriage, or of your—anything else about you." She took a deep breath and hurried on. "I certainly don't want to hear any more lies."

"I've never lied." His voice dropped to a husky growl. "I've only not told the whole truth."

"I don't see any difference." She folded her arms across

her chest in a lame effort to guard her heart. It was too late for that, much too late.

"I don't suppose you do. You're a woman who sees things in black and white, without the grays or the shadows. Life isn't always that simple."

Unable to help herself, she twisted to look at him. By now her eyes had adjusted to the darkness, and she spotted a look of apprehension in his eyes. "I know it isn't."

He continued as if she hadn't spoken. "I've told you about my twin, how Arthur died because of my carelessness."

The desire to relieve some of his pain swelled in her chest. No matter what he'd done to her, or what he might yet do, nobody deserved to suffer as he was suffering over his brother. "It was an accident. You didn't kill your brother." Her hand covered his, and she squeezed gently.

"Thank you for listening." He entwined their fingers and pulled her closer to his side. "I'm really not a peer, Maggie. My father is a duke, and my older brother Richard will inherit the title. I'm merely the ne'er-do-well younger son. I don't deserve the title."

Maggie stared at him, confused. "Then you aren't a wealthy nobleman?"

He let out a long sigh. "You're half-right. I'm wealthy, but I'm not a nobleman. After Richard's mother died, the duke married a very wealthy young woman—my mother. Her father was a baronet, not a peer, but he was proud his only child had married into a noble family. In the normal course of events, my mother should have outlived my grandparents, thereby giving my father control of the estate."

His head fell back against the leather seat back. He closed his eyes for a second, then opened them to study their entwined hands. Maggie felt his anguish, wishing she could do something to ease his pain.

In a strained voice, he continued. "As it happened, my mother died, leaving Arthur and me the heirs. At my twin's death I became soul heir to a considerable fortune. My grandparents lived until I came to majority, and I inherited."

"If you're so wealthy, why are you pretending to be a

poor writer?" And why did you let me fall in love with you? The question lodged in her throat.

Wex weighed his options. He had few. Maggie deserved to know the truth. Her warm touch inspired confidence. "Until recently, the estate was kept in trust for me. Appleton managed the funds, and I received a monthly allowance. It was more than generous and allowed me to travel and lead a life of extravagance and frivolity. Often during my travels I wrote amusing stories to my friends and half sisters. Somehow a London periodical learned about them and showed an interest in publication."

"You weren't lying? You are a writer?" she asked.

Lifting her fingers to his lips, he planted a brief kiss on her knuckles. He suppressed his need to hold her close and love away all her doubts. "Yes, I am a writer. During my travels, I've gotten into trouble more times than I care to recall, and my father was always able to use his influence to get me out of embarrassing predicaments. Until last winter."

He shivered at the reminder of what he'd done, or almost done. The idea of killing a man brought a chill to his heart. Next to him, Maggie remained silent, waiting for him to continue. But how to tell her without turning her completely against him. She'd been reared by a spinster aunt, adhering to a strict moral code. What would she think of his decadent life? Wex wasn't very proud of his past.

"To make a long, ugly story short, I became involved with a married woman. Her husband came home unexpectedly and caught us in"—he drew a deep breath—"a rather intimate position."

"You were in bed with her?" Maggie asked without condemnation. For that he was grateful.

"Yes. He pulled a gun on me. We struggled, and the gun went off accidentally. He was badly wounded, and for a while I didn't think he would live. I would have been tried for murder." The thought of being incarcerated for even a short time made his blood run cold. He knew he would go mad if he was unable to feel the sunshine on his face and the wind in his hair. Thank God it hadn't come to that.

She gasped. "Did you intend to harm him?"

"Of course not. I have my faults, but I'm not a murderer. When he began to recover, he demanded a large sum not to press charges against me. My father handled the negotiations and used his influence to keep me from being charged with attempted murder.''

Guilt and shame washed over him as well as anger for getting into the situation in the first place. "To avoid a scandal, my father recommended that I come to America and inspect his investment in a Wyoming cattle enterprise. It was the perfect opportunity for me to get away and allow the gossip to die down. I contacted an agent who agreed to handle my stories. That was how I ended up in your camp with a bullet hole in my shoulder.''

Unconsciously he rubbed the spot, now healed thanks to Sarah. Although he couldn't see Maggie's face, he sensed her softening. Her thumb brushed lightly along his hand, giving him courage to go on. Lord, he longed to crush her in his arms, feel her soft lips under his, let her sweet warmth melt away the ice in his heart. For now he comforted himself with the touch of her hand—more than he deserved.

"Were you betrothed while you were with the other woman?" Her voice sounded raw and strained.

A new wave of remorse swamped him. Inadvertently he'd hurt her, something he never intended. "No. And I'm not betrothed now. I don't know Grace Ferguson. I've never met the woman." He heard the harshness in his voice.

She pulled her hand free and twisted it in her lap. "Then what was Mr. Appleton talking about?"

The loss of her touch was like stepping from a cozy cabin into a frigid ice storm. Up to now Maggie had been amazingly understanding about his sordid past. He doubted she would have the same compassion about his ignoble future.

"It seems my father made some bad investments, and he's on the verge of bankruptcy. He may even lose our ancestral home in Allenshire—everything that the Wexfords have possessed for hundreds of years. He borrowed heavily from this Ferguson, and now the man is demanding payment.''

"What does that have to do with you?"

He let out a sharp bark of mirthless laughter. "I'm the chattel, the payment, if you please. Ferguson is demanding a pound of flesh. He wants a titled husband for his daughter, and the prestige that goes with it.''

She turned to face him. Even in the dark carriage he could read the shocked look on her face. "You?"

"Yes, dammit, me. My father has made it clear that it's my responsibility to save the family estate and keep the proverbial wolf from the door." He looked past Maggie, out the window. In the growing twilight, the moon was slowly coming to life over the city. Unable to stop himself, he caught her hands. He squeezed, not sure if it was he or she who was trembling. "My father also reminded me of all the times he's gotten me out of trouble over the years. I owe him my life."

Her fingers were cold and stiff. "Your father has arranged your marriage to Ferguson's daughter."

"Arranged marriages aren't unheard of, even here in the United States."

"Somehow I'd thought you were more independent—your own man. What are you going to do?" She slipped her hands free, and he suspected he'd lost her forever.

His heart sank. He'd disappointed her by not being the man she'd thought he was. The pain was far worse than he'd envisioned.

"For the first time in my life, my father needs me. I've failed him so many times, but now I have a chance to prove I'm something other than a degenerate prodigal son. It isn't only for him, but for my stepmother and my sisters. They're used to a certain standard of living, and I couldn't live with myself if I took that away from them."

"Is that why Mr. Appleton came to Denver? To take you back to England?"

"Yes, he explained the situation. The ironic part is that if Arthur had lived, he would have inherited the bulk of the estate, and I would be a poor writer, free to pursue my own life. Damn, looks like it's time to pay the piper."

She tilted her chin to a haughty angle. "Then by all means you should leave for England immediately. You certainly don't want to keep your Grace waiting."

"She isn't *my* Grace." He squeezed his eyes shut to stem some of the pain. Not only would he be leaving Maggie behind, but also the independence and freedom to be his own man. He liked being known only as "Wex," a man accepted or rejected on his own merits, not because of who his father was or wasn't. "I'm going to miss America," he said finally.

A huge ache settled in Maggie's chest. She turned her head and avoided his gaze. "Please direct the driver to the Windsor. My aunt will be worried." She needed to get away from him before she did something foolish—like tumbling into his arms and begging him to stay.

On a sigh, he knocked twice on the roof of the carriage. "Look at me, Mary Margaret." Gently he cupped her chin and turned her face to his. "I'm going to miss you, and Sarah, and Tim."

Maggie bit her lip to keep it from quivering. Why did she have to love him so much when he didn't care a whit for her? "I'm sure they'll miss you, too." The words stumbled around the lump in her throat.

"And *you?* Will *you* miss me?" he whispered in the darkness.

With all her heart, soul, and spirit, she wanted to confess. But speaking her heart would leave her open, vulnerable to further pain. Soft ironic laughter bubbled from her throat, raw now from unshed tears. "Who would ever imagine a wealthy, sophisticated gentleman traveling in a covered wagon and acting as an itinerant photographer's assistant."

He stroked his thumbs across her lips. "I loved every second of our gypsy lifestyle."

Maggie met his gaze. Even in the dark carriage, the longing was visible in his eyes. He wanted to kiss her, and she was afraid she was too weak to refuse. Summoning all her resolve, Maggie captured his wrists in her fingers.

"No, don't try to kiss me again. Save them for your be—" She swallowed the word. "Miss Ferguson."

For a long moment he continued to stare into her eyes. She lowered her eyelids, not wanting him to see into her soul or learn of the love hidden in her heart. He loosened his grip and moved away. A chill raked her at the sudden loss of his warmth.

From the far side of the leather seat, he said, "Don't concern yourself, Miss Callahan. Your honor is quite safe with me. We'll arrive at the hotel shortly."

Maggie twisted her fingers together. Through blurry eyes she watched as they joined the line of carriages in front of the elegant Windsor Hotel. Built to resemble Windsor Castle, the five-story hotel was acknowledged to be one of the finest in the West. No wonder Lord Geoffrey chose to stay here, she thought. It probably reminded him of London with its richly appointed furnishings.

The instant the door opened, Wex exited and held out his hand for Maggie. Hesitantly she placed her palm in his. She allowed him to take her arm and escort her into the hotel. He hadn't spoken a word after she'd rebuked him for trying to kiss her. It was just as well. She didn't want her family to learn about their arguments.

He ushered her into the lobby filled with beautifully dressed women and handsome men. Laughter and voices swelled around them. After all that had happened that day, Maggie was in no mood for dinner with Wex or her family. But she wasn't going to spoil the evening for the others. She would laugh and smile and never let them know her heart was breaking.

The quiet house wreaked havoc with Maggie's nerves. With Tim and Sarah in school, and the housekeeper shopping, an abnormal silence shrouded the house. Jeremy Appleton had come by earlier and insisted that Olivia tour Denver with him. On her way out, Olivia whispered for Maggie not to expect her until dinner.

Maggie arranged and rearranged the cameras, the potted plants, and the painted scenery panels. So far, not a single customer had graced the premises of Callahan and Company. In the first-floor reception area, she paced until she suspected she would wear the floral pattern off the rug. She jumped every time a horse-drawn streetcar rumbled past.

Even Wex hadn't shown up. Not that she expected him. After their confrontation the previous night, she doubted he would come to the studio again. In spite of the strained atmosphere, the dinner had gone well. Maggie had sat beside Harry, and Sarah had been delighted when Wex had taken her arm and escorted her into the dining room.

Whenever Maggie looked up, however, she'd found Wex staring at her, a dark scowl on his face. It wasn't fair to use Harry, but if Wex was just a little jealous, so much the better. Let him know how rejection felt.

A noise from the street drew her attention. Shoving aside the drapes, she watched an elegant carriage, pulled by matching black horses, stop in front of the house. Finally, she thought, a customer. With a quick check in the mirror, she tucked a stray lock of hair back into the bun and pasted on a smile. She puffed the sleeves of her starched white shirtwaist and wiped her damp palms on her gray-and-black skirt. Ready to greet her customer as a businesswoman, Maggie folded her hands docilely in front of her and waited.

The high-pitched twitter of feminine laughter drifted from the doorway. Maggie didn't recognize the woman's voice, but the deep resonant voice of the man accompanying her was all too familiar. Maggie's heart stopped for several seconds before she willed it to start up again.

"This way, lovely lady," Wex said, holding the door open.

A pretty young woman attached to Wex's arm giggled again. "Is this the picture studio, Your Lordship?" she asked. Dressed in an elegant maroon velvet gown, the woman swept the room with her gaze. Twin strands of marble-sized pearls draped the lacy inset of her bodice. Blond ringlets danced from under a large hat covered with silk flowers and a dozen feathers.

Wex smiled down at her. "Yes, Miss Miranda. May I introduce Miss Callahan, the finest photographer in the West."

Maggie stood stock-still. She coiled her fingers into her palm to keep from snatching the woman away from Wex. Instead of the denims he'd worn for months, he was now attired in a black tailored suit and immaculate white shirt. Gone was the man with whom she'd fallen in love. In his place stood Lord Geoffrey. And he was devilishly handsome.

"Miss Callahan." He turned his gaze to Maggie. The warmth she'd never expected to see glittered in his eyes. "Meet Miss Miranda Brown. Your first customer."

A thousand emotions assailed Maggie. Gratitude mingled with jealousy and turned her heart upside down. Just when she'd thought Wex didn't care at all for her, he'd brought her a customer—a wealthy customer.

Keeping her arm firmly attached to Wex, Miranda glanced at the framed portraits on the walls. "My papa's birthday is coming up soon, and I want to give him a picture of me to put in our new house."

"Then I'll turn you over to Miss Callahan." Wex deftly disengaged himself from Miranda's grip.

"But, Lord Geoffrey," she said, reaching for him again. "I thought you were going to take my picture."

Maggie groaned inwardly. Her first customer, and the woman was smitten with Wex. Common sense shoved away the jealousy and made her think clearly. This woman could bring other customers to the studio. "Please come in, Miss Brown. Lord Geoffrey will be assisting, and he'll stay right at your side."

During the session, Wex did more than assist. He removed his jacket, rolled up his sleeves, and took over. He posed the subject, arranged the cameras, and Maggie found herself working as his assistant. She bit back her pride and followed instructions. Her business depended on satisfied customers, and given the smile on Miranda's face, the young woman seemed more than happy with the attention being paid her by the handsome nobleman.

Miranda, who was barely twenty years old, became talkative. Her father was a prospector who'd dragged his only daughter from mining camp to mining camp for years. He'd made small strikes, barely enough to keep them alive, until one day he discovered a mother lode.

Unlike other miners who wasted their wealth or had it swindled from them, he'd had enough education and intelligence to manage his finances. He'd invested in other mines and was one of the wealthiest men in Denver. Until their mansion was complete, Miranda and her father occupied a suite in the Windsor Hotel. Wex had met her that morning in the dining room.

By the time they'd taken a dozen poses and carried the plates into the darkroom for developing, Maggie was exhausted. Normally they would take only three or four poses. Miranda insisted on at least a dozen to choose from, however, and she was willing to pay the price.

A few minutes after the clock struck two, someone knocked on the studio door. Maggie opened it to find Harry, hat in hand, standing on the landing. A wide smile lit his face.

"Good afternoon, Maggie," he said.

"Hello, Harry." Not sure how to deal with him, she blocked the entrance with her body.

"May I come in?" He shoved a small bouquet of flowers into her hand.

She was about to tell him she was busy when she heard Miranda's giggles. Inspiration struck her like a bolt of lightning. Here was her chance to kill two birds with one stone.

"Of course, Harry. We were about to serve tea." She took his arm and led him into the studio. "There's someone I think you should meet."

Chapter
Sixteen

"*That was a clever move, Mary Margaret,*" Wex said.

Inside the close confines of the darkroom, her arm brushed his as she set the glass negative in the fixing bath. "I'm afraid I don't know what you're talking about."

He chuckled softly. "Pairing Miranda with Harry. You should get a license as a matchmaker."

Proud of her handiwork, Maggie couldn't hide the smile in her voice. "Harry's been looking for an heiress since we broke our engagement. Miranda more than fills the bill."

She sensed rather than saw him turn toward her. "You were engaged to marry that chap? Somehow I can't quite picture the two of you together."

Maggie struggled with her temper. For hours she'd been working with Wex, and being cooped up with him made her as jumpy as a nervous bullfrog. "Why is that, Your Majesty? Do you think a twenty-four-year-old spinster is undesirable?"

He swung toward her and trapped her against the counter, his hard chest meeting her soft breasts. Her nipples puckered at the intimate contact. She clutched the tongs in her hands to keep from touching him.

"Mary Margaret, you are without question the most desirable woman I've ever met." Since they were both wearing protective gloves, he didn't touch her, but wedged his body into hers. Through their layers of clothing, his male hardness pressed against her. Her breath caught in her throat. "I simply thought you were much too intelligent and clever to become involved with the likes of a fortune hunter like Harry."

Perspiration broke out on her forehead, her pulse raced out of control, yet she continued the conversation as if nothing was happening between them. "I found out before the wedding that all he really wanted was control of me and my inheritance. He didn't love me. He loved my money."

"And now you've turned him over to poor Miranda." He slid side to side, increasing the friction between their bodies. The erotic movement sent quivers of sensation to the pit of her stomach.

Maggie fought a losing battle with her emotions. Unable to move away, she swallowed down the longing in her heart. "Rich Miranda, you mean. I think she can handle Harry. You would only break the young thing's heart." Like you've broken mine, she thought.

"Mary Margaret, you sound almost jealous." He lowered his head and brushed a light kiss on her forehead.

In spite of the harsh chemical smell in the tiny room, his distinctive male fragrance made her hungry for all of him. A craving that would go unfulfilled. "Ha. I'm only thinking about Miranda. You really should at least try to be faithful to your Grace."

On a loud moan, he moved away. "Can't you forget that . . . that situation? The woman is probably homely, stupid, or very young to let herself get trapped into marriage with the likes of me."

By the light of a tiny gas flame, Maggie watched the reverse image of Miranda take shape on the glass plate. The perfect exposure, a contrast of lights and shadows, would make an outstanding portrait.

"What about you? You're neither homely, stupid, nor very young, yet you're going into a marriage with a woman you've never met."

Wex took the plate and set it into another washing tray. "I'd never intended to marry, ever. But I'll submit myself if it will save my father from ruin and help my family."

Carefully she began to dry the negatives. Maggie wished

she could wipe him from her heart as easily as she wiped the moisture from the glass. "That's all quite noble, but you sound more like a man condemned to the gallows than a blushing bridegroom."

"Damn, that's exactly how I feel." He removed his gloves and wiped his forehead with a handkerchief. "I wish you'd quit talking about it and let me have a few minutes' reprieve."

Maggie sighed. "When will you be leaving for England?" With the negatives developed, she reached for the door. After the heat and the overpowering odor of the chemicals, she needed a breath of air. And she needed to put some space between her and Wex.

He followed her into the studio. "Soon, I suppose. Jeremy wants to cross the Atlantic before winter."

Her heart sank at the thought. It was already the first of October. Yet the sooner he left, the sooner her heart would mend. If it ever would. "I understand he was quite seasick on the voyage over."

Wex moved to the window and stared at the mountains in the distance. All this talk about leaving made his nerves raw. He felt as if he'd been sucked into a vortex and was unable to fight his way out. In twenty-four short hours his entire world had been turned upside down, never to be righted again.

He'd planned to return to England—eventually, on his terms and on his timetable. There had to be some way out of this bizarre situation.

Behind him, Maggie bustled about the room, arranging and shifting things from one spot to another and chattering like a magpie. "I hope Miranda likes her photographs and that she tells her friends about us. I could use the business."

He spun to face her. Her face was flushed, and her damp shirtwaist clung provocatively to her breasts. Strands of her beautiful fiery hair had come loose and hung in damp wisps around her face. A band tightened around his heart. He'd heard about love, read about other men's feelings, even enjoyed the poems devoted to the emotion. But he'd never expected to know love for himself.

Did he love this woman? He swallowed hard to suppress

his emotions. No, love left a man vulnerable, weak. He was attracted to her, he wanted her, but he didn't love her.

If he did, it was too late to do anything about it. His fate had already been sealed by his father.

"Mary Margaret, will you please stop fluttering around like a hummingbird?" He took the tray of discarded teacups from her hands and set it on a rococo table. "I would like to talk to you."

She groaned aloud. "Haven't we talked enough?"

With a firm hand on her arm, he led her to the settee. As much as he wanted to hold her, he let her sit on one end while he took the other. "I've been thinking about us."

"Us? Your Majesty, there is no *us*. There's *you* and there's *me*. *You* are on your way to England and your lady, while *I* am staying here in Denver with my sister and brother."

"You can come to England with me." The words came out before he even thought about them. Yet it was the perfect solution, the only solution.

Her eyes grew wide. "Why?"

Tired of the space separating them, Wex slid across the brocade settee. She folded her arms across her chest to keep him from reaching for her hand. Undeterred, he cupped her chin with his fingers.

"I would say so I can look after you, but I know that would make you angry. You're quite capable of taking care of yourself. I've become very fond of all of you, however. Tim needs a man's influence in his life, and I'll see that Sarah attends the finest medical school in the world. I can give them this."

The pink in her cheeks turned crimson. She slapped his hand away. "You want to take Tim and Sarah away from me? My aunt would never allow it. She wants them to return to St. Louis with her."

"I want all of you to come with me. I can set you up with the best photographic gallery in London. Noblemen and aristocrats will be beating a path to your door for their portraits. Even the royal family. You'll be the toast of London."

"I see. And of course I can photograph your wedding and take the pictures of your wife and children." The last words came out on a raspy grunt. "What about us?"

He ran his hands through his dark hair. Damn, he was handling this all wrong. "Mary Margaret, I didn't intend to insult you or make unwanted advances. We can be friends, lovers, or enemies. It isn't uncommon for married men to have . . ." How to phrase it without scandalizing her sensitivities? "To be friends with women."

Her eyes deepened to the darkest green he'd ever seen. "You once told me women and men couldn't be friends. You want me for your mistress, don't you?"

"My father has been married three times, and he's always kept a mistress."

"And his wives didn't mind?"

"I don't know about Richard's mother or my mother. But Frances, my stepmother, either doesn't know or doesn't care. She has her home, her children, her social standing, everything she needs. What my father does in his spare time is up to him."

Maggie jumped to her feet. "And you assume that your Grace will be as open-minded?"

"Mary Margaret, I didn't ask you to be my mistress. I feel responsible for you and I want to help you."

"I'm quite able to take care of myself, thank you." She lifted the tray from the table. "If you'll excuse me, I'd like to discuss dinner with Flora."

Nothing had gone right. "Think about it. You can become one of the most famous photographers in the world."

"I will," she shot over her shoulder. "Without your help."

Aware he'd lost the battle and hurt her in the bargain, he rolled down the sleeves of his white shirt. "When Tim comes home, tell him I'll meet him in the meadow for his polo lesson. He's quite a horseman."

The cups on the tray rattled. "It's natural considering he's Indian and Irish."

"A potent combination," he said. "Good day, Miss Callahan."

Without a backward glance, he marched out of the house into the sunshine. He couldn't wait to feel the power of the stallion under him, to race the horse until both animal and man were winded. Maybe then he would be able to clear his head and gain some perspective on his situation.

Maggie continued to fume all night. The insufferable Brit

infuriated her beyond belief. Unable to sleep, she got up early the next morning and went into the kitchen. The housekeeper hadn't arrived yet, and everyone else was still asleep.

Olivia had invited Wex and Jeremy to dinner the previous night, but Maggie had feigned a headache and remained in her room. Sarah, concerned as ever, had mixed a special potion. When Sarah left her alone, Maggie poured the drink into her chamber pot. She was heartsick, and there was nothing Sarah could do for her.

Thoughts of the Englishman haunted her all night. He was conceited and cavalier totally beyond belief. The idea of asking her to be his mistress. To take a backseat to his wife. To be subjected to a few stolen minutes when he could get away from his family. To live in the shadows while another woman had his name.

Well, His Lordship had better think again if he thought Maggie Callahan would take a backseat to any woman. As much as she loved Wex, she would live to be a hundred-year-old virgin before she'd give herself to that man. Even if they were the two last people left on earth.

A devious smile curved her lips. Damn, she hoped Grace looked like his horse, and he'd be forced to remain totally faithful to her for the next fifty years. That would serve him right.

Maggie set the enamel coffeepot on the wood-burning stove. She added wood and stoked the fire. As she waited for the coffee to brew she wondered if she could face Wex again. Undoubtedly he would show up again to act as her helper. They needed to print the negatives and show the proofs to Miranda.

So much to do, she thought. But not today. Today she needed some time and distance to pull herself together.

She glanced out the window. In the gleaming dawn, the sun was peeking over the horizon, firing pale golden streaks across the sky—a perfect day for photography. In an instant she made a decision.

Racing back to her room, she threw off her dressing gown and donned the trousers and boy's shirt she'd worn in the mountains. She slipped into Papa's old jacket and shoved

the derringer into the pocket. On her way out, she grabbed
her rifle.

From the studio she picked up the five-by-eight camera
with the Dallmeyer lens and a tripod. She added a half-
dozen plates and a double book-plate holder to the pile.

After filling a large basket with bread, a jar of jelly,
leftover chicken from supper the night before, some pickles,
and cold potatoes, she left to get the photographic wagon
from the nearby livery. By the time she returned to the
house to collect her camera and food, Tim had come in from
the privy out back.

"Maggie, what's going on?" he asked, rubbing the sleep
from his eyes.

Her spirits sagged. Nothing was going her way. To avoid
explanations, she'd planned to get away before anyone was
up. Aunt Olivia would never approve of her going into the
hills alone. "It looks like a glorious day, and I want to go out
and get some photos of the mining towns. I'll be back in
time for supper."

He shook his head and watched her load the wagon.
"Gosh, Maggie, do you think it's safe for you to go alone?
I can stay home from school and go with you."

She hefted the rifle. "Don't worry, I'll be safe. Here's a
note for Aunt Olivia."

Tim took the paper and shoved it into his pocket. "I wish
I could go with you."

She smiled and tousled his thick black hair. "Aunt Olivia
would be furious if I kept you out of school. I'll be back
later."

"Okay, sis," he said as she climbed into the seat of the
wagon. "Be careful."

"I will." She clutched the reins in her gloved hands,
happy to be in her own element. This is where she belonged.
The American-born daughter of an Irish immigrant would
never fit into London society. Leave it to his precious Grace
to receive visitors and serve tea. Maggie Callahan had
more interesting things to do with her life. Someday
everybody would remember the woman who photographed
the Rockies.

With a wry smile she snapped the reins, and the photo-

graphic wagon pulled onto Larimer and moved along the
South Platte River to the mining camps beyond.

"Has Maggie returned, Lord Geoffrey?"

At the sound of Olivia's worried voice, Wex spun to face
her. Jeremy stood at her side, concern on his face.

"No." He glanced toward the mountains. For hours he'd
kept a vigil at the front windows. In the west, gray clouds
gathered across the sky. The sun that had been so bright
only hours ago was now obscured by the clouds. "I've
looked everywhere I can think of, and nobody has seen her
today. I even checked with Harry."

That fact alone burned in his gut. But Harry was
entranced by Miranda and had spent the entire day with the
young heiress.

Olivia removed her wide flower-trimmed hat. "She
wasn't here when I arose this morning, and Flora said she
hasn't seen Maggie either."

"Do you think we should call the constables?" asked
Jeremy.

Wex ran his hand along the back of his neck to ease the
tension. "Not yet. Let's give her a little more time." Lord, he
hoped she showed up soon. Since he arrived at the studio
that morning, he'd known something was wrong. He'd
assumed she was simply avoiding him. But when nobody
had seen neither hide nor hair of Maggie, he began to worry.

While at the Windsor, he'd changed from his tailored suit
into his denims, flannel shirt, and boots. He dropped his
hand to the Colt .45 low on his hip.

He continued to stare out the window. Damn, where the
hell was the stubborn woman?

The front door opened and slammed shut. In a few long
strides, Wex entered the front hallway. "Mary Margaret," he
whispered. Thank God she was home.

He came to an abrupt halt when he spied Tim and Sarah
with their schoolbooks in their hands. His stomach lurched.

"Wex," Tim said, a wide smile on his face. "Are we going
to practice again today?" He shrugged out of his jacket and
tossed it on a chair.

Sarah snatched her brother's jacket and hung it neatly

beside hers. "Tim, his name is Lord Geoffrey. Please mind your manners."

For the first time that day, Wex felt like smiling. "No practice today, Tim. I'm waiting for Mary Margaret to come home."

Tim headed toward the kitchen. "She isn't back yet?" he called over his shoulder.

Something in the way he spoke struck Wex like a kick from a mule. "Tim, do you know where Maggie went?" Wex followed in the boy's wake.

"I'm not sure. She said she would be back this afternoon."

Wex stopped the boy with a hand on his shoulder. "When did you last see your sister?"

"Maggie?" He shrugged and dug his hands into his pockets. "This morning. She went off in the photography wagon, said she was going to the mining camps. Holy cow." His eyes grew wide as he drew out a piece of crumpled paper. "She gave me this note, but I forgot to give it to Aunt Olivia."

By then Olivia, Jeremy, and Sarah had caught up with them. "Tim, Maggie gave you a note?" Olivia stuck out her hand.

Tim bowed his head. "Yes, ma'am. You were still in bed when I left for school, and I guess I forgot."

Olivia took the paper and handed it to Wex. "'Aunt Olivia,'" he read aloud. "'I'm going out for a while to take some pictures. I'll be home in time for supper.'"

A wave of relief poured over Wex, his fears temporarily allayed. He'd been right about one thing. She'd left to avoid seeing him.

"I'm going to find her," Wex said. "It looks like a storm is brewing over the mountains, and I want to make sure she doesn't get caught out in the weather."

Sarah caught his arm. Her green eyes darkened to jade. "Wex, I think she's gone to that mining camp near Golden. Be careful."

He planted a quick kiss on the girl's cheek. "I will."

The foreboding that had nagged him all day grew stronger. Maggie was in danger, he knew it. He shoved his arms into his jacket on the run, not stopping until he reached the livery where he'd stabled his horse. Within minutes he had the stallion saddled and he was riding out of the city.

The wind whipped the branches of the willows along Cherry Creek and stung his cheeks. If Maggie was high up in the mountains, the storm could hit before he reached her. Fear burned in his stomach. With the wagon, she would be forced to remain on the roads. He hoped she hadn't veered off where she would never be found.

Wex had never been a religious man, but as he began his ascent into the mountains, he prayed he would meet her on the steep winding road. He hunched over the neck of the horse, urging the animal against the wind. As he reached a hilltop he shielded his eyes to scan the clearing below him.

His heart stopped beating. About a hundred feet down stood the familiar black wagon. The horses nibbled at the low grass, but Maggie was nowhere in sight. Spurring his horse into a gallop, he forced himself to believe she was all right. He'd promised to protect her, and he couldn't fail again.

He knew of the chances Maggie often took when she wanted to get a photograph. She thought nothing of leaning over the edge of a precipice for the best angle. A thousand fears rushed through him. She could have fallen, she could have been attacked by an animal, or worse, by a man.

When he reached the wagon he jumped from the horse and dropped the reins. "Maggie? Where are you?" The rising wind flung his words back into his face.

Terror lodged in his throat like a huge stone. Surely she had to be nearby. With a quick glance around the clearing, he spotted a splash of red through the thin stand of trees. He grew weak with relief. Perched on the edge of a cliff, her head under the dark cloth of her camera, Maggie was totally oblivious to the rages of nature around her. Her red wool scarf flew behind her like a banner.

Within seconds he was at her side. Frustration drove him to the limits of his control. "What the hell are you doing here?"

With slow precise movements, she slid the plate into the camera and uncapped the lens. Only when she finished the procedure did she turn to face him.

Her eyes narrowed, and her mouth pulled into a straight line. "Does it look like I'm attending a ball in Buckingham Palace? For your information, Your Lordship, I'm taking a photograph."

He caught her by the shoulders and shook her. "Woman, can't you see there's a storm brewing?"

She threw off his hands. "The clouds were forming such an interesting pattern, I couldn't resist photographing them over the mountains. What are you doing here?"

"Looking for you, dammit."

Her hair had come loose from her braid and was flying wildly about her face. She caught a flyaway strand and tucked it under her hat. "I can take care of myself. I don't need a guardian."

"Mary Margaret, you're the most obstinate creature I've ever had the misfortune to encounter. Can't you feel the chill? It could snow before we reach the city."

Eyes wide, she glanced around. "I hadn't noticed. It's always windy in the mountains." She folded the leather bellows of the camera. "I suppose I had better get back home."

Impatient, Wex folded the legs of the tripod and flung the apparatus over his shoulder. He grabbed Maggie's arm with his other hand. When they reached the wagon, he stored the equipment in the back.

The first white snowflakes landed on the black wagon. "We'll never get back before the storm hits."

Maggie propped her hands on her hips. "You worry too much. We'll make it with time to spare."

Tired from the long worrisome day, and sick of arguing, he lifted her in his arms and plunked her on the seat of the wagon. Her mouth dropped open, and anger flashed in her eyes. "Stay there and don't say a word."

On a run he grabbed the reins of his horse and tied the animal to the rear of the wagon. Then Wex climbed into the driver's seat and picked up the lines. He shot Maggie a stern look, daring her to protest. A steady flurry of snow swirled around the wagon. "You had better pray we get off this mountain before the snow makes the road impassable."

She pulled the ragged hat low on her forehead. "May I have permission to speak, Your Lordship?"

He snapped the reins, and the horses began their slow prodding gait. "What?" he grunted between his teeth.

"I spotted a cabin about a half mile off the road. We may find shelter there." She stuffed her hands into her pockets an shrugged deeper into the coat.

The horses whinnied and protested against their burden. The wind whistling in his ears, he turned the wagon in the direction she indicated.

One of two things was certain. By the time the storm blew over, they would end up bitter enemies or lovers.

Either would be disastrous for him.

Chapter
Seventeen

Maggie huddled deep into Papa's old gray coat and
pulled the red scarf over her mouth. Snowflakes pelted her
exposed skin like a thousand tiny pinpricks. In the past few
hours the temperature had dropped at least twenty degrees.
Nightfall would surely bring the full force of the storm.

Only a total idiot would get caught out in the inclement
weather as she had. The idea that "his nibs" had found her
and was playing the knight in shining armor rankled her
even further.

She shoved her hands into her pockets and closed her
fingers on the icy metal grip of the derringer. If somehow
they managed to survive the storm, the fox had better
beware of the hunter.

Dark swirling clouds blotted out the sun. Progress grew
agonizingly slow with visibility limited to a few dozen feet
on the curving hillside. The wagon bumped over the rocky
road and shook from side to side. Wex expertly handled the
shying team in the face of the adverse wind.

He hadn't uttered a word since she'd steered him in the
direction of the cabin. From the corner of her eye she
sneaked a glance at his face. His jaw was set in a determined
line, and his expression was unreadable under the brim of
his black Stetson. White snowflakes dotted his buckskin
jacket like stars in the night sky.

By the time they reached the clearing, several inches of snow blanketed the ground. Maggie's spirits sagged at the close-up view of the cabin. Little more than a clapboard shanty propped against the hillside, it appeared to be held together by the brambles and bushes growing from the cracks in the walls.

Wex pulled hard on the pole brake, tied off the reins, and jumped to the ground. Maggie followed in a single bound. "Do you think this place will stand up against the storm?" She shouted to be heard.

"It's a shelter. That's all we can hope for."

Maggie shivered, more from the chill in his voice than the frosty air. What right did he have to be angry? she wondered. She hadn't sent for him or asked him to come looking for her. In spite of her bravado, some deep-down part of her was glad he had found her. Being caught out alone in a blizzard held no appeal.

In a few long strides, Wex approached the shanty and reached for the door. Hooked to the wall by one rusty hinge, it groaned and protested as he opened it enough to squeeze through. Maggie followed him inside. In the near darkness, all she saw was dust, cobwebs, and chunks of wood that had once been crude furniture. From the looks of the place, no one had lived here in ages.

Wex gestured to the rustic stone fireplace. "See if you can start a fire." He gathered a pile of wood and took a box of matches from his pocket. "I'll unhitch the horses and put them in the lean-to out back. They should be safe from the full force of the storm."

Aware they would have to work together if they were to survive, Maggie didn't protest his harshly given orders. Hastily she stacked the wood in the fireplace. Her fingers stiff from the cold, she wasted half the box of matches before the kindling caught fire. The dry wood ignited, and the smoke poured up the chimney.

With a sigh of relief, she ventured into the steady snowfall to unload the wagon. The force of the wind bit through her clothes, and she had to make three trips to retrieve the food basket and blankets from the wagon. Thank goodness she'd packed a lunch and had left the blankets in the wagon.

Shivering from the chill that seeped through the many cracks in the cabin's walls, Maggie stretched her hands toward the fire to warm them. She wondered if she should go outside and help Wex with the animals. When she'd last seen him, he'd been struggling against the wind to get his stallion to the makeshift stable. But she was afraid she would only get in the way and cause him even more trouble than she had already.

Her shoulders slumped, and she looked around the dilapidated shelter, their only protection against a winter storm. Small snowdrifts gathered on the floor near the walls. Any moment she expected a strong gust to pick up the cabin and toss it down into the valley, inhabitants and all.

If she'd used a tiny bit of her common sense, she would be safe in the warm house in Denver, waiting for Flora to serve dinner. Instead she'd tried to run away from Wex, and now she would spend the long night alone with him. The wind whistled through the cracks like ironic laughter mocking her foolishness.

A sudden blast of frigid air ripped through the cabin. Maggie spun around to see Wex silhouetted in the doorway, his jacket and hat covered with a light powder of snow, his cheeks red from the cold.

He shouldered the broken door shut and propped a wooden bar against it to keep it closed. Striding toward Maggie and the fire, he left a trail of wet footprints on the dirty floor.

"Damn, it's not much warmer in here." Hunkering down, he tore off his gloves and shoved his hands toward the fire.

Maggie stared down at him. Moisture clung to his thick eyebrows and rolled from the brim of his hat. A falling drop pulled her gaze to his wide, strong shoulders. "Nobody asked you to come."

His head snapped up, and his eyes narrowed. Immediately she regretted the rude remark. After all, it was her fault they were in this predicament, not his.

"Your family was worried about you. And I felt responsible for your running away from me." He returned his gaze to the fire.

"You're even more arrogant than I'd thought. I didn't run away from you. It looked like a beautiful day to take photographs. How was I supposed to know a storm would come up unexpectedly?"

"By watching the sky."

She bit her tongue against a sharp retort. "At least I had the foresight to bring food and blankets."

He shifted his gaze to the basket. "Good. I'm starved."

Puddles from the melting snow gathered on the dirty floor. "You'll be warmer if you take off that damp jacket and wrap yourself in a blanket."

At her suggestion Wex shed his coat. Maggie averted her gaze, not wanting to see the way his muscles flexed in his back when he moved. Her fingers itched to feel the varied textures she'd only just begun to learn when Aunt Olivia had interrupted them days ago. Silently she cursed herself for the desire she couldn't control.

Maggie draped a blanket over her shoulders and joined him on the floor, the picnic basket between them.

Neither spoke while they shared the lunch, leaving some of the bread and jelly for breakfast. Maggie kept her gaze averted and stared into the glowing fire.

The wind forced the snow through the many cracks in the walls, and the cabin shook with the force. Maggie wondered if she could survive the long night alone with Wex. In spite of her anger and her feeling of betrayal, her desire for him was as strong as ever. Maybe stronger, considering he'd risked his life to find her.

By the yellow glow of the fire, she watched him. From time to time he slanted his gaze toward her, yet he remained silent, and she wasn't about to be the first to speak. She shivered and snuggled deeper into the jacket under the blanket.

He moved the basket aside and stretched out an arm. "You're cold. Come, let me warm you with body heat."

Body heat? At his words, excitement coiled through her. As wonderful as it sounded, Maggie was afraid of what she would do if she were to give in to his request. "I'm not cold."

His lips thinned to a narrow line. "Don't be so stubborn, Mary Margaret. The only way we're going to survive is to work together."

"Sleep together, you mean."

He turned his gaze to her. The golden firelight reflected the desire in his bright eyes. "Once I was caught in a Russian hunting lodge during a particularly severe blizzard. I learned that two bodies nestled together can endure the cold much better than one alone."

Indignation rose up in Maggie. "Like your other proposals, this one isn't worth a pile of bull—cow manure."

"Are you referring to my inviting you to return to England with me?" His voice remained softly coaxing.

Which only added fuel to her temper. She knelt to face him eye to eye. All the misery she'd stored up since learning of his deception spilled out like fire spewing from a dragon. "You arrogant, lily-livered Brit. Do you think I would allow my brother to be influenced by the likes of you? Or let my sister become part of your hedonistic society? You ask me to be your mistress to satisfy your carnal desires while your wife sits in her mansion and serves tea to your guests."

"I said we can be friends." His lips barely moved when he spoke.

Maggie shoved her hands into her pockets and wrapped her fingers around the derringer. She wished she had the courage to put a bullet between those mocking eyes. "Well, I don't want any part of you or your society. The sooner you leave for England and your precious fiancée"—unable to hide the lie in her eyes, she slid her gaze to a dark place over his shoulder—"the happier I'll be."

Wex refused to let her look away. With one strong hand, he cupped her chin and turned her face to his. Moisture glistened in the corners of her eyes. "Mary Margaret, I'm afraid I've insulted you, although that was never my intention."

Green fire flashed in her eyes. "Don't deny your intentions were less than honorable. Did you expect me to be pleased by your offer?"

His thumb brushed lightly across her lips—soft, full, and inviting. Tentacles of desire gripped him so hard he almost groaned aloud. Since the night he'd met her, not a moment had passed that he hadn't wanted her. He prayed his torture would soon end. "Some women would be flattered."

She slapped his hand away. "We both know what kind of women they are. I'm not one of them, Your Highness."

Her sarcasm didn't surprise him, but understanding her motive didn't help his cause. "I'm afraid I handled the situation without finesse. I'm fond of you and I thought I could repay you for saving my life." Fond was too weak a word for how he felt, but he wasn't sure how deep his emotions for her went. He'd guarded his heart against love for too many years to recognize the sensation.

"Something I lived to regret," she muttered.

Under the jacket and blanket, she was coiled as tight as an overwound clock spring. Something about the gleam in her eyes told him to beware. Reaching out, he snagged her wrist and pulled her hand from her pocket. As he'd suspected, the derringer came out with her fingers. "I'll take this, if you don't mind. If I'm going to die tonight, I would prefer to freeze to death." He tucked the gun into the waistband of his denim trousers.

She let out a string of curses that would do a Liverpool longshoreman proud. "I hope your precious . . . *lordship* is the first thing to freeze off."

"Such language for a lady, Mary Margaret."

"Such arrogance for a popinjay, Your Majesty."

A man could take only so much abuse before his own spring snapped. Wex had long since passed his limit. "This from a woman who had planned to marry the likes of Harry Seymour?"

She curled her fingers into fists and shook them at him. "At least I wasn't selling myself to the highest bidder. I chose him and I rejected him. Both were *my* choices."

"Do you think I'm selling myself by marrying Grace Ferguson?" Once spoken, the truth of the words tightened like shackles on his heart. The trap had been sprung the moment Appleton had revealed his father's plans.

Turning away from him, she tossed another stick on the fire. The wood snapped, and sparks flew upward. Tension hung like a heavy curtain between them. "What I think doesn't matter. It's your life. You and this woman probably deserve each other." Her voice dropped to a husky whisper. "I'm sure you'll find someone else to be your mistress. I wouldn't want a man like you, anyway."

He remained silent for a long moment, fighting a battle

within himself. "What kind of man do you want, Mary Margaret?"

Maggie turned and locked gazes with him. He'd challenged her, and she wasn't sure she was up to the confrontation. Her heart cried out that she wanted him, only him. But it could never be unless he was willing to stand up and be counted as his own man. Anything less wasn't worth having.

"What do I want in a man?" Pure deviltry sprang up along with the desire to reject him as he'd rejected her. "A strong red-blooded American man. A Westerner. A man who knows what he wants and isn't afraid to go after it."

"A man like Ross Elliott? Or his son, who'll rape a girl to get what he wants." The fury in his tone chilled worse than the fury outside the cabin.

Maggie shivered at the memory of Sarah's ordeal. "Of course not."

"Then what, Mary Margaret? Be sure of what you ask for, you may get it."

Spurred on by his taunting words, she tilted her chin a notch higher. "A man of action, one who won't bore me with words and silly games."

A strange gleam sparkled in his eyes, and a wry smile curved his lips. A day's stubble shadowed his jaw. He twisted his hand in her long braid. Before she could protest, he pulled her head toward him. "What—" tore from her lips the second before he captured the word in his mouth.

Caught off guard, Maggie opened her mouth in surprise. With the swiftness of a striking cobra, he slid his tongue between her parted lips. Heat sizzled in her like a branding iron. He gripped her arm and held her tight against him.

Need sliced through Maggie with a force as powerful as any tempest that nature could supply. There was no gentleness in his kiss. His lips crushed hers with power and possession, demanding and accepting nothing less than complete surrender. He tasted of the sweet raspberry jam he'd spread on the bread. She drank of him with the voracity of a woman dying of thirst.

The kiss went on and on, his tongue dominating hers with thrust after thrust into the recesses of her mouth. In spite of the frigid air in the cabin, fire raged through her. Although their mouths were the only contact of flesh upon flesh, Maggie felt as if he'd seared every inch of her body. Her stomach muscles tightened, and her breasts swelled. Under her heavy clothes her nipples tightened into hard, tight buds.

From some niche of her mind, a voice warned her to protest, to stop before it was too late. But the feeling was too good to let it end.

Just as she was melting he jerked his mouth from hers. Tugging gently at her braid, he pulled her head inches from his. "I warned you, Maggie. Be careful what you ask for, you may get it."

With an abruptness that startled her, he released his hold. She sagged forward at the loss of support. In one quick movement he stretched to his feet and shrugged off the blanket.

Maggie's mouth hung open. The unexpected loss of his warmth left her weak. "What are you doing?" Coherent thought escaped her.

"I'm going to check on the animals." He slipped on his jacket and moved into the shadows beyond the light of the fire.

Too stunned to move, she listened to the roar of the wind as he opened the door and disappeared into the storm.

For a long moment Maggie stared at the broken door where the snow blew onto the floor. Jumbled thoughts left her frozen in place. Her insides were trembling, and she knew her cheeks must be crimson. How could he work her up into a frenzy by his kiss, then walk out and leave her deprived of her very breath?

She picked up a piece of wood intended for the fire and flung it toward the door. "Damn you, Wex," she shouted, although nobody could hear. Her voice lowered to a whisper. "Damn you for making me love you and not loving me back."

The frigid wind stung his lungs as Wex gulped mouthfuls of the life-giving air. He'd known the moment Maggie had let down her barriers, the moment she was his. His to take, his to love, his to do with as he pleased.

And that alone had frightened him. What an ironic twist this was, he thought. The man who'd wooed and won duchesses, countesses, and a princess or two was reluctant to make love to a common American woman.

No, he told himself as he ran his bare fingers over the frosty whiskers and along the scar on his cheek. Mary Margaret Callahan was far from common. She was the most special creature he'd ever encountered. A woman full of fire and spirit, Maggie deserved more than what a scoundrel had to offer. She deserved love, devotion, and complete fidelity. Things he knew he couldn't share with any woman.

With love came responsibility and trust. And as his father had reminded him so many times after Arthur's death, he wasn't worthy of any of it.

The wind propelled him toward the small stall that sheltered the horses. Their snorts carried over the storm's mournful song. Other than scratch up more hay, there was little he could do for them. He brushed his hand across the stallion's velvet nose. Sheltered as they were from the full brunt of the wind, he was certain the horses could wait out the storm without harm.

He studied the sky for a moment. The snowfall seemed to be lessening, and the force of the wind not as strong as earlier. The liveryman had warned him of the fierceness of the early mountain storms, but he said that their fury often abated as swiftly as it came. By morning the storm should be over.

Satisfied the horses were all right, he bent his head against the wind and returned to the cabin. All this self-reproach had his thoughts in a jumble and his feet about to freeze off. But it had done little to cool the fire that burned in his gut or ease the pain in his groin.

His steady seduction of Maggie had backfired and ensnared him in the silvery web of passion. Like a fly mesmerized by the beautiful spider, he had nowhere to go but into her trap. With trembling hands, he shoved open the rickety door and stepped in.

He bolted the door and stood for a moment to bolster his courage. Maggie was lying on the floor before the fireplace, cocooned in a blanket. She didn't move, but he felt her gaze on him.

"Wex?"

"Yes, Maggie, it's me."

"Good. I'd hate to shoot a stranger."

A slow smile snaked across his face. The cold hadn't extinguished a bit of her fire. "With what? I have the derringer."

"But I have my rifle."

The dim light from the fire glinted on the rifle's barrel. "Do you mind if I come to the fire? I'm about to freeze my . . . *lordship* off."

The twitter of gentle laughter welcomed him to the spider's parlor. "No great tragedy, I'm sure." She stroked her fingers slowly on the long barrel of the rifle.

He swallowed hard to quell the tremor that shot through him. "That, dear lady, is a matter of opinion." Striving to appear unconcerned, he took the rifle from her fingers. He set the weapon aside, along with his cartridge belt and the derringer. "We'd better get some sleep. Never know how long the storm will last. Sometimes these things go on for days and days."

"Whew. If it gets any colder, I'll freeze my . . . nose off."

Picking up one of the quilts beside the fireplace, he shook it out and spread it on the cold floor. Then he stripped off his jacket and tossed it atop the quilt.

His wet denims clung to his legs, chilling him to the bone. His gaze fixed on Maggie, he unbuttoned his fly, welcoming the relief from the pressure. In the firelight he noted Maggie's wide eyes reflecting the flames like an emerald mirror.

"What are you doing?"

"I told you how we'll keep warm tonight." Without giving her a chance to protest, he threw off her blanket and reached for the buttons on her coat. "We'll make a mattress of our coats and wrap ourselves in the blankets."

She shoved his fingers away. "You're mad. We'll freeze without our clothes."

He dropped his voice to a husky growl. "Maggie, I promise you'll stay warm. In fact, by morning you'll forget all about the cold."

Indecision danced across her face. "All right. But that's all I'll take off."

Satisfied to have his way, he added her coat to his and

stretched out on the floor. By the time she lay down, he'd removed his trousers.

The knowledge that he was playing with fire didn't deter him. He'd made his decision, and it was too late to stop. He was ready when she slid next to him.

A small gasp of surprise came from her lips when he covered her legs with his. Face-to-face, chest to chest, legs entwined, the blankets wrapped about them like a warm cocoon, there was no way he could hide his arousal.

His fingers twisted in her braid, freeing her silky hair. "What are you doing now?" Her words came out like the mewing of a kitten.

"Giving you what you asked for. Wex is making love to Maggie."

Chapter Eighteen

The husky timbre of Wex's voice rekindled the fire in Maggie as quickly as a match to dry brush. Wex rarely called her Maggie, and an undercurrent of danger whispered in the air.

Maggie pressed her hands to his chest. His heart thundered against her fingertips. "I didn't give you permission to touch me." The feeble attempt to take control only brought a deep chuckle from his throat.

He twined his fingers in her hair, while his other hand settled low on her backside. "Maggie, *macushla*, I'm giving what you asked for."

Distracted by the use of the Irish endearment, she allowed him to pull her closer into his embrace. "How do you know Gaelic?"

His fingers grazed along her nape. "I could make love to you in a dozen languages, but you wanted a Westerner, a man of few words and a great deal of action."

Pleasure rippled across her shoulders. She remembered his warning about being sure of what she asked for. He was giving her what she wanted. And Maggie was more than willing to take. Still, she couldn't resist a parting jab. "With that crisp British accent, no one would mistake you for an American." Or with his courtly manners, she added to herself.

"Then I'll not say another word." Tightening his grip, he snuggled her closer.

"I'm not making love with you," she said, knowing full well that it was too late to stop.

A gentle growl rumbled from his chest as his mouth claimed hers. He shifted his legs so his arousal settled against her stomach. The thick barrier of her canvas breeches and his underdrawers provided no protection from the sensations that took her breath away.

His lips moved gently, coaxing a response. He'd already claimed her heart and soul; all that remained was her body. A body rapidly betraying her with its own needs.

With a final token of resistance, she clamped her teeth closed and pressed her fingers against his chest. But the warm flesh under her hands invited further exploration. Instead of pushing him away, she clung like a drowning sailor to a lifeline.

At her back, his hand tugged her shirt from the trousers. One touch of his fingers to her bare bottom broke her last thread of defiance. Fighting her needs was as useless as putting out a raging inferno with a single teaspoon of water.

His tongue stroked the seam of her lips, seeking entrance. Wanting, needing the intimate contact, she opened her mouth and welcomed him. A low groan came from somewhere deep inside her. With slow thrusts, his tongue imitated what she knew was soon to follow with their bodies.

Fire settled deep in her stomach. She fitted her body against his, hating the barrier of her clothes. Her fingers grazed across his shoulders and found the deep scar from his wound.

A wreath of love tightened around her heart. Since the moment she'd gotten his blood on her fingers, there had been a bond between them. Making love was the consummation of that bond, the binding of their bodies, if not their lives.

The kiss ended, and Maggie felt lost without the fusing of their bodies. She moaned, unable to voice her needs. He released her hair, his hand moving between them to the buttons of her shirt while his lips traced a line from the corner of her mouth to the hollow under her ear.

Her breath caught in her throat as she waited. Once loose, the shirt parted under his seeking fingers. Restless, she shrugged to become free of the restricting garment. Wex tossed the shirt aside. In short order, her tight trousers followed.

Clad only in her chemise and pantalets, Maggie pressed against his strong, warm body. Her fingers trailed across his shoulders, tangled in the furry mat on his chest, and down to the washboard hardness of his stomach. Where she was soft, he was hard. Where she touched, he answered in kind. Instinct goaded her to search the varied textures of his body.

He dipped lower, and heat followed the trail of his tongue to the swell of her breasts. With slow precision, he kissed and nipped at the full mounds that spilled over her chemise. Maggie arched toward him, wanting more, but not sure she could bear the exquisite torture.

"Please," she whispered, twisting her fingers in his dark hair to draw him closer.

In response he closed his mouth over the sensitive tip of one breast. He suckled gently, his teeth and tongue teasing the nipple until it strained against the damp cotton garment. Nothing in her past had prepared Maggie for the sensation that vibrated along her ribs, past her stomach, and settled in the nest between her thighs. Like a butterfly unable to choose between two luscious flowers, he fluttered from one taut nipple to the other, until Maggie thought she would melt.

Lovemaking couldn't get any better, she thought. But her female intuition told her it could. It would.

Wex didn't know how much longer he could hold his passion in check. This beautiful woman had opened herself to him, made herself vulnerable to his touch, and given freely. Never had he wanted a woman more than he wanted Maggie. *His* Mary Margaret.

He'd purposely gone slowly, readying her for their completion. Her hand slipped between them, touching his stomach where his arousal waited for sweet release. At the first touch of her fingers, she jerked back, and he felt as if he'd been seared with a hot iron.

Taking her wrist in a gentle grip, he pressed her hand to him. "Touch me, Maggie. I won't hurt you."

The room was dark, with only the palest glow from the fire, but he saw no fear or apprehension in her eyes. Her hair gleamed like a halo around her head. Without hesitation, she used first one finger, then another, until her entire hand was pressed against him. Intense pleasure surged through him.

He covered her lips and worshiped her with his kiss. Her tongue met his, boldly seeking entrance to his mouth. One of his greatest assets as a lover had been his control. He took pride in always bringing the woman to a climax before he had his own. Now, with the woman who meant more to him than any other, he was on the verge of losing that control. Maggie's love offering drove him to the brink.

Within seconds, he removed their remaining garments, and the full glory of her flesh pressed against his. Not breaking the kiss, he dropped his hand to the apex of her thighs. She gasped at the intimate contact and pressed herself against his palm.

"Now," she whispered against his lips. "Don't make me wait."

He needed no further invitation. She was warm and damp; he was hot and heavy. With the utmost care, he parted her knees and settled gently between them. At the first brush of his shaft against her, she stiffened.

Sensing her wavering, he rested on his elbows and allowed her to become accustomed to his weight and the feel of him. He kissed her gently, sipping at the sweetness of her mouth. Her hands cupped his buttocks, and her fingers drew him closer.

She shifted her hips and offered herself. Taking a deep steadying breath, he eased into her. A barrier stopped him. Emotion swelled in his chest. Humility surged through him at the reminder that he was her first lover.

Containing his needs, he waited until she adjusted to him, then with a single bold thrust, he accepted the gift she offered. A deep moan came from her throat. He stopped and captured the sound with his mouth.

The momentary twinge of pain startled Maggie. Although she'd read what little she could find on love and sex, she'd been ill prepared for the overpowering wonder of the actual act.

She relaxed, and pleasure flowed over her like a warm

summer rain bringing life to a flower. Under his gentle
touch she blossomed and opened to him. She'd never in her
wildest dreams imagined that joining with a man could be
so splendid. But Maggie knew that it was like this because
of her love for Wex, and would never be the same with
another man.

He moved slowly, and the long thick length of him filled
her. The trembling deep inside started with a gentle stirring
until the ripples spread outward and she convulsed around
him.

As she reached her peak he plunged his tongue deep in
her mouth. She met his tongue and wrapped her legs around
him, wanting to lose herself in him. Her heart pounded as
loud as the blast of wind that rocked the cabin.

He lifted his head and gazed into her eyes. A look of
wonder, of gentleness, swept his dark features. Was it love?
she wondered. Her own passion threatened to swamp her
with its intensity. *I love you, I love you,* she repeated over
and over in her mind.

The tremors went on and on, and he began another series
of thrusts, each one stronger than the last. Maggie moved in
harmony with him, the rush of the wind through the cracks
in the cabin walls a love song in her ears. He moved faster
and faster until Maggie was unable to hold back her cry of
pleasure.

Driven wild by Maggie's whimpers of gratification, Wex
could no longer contain himself. With a loud grunt, he
shoved to the hilt, and powerful shivers racked his body.
The completion was stronger than anything he'd experienced in his long sordid life. Perspiration broke on his back.
Ecstasy washed over him. He didn't want to move or break
the spell that had been woven around them.

"Maggie, Maggie." He whispered her name with the
reverence of a prayer. Long lashes shaded her green eyes.
"Are you all right? Did I hurt you?"

She brushed a damp strand of hair from his forehead, her
touch like the brush of a butterfly's wing. "It was wonderful."

He looked into her face, flushed and beautiful as an
angel's. At that moment he felt like a man dying of thirst in
a desert who'd stumbled into an oasis flowing with cool

clear water. An awareness of awe stole over him. As unworthy as he was, she'd given willingly and completely.

Dipping his head, he planted a light kiss on her mouth, now swollen from his kisses. Reluctant to leave her, he shifted to his side, his still-hard shaft nestled in her warmth. "Maggie, love, my sweet virgin. So good, so giving."

A worried look crossed her face. "Did it matter that I was a virgin?"

Pulling the quilt around them, he stroked a lock of coppery hair from her cheek. "I'm honored that you trusted me with your love."

Her fingers wandered to his hip, stroking lightly from his waist to his thigh. "I wanted you."

The simple statement fired the blood in his veins. Her nipples pressed into his chest, and her touch had him getting hard again. He began to move his hips in slow gentle strokes. This time it would be better, if such a thing were possible.

Maggie awoke slowly the next morning. She snuggled closer into the warmth next to her. After making love, she'd settled into Wex's arms and fallen into a short but peaceful sleep.

She was reluctant to open her eyes, to see the idyllic time come to an end. Sometime during the night the wind had dropped to a steady, mournful roar. If the storm had played itself out, she would be forced to return to Denver and watch the man she loved leave her forever. The thought brought a tinge of sadness to her heart.

Venturing a quick glance around her, she noted the thin gray light seeping through the cracks in the wall. The fire had died to a pitiful glow. Cold bit at her face, and she turned back into the cocoon of the blankets.

Wex touched her face, warming her with his big hand. "Wasn't I right about the way to survive the storm?" he asked against her hair.

Her long tangled strands clung to the day's stubble at his jaw. She traced a finger around one hard male nipple. He trembled slightly under her touch. The question that had bothered her all night slipped to her lips. "Wex, who was she?"

"She?" he asked in a voice lacking guile. "Who, Maggie? I don't deny I've known many women. But all memory of them was lost last night."

His beautiful words did little to allay her curiosity. "The woman in Russia. The one who taught you how to keep warm during the long cold nights."

He threaded his hand in her hair, skimming her face with his thumb. "He was a big, ugly Cossack with hair on his back and all over his face."

Maggie gasped, and her eyes widened.

With soft laughter, he continued. "I stretched the truth a bit. We slept with our clothes on."

Her own laughter joined his. How foolish of her to be jealous of his past. It was his future that never left her thoughts. Shoving her anxiety aside, she asked, "How are we going to get dressed without freezing to death?"

He kissed her gently on the lips. "Since I'm too exhausted for anything else, I'll get up first and build up the fire. Then you can get dressed in the warmth."

A soft moan issued from deep in her throat. "I wish we could stay here all day."

"So do I, but your family will be worried about you, and I have business to attend."

"Of course, you have to make arrangements to return to England." The instant the words escaped her lips, she wished she could call them back. But it was too late.

He pulled back and met her gaze. Tiny silver flecks danced in his blue eyes. "Have you reconsidered my offer?"

Maggie's heart constricted. She lowered her lashes and looked at the red scar on his shoulder. "I've thought of little else, but I haven't changed my mind." After the night of love, he deserved complete honesty, although he'd shared little of the truth since she'd known him. "I wouldn't be happy living in the shadows of your life. It wouldn't be good for me, or Sarah and Tim."

"I was being selfish." He cupped her chin so their eyes again met. "It's a bad habit of mine."

Emotion glittered behind his dark lashes. If he would admit he loved her, Maggie doubted she could refuse him. But to give her heart without receiving his in return would cause more pain than simply letting go.

"We all have our crosses to bear."

After one brief kiss, he tossed off the blanket and jumped to his feet. Maggie snuggled in the still-warm covers, but without his body heat, the cold seeped through her.

With a few quick movements, he slipped into his pants and shirt and huddled in his jacket. Pulling on his thick wool socks, he shoved his feet into the Wellington boots. In seconds he had the fire built to a roaring blaze.

Wex turned and looked at her. "I'll go check on the horses and the weather. Wait a few more minutes before you try to get up."

Maggie nodded. A cold band tightened around her heart. He strode to the door and out into the cold as casually as if they hadn't spent the night making love. What meant so much to Maggie clearly meant little to him. Hadn't he admitted she was only one in a long line of lovers? Determined to act as unconcerned as he, she set her resolve and reached for her clothes.

By the time he reappeared in the doorway, she'd regained her composure and was huddled in front of the fire. "We have some bread left over and some jelly. Sorry I didn't bring a pot for some tea."

He closed the space in a few long strides. "Thank you, Mary Margaret. This will do quite nicely."

The sound of her full name brought a twinge of despair. Wex had disappeared, and Lord Geoffrey had taken his place. "How are the horses?" she asked in an effort to distance herself from the pain in her heart.

"They survived quite well." He removed his gloves and took the two slices of bread from her hand. "The storm passed over, and the sun is breaking through the clouds."

"When can we leave?"

"As soon as I hitch up the wagon."

Maggie put a smile she didn't feel into her words. "Good. Then we should get started right away. Aunt Olivia will send out another search party if I don't get back home."

"Maggie." He reached out and touched her cheek. "About last night, it . . ." His bushy brows knit together under the brim of his wide Stetson.

With a cavalier shake of her shoulders, she moved away. She couldn't bear to hear him apologize or make excuses for their lovemaking. "Think nothing of it. At least we were able to keep warm during the storm." Turning away to avoid his hard stare, she began to fold the blankets. "Now that it's over, we can go back to where we belong." *You to Grace Ferguson, and me to . . . nobody.* She bit her lip to keep her despair contained in her heart.

His gaze remained locked on her for a long moment. When the blankets were piled in a low stack, she chanced a glance at him. Bathed in shadows by the hat, his face was unreadable.

"Hell," he grunted. He picked up his gun belt and hooked it to his waist. While she watched, he removed the Colt, swung open the cylinder, and checked the cartridges. Her breath caught in her throat. Something was wrong; she saw it in the way he coddled the gun in his palm before easing the weapon back into the holster.

Stretching out his hand, he offered the derringer. "Take this, Maggie. Never know when you'll need it."

She covered her shock with a wry smile. "You never know." Grateful to have the firearm back, she shoved it into her jacket pocket. "Thanks."

"While I hitch the horses try to put out the fire. We wouldn't want to burn down this magnificent mansion."

His strained attempt at humor eased the tension building between them. She swept the room with her gaze. The cabin was filthy, full of cobwebs, and she was certain rats inhabited the spaces under the floor. But she would always remember the ramshackle cabin and the love she'd found during a long, stormy night. "Another poor soul may need to find shelter here."

"Ha. A hard gust of wind will topple this place over the hillside and any inhabitants with it." He disappeared through the door into the cold, gray dawn.

Snow and ice crunched under her boots as Maggie made her way to the wagon. She climbed onto the seat with the rifle at her side. Wex tied his horse to the rear of the wagon and climbed in beside her. Few words had passed between them while they prepared for the return to Denver. Gloom as depressing as yesterday's cold, drab sky settled over Maggie.

Wex took the reins and turned the wagon down the

mountain. In the pale morning light the newly fallen snow
weighed heavily on the pine boughs; the tops of the trees
pierced the sky like the silver spires of a cathedral. Maggie
slouched down in the heavy coat as protection against the
chill wind, too depressed to appreciate the winter wonder-
land.

The farther down the mountain they went, the less snow
they saw and the warmer the air felt. Maggie loosened her
coat and tried to temper the pain that was growing in her
chest. During the long ride, she'd examined the future.

She had two choices. A bleak life without Wex or a
shadowy one with him. If she were alone, she had little
doubt which she would choose, but she'd promised Papa to
look after Sarah and Tim. With a mental shake, she knew
she'd made the right decision. Wex could leave, but she was
staying in America where she belonged.

The road widened, and the forest grew thicker. When they
reached the crossroads that led toward Denver, Wex pulled
on the reins and stopped the horses. He tied off the brake
and turned toward Maggie.

"Maggie," he said, his gaze on her face, "keep your rifle
handy and follow this road." Gesturing with his hand, he
pointed to the east. "You'll reach Denver by this afternoon."

Shocked, she studied the cold expression on his face.
"What are you talking about? Aren't you coming home with
me?"

"No. I have some business to take care of. Tell Appleton
I'll be back in a few days."

Fear wrapped its ugly fingers around her heart. "What
kind of business?" The look in his eyes frightened her.
"You're going to Sherman, aren't you?"

He caught her shoulders with his strong hands. "It's
nothing to worry about. I can't go back to England until I
get a few things settled."

"Don't go. Hillcroft will be all right. Wire him some
money if you have to. Elliott will be waiting for you." The
words twisted around her heart. "You could get yourself
killed."

A strange smile curved his mouth. "Maggie, you should
know I live a charmed life. Nothing will happen." He tilted
his head toward hers.

Unable to help herself, Maggie flung her arms around his neck and covered his mouth with hers. The kiss was long and deep, filled with all the love and passion in her heart.

"Please," she whispered against his lips.

He set her away from him and smiled. "Hold that thought until I get back. I'll meet you in Denver in a few days."

In one quick motion, he leaped over the side and landed on his feet with the agility of a cat. Without looking back, he sauntered to the rear of the wagon and untied the horse. Maggie's gaze followed him as he mounted the stallion. Restless from following the slow-moving wagon, the animal pranced and pawed the ground.

Wex tipped his hat to Maggie, then dug his heels into the horse's side. As she watched he started at a trot before he urged the horse into a gallop. Within seconds he went around a curve and disappeared from her sight.

Maggie picked up the reins and looked from the right to the left. With a shake of her head, she snapped the whip and turned the wagon away from Denver and safety southward toward trouble.

Chapter
Nineteen

Wex settled Midnight at a steady gait and breathed deeply of the fresh clean air. He loved the freedom and power of the stallion under him. Someday he hoped to teach his sons to love and appreciate horses as he did.

If he ever had children. The thought of bedding Miss Grace Ferguson held no appeal. Especially after the feast of passion he'd shared with Maggie last night. Thinking about her brought a twinge somewhere in his chest.

He'd hated leaving her to make her way alone, but he knew if he returned to Denver, too many forces would keep him from completing the task.

For days he'd thought about this mission. Although he wasn't sure how he would handle the problem between Hillcroft and Elliott, he had to try. He couldn't return to England and leave unfinished business behind. At his current pace, he should reach Sherman by nightfall.

Lost in his thoughts, he slowed the horse to a trot. The newly fallen snow crunched under Midnight's hooves. There was no use hurrying; he would meet trouble soon enough.

With the passing of the storm, the air was crisp and cool and smelled of pine. As the morning wore on, the sun burned away the fog, and the sky turned a brilliant blue.

White-tipped aspens and pine guarded the narrow road through the mountain pass.

After several hours Wex stopped beside a swiftly moving stream to let Midnight drink from the clear water. They both needed a break. The storm had passed farther north, and the ground was clear. He sank to a bed of pine needles and rested against the trunk of a slender pine. The boisterous sound of the water tumbling over the rocks kept him company.

During the past months he'd learned to love the rugged land. Above him the jagged mountains zigzagged against the azure sky. The snow-tipped peaks glittered in the sunshine like a ring of ermine above the dark green tree line. Huge boulders thrust from the forests as if strewn by a huge hand in a fit of anger.

He would miss Colorado. Most of all, he would miss Maggie. Damn, why did the woman have to be so stubborn? After their passionate lovemaking, he'd assumed she would be willing to accept his terms and accompany him to England. Now, thinking about the situation without his mind being clouded by emotion, he should have known her answer before he asked.

Fiercely independent, Maggie had her own mind and her own calling. For a reason he couldn't quite understand, she wanted to make her name as a photographer and she steadfastly refused to accept his help in achieving her goal. A strong woman like Mary Margaret Callahan deserved to stand at a man's side as his equal, not live in the shadows as his mistress.

Maggie hadn't been taunting him about the kind of man she wanted. Only a truly stalwart man would be able to stand up to her. And a "lily-livered Brit" would never fit the bill.

He took out his watch and flipped open the lid. The tiny portrait of his brother renewed his determination to avenge the wrongs done to Maggie and Sarah. Perhaps then he could redeem himself for his part in his brother's death.

With a start, he realized that time was slipping by. Quickly he stood, grabbed the horse's reins, and swung into the saddle. Striving to center his thoughts on the problems facing him in Sherman, Wex returned to the road.

He'd ridden about a mile when the hairs on the back of his neck began to prickle. Somebody was following him. The clatter of wagon wheels carried a long distance in the quiet mountains. Since he'd only passed one slow-moving farm wagon that morning, he became immediately alert to danger. Although this was the most direct route to Sherman, the old stage road was seldom used since the coming of the railroad.

Unwilling to take any unnecessary risks, he urged the horse to the grove of pines to allow the wagon to pass. Hidden behind a huge boulder, he had a clear view of the road. After several short minutes the horses came into view, then the wagon.

He cursed aloud when he spotted the unmistakable black vehicle with CALLAHAN'S PHOTOGRAPHIC VIEWS in huge white letters emblazoned on the side. And there was no mistaking the woman at the reins—Maggie.

The bullheaded woman had followed him.

With an angry grunt he goaded the horse to a gallop and within seconds he was alongside the wagon. "Stop this damn thing," he shouted.

Her eyes widened, and she immediately pulled on the reins. The horses slowed, and the wagon came to a halt. She looked at him and smiled. "Never know who you're going to meet on the road, do you?"

He leaned forward in the saddle and propped his arm on the horn. Biting the inside of his mouth to control his temper, he said, "What the hell do you think you're doing?"

She shrugged, her shoulders barely moving in the heavy coat. "What does it look like? I'm driving my wagon."

Her attempt at innocence riled him further. He narrowed his eyes and leaned closer. "I told you to go back to Denver. You're on the wrong road."

She tugged off her old felt hat and glared at him. The wind whipped the loose tendrils of russet hair about her face. "Who are you to give me orders? If you can go to Sherman, so can I."

Fury threatened to choke him. He clutched the reins to keep from wringing her pretty neck. "Maggie, this is my battle. Go back where you'll be safe."

She tilted her chin. "It's my battle, too. Sarah is my sister, and it was my wagon they vandalized."

"You could get hurt."

"So could you."

"I'm a man."

"I'm a woman." She folded her arms across her chest and set her jaw. "Now that we have our genders settled, let's go. I want to get a bath and some clean clothes tonight."

The urge to strangle her grew stronger with every outrageous word. "You'll get both when you reach Denver. Your family is waiting for you."

"I'll send a telegram at the next town."

"Mary Margaret Callahan, turn this damn wagon around and go back where you belong."

"Where I belong?" She came to her feet, her eyes blazing with green fire. "Who are you to tell me what to do? This isn't England." She poked a finger into his chest. "You aren't a feudal lord, and I'm not your chattel."

"Did anybody ever tell you that you're the most stubborn, obstinate, bullheaded, willful woman God ever saw fit to put on this earth?" By now his voice had risen to a shout, and his horse began to paw the ground.

"Yes, you. And before you run out of words, add tenacious and persistent. You won't get rid of me so easily, Lord Geoffrey." She folded her arms across her chest. "This is a free country, and I can go wherever I please."

He squeezed his eyes shut to gain some semblance of composure. When he opened them, she was glaring at him with murder in her gaze. "Go home," he repeated between his teeth.

Defiance shot at him like daggers. "No."

As he reached out she flicked the reins and shouted. The team took off on a run. The shock almost unseated him from the horse. He choked on the dust billowing from the wagon. He was definitely going to strangle the woman the instant he got his hands on her beautiful neck.

Maggie knew the awkward wagon and two horses couldn't outdistance the Thoroughbred stallion. But she sure as hell could give him a run for his money. She fell back in the seat and urged the horses faster.

The wind tore at her bare head, pulling the hair loose from the braid. Her cheeks burned with fury in spite of the chill autumn air. Whatever gave the insufferable, demanding Englishman the idea that he could order her around like some kind of lackey? Someday he would have to learn that Maggie Callahan had a mind of her own.

Why couldn't he admit he needed her—that it wasn't a sign of weakness to accept a woman's help? Hadn't she saved his life once? Only a complete fool would try to face Elliott and his henchmen alone. Some men didn't use the brains God gave a jaybird.

From the corner of her eye she saw him gaining on her. She didn't dare urge the horses faster on the rutted road and take a chance on upsetting the wagon. To her surprise, when he pulled up beside her, he kept going.

She laughed. Let him go. She would just catch up with him in Sherman.

The laughter died on her lips when he drew beside the team and slowed. For several moments Midnight raced neck and neck with the team. Then she watched in horror as Wex leaned far to the side, his arms outstretched. In a split second he flew from the saddle.

For a long moment time stood still as he hung suspended in the air like an acrobat in the circus.

Fear threatened to choke her. One slip, one miscalculation, and he would be trampled by the team or crushed under the wagon's wheels. A cry tore from the pain in her chest.

Somehow he managed to land squarely on the back of the horse nearest him pulling the wagon. She had never seen, nor had she ever expected, such acrobatics. He yanked the reins and pulled hard. The slack in her hands was useless as he took control of the team.

Gradually the wagon slowed with Midnight keeping in perfect step. Admiration for Wex's superb horsemanship was lost in her fury at him for risking his life. The instant the wagon came to a complete halt, she pulled the pole brake and jumped to the ground.

A thousand curses bubbled into her throat, words that would scald the ears of a trail-hardened bullwhacker. The arrogant foolhardy man had scared ten years off her life.

Wex slid off the horse and waited with his hands propped

on his hips. Murder flashed in his eyes. Not allowing him to intimidate her, she met him toe to toe, face-to-face. He gripped her arms and glared at her through narrowed eyes.

A wide-eyed doe followed by a buff-colored fawn strolled out of the trees and stared at the man and woman who'd invaded their domain. Then, as if realizing they were about to be caught in a cyclone of angry words, they darted across the road into the safety of their forest.

Wex yelled first. "Woman, are you crazy?"

"Man, have you completely lost your senses?" Maggie returned with equal fervor. "You could have been killed pulling a stupid stunt like that."

"I know what I'm doing, which is more than I can say for you." He shook her until her teeth rattled.

His caveman antics didn't impress Maggie. She shoved hard against his chest, but he didn't budge. "I'm trying to help, you pompous moron, though I don't know why I should bother with a crazy Brit who doesn't give a fig about his own life."

A muscle twitched in his jaw. "Don't you understand this is something I have to do, and you could get hurt if you follow me?"

Tilting her chin an inch higher, she met his gaze squarely. "Is this some sort of code of honor? You think you have to defend your name?"

For a long moment he stared into her face. "Yes. A Wexford has never backed down from a fight, and I would be less than a man if I didn't set things in order with Elliott."

"Is your honor worth dying for?" She choked the words around the lump in her throat. To her dismay, a tear slipped from her eyes. She clutched the soft buckskin jacket in her fingers as if she could stop him by sheer force of will.

He pulled her into his chest, and she rested her head against his wide shoulder. His hands moved to her back, stroking gently. "I'm not going to die," he said in a husky voice. "I don't suppose I can convince you to go back to Denver."

She sighed and breathed in the smell of leather and pine. "Not without you." Lifting her head, she met his gaze.

A new emotion glittered in his eyes. "Mary Margaret, what am I going to do with a stubborn woman like you?"

Love me, she wanted to say. Love me as I love you. But this wasn't the time or place to confess her deepest feelings. "Take me with you."

"Do I have a choice?"

"No."

He snuggled his lips in her hair. His breath was warm on her ear. "You'll have to promise to stay out of trouble and let me handle Elliott."

Grateful something was finally going her way, she reached up and pulled his head down to hers. She planted a quick kiss on his startled lips. "Then let's be on our way."

"Not so fast, Miss Callahan." His hands low on her hips, he tugged her intimately against him.

The bulge pressing into her stomach came as a surprise. Her eyes widened. He might not love her, but he couldn't deny he wanted her. "Oh?" A smile eased across her mouth.

"I want your promise, or I'll tie you up and hire a teamster to take you back to Denver."

In spite of her heavy coat, his touch sent a wave of yearning through her. "Yes, Your Majesty," she said, without the usual mockery in her voice. "I'll do whatever you say."

He looked at her as if he didn't quite believe her. And with good cause. Maggie had no intention of letting him face danger alone. A rifle made women and men equal. And she had learned to handle firearms from the best teacher.

On a long sigh, he shook his head and covered her mouth with his. The kiss was long and hard, filled with the promise of more to come. His tongue slipped past her teeth, and she welcomed the intimacy. When the kiss ended, he cradled her in his arms for a long moment before he released her.

A dusty road was no place to make love, but the hotel in Sherman had wonderful, soft feather beds.

The tinkling of a player piano and loud male laughter greeted them as they rode down Sherman's main street. Lights slanted from the windows of the various saloons competing for the cowboys' hard-earned wages. Dusk had descended early, and Wex felt relieved that they had reached the town before the road became too dark for safe travel.

They'd stopped at a small way station and sent the

telegram to Olivia and Appleton informing them of his and Maggie's whereabouts.

With a weary sigh, he pulled the team to a halt in front of the general store. Maggie placed her hands on her back and stretched. "I don't think I can spend another minute on this seat," she said.

He flashed her a wry grin. "It was your choice, remember?"

She set her jaw. "I'm not complaining, but clean clothes and a bath will make a new woman out of me."

Reaching into his jacket pocket, he pulled out a small bag of gold coins. "I'll leave you to purchase some apparel while I stable the horses. We can meet back at the hotel."

For once she didn't argue. "Fair enough." She jumped to the muddy street and stepped onto the boardwalk. "Wex, be sure you bring my camera in. I don't want another 'accident.'"

"Certainly." He glanced into the window of the store and the red gingham dress on display. "And Maggie, get a dress. I'm sick of those trousers."

She opened her mouth to protest, but he'd already flicked the reins and was on his way to the livery.

Wex felt fortunate that the trip had passed without incident. They had encountered a few travelers, mostly ranchers on their way to Denver. A chill raced up his spine. If things went as well here, they could be on their way to Denver in a few short days.

Thirty minutes later, Maggie's camera slung across his shoulder and her rifle in his hand, he stepped into the lobby of the Sherman Inn. Nothing had changed in the past month. The same faded furniture filled the lobby, and behind the long mahogany desk Mr. Klein waited with a look of apprehension on his face.

"'Evening, Mr. Wexford."

Wex nodded in greeting and looked around for Maggie. She should have returned by now. An uneasy feeling gnawed at his stomach.

"If you're looking for your wife, she's already in your room." The man took a key from a hook on the wall and shoved it across the counter at him.

His wife? Wex stared at the register and spotted the last line. "Mr. and Mrs. Geoffrey Andrew Wexford."

A smile inched across his face. He'd fully expected Maggie to insist on separate rooms, not that he would allow it. The thought of spending another night with her, this time on a real bed, made him hot and hard in anticipation.

Mr. Klein chuckled softly. "Since you're newlyweds, I gave you our largest room. My son brought up the hot water, and the missus is preparing a special dinner for you."

His thoughts on the night to come, Wex didn't hear the man approach until a heavy hand clamped his shoulder. "Hope you're not here to cause trouble, Wexford."

Wex turned slowly and met Wade Steward's angry gaze. The sheriff's hand dropped to his gun.

"Wouldn't want to run you and the little lady in since you're on your honeymoon and all. 'Course, I can think of a whole lot better places to take a bride than Sherman."

"I'm not here to cause any problems for you, Sheriff." He forced a smile. "I have business to tend to, and . . . you know how it is. I didn't want to leave . . . the little woman."

Sheriff Steward nodded in agreement. "Just make sure your business doesn't concern Ross Elliott. He didn't take too kindly to your last visit."

Wex squeezed his fingers around the room key. "My previous encounter with Elliott wasn't particularly enjoyable for me—or the Callahans, for that matter." About to lose control of his temper, Wex turned and started toward the stairs.

"Wexford!"

At the sheriff's harsh tone, Wex shot a glance over his shoulder. He lifted one bushy eyebrow.

"I'd hate to see that little gal become a widow on her honeymoon." He tipped his hat and sauntered out the door.

Pure fury propelled Wex up the stairs two at a time. He hadn't come looking for trouble, but trouble had already found him. Undoubtedly Elliott had been informed of his and Maggie's presence in town.

His hand shook as he fit the key into the lock. He stepped into the room and slammed the door behind him.

"What took you so long?" came the soft purring female. voice.

All thought of Elliott, Steward, and revenge vanished from his mind.

Seated in a copper bathtub, her hair pinned loosely on top of her head, a waiting sea nymph flashed an alluring smile to snare an unsuspecting voyager into her net. Ivory shoulders gleamed in the lamplight, and water dripped from her rosy cheeks. She was Lorelei, the siren sent to steal away his very soul.

He was ready to relinquish it without a fight.

Chapter
Twenty

Maggie gazed at Wex through lowered lashes. For a man experienced with women, he was staring at her like a boy seeing a naked female for the first time. A charming blush tinged his cheeks.

"Would you mind handing me a towel?" She stretched out her arm toward the stack that Mrs. Klein had sent. "I saved you some hot water." The teasing smile came surprisingly easy. If only her pounding heart wouldn't betray her nervousness. Playing the siren was a new role for Maggie, and life or death depended on her ability to pull off the act.

Wex propped the rifle against the wall and set the camera on the floor. He strolled slowly toward her, the gleam in his eyes anything but innocent. Maggie's toes curled in anticipation, and heat rose in her stomach. Control of her body was becoming increasingly difficult.

"Certainly, *Mrs. Wexford.* Your wish is my command." He picked up the towel and knelt beside the tub, his eyes level with hers.

Heat rushed to Maggie's face. "I hope you didn't mind . . . registering as your wife, I mean. I knew we would . . . well, I had to think of my reputation."

Conscious of the desire in his gaze, she slipped lower into the tub, her knees nearly touching her chin. A tiny row of soap bubbles floated on the water, outlining the swell of her breasts. The nipples tightened into hard buds under Wex's perusal.

"I'm honored you thought so highly of me. Would you like me to wash your back?" His voice dropped to a husky growl.

A sudden attack of shyness assailed Maggie. "No, thank you. I'm clean." She reached out for the towel. "Would you mind turning your back while I get out of the tub?"

He stood and stretched the towel between his hands, open and inviting. "I most certainly would mind. It's a husband's duty to assist his wife in any small way he can." He caught her hand and pulled her to her feet.

Maggie resisted the urge to cover herself with her hands. For the first time in her life she stood before a man completely naked—exposed and vulnerable. She'd known the consequences when she'd ordered the single room. After the wild and wonderful things she'd done the past night, there was no reason to be timid with the man she loved.

His gaze drifted slowly over her. A thousand insecurities tugged at her confidence. What if he found her unattractive? What if he compared her to other women and found her wanting?

"Beautiful," he whispered in a soft reverent voice. His gaze swept over her like a ray of sunshine, covering her with warmth and pleasure. Tingles ran over her skin, pink from the water. Her self-doubts flew away on the wings of her love.

With a touch as gentle as the brush of a butterfly's wing, he wiped the moisture from her forehead, her nose, and her cheeks. Her mouth went dry, and she swiped out her tongue to moisten her lips. By sheer willpower she remained motionless and allowed him the pleasure of serving her. Maggie had never felt so loved or wanted. Or so incredibly sensuous.

They must be a strange sight, she thought. Her, naked, shiny, and wet, standing in a tub—him, fully clothed in a buckskin jacket and wearing his black Stetson and the six-gun.

He moved his attention to her shoulders, patting the flesh with slow precise movements. His mouth followed the

towel and scattered a row of light kisses along her skin. The
stubble on his jaw added a strong degree of sexuality to his
actions. He was hard and all male. She pressed her legs
together to keep the tingling from spreading down her
thighs. The lovemaking she'd anticipated all day had begun.

Her insides quaking, she waited for his next move. The
towel grazed the tops of her breasts, and she was surprised
to see his hands shaking.

Maggie memorized his every move, planning the same
exquisite torture for him. She snatched the hat from his head
and tossed it across the room. Her knees grew weak, and she
dug her fingers into his thick black hair for support. The
fragrance of her lilac soap wafted around them.

"Such soft skin," he said in that crisp accent that never
failed to send quivers up her spine. "I'm very glad I didn't
give in to my carnal needs this afternoon and take you on
the ground in the woods." He nipped lightly on her shoulder.
"This is more than worth waiting for." Bending his head, he
continued his worship of her body with hands and mouth.

His voice, his touch, the belief that he desired her sent her
soaring higher than an eagle caught in the mountain breeze.

So far her plan was working to perfection. None of the
many arguments they'd had that day had diminished one
iota of their desire. Their lovemaking of the previous night
hadn't sated his ardor, or hers.

She planned to keep him in this room and out of trouble
if they had to stay in bed until he was too weak to confront
Elliott or anybody. The idea brought a self-satisfied smile to
her lips.

Lost in a fog of sensuality, she almost didn't hear the
knocking on the door. "Mrs. Wexford," called the voice
from the hallway.

Wex jerked away, and Maggie caught her breath. She bit
her lip to keep from groaning aloud.

"I have the dinner you ordered." Mrs. Klein knocked
again.

"One moment, please," Wex answered, his voice shaky.
He shook his head and dropped the towel across her
outstretched arms. "Don't move. I'll get rid of her."

Maggie draped the towel across her shoulders and
stepped behind the dressing screen. While Wex accepted the

tray from the proprietor's wife she hastily dried herself and slipped into the white batiste gown she'd purchased from the mercantile.

She'd searched through a pile of flannel and muslin nightdresses to find one pretty enough for tonight. She tied the ribbons at the front clear to her neck. A narrow row of lace was the only adornment on the yoke and the edges of the long sleeves.

Closing her eyes, she wished for something better. If this were truly her wedding night, she would have a sheer silk nightdress with a matching wrapper trimmed with French lace and delicate embroidery. And she would be in a suite in a hotel like the Windsor.

On a sigh she stepped from behind the screen, her bare feet silent on the worn rug. When she'd registered as Mr. and Mrs. Wexford, Mr. Klein had offered what he called the finest room in the hotel. Though lacking the luxury of a room in the Windsor Hotel, this bedchamber was larger than the one she and Sarah had shared on their last trip. The big four-poster bed, the dresser, and bureau were finely made and had been imported from Europe. A roaring fire lent an air of warmth and comfort to the room.

Wex stood in the sitting area beside a small settee. He set a large tray on the table and pulled out a chair. The aroma of roasted chicken filled the room. Her stomach rumbled with hunger. But her body ached with a deeper need, one only Wex could satisfy.

Wex turned and stared. In his wildest dreams, he'd never expected this kind of acquiescence from Maggie. She was warm, willing, and judging by the look in her eyes, eager for him. Playing her game had been sweet agony, but he knew he would win in the end.

"I'm torn with indecision, Mary Margaret. Should I eat, take a bath, or . . ." His gaze slid leisurely over her. Her damp hair clung to her cheeks, and her skin glowed in the pale light from the fire.

She stepped closer, her bare toes sticking out from the hem of the simple cotton gown. This woman was clearly unaware of her own sensuality and beauty. The fabric fell in soft folds across her breasts, her nipples hard and dark under the material. At the vee of her legs, the copper nest was

clearly visible. Perspiration beaded on his forehead. He
found himself salivating, not over the food, but over the
anticipated womanly feast moving slowly toward him.

"Since we're both starving, may I suggest you wash your
face and hands so we can eat?" She settled in one of the
straight chairs at the table. "Then you can bathe and . . ."
After a long, meaningful pause, she lifted the cover from the
tray and sniffed in appreciation. "Doesn't this smell delicious?"

He turned away to gain some semblance of composure.
All day he'd planned his seduction, but now that Maggie
had turned the tables on him, he had only to relax and let her
lead him into paradise. He glanced at the bed, the counterpane thrown back. He had no doubts concerning the
outcome of the evening.

While he poured water into the washbowl, he listened to
the gentle sounds behind him. The wood in the fire cracked
and snapped. Maggie was humming an Irish ditty, slightly
out of tune. He let the sound flow over him, more beautiful
to his ears than Adelina Patti's performance as Verdi's Gilda
when he'd seen her at La Scala. This was a Lorelei's song,
drawing him toward heaven or hell. Either way, he was
already lost.

He removed his jacket and cartridge belt and doused his
face and arms with the cold water. By the time he returned
to the table, he'd gained a modicum of control over the fire
in his loins. Maggie was waiting for him with two plates full
of the delicious-smelling food. Yet the most appetizing
morsel at the feast was the woman herself.

She handed him a glass of sparkling wine. "Mr. Klein
assured me this is the best available in his cellar," she said,
her green eyes glittering with promises unspoken.

His fingers brushed hers as he took the offered glass, and
his hard-earned control snapped. Before she could pull
away, he caught her fingers and brought them to his lips.
"Thank you, Mary—" He caught his slip. "Maggie. I'm not
sure which smells better, you or this feast." He stroked his
tongue over the warm flesh of her palm. She quivered
slightly at the touch. To his surprise, he found his own hand
trembling. He felt like a lad on his first rendezvous.

Her already pink cheeks turned crimson. She eased her

fingers from his. "The chicken, of course. Mrs. Klein is an excellent cook."

He sipped slowly from the wine, letting the warmth settle in his stomach. Mr. Klein's best was surprisingly good. As was the meal. Until he dug into the chicken, he hadn't realized how hungry he really was. He spoke little, aware of the tension building between them. He knew where the evening would lead and wasn't willing to rush.

Maggie's eyes darkened to jade in the candlelight. Occasionally she shot a glance at the bed. Things were going much more easily than he'd planned. All he had to do was make love to this beautiful woman until she was too weak to protest when he left her in the morning.

"I hope the water isn't cold," she said as she sipped the last of her wine.

With a glance at the tub, he almost hoped it was. Considering the raging inferno in his body, he would welcome a douse of cold water. He stood and stretched, his muscles stiff from riding on the bouncy wagon. "I must smell like a horse," he said, unbuttoning his shirt.

Standing before him, Maggie shoved his fingers aside and began to loosen the buttons. "Let me help you."

Her touch was like a spark to a powder keg. Exerting all his willpower, he remained stationary while she slowly slid the garment form his shoulders and down his arms. She swiped her fingers over his chest, tugging lightly on the curly, dark mat of hair. His stomach muscles tightened, and if possible, his swollen manhood grew harder.

When she reached for the buckle of his belt, he squeezed his eyes shut and prayed for control. Unable to bear the fierce pleasure, he captured her wrists in his hands. "Please, Maggie. Let me wash."

Understanding glittered in her eyes. She nodded and stepped away. He turned his back and shed his trousers and underdrawers in one quick movement. His arousal was there, full and hard for her to see. Swiftly he slid into the tub, bending his knees to fit into the tight space. The lukewarm water did little to cool his ardor.

"Would you like some hot water?" Maggie asked, standing over him.

He jumped at the sound of her voice. A chunk of ice

would be better, he thought. "This is fine." Lifting his head, he found her gaze locked on him. Damn, he would never get through the bath the way she was looking at him. "Maggie, I could use another glass of that wine, if you please."

With a brief nod, she moved to the table and refilled his glass. When she returned, he'd partially won the battle with his desires. But the war was far from over.

Kneeling beside the tub, she pressed the glass against his lips. "Let me help you."

He swallowed the wine in one gulp and choked when it went down too quickly. Snatching the glass away, she patted him on the back. "I'm all right," he sputtered. Or he would be if only she would move away.

"Would you like me to wash your back?"

Fire surged through him. "You'll get wet."

"Not if you don't thrash about like a fish."

On a long sigh, he gave up the fight and lost the war. He pressed the wet cloth into her hands and smiled over his shoulder. "You will be gentle, won't you, madam?"

Her seductive laughter tightened the web around his heart. "Of course. I'll be especially careful of your . . . lordship."

To the victor go the spoils, he reminded himself as he settled back and accepted defeat like a man.

Maggie couldn't believe her own wantonness. She'd spent the hours riding beside him in the wagon planning the evening, but she'd never expected his complete acquiescence.

Nor did she expect the fire to ignite in her own body the instant she touched his wide back. The muscles twitched slightly when she wiped the cloth across his shoulders. He was the most beautiful man she'd ever seen. Or ever would know. A tear sprang to her eyes at the thought of losing him forever.

She shoved the depressing thoughts aside. She had tonight, now, to love him and be loved by him. To keep him safe, if only for another woman.

When she reached for his chest, he shoved her hands away. "Enough, love. I can't take much more."

Hands trembling, Maggie relinquished her grip on the soft cloth. "Neither can I," she whispered.

She backed away until her legs touched the bed. A tiny shock jolted her. This was no time to flinch or become timid. This might be their last night together, and she vowed to make it memorable for both of them. The gleam in his dark eyes assured her this would be a night she would never forget.

Maggie had lost all track of time and place. The man next to her became the one real thing in her world. Through the night they'd made love then slept, only to awaken and begin the cycle all over again. In a half-dreamy state, she reached out to confirm that this hadn't been an erotic fantasy. Her hand touched the space next to her, the feather mattress warm and . . . empty.

She choked back the disappointment that surged through her. It couldn't have been a dream—the tingle between her legs and her swollen lips felt very real.

With a tiny moan she opened her eyes a slit. The mattress and pillow held the impression of a large body. She widened her eyes and strained to study her surroundings.

Darkness shrouded the room; the fire in the hearth cast only a pale orange glow. Beyond the foot of the bed, she spied a shadow at the window, the curtains pulled aside. She bit her lip to keep from crying out. Wex was preparing to leave.

She sat up and slipped silently from the bed. Pulling the blanket with her, she wrapped it around her shoulders and padded across the room.

Wex was staring into the night at the moon, now low on the horizon with the coming of dawn. Maggie forced back the tears that pooled in the corners of her eyes.

"You should be sleeping, love," he said over his shoulder.

"So should you." Stretching out a hand, she reached for him. The taut muscles of his back quivered at her touch. "You're freezing." She wrapped the blanket around both of them, crossing her arms over his hard, flat stomach.

"I'm fine." He covered her hands, anchoring her in place. "I thought I'd worn you out last night." Lifting her fingers, he placed her palm on his pounding heart. "I must be losing my touch."

Crushing her breasts into his back, she smiled into the

crook of his shoulder. "How is your . . . lordship this morning?"

With a burst of laughter, he spun around and lifted her up in his arms. She yelped in surprise as he fell on top of her in the middle of the bed. "Find out for yourself."

Satisfied to have her way, she laughed softly. "I think he's ready, willing, and . . ." With a boldness that brought a gasp from his lips, she circled him with her fingers. "More than able."

This time the loving was slow, sweet, and so sensuous that Maggie thought she would faint from pleasure. She fell asleep with the thought that he wouldn't leave her, not now, not ever.

Wex gazed down at Maggie snuggled peacefully into the quilt. The angelic smile on her face belied the passion that had been unleashed during the past two nights.

As unworthy as he was, she'd given herself over and over with a fervor that had left him breathless. Untangling himself from her arms proved to be the hardest thing he'd had to do in years.

He strapped the cartridge belt at his waist and stroked the handle of the Colt. The gun weighed heavy, but responsibility weighed even heavier.

She would be angry, and he couldn't blame her. A woman like Maggie wouldn't understand that a man had to stand up and be counted. It was the least he could do before he returned to England.

Slipping his arms into his jacket, he chanced one last glance at the bed. When his eyes locked with Maggie's, he stopped. A chill settled in the center of his chest. Her eyes were wide with fear.

"Wex . . ." She clutched the quilt to her chest. "Where are you going?"

He sat on the edge of the bed and stroked her cheek with one finger. She was warm and soft and smelled of woman and love. He felt like a thousand fools for leaving her. "I have business to tend to."

Fear chased away the softness in her eyes. "Please." She released the covers and caught both his arms in a strong grip. "Don't leave me . . . don't get yourself killed."

The anxiety in her eyes almost changed his purpose. "Love, I have no wish for death. I've thought about the situation, and you're right. It would do no good to confront Elliott." He bent his head and kissed away the single tear at the corner of her eye. "I can't prove anything against him, and I doubt he'll confess."

"Then where are you going?"

"To the Double H. I have to see Hank Hillcroft and find out what he plans for the ranch."

"Before you return to England." The words were flat, without emotion.

A band tightened around his chest at the reminder that he would soon be leaving her forever. "Yes," he said around the lump in his throat. "I want to learn if Hillcroft needs anything, and to give him the name of my solicitor in New York."

"I see." She met his gaze as if to see into his soul.

Her intense stare shot clear to his heart. "I give you my word that if I even see Elliott on the street, I'll cross to the other side."

"Wait until I get dressed, and I'll go with you."

He kissed her lightly on the mouth. "It's cold and windy. Stay here and keep warm for me."

"Wex . . ."

"Go back to sleep. I promise I'll be back in time to have a noonday meal with you." He twisted a finger around one long coppery strand of hair. "I won't object if you ask Mrs. Klein to serve us in this room like last night."

She wrapped her arms around his neck and pulled his head down hard to hers. Her kiss was full of passion and promise. Only a fool would leave a woman like Maggie. "I'll be back, love. Promise."

Before he could change his mind, Wex spun on his heel and left Maggie and part of his heart behind.

Chapter
Twenty-one

Stunned by Wex's abrupt departure, Maggie stared at the solid wooden door, unwilling to believe what had just happened. She chewed at the inside of her mouth to keep from calling out to him.

Defeated, she bowed her head. He wouldn't hear her. He'd never really heard her, never listened to her warnings or understood her fears.

Wanting, needing a last look at him, she slipped into her nightgown and hurried to the window. From the third floor of the hotel, she studied the main street below.

The first gray fingers of dawn stretched across the sky, bathing the town with a pale glow. A lone figure stepped from the boardwalk to the center of the street. The tall man clad in the buckskin jacket would stand out in the midst of a thousand men. And Maggie's heart would recognize him among millions.

Wex tugged his hat low on his forehead and bent against the wind. In a few long-legged strides he stepped over a mud puddle and continued across the street. Then he disappeared down the alley that led to the livery where he'd stabled the horses.

Frozen in place, she continued to stare into the dawn. One by one lights came on in the various businesses along the boardwalk. A farm wagon rumbled up to the feed-and-grain store. The driver jumped down and strode into the building.

A horse and rider materialized from the alley. Wex and Midnight moved like one shadow toward the hotel. Her heart leaped into her throat. As if he sensed her watching him, he glanced toward the window and tipped his hat. Then he nudged the horse to a gallop and continued on his mission.

"Be careful," she whispered, her warm breath leaving a small cloud on the windowpane. "I love you."

After washing in the cold water in the basin, she donned the gingham dress she'd found at the general store. The simple ready-made garment was a poor substitute for the clothes she'd left behind in Denver. Too large in the bodice, the dress hung like a flour sack. She wrapped a sash around her waist that hiked up the hem above her ankles. The sight that greeted her in the mirror brought a wry smile to her lips. At least it was a dress, and that was what Wex had wanted.

Downhearted, she moved slowly about the hotel room, unconsciously straightening the bed where they'd made such glorious love, picking up the wineglasses from the table and the dirty clothes tossed near the tub.

With every moment the pain in her chest grew stronger. The walls of the room had begun to close in on her when a knock sounded on the door.

"Wex," she whispered, her pulse racing in anticipation. She flung open the door, and the smile faded from her face. Mrs. Klein stood in the hallway with a large tray in her hands.

"Your husband ordered a breakfast for you, Mrs. Wexford."

At the sound of the name she would never truly possess, Maggie bit back a groan. Mr. Wexford, *Lord Geoffrey,* was soon to wed another, and Maggie would be alone.

Mrs. Klein stared at her with a puzzled expression. "Are you all right, my dear?" the older woman asked.

Taking the tray from the woman, Maggie smiled. "I'm well, thank you. And thank you for the breakfast."

Mrs. Klein glanced over Maggie's shoulder into the room. "May I send up the maid?"

"Yes, of course. My . . . husband will be back later."

"Mrs. Wexford, it certainly is a pleasure having you and

Mr. Wexford back with us again." Mrs. Klein folded her hands over her pristine apron. "How is your young sister?"

The memory of Sarah's ordeal cut into Maggie's heart. "She's in Denver with my aunt, and she's doing very well. Sarah is a strong young woman." Maggie backed up a step, not wanting to gossip or discuss her personal affairs. "Thank you for the breakfast, Mrs. Klein. We appreciate your fine hospitality."

A satisfied smile spread across the woman's round face. "We do our best to please our patrons. Let me know when you want your dinner served, and I'll prepare something special for you and the mister."

Maggie returned her smile. "I will." Closing the door behind her, she stared at the empty room. She wished she could make plans, that she knew when Wex would return to her. *If* he returned to her.

Although the eggs, bacon, and fluffy biscuits were delicious, Maggie had little appetite. Restless, she moved to the window, hoping to see Wex riding back into town.

Sherman was alive with activity. Farm wagons and buggies rolled from one end of the town to the other, stopping at the various merchants. Men on horseback competed for space at the hitching posts. But Wex wasn't among them.

While she watched, a particularly handsome carriage rolled into town and stopped in front of the sheriff's office. Her heart slammed against her ribs as she recognized the owner of the carriage. Ross Elliott jumped down and hurried across the boardwalk and into the office.

News traveled fast in a town this size, and he surely knew that she and Wex had returned to Sherman. Would he cause trouble for Wex? With the sheriff as his ally, he could get away with anything—even murder.

Unable to bear the inactivity a minute longer, especially since Wex could be in danger, she grabbed her jacket and rifle. He may not think he needed her, but she needed him. She had to make sure he was safe.

She hurried down the stairs and out of the hotel. When she crossed the street, she noticed Elliott leaving the sheriff's office. He leaped into his carriage and sped away into the direction from which he'd come.

Trouble. The word roared into Maggie's ears as loud as a clap of thunder. She ran the remainder of the way to the livery stable.

With the directions from the stableman, she was soon on her way to the Double H ranch. She prayed she would reach Wex in time to warn him about Elliott and convince him to be on guard.

Gray skies hung low over the valley; the wind whistled through the trees. With dogged determination, Maggie set the team at a trot. The chill in her heart was far worse than the bite of the wind on her face.

Relief surged through her when she spied the gate and the sign announcing her arrival at the Double H. Without slowing her pace, she rode directly into the compound. A series of neatly arranged barns and stables sat back from a sturdy log cabin. A snowcapped mountain guarded the valley.

She pulled to a halt in front of the house and looked around for Wex or his black stallion. Her heart sank when she spotted neither.

The door opened, and a woman stepped onto the porch, a shotgun in her hands. "May I help you?" she asked in a slow drawl. A few years older than Maggie, the woman showed a fierce determination in her stance and in the way she brandished the weapon. Her hair was pulled into a severe bun, without a single strand escaping the strict confines. Not like Maggie's unruly locks that refused to be bound in any fashion.

"Mrs. Hillcroft?" Maggie called from her perch on the wagon seat. "I'm Maggie Callahan. Have you seen Mr. Wexford?"

The woman nodded. "Yes, Mr. Wexford was here earlier. I believe he and my husband are inspecting the herd."

A thousand-pound weight lifted from Maggie's chest. But she wouldn't be content until she saw for herself that he was safe. "Do you know where they are?"

"I'm not sure." Matilda Hillcroft lowered the shotgun, and two little girls skittered around their mother and stared at Maggie. "Please come in. You look as if you can use a warm drink."

At first Maggie thought she was seeing double, until the

girls stepped forward in unison. "That's a funny wagon," one of them said. "What does C-A-L-L-A-H-A-N mean?"

Maggie jumped down and stooped to eye level with the girls. "That's my name, and this is the wagon I use to take pictures." She removed her dusty hat and tugged her braid over her shoulder.

They stared at her with wide golden eyes. "Are you going to take our pictures?"

Mrs. Hillcroft laughed. "Girls, quit bothering Miss Callahan. Let her come in and get warm."

Neither moved. "Well, are you?" asked the child to her right.

"I would love to. But I'm afraid I forgot my camera in town. Next time I would be honored to photograph two pretty girls like you."

They giggled and each caught one of Maggie's hands. "I'm Elizabeth, and she's Victoria."

"Mr. Wexford said we were named after two great British queens," said Victoria. "Papa said we were named after our grandmothers."

Maggie rose and followed the twins into the cabin. The main room was spotlessly clean, and the aroma of fresh coffee wafted from the stove.

"Take Miss Callahan's coat," Mrs. Hillcroft ordered as she reached for two cups. "Tea or coffee, Miss Callahan?"

"Coffee, if you don't mind."

The twins both reached for Maggie's coat, working together to ease it from her shoulders. A twinge shot through Maggie's heart. Would Wex father twins like these? she wondered. Unconsciously she touched her stomach. Were they already growing inside her? The sobering thought sent a shiver through her body.

Maggie settled on a bench at the long wooden table, Victoria on her right, Elizabeth on her left. The embroidered linen cloth covered the table, a surprising bit of elegance in the rustic cabin. Probably a part of a trousseau, Maggie thought.

Maggie's heart sank further at another reminder of what she would never share with Wex. Another woman was at this moment gathering linens and goods for their impending marriage.

Angry at herself for entertaining such disparaging thoughts, Maggie turned her attention to the problem at hand—keeping Wex safe, even if for another woman.

Mrs. Hillcroft set two steaming cups on the table. "It's a pleasure to finally meet you, Miss Callahan. I've heard so much about you." The woman flashed a warm, knowing smile.

A tinge touched Maggie's cheeks. "Please call me Maggie."

"My friends call me Tillie." She patted Maggie's hand. "I feel as if we're already friends, after what Mr. Wexford is doing for us, and since Grady stopped by."

"Grady? Is Grady here?" Happiness surged through Maggie.

"He only stayed a few days to ask permission to look for gold on Sunshine Mountain. Hank tried to convince him there's no gold here. But Grady insisted he had to see for himself."

Maggie smiled. "I think he just likes to be out in the mountains doing something."

Tillie set a plate of cookies on the table. Instantly two small hands snaked out. "Girls!" Tillie slapped Victoria's—or was it Elizabeth's?—hand from the tray of cookies. "Let Maggie have the first one."

"Thank you." Maggie took a cookie from each of the girls and bit into one. "These are delicious," she said.

Tillie sipped her coffee and studied Maggie over the rim. The close scrutiny made her uneasy. The woman was clearly not given to idle chatter. "I saw you at the dance. I'm sorry about what happened to your sister."

Maggie flinched. Did everybody in the county know? "Thank you for your concern. But Sarah is doing fine."

"It was Cole Elliott, wasn't it?"

At the icy tone, Maggie's head snapped up. "We suspected him, but we can't prove it. Why do you think that?"

"The Elliotts have been behind most of our troubles, and Cole is a wild boy. Maybe he'll go away to college like his brother and leave us alone."

"Can't you do something about it?"

"Like you, we don't have any proof. Ross Elliott wanted to buy our land. Now, thanks to Mr. Wexford, we won't

have to sell. Hank is already making improvements, and
he's looking for a bull to upgrade the herd. We hope to turn
this into a breeding ranch.''

Her plans for the future warmed Maggie. Plans that Wex
had helped to bring to life. At the sound of the door opening,
she spun around. "Wex." The name escaped unbidden.

Disappointment flooded her when a young boy, about
Tim's age, entered and shut the door behind him.

"This is my son, Shane," Tillie said. "Are your father and
Mr. Wexford with you?"

The boy grabbed a handful of cookies. "No, ma'am.
They're out on the south range checking the fence."

The color disappeared from Tillie's cheeks. "Are any of
the hands with them?"

"No. They're alone."

Maggie caught the anxiety in the woman's voice. "What's
wrong, Tillie?"

"Nothing. It's just that the south range borders the Lazy
E—Elliott's ranch. Most of our troubles have come from
that direction."

Talons of fear tore at Maggie's heart. Wex could be riding
unaware right into danger. She jumped up and upset the
bench behind her. The girls squealed as they tumbled to the
floor.

"I'm so sorry," Maggie groaned. She reached for a twin
with each arm. "Are you hurt?"

Laughter bubbled from them. "That was fun. Can we do
it again?"

Tillie caught both girls by their arms. "Run along and
play. I have to talk to Maggie."

"I'm sorry I'm so clumsy." With Tillie's help she set the
bench back under the table.

"Maggie, what's wrong?" Tillie touched her arm and
stared into Maggie's face. "You look scared to death."

With a quick shake of her head, Maggie forced a smile.
"It's nothing. It's just . . . I have to find Wex."

Tillie's eyes warmed with understanding. "Don't worry.
They'll be back soon. Hank didn't take food with him, and
he never misses a meal."

Panic made Maggie's stomach clench. It could already be
too late. "I have to find him."

"Shane." Tillie turned to her son, still munching the cookies. "Go with Miss Callahan to find Mr. Wexford." She held Maggie's jacket. "You really love him, don't you?"

There was no use lying to the woman. "Is it so plain?"

Tillie laughed. "Only a woman who's either crazy or in love would drive a wagon in the cold wind to see a man. And except for being in love, you don't appear to be insane."

Unable to control herself, Maggie laughed. She must be crazy to love a man who didn't care at all for her. "Thanks, Tillie." Buttoning up the jacket, she moved toward the door. "Shane doesn't have to go with me. It's cold, and he's just come in. All I need are directions." The boy preceded her into the chill wind and gave simple directions.

"And Maggie." Tillie's voice drew her attention. "For what it's worth, I think he loves you, too."

Although she knew it wasn't true, the thought warmed Maggie's heart as she climbed into the wagon seat. With a wave to Tillie and the twins standing on the porch, Maggie turned the wagon toward the south pasture and Wex.

Without roads, the wagon had to go slowly over the rutted pastures. Frustration welled up in Maggie, but she carefully followed Shane's directions. Herds of white-faced Herefords grazed at the lush grass, now turning brown with the coming of autumn.

The Double H boasted a fine stream, which was probably the reason for Elliott's interest in the property. Water was as valuable as gold to a cattle rancher.

The wind bit at Maggie's exposed cheeks, but she ignored the cold. The afternoon sun had somehow managed to peek from behind the clouds. Afraid she'd taken a wrong turn, Maggie searched for Wex and Hillcroft. She continued slowly along the fence line.

Then she heard it—gunfire.

Her worst nightmares were coming true. She yelled, urging the horses toward the sounds. Shot after shot carried over the narrow valley.

She prayed as she'd never prayed before for Wex's safety. If he survived, she would let him go, to Grace Ferguson, to any woman he chose.

Heedless of possibly upsetting the wagon, she kept the

pace. The wagon shook and bumped on the rutted ground.

Suddenly the gunfire ceased, and a deadly silence filled the air. Maggie pulled the team to a halt. Wex and Hillcroft were standing over a body, Wex with his six-gun drawn, Hillcroft a rifle in his hand.

Maggie breathed a prayer of thanks. She opened her mouth to yell a greeting when the glint of sunshine on metal caught her eye. Someone from behind a boulder had his sights on the men.

In a single movement, she grabbed her rifle, cocked it, and fired. The shot struck the rock and shattered pebbles into the air. She fired again, and a gun clattered down the boulder.

At the sound of renewed gunfire, Wex and Hank threw themselves on the ground. Wex rolled over and aimed his Colt in the direction of the sound. He'd already taken aim when he noticed the black wagon and Maggie with her rifle pointed over his head.

His gaze followed hers, and he saw a shadow behind a boulder. A six-shooter rolled to the ground.

Hank was the first on his feet, bending low as he ran to the copse of trees where the initial shooting had originated. They reached the spot in time to see a man mount a horse and take off on the run. Wex took aim, but only a loud click came from the weapon. He hadn't reloaded.

A thousand curses erupted from his mouth. The rider, bent over the neck of his horse, headed toward the Lazy E.

"Damn." Hank stood beside him, fury written on his face. "We couldn't get our horses and catch him before he reaches the Lazy E. There must be a thousand places a man can hole up in this country."

"The way he was holding his shoulder, I think he was hit." Not wanting to make the same mistake twice, Wex pulled the bullets from the cartridge belt and reloaded the gun.

"Did he get away?" Maggie, her dress hiked to her knees, ran toward them.

Only then did Wex allow himself to consider what had happened. Maggie had ridden right into the middle of a gun battle. His stomach tightened into knots. Unable to control his anger, he caught her by the arms and shook her. "What the hell are you doing here? I told you to wait for me in town."

Her hat fell off, and the hair escaped her braid. "You idiot. I saved your life."

He dug his fingers into her soft flesh. "He could have hit you first, you little fool."

"You are the damnedest most unappreciative man I've ever had the misfortune to meet," she yelled. "I'm sorry I even worried about you. I should have let Elliott's henchmen kill you."

As the importance of what had happened washed over him, he pulled her hard against him and enfolded her in his embrace. "Damn, Maggie, when are you ever going to listen to reason?"

She sagged against him and wrapped her arms around his waist. "I had to warn you that Elliott knew you were back. You promised to come back safe."

"You put yourself in danger."

"I saved your life."

"Thank you." He kissed the top of her head.

"What happened?" She pulled back to gaze into his face. Her eyes were dark with concern.

"We were ambushed. Must have been at least six of them and two of us."

Hank began to laugh. "But one Johnny Reb and one bloody Englishman can take on at least a dozen paid killers. But we do appreciate some help from the lady."

The observation brought a groan from Wex. He set Maggie from him. "A lady who shouldn't have been here in the first place."

Maggie clutched the sleeve of his jacket. "Did you . . . kill them?"

Hank moved to the body on the ground. "He's still alive, but not for long if we don't get him to a doctor."

Wex knelt over the man, sticking his fingers into his shirt to check his heartbeat. The beat was weak, and the wound in the man's side was bleeding profusely. "We need to stop the bleeding."

"You can use my petticoat," Maggie offered. "Do you have a knife?"

"Yes," Hank said, pulling a long-bladed bowie knife from a sheath at his waist.

Without a thought for modesty, Maggie lifted her dress and sliced off the bottom half of her white cotton petticoat. While Hank bound the man's wound, Wex studied his face. Somehow the man's hard rough face looked vaguely familiar. "Do you know him?"

Hank tugged on the man's shaggy back hair and turned his face. "I don't recognize him. Must be a drifter."

"Let's get him to the doctor. Maybe he can tell us why he fired at you," said Maggie.

A stubborn streak rose up in Wex. His nerves couldn't take much more of this. "We, Mary Margaret? I think you've gotten into enough trouble already."

She planted her hands on her hips and flashed him an angry glare. "I happen to have the only wagon out here, Mr. Wexford. And if we don't hurry, he may not live to talk."

"She's right, Wex. Let's load him in that strange wagon and head for town."

As much as he hadn't wanted Maggie involved in his troubles, Wex had to admit this was the only thing to do. "All right, but you'll go directly to the hotel and wait for me there."

"Yes, sir." She ran toward the wagon and pulled closer to the wounded man.

They loaded the man into the rear, and Maggie took up the reins. Wex and Hank rode beside her, each with a rifle in his hand.

The road into town seemed interminably long. If the outlaw talked, they might be able to solve the problems plaguing Hillcroft, although Hank reported that he hadn't been harassed until today. Wex knew the gunmen were after him, not Hank.

When they reached the edge of town, he rode ahead to warn the doctor to prepare for a gunshot wound. Fortunately the doctor was in his office reading a medical journal. In a few seconds, the physician had the operating room ready for the outlaw.

Ordinarily Wex wouldn't care if the man lived or died. But this was their only link to the man behind the problems, and maybe he could reveal who'd attacked Sarah and vandalized Maggie's wagons.

Since Hank had been a medic in the Confederate army, he assisted in the operation. Maggie and Wex waited outside for word. He'd ordered her to the hotel, but as usual she'd refused to leave his side. He was forced to admit he liked having her with him.

They had been in town less than thirty minutes when the sheriff burst into the room. "What kind of trouble are you causing now, Wexford?" he asked in place of a greeting.

Wex sprang to his feet with Maggie close behind. "I'm not in any trouble, but somebody is." He gestured to the closed door behind him. "If he survives the operation, he'll be able to tell you who's behind all the problems Hillcroft has been having."

The sheriff set his hand on the gun at his side. "Trouble follows you, doesn't it, Wexford?"

Wex curled his fingers into his palms to keep from punching the smirk off the man's face. "Hank and I were inspecting his cattle when we were ambushed by half a dozen men. Most of them got away, but this one didn't. We think another one was wounded."

Steward let out a long string of curses before he clamped his mouth shut. "Sorry, Mrs. Wexford. Did you recognize the men?"

Folding his arms across his chest, Wex merely glared at the man. "Since I'm a stranger here, I don't know many people."

"Maybe I'll recognize him." The sheriff shoved through the other door with Wex at his heels.

The outlaw was stretched out on a long table, his lower body covered with a white sheet. His eyes were closed, and his face was deathly pale. The doctor didn't look up, but continued stitching the hole in the man's side. Hank, his sleeves rolled up, was handing the doctor the required instruments.

"Wex tell you what happened, Wade?" Hank asked, not taking his eyes off the doctor.

"Yeah." The sheriff studied the man for several minutes before he turned to leave.

"Well, Sheriff," Wex asked, "do you know who he is?"

"Name's MacKenzie. He works for Ross Elliott."

Chapter
Twenty-two

A shiver raced through Maggie as the sheriff confirmed what she'd suspected all along. Ross Elliott, of course. The man had his hand in everything that happened in Sherman—good or bad.

Wex nodded and hooked his thumbs in his gun belt. "Then it's time we paid Mr. Elliott a visit."

A hard line slashed across the sheriff's mouth. "This is my job, Wexford. I'll talk to Ross and find out if he knows anything."

Hank rolled down his shirt sleeves and wiped his bloodied hands on a towel. "We'll ride along with you, Wade. Never know when you'll need reinforcements."

Under the brim of his gray hat, the sheriff's eyes hardened. "Stay out of this, Hank. Go home and take care of your family."

Hank stood his ground under a look that would wither a lesser man. "Wade, somebody tried to kill me today, and I don't take lightly to being shot at. We'll either go with you or on our own."

Wex stood shoulder to shoulder with Hank. "We know at least one of them was wounded and rode toward the Lazy E. He probably went back for medical aid."

"Why don't we question this man?" asked Maggie. The last thing she wanted was for Wex to ride out to Elliott's ranch and possibly into another trap. Especially with the sheriff she didn't trust.

The doctor looked up. "I gave him enough ether to keep him knocked out until tomorrow. You can't question him until he wakes up."

"These men didn't act without orders," Wex said. "If Elliott isn't behind this, somebody on his ranch is."

Unable to stop herself, Maggie clutched the sleeve of Wex's jacket. "Like his son."

Sheriff Steward shot a quelling glance at Maggie. "Keep your woman out of this, Wexford. This is man's business."

Indignation poured over Maggie like hot oil. The man didn't even have the courtesy to speak directly to her. "Sheriff, I'm as much involved in this as any of the men, maybe even more."

"Mary Margaret," Wex said, his tone issuing a warning. "Let me handle this. Go back to the hotel and wait for me."

Shocked at the reprimand, Maggie dropped her hand as if she'd been struck. "I'm going with you."

"No, you aren't." His dark eyes narrowed dangerously.

"Get out of here, all of you," the doctor scolded. "This man is my patient, and I won't have all this confusion in my operating room."

"I'll be back later, Doc." The sheriff led the way into the waiting room. "If you insist on coming with me, let's get going," he said in a cold voice. "But the lady stays in town."

Wex caught her arm and spun Maggie around. "Mary Margaret, there could be trouble, and I don't want you hurt. Wait for me at the hotel." Lowering his head, he whispered for her ears only. "I promise I'll come back safely. Order us a special dinner, and I'll make it all up to you tonight."

Maggie swallowed an angry response. All warmth disappeared from his eyes. His charming invitation was only a ploy to distract her from the danger he would be facing. "All right," she said.

He kissed her lightly on the forehead, then followed Hank and the sheriff out the doorway. Maggie watched as the men mounted their horses and headed to the edge of town.

Maggie shrugged into her coat and with a heavy heart moved toward her wagon. After all that had transpired between them, Wex still didn't think he needed her. She climbed into the seat and picked up the reins. Before the dust from the horses settled, she turned the wagon and followed in their wake toward the Lazy E.

The miles clipped off under Midnight's powerful hoofs. In one hand Wex clutched Maggie's loaded rifle. If Elliott wanted trouble, this time the man would meet his match.

He only hoped the stubborn woman had the good sense to remain at the hotel and out of harm's way. But Wex doubted Maggie had listened to a word of his warning. She didn't take well to being ordered by anyone, especially him.

They crossed onto Lazy E land and continued toward the house. Cows with their calves lounged under the cottonwoods near a stream. A few of the cowboys repairing the fence looked up when they passed. The sheriff waved, and nobody bothered to stop them.

The road curved into a long line of sturdy pines, leading up a hill. A white house, reminiscent of the Greek Revival mansions in the southern United States, stood tall and proud. Four graceful columns rose from the porch to the roof. The bunkhouse and barns sat almost a quarter mile below the mansion.

Everything about the compound lived up to Wex's expectations. More than before, Elliott reminded Wex of his own father with his showy display of his position and power. Tyrants and despots were the same the world over. He dismounted and walked between the sheriff and Hillcroft up the steps onto the verandah.

"Let me do the talking," the sheriff ordered as he lifted the shiny brass knocker and let it fall in a loud thud.

Wex half expected a liveried butler to pull open the wide-paneled double doors. Instead a plump Mexican woman acknowledged their presence. Her brown eyes widened at the sight of the three armed men.

"Señor Sheriff," she said, her voice heavily accented. "You come see Señor Ross?"

"Sí, Angelina. Is Señor Ross in?" Steward removed his wide hat as they stepped into the large foyer.

The house was every bit as impressive inside as it was out. Elliott had spared no expense in the crystal chandeliers and polished furnishings. Their boot heels clicked loudly on the Italian marble floor.

"*Sí.* Señor Ross in his study. His foot hurt again."

Angelina led the way down a short hallway and knocked on a heavy oak door. "Come in," called a gruff voice from inside.

"Ross?" The sheriff shoved open the door. "I want to talk to you."

Wex followed into the mahogany-paneled study. The walls were lined with overflowing bookcases, and a huge map hung behind a desk. It wasn't difficult to recognize Elliott's holdings. Wex swallowed hard. He felt as if he'd been transported in time and place to his father's estate in Allenshire.

Elliott faced the fireplace, his back to the door. One foot was propped on a padded hassock in front of his overstuffed chair. "This had better be important, Wade. This damn gout is acting up again." The man turned his head, and the cigar in his hand stopped halfway to his mouth. His eyes flashed a murderous glance. "What the hell is that Englishman doing in my house?"

Wex and Hank exchanged glances, but they held their tongues and let the sheriff speak. "There's been some trouble at the Double H, Ross. These fellows thought you might know something about it."

Taking a leisurely puff on his cigar, Elliott looked them over, malice glittering in his steely eyes. Wex gritted his teeth and stood his ground. He'd never allowed his father's authoritative looks to intimidate him, and he certainly wasn't going to cower before a man like Elliott.

"Trouble follows the Brit. What's it got to do with me?"

Unable to stand the man's contemptuous tactics, Wex shoved past the sheriff. "Somebody tried to kill Hillcroft and me. One of the wounded got away and headed this way."

Elliott narrowed his eyes. "This is a big ranch. Any kind of outlaw could hide here, and my men would never find him."

"Ross," Wade Steward interrupted before Wex could counter. "They brought in a wounded man for Doc to fix up. It was MacKenzie."

The color seeped slowly from Elliott's bronzed face. "MacKenzie? Hell, I fired him a week ago. Reckon he's working for somebody else. I can't be responsible for everything that goes wrong. I sure as hell didn't order anybody to shoot at you. If I had, neither of you would be here to tell the tale."

Wex stiffened. Threats had never worked for his father, and they sure as hell wouldn't work for Elliott. "Then you won't mind if we question your hands."

Elliott looked to Steward for his reaction. The sheriff shrugged. "We'll check the bunkhouse and see if any of the fellows know anything."

"Goddammit, I can hardly walk on this foot, and you troublemakers want to upset my entire operation." He swung his foot to the floor and flinched. "Let's get it over with. Most of the boys are out on the range. But you'll see for yourself." Grabbing a silver-handled cane, he hobbled into the hallway.

Clutching his rifle in his left hand, Wex followed Elliott down a path that led past a small grove of trees to a sprawling whitewashed building. Elliott flung open the door and bellowed, "Anybody here?"

"Just me, Pa." Cole Elliott swung his legs off the lower bunk. "The other hands are still out on the range."

Ross pointed his cane at his son. "What are you doing out here? What's wrong with your room at the house?"

The young man's face turned pale. He tugged at the kerchief around his neck. "Nothing, Pa. I just like hanging out with the men, that's all."

Wex followed the sheriff to the next room and scanned the empty bunks. Various articles of men's clothing hung from nails or pegs on the walls. He had started back to the main area when something on the floor caught his eye. Stooping down, he touched the blotch on the thin rug. The spot was damp and rust-colored. Blood.

Wex looked up and saw Steward watching him. He held up his finger. "Looks like our man was here." Nearer the rear door, he spotted another small dark stain. "Hank," he called.

Instantly Hillcroft was at his side. Wex pointed to the bloodstains and out the door. On a run, they entered the yard, the sheriff on their tail, Elliott following behind. Hank spotted the next blot and gestured to the large barn, the closest hiding place.

At the barn door they paused. Hank pulled out his six-gun as Wex cocked the rifle. Both men slipped inside and pressed against the wall. Elliott flung the door wide and stepped in. "Wade, you had better stop these two hotheads before they cause any more trouble."

Ignoring the warning, the sheriff slid along the wall behind them. They checked each stall, one by one. The horses whinnied and stomped at the intrusion on their domain. Hank spotted another drop of blood and gestured to the hay stacked in the far corner. In a single movement Wex kicked a bale aside and pointed the rifle at a man crouched in the corner. His face was pale, and his eyes wide with terror. One hand was pressed to a gaping wound in his shoulder.

"Looks like we found our hired killer," Hank said, his own gun trained at the man's chest.

"What the hell—" Elliott stopped when he spotted the man. "Ringo, what happened?"

The man struggled to his feet. "I was ambushed, boss." His voice dropped to a growl with the pain. "Help me."

Steward grabbed Ringo's gun from his holster. "Let's get him to the bunkhouse. Maybe we can stop the bleeding enough to get him to the doctor."

Weak from the loss of blood, the man had to be assisted by the sheriff on one side and Hank on the other. The instant they exited the barn and stepped into the open, a gunshot rang out. Ringo slumped and pitched forward. Wex and the others hit the ground. Wex spotted a figure running through the trees toward the house.

Maggie halted the wagon in front of one of the most magnificent homes she had ever seen. Never had she expected to see this large a house out in the middle of the valley. Usually fine homes were reserved for the city, or some of the large plantations in the South.

For a moment she studied the tall white pillars that supported the roof. Elliott was far wealthier and more important than she'd ever imagined—like an English lord who ruled his subjects from his manor house. Her heart sank at the memory of who and what Wex really was. She wondered if he lived in an elegant house and ruled his lands like a feudal lord? As much as he enjoyed playing cowboy, he didn't belong in the West or in America.

Or with her.

Heart sinking, she picked up her unwieldy skirts and prepared to step down from the wagon. Wex had to be somewhere nearby; his horse waited at the hitching post.

Suddenly a shot rang out. The horses snorted and jerked. Maggie fell back into the seat. Don't let it be Wex, she prayed.

From out of a grove of trees, a man ran toward the wagon. Automatically Maggie reached for the rifle she kept at her side. This time it wasn't there. Wex had taken it.

Brandishing a six-shooter, the man pointed it at Maggie as he climbed on the wheel and into the seat. He jammed the barrel into her ribs. "Get going, lady."

The feral gleam in the man's eyes told her he meant business. He wouldn't hesitate to kill anybody who stood in his way. The click of the hammer spurred her to action. Grabbing the reins, she yelled, and the team took off at a gallop.

Terror made her numb to the pressure of the gun in her side and to the chill wind that whipped her hair loose from the braid. A thousand thoughts flooded her mind as she guided the horses toward the road. Wex had warned her. He'd ordered her to stay in town and out of harm's way. Now she was tearing through the countryside with a killer. She had to do something to save herself.

Trees whizzed past, and the wagon shook and rattled on the bumpy road. At a fork the man yelled for her to turn left onto little more than a cow path. Her teeth chattered with every rut the wheels hit. If the man didn't kill her, surely the ride would shake her head off.

The effort to control the team took all her concentration. Her head was spinning. Maggie put Wex, her past, and her future out of her thoughts. She focused her attention on survival.

"We have to slow down," she yelled at the man beside

her. "The wagon can't take this kind of abuse." Panic lodged in her throat like a huge stone.

He waved the gun at her. "I'll tell you when to slow down."

The clatter of the wheels loud in her ears, Maggie didn't hear the approaching horses until the man began to curse. "Somebody's following us. If they catch up, you're the first one to die."

From the corner of her eye, Maggie spotted the black stallion. Wex drew up beside them and reached for the reins. The man beside Maggie pointed the gun at Wex. Thought for her own survival was forgotten. Wex was going to get killed after all she'd done to save his life.

She couldn't let that happen. She wouldn't let it happen. Turning the team to the left, away from Wex, she threw herself against the gunman, knocking him off balance. He fired, and the bullet shot into the air, missing both of them.

After that everything happened so fast Maggie was never sure of the sequence of events. The reins jerked from her hands, and the wagon listed to the side. While she struggled for possession of the gun she sensed the wagon slowing. A voice rang out, but the words didn't register in her mind. The wagon skittered like a sled and hit a boulder.

She felt herself flying through the air, then darkness descended.

Wex pulled hard on the slack reins, using all his strength to control the runaway team. From the corner of his eye, he saw Maggie wrestling with the killer, but he was powerless to help her. If he didn't stop the horses, the wagon would surely overturn, killing her in the process.

Somehow he managed to remain seated on the horse while gathering the leather straps in one hand. Winded and exhausted from the wild ride, the team gradually slowed. The wagon careened sideways and struck a boulder. He watched in horror as Maggie and the killer were both thrown to the ground.

His stomach knotted, and the air whooshed from his lungs. Before the team came to a complete halt, he flung himself from Midnight and ran the remaining yards to

Maggie. Like a rag doll, she lay crumpled on the stony ground, blood dripping from a wound on her forehead.

For a brief instant he saw not Maggie but Arthur lying in a silent heap, his body twisted and broken. Wex shook his head to clear away the frightful image. He couldn't lose another person he loved because of his carelessness. His heart couldn't take that kind of pain.

The realization that he loved her hit him squarely in the center of his chest. Dammit, he wasn't going to let her die.

Maggie's eyes were closed, and a huge knot was forming on her forehead. He tore open her coat and pressed his hand to her heart. Thank God she was alive, but he had no idea of the extent of her injuries.

Behind him he heard the sound of hooves and his horse's loud snort. Bullets whizzed past his head, and he threw himself across Maggie to protect her. He was more than willing to take a shot to save her life.

"Wex, you hurt?" Hank's voice was followed by the jingle of spurs and the sound of running feet.

Easing away from Maggie, Wex chanced a glance over his shoulder. The sheriff, Cole Elliott, and Hank were running in his direction. The killer lay in a heap on the ground.

"I'm all right, but Maggie's injured."

Hank knelt beside him and expertly ran his hands along her arms and legs. When he ran his fingers under her coat and pressed under her breasts, her mouth pulled into a frown. Carefully Hank closed her coat and looked up.

Wex held his breath, waiting for the verdict like a man facing a hangman's noose. "Does she . . ." The words died in his throat.

"No broken bones, but she may have bruised ribs. The heavy coat kept her from getting skinned up." Hank lifted his gaze. "And she had a pretty bad lick on the head." He covered Wex's trembling hand. "I won't lie. It could be serious."

Pain sliced through Wex. He should be the one hurt, not Maggie. Cradling her head in his arms, he dabbed gently at the cut across her forehead. The sight of her blood on his hands fueled his anger like a white-hot poker in his gut.

If the killer wasn't dead, Wex would personally strangle the life from him.

"He's dead," Hank said in answer to Wex's unspoken thoughts. "He had a bead on you, and Cole killed him."

Wex jerked his head to see the sheriff and the younger Elliott leaning over them. "It's all over, Wexford."

"Is it, Sheriff? Did we get the ringleader?"

"Yeah." Cole's face was white as he looked down onto Maggie's still body. "I overheard some of the hands talking about stealing some cattle and horses. Guess they were the ones who shot at you."

Wex studied the nervous young man. His gaze shifted from side to side, unable to look at either Wex or Hank. The boy was lying. Wex would stake his life on it. But the sheriff seemed willing to accept the explanation and close the case. There was always the wounded outlaw at the doctor's office. It would be interesting to hear what he had to say.

Maggie groaned, and Wex returned his attention to the woman in his arms. "Sweetheart, can you hear me?" He stroked a finger gently across her lips.

She blinked and pressed her hand to her forehead. "What happened?"

"Hush, love," he whispered, relief flooding him. "You were hurt, but I'm here to take care of you."

Her eyes glazed over, and her pupils widened. "He was going to shoot you."

"He's dead, and we're alive."

She tried to sit up, but he held her close. "My head hurts."

"You have a nasty bump on your temple. Don't try to move. We'll get you to the doctor."

"Don't need a doctor—"

Her words were cut off by the clatter of a carriage escorted by a half-dozen riders. Ross Elliott stepped down and limped over to where Maggie still lay on the ground.

"Get them back," Wex growled, unable to contain his fury a second longer. "This isn't a show. Take care of your dead wrangler, and I'll take Maggie to the doctor."

Ross's cold gaze swept over the scene. "Put her in my carriage and take her up to the house."

Wex swept Maggie up in his arms, careful not to hurt her ribs. She looped her arms around his neck. Warmth flowed through him. "Thank you." The words came reluctantly. "I'll take her to town and to the doctor."

Hank touched his arm. "My place isn't far. Tillie can look after her. She's a good nurse."

He set Maggie on the smooth leather seat and wrapped the lap blanket around her. Hank mounted his horse and caught Midnight's reins. As Wex pulled away he spotted Elliott bent in conversation with his son. Wex was certain one or the other was involved in the troubles. But unless the man in the doctor's office would talk, he'd reached the end of the line. Now his concern was for Maggie, the only woman he'd ever loved, the woman he had no right to claim.

Chapter
Twenty-three

Maggie rubbed the huge lump on her forehead and winced at the pain. The pounding behind her eyes had subsided to a dull roar, but her arms and legs ached as if she'd been beaten with a club.

In the darkness voices surrounded her—some familiar, others foreign. A deep masculine tone remained constant. "I love you, Mary Margaret," it repeated over and over. "Don't leave me."

Comforted by the tone, she struggled to open her eyes to strange surroundings. Nothing was familiar—not the wide bed, the lace curtains, the oak bureau and washstand, or the white nightgown she was wearing. Struggling to sit up, she pressed her fingers to her temples to stop her head from spinning.

Strong hands caught her shoulders and urged her back against the pillows. "Lie still, love. I'll take care of you." It was the same voice she'd heard in the darkness. Wex was with her. He hadn't been killed, and neither had she. Unless . . . She closed her eyes.

"Am I dead?" she whispered, afraid to open her eyes.

Cool fingers touched her cheek. "No. But I'm afraid you frightened ten years off my life."

She turned her head and opened her eyes. Wex moved from a straight-backed chair to sit on the edge of the bed.

His dark hair fell across his brow, and shadows lined his eyes. Yet Maggie had never seen a more handsome or welcome sight.

"Where are we?" Lifting her hand, she covered his long fingers and squeezed with her limited strength.

"At the Hillcroft ranch. Tillie's been taking care of you."

"Why? What's wrong with me?" A thousand frightening thoughts surged through her mind.

"You had a nasty fall from the wagon. After a few days' rest you should be good as new." He swiped a stray wisp of hair from her forehead.

The wagon . . . a fall . . . One by one the memories trickled back. The outlaw with a gun pointed at Wex . . . the shots . . . riding in a carriage with Wex's arm around her. Slowly the fear began to abate. "You saved my life," she whispered.

His dark eyes held a tenderness she'd never seen before. "No, for the third time you saved *my* life." He stroked his thumb across her dry lips. "Would you like some water?"

She nodded, unable to speak around the lump of emotion in her throat. He shifted his arm to the back of her neck and gently tilted her head. A feeling of well-being, of being loved, swirled over her. She took a few sips of the water, then shook her head. "I wish I had one of Sarah's magic potions for my head."

"As soon as the sun comes up, Hank and I are going to the doctor's office. I'll bring something back for pain."

More memories of the past days poured over her. "Did you capture the man who . . . the one in the wagon?"

On a long sigh he removed his arm and set the glass aside. "No, Cole Elliott killed him."

Her head started spinning again, her mind unable to comprehend the situation. "It was my fault. I should have stayed in town like you told me."

Gently he laid a cool cloth on her forehead. "I won't argue that point." He lowered his voice to a whisper. "If you had, we would this minute be making love in that hotel room, and you wouldn't be suffering from such a severe bump on the head. But I should have known you wouldn't stay away."

Maggie relaxed against the pillows. He was right. When

was she ever going to learn to stay out of trouble? "What about my wagon?"

He drew his eyebrows together and bit his lip. When he finally answered, his voice was soft and full of remorse. "I'm afraid it was destroyed. When you tumbled off, it careened into a boulder and was smashed beyond repair. Elliott sent your horses over here."

A tear slipped from the corner of her eye. "All Papa's work, gone, all because of me and my stupidity."

"Hush, love. Don't worry about a thing. With the gallery in Denver you won't need to wander in the mountains. Never know what kind of creature you could meet on a dark night."

She nodded, remembering the night he'd wandered out of the shadows into the camp. "You never know."

With the backs of his strong fingers, he swiped the dampness from her cheek. "We can still question the wounded man at the doctor's office. In fact, Hank and I are going to do just that."

A shiver raced up her spine. For some odd reason, she suspected they would never get to the bottom of the incident. "How long have I been sleeping?"

"Since yesterday afternoon." He pulled his watch from his pocket and flipped it open. "About fifteen hours. We were wondering if you would ever wake up."

A new surge of sadness covered her when she glimpsed the miniature of his brother inside the cover of the watch. Would he blame himself for this accident, as he blamed himself for his brother's death?

She forced a smile. "We Callahans have pretty hard heads, but the rest of me hurts like the devil." One by one she wiggled her toes, her feet, her hands, and arms. "Is anything broken?"

"Fortunately no. But the bruises will take a while to heal. I'll bring the doctor back and let him make a professional diagnosis."

"I don't need a doctor."

"Let me decide."

The decisive tone of his voice was strangely comforting. In her present condition, she needed—welcomed—his care, if only for a few days.

"Is she awake?" A woman's soft voice came from the doorway.

Wex turned, and Maggie followed his gaze. Tillie Hillcroft, fully dressed, not one hair on her head out of place, held a tray in her hands. "I brought something to eat."

Maggie pushed up on her elbows, ignoring the pain in her side. "Tillie, is this your bed? I'm so sorry."

"For what? I slept with the girls, and Hank bunked down with Shane." She set the tray on the table next to the bed. "But that man of yours refused to budge from your side."

At Tillie's words, Maggie groaned. He wasn't *her* man. They were lovers, but he would never belong to her. The declaration of love must have been her imagination, a dream caused by the accident. The ache in her chest wasn't from her injuries; the pain went much deeper.

Wex spotted the flash of pain in Maggie's eyes when Tillie had called him "that man of yours." More than anything, he wished it could be possible—that he was free to be her man, that he could openly confess his feelings. Wishes were for children, however. As a grown man, he'd agreed to accept the responsibility for his family and put the good of others before his own needs and wants.

"Tillie, do you mind staying with Maggie for a few minutes? I would like to speak to Hank." And put a little distance between himself and his emotions.

"Certainly. He went down to the barn to saddle the horses. He wants to get to Doc's as soon as possible, but he didn't want to disturb you as long as Maggie was asleep."

He slanted a glance at Maggie and noted the anxiety on her face. "Don't worry, love." He cupped her face in his hands. "I won't get into any trouble. We're just going to talk to MacKenzie and let the sheriff handle it from there."

"Be careful," she whispered, a single tear rolling from her eye.

Unable to help himself, he caught the tear with his tongue and planted a quick kiss on her cheek. "Be a good girl and do everything Tillie says. I'll be back in a few hours."

She nodded, and before he could change his mind, he walked into the kitchen.

"Wex," Tillie called after him. "Get some coffee before you go out. There's a real chill in the air."

He heard the soft murmurs of the women as he filled a cup with the thick brew. He could no longer deny that he loved Maggie. All night he'd sat beside her, listened to her steady breathing, and prayed she would be safe. In spite of his resolve after Arthur's death not to care for another person, he cared more for Maggie than for life itself. He would gladly have traded places with her if he could. Instead he'd almost gotten her killed. He should have stayed in town with her to protect her and keep her out of harm's way. Instead he'd insisted on going with the sheriff and Hank. Guilt washed over him. Yes, her injuries were his fault.

The door opened with a burst of cold air. Hank pulled off his gloves and reached for the coffeepot. "How's your little lady this morning?"

"Maggie is awake, but aching from the bruises." He picked up a hot biscuit and took a bite. "Are you ready to go into town?"

"As soon as we eat. Get yourself a plate and sit down."

The first glimmer of daylight broke across the horizon as Wex and Hank galloped toward Sherman. Maggie had begged to come with them, but Tillie had convinced her to remain in bed for another day. For once Maggie had listened to reason. Besides, she could barely walk, much less sit on a horse.

Wex knew something was wrong when they reached the doctor's office and spotted the sheriff's horse tied at the hitching post. He and Hank exchanged questioning glances and darted into the house.

The doctor was seated behind his desk, holding a cloth to his head, while the sheriff leaned over him. Both looked up when Wex and Hank entered.

"What's going on?" Wex asked. He touched the gun in the holster.

Steward shot them a hard look. "You don't know?"

"How the hell would we? We just rode into town." He glanced at the open doorway leading to the inner examining room. "Where's MacKenzie?"

"He's gone." The doctor gazed at them from over his eyeglasses. "Two men came in, knocked me out, and carried MacKenzie off."

Hank spit out a long string of profanities. "He got away? Where the hell were you, Steward?"

Hooking his thumbs in his belt, the sheriff locked gazes with Hank. "Trying to get some sleep. After the ruckus you two caused yesterday for Ross Elliott, I was dead on my feet."

Wex bit his lip and curled his fingers into fists. Now they would never learn who was behind the troubles. "What are you waiting for? Let's get after them."

"Goddamn you, Wexford. They had hours' head start, and we have no idea which direction they went. By now they could be halfway to New Mexico."

"Wade's right, Wex." Hank picked up an overturned chair and flopped down on it. "We'll never find their trail."

Wex nodded, reluctant to give up. "So where do we stand? Two dead, one wounded, and two or three others on the run."

"I don't reckon they'll cause any more trouble for you, Hank. But I'll wire the sheriffs around the state to be on the lookout for them." Steward moved toward the door. "Wexford, how's your woman?"

Wex's head jerked up. The tone of the sheriff's voice told him that the man had anything but sympathy for Maggie. "She'll be all right. She'll have a headache for a while, and the bruises will eventually go away."

"That was no place for a woman. We might have caught the outlaw if she hadn't interfered." With a brief nod he continued through the doorway into the chill morning.

Wex wanted to hit something, anything, especially the sheriff's smug face. Although he agreed with Steward, he couldn't blame Maggie for what had happened. She wasn't a woman to sit in the parlor and pour tea while life passed by. She would always be in the middle of whatever was going on around her. He wondered if his nerves could take the pressure.

"Mr. Wexford." The doctor's voice drew his attention. A huge lump protruded from his balding scalp. "I'll get my bag and go out to see the lady."

"It looks as if you need medical attention yourself. If you have a painkiller, I'll take it to her."

Setting the bloodstained cloth on the desk, the doctor got

up and retrieved a small vial from a glass cabinet. "This should help. Think I'll take a little myself."

"Thank you, Doctor," Wex said. He took a gold coin from his pocket and pressed it into the doctor's hand. "This should cover your fee for the operation yesterday and for the medicine."

Eyes wide, the doctor stared at the coin. "This is twice my usual fee."

With a tip of his hat, Wex followed Hank out of the office. He wanted to get back to Maggie as soon as possible.

The afternoon passed slowly while Maggie waited for the men to return to the ranch. Against Tillie's wishes, she insisted on putting on her dress and going out onto the porch. With the other woman's wool shawl wrapped around her shoulders, she sat on a rocker and read stories to the twins.

Although the pain in her head was gone, she ached in places she didn't know she had. She'd been shocked when she'd taken off the nightdress and seen the many purple-and-black bruises that marred her legs, her shoulders, and her ribs. She was thankful Papa's heavy old coat had protected her from torn skin and lacerations.

Victoria and Elizabeth took it upon themselves to entertain Maggie while their mother tended to ranch chores. She read the two fairy-tale books over and over. When she recited the story of Cinderella, both girls giggled with delight. Didn't Maggie think that Mr. Wexford looked exactly like Prince Charming? they asked.

The idea startled her, until she realized that he was indeed a lord, if not a prince. That made Maggie a Cinderella, the American-born daughter of an Irish immigrant who had no place in a nobleman's life. Unlike Cinderella and her prince, there was no "happily ever after" for Mary Margaret Callahan and Lord Geoffrey Andrew Wexford.

The twins were bright and lively, and Maggie promised to send them some new books when she returned to Denver. Something by Mark Twain or Stevenson. Forget Hans Christian Andersen and Charles Perrault.

After every page she looked toward the road for the sight of Wex and Hank. The sky was blue and cloudless, and in the distance the snow on Sunshine Mountain seemed closer to the base than yesterday.

With every glance she grew more wary. What if something had happened to them? What if . . . ? She forced away the fear that formed in her mind. Wex and Hank were quite capable of taking care of themselves.

Like yesterday? They would have been killed if she hadn't been there.

The sun had begun its descent toward the west by the time she spotted a puff of dust near the end of the lane.

She heard a loud, shrill whistle, and the twins leaped to their feet. "It's Papa," they sang in unison. "Maybe he brought us something from the store." Ignoring Maggie and the story, they leaped to the ground. Skirts flying around their slim legs, the girls raced down the road and met the two horsemen.

Maggie's heart pounded in anticipation at seeing Wex. She rose, though much more slowly than the girls. How could one fall cause so many aches and pains? she wondered. The door to the cabin opened, and Tillie joined her on the porch. Together they watched the men; each scooped up a girl in his arms and set her in front of his saddle. From the distance Maggie wasn't sure which twin Wex carried, but the child seemed delighted with the attention from her guest.

A lump formed in Maggie's throat. She could picture him with his own offspring—twins—Grace's children. She shivered, not from the cool air, from the chill in her heart. She fixed a grin on her face to cover her pain.

Victoria—at close range now, Maggie could identify the girl—kept her arms tightly around Wex's neck as he dismounted and approached the porch. His eyes locked on Maggie, he pulled his lips into a grim straight line. "What are you doing out of bed?"

No greeting, no "how are you feeling," simply his censure for disobeying his orders. She quelled the stirring in her stomach and met his gaze with a shrug of indifference. "I was tired of being cooped up indoors, *my lord,* if you don't mind."

He flinched at her sarcasm, but didn't rise to the bait. Instead he flashed a look that warned he would deal with her later. Maggie folded her arms across her chest, ready for battle.

Ignorant of the tension between the adults, Victoria squirmed out of his arms and lunged for her father. "Papa, what did you bring us from town?"

Maggie tore her gaze from his and watched the children interact with their father.

Hank tugged on the young girl's braid. "What did I bring you?" With a fake frown, he dug his hand into one pocket and pulled it out empty. The girls squealed when he repeated the gesture with his other hand. "Have you been good? Did you help your mama with the chores?"

"Yes, Papa," Victoria said, a bit of worry darkening her golden eyes.

"We took care of Maggie," added Elizabeth. "We let her read stories from our books."

Hank let out a roar of laughter. "Then I suppose you deserve a present. What do you think, Wex?"

Maggie lifted her eyes and found him still staring at her with the dark scowl on his face. Surely her being out of bed wasn't serious enough to warrant this much displeasure.

After a second he answered, "Since they took such fine care of Maggie, they deserve a treat. Where did that storekeeper put those lollipops?"

By now Shane had come out and was watching with interest, his eyes shiny with the prospect of eating the store-bought candy. Maggie knew that if Wex had anything to do with it, they would have enough treats to give all three children stomachaches. She tamped down her emotions and steeled herself against him. His charm and generosity made her much too vulnerable.

"In the package on your horse," said Shane, running toward the horses. In seconds he had the bundle from the back of his father's saddle and was reaching inside. The smile left his face when all he found was some tea, coffee, and a few lengths of cloth. His eyes questioned his father.

At an unspoken signal from Hank, Wex reached into the inside pocket of his jacket. "What do we have here?" He pulled out a paper package tied in string. "How did this get into my pocket?"

Elizabeth flung herself at him and grabbed for the packet.

Reaching Wex first, Shane held the parcel out of his sisters' reach. "I'm the oldest, so I'll open it, and if you're quiet, I'll give you some."

"Shane," his mother admonished with a smile. "Don't tease your sisters."

The boy sat on the porch and broke the string. At the sight of the contents, the hardworking young boy's smile transformed him into a child. Inside the paper was a youngster's dream assortment of peppermint sticks, lemon drops, licorice, and three huge lollipops. With wide grins, each youngster scooped up a handful.

Her arm around her husband's waist, Tillie watched her children. Maggie envied the couple. Their love was as much a part of them as the smiles on their faces. And the three children were a result of that love. "Aren't you going to thank Mr. Wexford?" Tillie asked.

Three shiny faces looked up in wonder. "Thank you," they said in one voice before they darted to the far end of the porch with their treasures.

Maggie slanted a glance at Wex. One foot propped on the upper step, he leaned forward with his forearm resting on his knee. The tight canvas breeches hugged his slim hips and muscular legs. His bold masculinity brought a flutter to her stomach, and his kindness caused her heart to melt.

How could she remain angry at him for his arrogance? Would she want him any other way? He couldn't help being born into the peerage any more than she could help loving him.

Tillie picked up the bundle her husband had brought home. "Let's go inside out of the wind. I just took a fresh apple pie out of the oven."

Wex snaked out a hand and caught Maggie's arm as she spun to follow the couple. "Aren't you going to ask what I brought for you, Mary Margaret?"

In spite of his warm touch, a shiver coursed up Maggie's back. With the use of her full name, he'd resurrected the barriers between them. He had relegated the passionate lovemaking between them to the shadows of his life. Where Mary Margaret didn't belong.

Feigning nonchalance, she shrugged. "I didn't ask for anything from you."

His eyes turned a glacial blue. "I apologize for the way I snapped at you. Things didn't go at all well in town."

A surge of remorse flooded her. "What happened? Did Elliott cause trouble?"

"We'll tell you and Tillie everything when we go in. Aren't you the least bit curious about your gift?"

Warmth inched up her arm from his touch. "Your last gift was a pistol. I already have a rifle, so I can't imagine what you can give me." She wished her heart wasn't beating so fast. Surely he could see the pounding in her chest.

With a bare hint of a smile, he released her arm. "Wait here." In a few long strides he returned to the horse and retrieved a bundle tied to his saddle. His package was larger than the one Hank had carried. Maggie sat on the top porch step and tried unsuccessfully to suppress her natural curiosity. She hugged the shawl closer to her chest.

Sitting beside her, he set the package on her lap. "I hope you don't think it improper, but I purchased you another frock. It isn't elegant or worthy of a woman like you, but it's the best the mercantile had on hand."

She touched the printed calico fabric, the dress similar to the one she wore. What kind of gown did he expect for a woman like her? What kind of woman did he think she was? His fancy piece, of course. The woman who'd given herself freely out of love. A love that would never be returned.

"Thank you," she said in a tight voice. "I'll repay you when we reach Denver."

"I don't expect repayment. If it hadn't been for you, I wouldn't be here." He reached farther into the parcel. "That isn't your gift, however." Holding out a box tied with a piece of blue ribbon, he smiled. "This is."

Maggie's mouth dropped open. She blinked and stared at a box the size of his hand. A painting of pink roses decorated the slightly crushed box. She was sorely tempted to snatch it from him. Summoning her ladylike manners, she slowly reached for the gift.

Their fingers touched, and a spark kindled in her blood. No matter how hard she tried, Maggie couldn't control the sensations he evoked in her with a touch or a look. She lifted her head and detected the change in his eyes. Gone was the anger, replaced by something much more dangerous—desire, raw and hot.

For long succulent moments their gazes met and held. Maggie's chest tightened, and her breathing became shallow. Tension crackled between them like the air before a thunderstorm. She dropped her gaze to his lips, parted and inviting. All she had to do was lean forward and accept the kiss that waited inches away.

Time stood still as Maggie fought the battle within herself. *One kiss,* her inner self said, one kiss to quiet the storm raging within. What harm could one kiss do? Besides mark her as his forever.

He reached out and touched her arm. Though gentle, he inadvertently met one of the large bruises from her fall. An involuntary grunt came from her throat. His hand fell away.

"I'm sorry, Mary Margaret. I didn't mean to hurt you." He dropped the box in her lap and shifted away from her side.

Maggie felt the loss. Her heart sank, and a chill raced over her. She took a deep breath of the bracing autumn air. Somehow her heart started beating again.

She lifted her gaze to his. The fire was still there, banked and smoldering just beneath the surface.

"Open your gift," he whispered, his lips barely moving.

She'd almost forgotten the decorative box. Focusing her attention away from the man, she pulled on the ribbon and slipped it from the box. She lifted the lid and folded back a layer of white tissue paper. Nestled in the crushed paper was a row of dark, smooth chocolates.

"Where in the world . . . ?" Dumbfounded, she lifted her eyes.

"A drummer from Boston came by a few days ago and convinced the storekeeper to purchase a few boxes. I was lucky he had two left, one for you and one for Mrs. Hillcroft." With his thumb and forefinger, he picked one round bonbon from the box. "I know how much you love chocolates."

She offered a wide smile. He'd been with her the many times she passed the confectioners on Larimer Street and stopped in for a single, delicious treat. He'd called it

Maggie's one vice. But he was wrong. *He* was her greatest and most devastating vice.

Her gaze followed his hand as he lifted the sweet to her lips. She opened her mouth and accepted a bite of the candy. She swirled her tongue around the creamy, sweet treat and let it melt slowly down her throat.

Her eyes locked with his, she took the remainder of the confection from his fingers and carried it to his mouth. Like a hungry child, he opened for her offering. His teeth nipped the candy, and his lips closed on her fingers. Maggie felt the tugging of his mouth sucking gently. The stroke of his tongue sent wave after wave of sensation through her body. Her nipples stiffened, and a sweet heat settled deep in her femininity.

A powerful sweep of excitement rolled over her. There in broad daylight, with the children only a few feet away on the porch, the erotic feelings made her feel wicked, wanton. A flush sneaked up her neck. She tried to pull her hand away, but she didn't want to break the thin thread binding them together.

His gaze caressed her face while his hands remained innocently on the box. She watched his Adam's apple bob and knew he'd swallowed the candy. His teeth joined his tongue, nipping lightly at the two fingers as if they were some scrumptious delicacy given to him alone. A gust of wind cooled her heated skin.

"Would you like another?" Maggie whispered.

The fire in his eyes ignited to a roaring inferno. "Thank you, but I believe I've had all I can handle."

Reluctantly Maggie pulled back her fingers. She'd had more than she could handle also. Neither moved or spoke, each struggling to regain some semblance of composure for propriety's sake. Maggie was dangerously close to flinging herself into his arms and begging him to take her. And she could tell by the look in his eyes that he would not refuse.

"We had best go inside, Maggie." His raspy words were softly spoken. "You're much too bruised for what I would like."

Catching her fingers, he pulled her to her feet. "I'll never be too sore for that," she shot over her shoulder on her way to the door.

He grunted loudly, clearly having a difficult time controlling his arousal. A small wave of satisfaction bolstered Maggie's spirit. They may not get happily ever after, but the now was more than she'd ever dreamed she would have.

Chapter
Twenty-four

The rhythmic click-clack of the steel wheels droned on and on as the train raced through the Rocky Mountains. A week ago, Maggie had left Denver in the photographic wagon. Now she was going home on the Denver and Rio Grande Railroad.

She slanted a glance at Wex seated next to her. With his face covered by his Stetson, he looked like any ordinary cowboy asleep on the train. No one would suspect the man dressed in black was a wealthy British gentleman. But Maggie knew, and her heart beat out of control because his station in life diametrically opposed hers.

So much had happened in the past week. So much had changed. So much remained the same.

They had become lovers, and Maggie would never be the same. Would Sarah and Aunt Olivia suspect? She stuck her thumb in her mouth and troubled the nail. Their suspicions didn't matter; she knew, and so did he. Yet the situation between them had not changed. He planned to return to England and marry another woman, while Maggie would remain in the United States and become the most famous female photographer in the country. Her goals had been set long before His Highness had interfered with her life. Now, if only she could convince her heart.

She let her gaze skim across his wide chest encased in his

buckskin jacket, down his tight denim trousers. His long legs stretched out into the aisle, and the shiny Wellington boots were crossed at the ankles. The usual stirrings began in her chest and melted down to her most intimate parts.

Images flashed across her mind, thoughts of his beautiful body covering hers, loving her, her loving him. Thoughts a decent woman had no business entertaining. Things she had never imagined before he stole his way into her life and into her soul.

In less than three months he'd turned her world upside down. And only a miracle would right it again.

"Is something wrong, Mary Margaret?"

At the sound of his voice, she pulled her thumb from her lips. In the past month she'd bitten the one nail down to the quick. She jerked her gaze from his muscular legs to his face. With the slow deliberate movements of a panther on the prowl, he shoved the hat from his eyes. A conceited male smile curved his lips. He'd caught her staring at him like a child with her face pressed to the window of a toy store. She wanted everything she saw, but all was beyond her reach.

"Nothing's wrong now that we're safely on our way to Denver. Do you think Sheriff Steward was telling the truth? Are the outlaws who'd stolen Hank's cattle and tried to kill you dead?"

He shrugged. "Steward said he'd gotten a telegram from a sheriff in New Mexico that three men were killed during a bank robbery. One was identified as MacKenzie, the man who'd escaped from the doctor's office. Steward was certain the others were MacKenzie's accomplices. It's all over, Maggie, love." He covered her hand with his and squeezed gently.

"But you didn't get back your horse, and Sarah lost her medallion. And what about Cole Elliott? Surely he was involved in some way."

Anger flashed in his eyes and was gone as quickly as a bolt of lightning. "We would never be able to prove anything against him. Besides, his father owns Sherman, and nobody would dare cross Ross Elliott."

"Except you. Only a crazy Brit would try to buck a man like Elliott." Pride filled her heart to know and love a man who was willing to risk his life for others.

"I almost managed to get you killed." A frown tugged at his mouth as he lifted his gaze to the purple bruise on her forehead. "How are you feeling?"

"I told you a hundred times, I'm doing fine. The headache's gone, and the bruises are healing." She shifted on the hard wooden bench, striving for relief from the discomfort on her backside—not to mention the tingling between her thighs.

He'd been more than solicitous since the accident. Although she'd enjoyed his attention, he'd been treating her like a china doll, afraid she would break in pieces if held too tightly.

Maggie didn't want his sympathy or patronage. She wanted his love. The one thing far beyond her reach.

She'd hoped they would get to spend at least one night alone before they returned to Denver, but Wex and Hank made other plans. They had remained at the Double H ranch until early that morning when Hank had driven them to Sherman for the rest of their things and then to the station in Ross Elliott's elegant carriage. During the drive Hank and Wex had discussed the plans for the ranch while Maggie dozed in the rear seat.

Wex had left his stallion with Hank for stud, and Maggie had left her team for their use. Without the wagon, she had no use for the horses.

"Are you comfortable?" He reached over and tucked the blanket around her legs. She hadn't even noticed the chill draft in the passenger car. His fingers brushed her hip, and a new surge of heat roiled through her.

Retaining her composure was getting harder every minute. If only they'd had time to make love just once more before returning to Denver. Staying with the Hillcrofts had severely inhibited their time for any intimacy. And in Denver they would surely not have a moment's privacy. Struck with an idea, she lifted one end of the scratchy, gray wool blanket that had once been in the Elliott coach.

"If you're cold, you can crawl under here with me." She flashed him a smile that she hoped was at least a little seductive. "There's room for both of us."

Leaning closer, he whispered, "Thank you for the offer, Mary Margaret. Cuddling under a blanket with a beautiful woman has always been one of my favorite pastimes." His warm breath tickled her ear. "I'm afraid that if I take advantage of your offer, however, I'll end up embarrassing both of us by making love to you right here in this seat."

The husky timbre of his voice sent shivers of delight through her. She glanced at the other passengers in the crowded car. Miners with their gold, ranchers and their wives headed for Denver, and drummers with their samples in large suitcases filled the coach almost to capacity. In the seat across from her, a young mother nursed her baby, modestly covering herself with a large shawl. Her two young children jostled each other for space near the window.

The idea of making love in such an improper place sent a flutter of excitement across her chest. Her nipples stiffened and pressed against her dress. She hugged her cashmere shawl tighter to her traitorous body.

A sly smile sneaked across her mouth. "It would certainly be a shock to some of our fellow passengers, I'm sure."

She slanted a glance at the two elderly ladies seated a few benches behind them. Dressed in dark brown dresses, their ugly bonnets tied under their sagging chins in a huge bow, they sat as rigid as statues in the jerking, swaying train. Why, they would probably faint if they had an inkling of the conversation between Wex and Maggie.

Wex's hushed chuckle threw out more heat than the potbellied stove at the rear of the car. "It's a shame there weren't any private compartments available on this train."

Maggie turned her face to the window to hide her smile. Her imagination ran wild with the thought of making love with the swaying of the train adding to their enjoyment.

The train slowed as it neared a high trestle over a gorge. With a loud screech, the engine lurched, and Maggie tumbled sideways into Wex's lap. She gasped, and he wrapped his arm around her.

"Are you all right, Maggie?" he asked, a worried expression on his face.

She snuggled against him, reveling in his strength. Caught off guard, he'd called her Maggie. Her heart drummed into a loud staccato. "I think so."

His chin rested on her head as if he didn't want to let her

go. He still wanted her, she was sure of it. But leaving her
was his choice, and staying was hers.

Allowing the strength and warmth of his arm to comfort
her, she glanced out the window. They were chugging
slowly across the high bridge. Through the dirty, soot-
coated window she could see nothing but blue sky and white
clouds. She felt as if she were flying through the air in the
close train car.

At the end of the trestle the locomotive picked up speed,
spewing black smoke and ashes into the clean mountain air.
Wex nipped gently at her ear. "You can release your breath
now, love. We're back on solid ground."

She twisted to look at him and caught the smile on his
mouth. "I wasn't afraid. But it certainly was a strange
experience."

Tightening his hold, he pulled her closer. "I've been over
similar bridges in the Alps. I would love to show them to
you, Mary Margaret. From our own private compartment
we could look at the mighty snowcapped peaks and warm
each other with our love."

There it was again, his offer to make her his mistress.
Squeezing her eyes shut, she prayed for the strength to
refuse. When she opened her eyes, she eased out of his grip.
"I haven't changed my mind. I intend to stay in Denver and
operate my studio." Without his touch, all the warmth
seeped from her body.

"We'll discuss this later, when we're alone." With a curt
nod, he tugged the hat over his eyes and folded his arms
across his chest.

Maggie gnawed on her lower lip to bite back a snide
comment. There was nothing more to discuss. She'd made
up her mind, and no amount of talk would change it.

She braced her elbow on the ledge of the dirty window
and watched the passing scene. The train rumbled through a
valley, the mountain blocking out the sun. Tall pines
perched on steep hillsides, interspersed with splashes of red
and orange of the aspens adorned in their autumn garb.
Around tight curves and up steep grades, the locomotive
lumbered along, belching black smoke like an angry dragon.

When the scream of the whistle tore through the air, she
shrugged deeper into her shawl. They were nearing another

town, another delay while the fireman loaded more coal and water to provide the steam power for the hungry fire-eating monster.

High above the town, tiny cabins perched on the hillside, cabins like the deserted shack where she and Wex had sought shelter during the storm—the place they'd first made love. Her limbs grew weak at the memory of being held in his arms, feeling the warmth of him, and the glory of becoming one with him.

The loud screech of the brakes pulled her out of her reverie. A uniformed conductor began his slow tour through the crowded car. "Castle Rock—thirty-minute stop."

She felt the movement at her side. Wex straightened and glanced at her. "Would you like to get off for a few minutes, Mary Margaret? We can get something to eat and drink."

Glancing out the window, she spotted the station and the few dingy buildings lining the muddy street. Above them a huge rock, like a stone fortress, stood guard over the valley. Snow flurries whipped by the wind flew in swirling circles. "I don't think so. It looks too cold."

As the train lurched to a stop Wex stood. "I'll bring you something." He buttoned his coat and rested his hand on the Colt at his hip.

Most of the men left the train and headed into the restaurant or to the next building, a saloon, where painted women peeked from the batwing doors. The lady across from Maggie had finally gotten the children settled down, and she and her husband were talking quietly.

From the corner of her eye, Maggie studied them. They appeared to be younger than Maggie, yet it was clear that they were very much in love. The children were clean and neatly dressed, and the father cradled the little girl in his arms.

Maggie swallowed the melancholy that stole over her. She loved Wex so much that she doubted she would ever be able to get over him and marry another man. Like her aunt, Maggie had relegated herself to the life of a spinster.

With most of the passengers gone from the car, the noise level had dropped to the deep rumble of the stationary engine. A few seats away, a miner slept, his lower jaw hanging open and an occasional snort erupting from his throat.

A movement in the aisle drew Maggie's attention. Thinking it was Wex, she shifted toward the window to give him room.

"What's a pretty lady like you doing alone?"

Startled at the strange voice, she swung her gaze to a man who was old enough to be her father. His black hair was slicked down with grease, and he held a fat cigar clamped between his yellow teeth. Close-set pale gray eyes slid over her, lingering in the vicinity of her breasts. Maggie shivered, as if he could see through her layers of clothing.

"I'm not alone," she said, turning her gaze back to the window to discourage the man.

Not easily dissuaded, the stranger sat down beside her. "Not anymore, you aren't."

She shot him a haughty look, as cold as the wind on top of Pikes Peak. "I did not invite you to join me."

He laughed, a high-pitched, abrasive sound. "No need to be shy, little lady. Name's Block, Jonas Block." With an exaggerated flourish, he tipped his dusty black bowler hat. "Barbed wire's my game." The drummer's black coat and plaid trousers, once the latest fashion in the East, were years out of style.

Under his close scrutiny, she grew uneasy. Short of being rude, Maggie had no idea how to get rid of him.

"And what can I call you, sweetheart?"

"You will call her gone." The deep voice was soft, but as dangerous as the rattle of a diamondback snake. Wex caught the man by the front of his shirt and with one hand lifted him from the seat.

Jonas Block's florid face turned deathly pale. His eyes bulged in fear. He made a choking sound, his lips forming unspoken words. His cigar tumbled from his mouth, leaving a row of ashes down the front of his coat.

"Wex . . ." Maggie gasped his name. Cold fury glistened in his steely eyes. Murder was written in his expression. "He didn't do anything. Let him go." She stood and gripped Wex's arm. The muscles were taut and unyielding. The blanket fell to her feet, unheeded on the dirty floor.

For a long breathless moment Wex stared at the man. His

jaw tightened and a muscle twitched. The civilized nobleman became the primitive savage.

"The lady is with me. Do you understand?" He lifted the
man until his feet left the floor. "Never come near her
again." As easily as tossing a rag doll, he shoved the man
halfway down the aisle, where he landed on his rear, his hat
at his feet.

For a long moment no one dared move or speak. Wex
glared at the drummer, and Maggie glared at Wex. Finally
the voice of the conductor broke the unnatural silence. "All
aboard," he shouted.

At once the noise level of the coach escalated. The baby
across the aisle began to cry, and the rumble of the steam
locomotive covered the anxious voices. Several other traveling salesmen helped Block to his feet. He shot an angry
glance at Wex and Maggie, then retreated to a seat near the
rear of the coach.

Maggie grabbed Wex's sleeve and pulled him into the
seat next to her. Now that the excitement was over, she was
able to think again. "You didn't have to be so rough with
him," she said. "He was just a harmless pest."

His eyes narrowed on her, the chill enough to freeze ice
cream on the Fourth of July. "Mary Margaret, a rat is a pest.
But no one is sure how many kinds of illness he may carry."

"What if he'd had a gun? Or one of his friends?"

He flashed her a crooked smile that didn't quite reach his
eyes. "I trust you have the derringer. You've saved my life
so many times, I suppose I'm getting accustomed to having
you rescue *me*."

The train took off and jerked her back in the seat. She
picked up the blanket from the floor and hugged it to her
chest. "Remember, Lord Geoffrey," she said, putting every
bit of the sarcasm she possessed into the words, "even a cat
has only nine lives. According to my calculations, you're
quickly running out of yours."

Wex thought on her words for a moment. "Then I had
better preserve the few I have remaining."

He flexed his fingers to loosen the tension. He'd literally
seen red when he'd entered the car and spotted the man
sidling up to Maggie. If a simple flirtation infuriated him so,
how was he going to cope with the possibility of her finding

another man when he left for England? The idea of another man making love to her left his insides shaking. He refused to think of her bearing some man's child. Dammit all, Mary Margaret Callahan belonged to him. How was he ever going to leave her? The quicksand he'd stepped into was slowly sucking him deeper. He saw no way out.

Turning, he found her studying him, concern darkening her green eyes to jade. He covered her hand and was surprised to feel her trembling. Squeezing gently, he moved closer to whisper, "I'm sorry I distressed you, Mary Margaret. Sometimes I act before thinking."

She jerked her fingers from his. "You're so damned impulsive. One day you're going to get yourself killed."

His shoulder pressed to hers, he inhaled the sweet, clean fragrance of her hair. The car was stuffy and crowded, filled with odors of unwashed bodies and different types of food. Yet, next to Maggie, he imagined himself in the middle of a meadow filled with spring flowers.

"That's why I need you, Mary Margaret, to keep me out of trouble and to have your marksmanship handy."

A pained expression colored her features. "Lord Geoffrey," she said, "I told you . . ."

Certain he'd lost another battle, he shifted away from her. A lonely chill raced up his spine. The barriers were again in place, separating them for all time. Agony sliced through his chest.

A hand tugged on his sleeve. He spun toward the aisle, expecting trouble. A towheaded boy stood beside him, a straw basket in his hands. "Mister, did you drop your basket?"

Wex sagged with relief. He didn't want any more trouble. "Thank you, I believe I did." In his anger, he'd forgotten the lunch he'd carried back for Maggie and himself.

He took the basket and rewarded the boy with a coin from his pocket. As he pulled out the money a folded piece of paper fluttered to the floor.

"What is that?" Maggie asked. "It looks like a telegram."

"It's nothing." Bending over, he retrieved the paper and started to shove it into his shirt pocket.

She lifted one eyebrow and snatched it from his hand. "It's from Mr. Appleton." The color drained from her face as she read the message. "It says he's booked passage for England in two weeks. I didn't think you were leaving so soon." Carefully she folded the telegram and gave it back to him.

The pain was there, in her eyes and in her voice. Wex felt like the worst of scoundrels for hurting her. He should never have made love to her, never seduced her. Becoming lovers had changed everything for both of them. But in spite of all his self-castigation, he wouldn't change a moment of what they'd shared.

"Appleton wants to cross the Atlantic before the winter gets severe."

"I see. And, of course, Madam Grace is waiting for her bridegroom."

He bit his lip against the anguish he'd caused her as well as himself. "I'm sorry, Mary Margaret, truly I am."

"There's no need for regret. As the proverb says, 'As you make your bed, so you must lie on it.'"

"It will be no bed of roses, I'm quite certain."

She shrugged. "Is that my dinner?" Picking up the basket, she set it on her lap. "I'm rather hungry."

With nothing more to say, he shoved the telegram into his pocket. Defeat swept over him. He was helplessly caught in a trap of his own making.

The chugging of the train grew louder as it picked up speed. In a few hours they would reach Denver. Counting the time it would take to reach New York, he and Appleton would have to leave almost immediately. The only woman he'd ever loved would be lost to him forever.

A black cloud hung over him. The rest of his life loomed ahead of him like a long dark tunnel. Without Maggie's sunshine, he was doomed to an existence devoid of love and empty of contentment.

There had to be a way out of this mess. Surely he and Appleton were intelligent men, able to come up with something.

His mind studying on the situation, he took a chicken leg from the basket and bit into it.

The hansom cab pulled to a stop in front of the building on Larimer Street. As eager as Maggie had been to reach

Denver, now that they had arrived, she wished she'd had more time alone with Wex.

They'd spoken little since leaving Castle Rock, with nothing to say that wouldn't start an argument. Wex appeared as distressed as she at their imminent separation.

Helped by Wex's hand, she stepped to the wooden boardwalk that fronted the building. The shingle above the door swayed back and forth in the rising wind. She was certain it would snow again by morning. But this time she would have only her feather bed and down quilt to keep her warm.

Maggie opened the front door for Wex. He carried his carpetbag, the rifle, and her camera that had been safely in the hotel room when the wagon had been destroyed.

She glanced at the windows and saw only a few dim lamps in the second-floor bedrooms—Tim and Sarah's bedrooms. Entering the central hallway, they set the burdens on the floor. Maggie looked at Wex. If possible, he looked more distressed than she.

"I suppose I had better get to the Windsor. Appleton should be waiting for me."

Maggie nodded, but remained rooted to the spot. "I wonder if anyone's home." With a glance toward the parlor, she spotted the pale glow of a lamp. She moved toward the doorway and heard the soft murmur of voices.

Entering the parlor, she stopped to adjust her eyes to the semidarkness. Someone was on the brocade couch; no, on closer inspection she spotted two people.

Maggie's eyes widened in shock. Would wonders never cease? The pair was entwined in an intimate embrace, the woman sprawled across the man's lap, her lips locked on his.

"Mr. Appleton!" Maggie forced the smile from her voice. "What do you mean, compromising my aunt's reputation?"

Chapter
Twenty-five

Turnabout is fair play, thought Maggie as the older couple jerked apart. Time they got a taste of their own medicine. She remembered too well when they had caught her and Wex in a similar position, and her aunt had announced that the guilty couple had to marry.

At her side, Wex folded his arms across his chest, but was unable to cover the amusement on his face. "Jeremy, what is the meaning of this unseemly behavior?"

A bright pink flush crept slowly over Appleton's face, from his stiff white collar to the receding line of his gray-streaked brown hair. The man looked more like an untried schoolboy than a pompous English solicitor.

"Lord Geoffrey," he sputtered. He jumped to his feet and almost tumbled Olivia onto the floor. Realizing his mistake, he reached out and steadied her on her feet. "We weren't expecting you."

Maggie tapped her foot on the Oriental rug and bit the inside of her cheek to hold back her laughter. After the emotional turmoil of the past week, the humor of the situation came as a welcome relief. "I'll arrange the marriage as soon as possible."

Olivia laughed softly, the gentle twitter of a refined woman. In spite of the crimson on her cheeks, she retained her composure. "Don't be concerned, Mr. Appleton. My niece has a bizarre sense of humor." She patted Jeremy's jaw. "I'm old enough to make my own decisions."

As casually as if welcoming guests for tea, she smiled. "My dears, it's good to have you home. We've been frantic with worry."

Without a wrinkle in her lavender silk gown or a lock of her light brown hair out of place, Olivia opened her arms, inviting Maggie's embrace. Maggie's admiration for her aunt grew by leaps and bounds. Not even being caught in a compromising position rattled the refined woman.

"I see." Maggie accepted her aunt's embrace, but she wasn't ready to drop the subject. "And was Mr. Appleton offering you his consolation?"

Maggie's gaze shifted to the solicitor. At least he had the good sense to look embarrassed. He rushed forward with his hand outstretched to Wex.

Wex took the offered hand and slapped the older man on the shoulder. "Congratulations, Jeremy. I didn't know you had it in you."

Jeremy's face turned as red as a rooster's comb. His warm brown eyes shifted to Olivia. "Miss Stanton has been quite distraught since you disappeared."

"I'm sure she has," Maggie said. She studied her aunt for a moment. Olivia's pale blue gaze locked with Jeremy's. Something was happening between the pair. The adversaries of a week ago had turned into more than friends. Maggie wondered what would have occurred if she and Wex hadn't chosen that moment to return.

Before she had time to consider the depths of her aunt and Appleton's relationship, footsteps clattered on the stairs. Sarah and Tim burst through the doorway. "Maggie— Wex," they shouted in one voice. Ignoring formalities, they flung themselves first at Maggie, then at Wex.

Maggie draped her arm across her sister's shoulder. "Did you miss me?"

Sarah laughed. "Of course. We missed you telling us what to do, bossing us around, and generally being a pest. Aunt Olivia was worried about you, but I knew you would be all right as long as Wex—I mean, Lord Geoffrey was there to look after you."

A deep chuckle came from Wex's direction. "You had

better revise your opinion, Sarah. Your sister only saved my life twice."

Tim's eyes widened. "She did? What happened?"

Maggie shrugged off her shawl. "Let's get some tea, and we'll tell you all about our adventures—or misadventures, as they may be."

Her gaze shifted to Wex, tall and handsome in the pale light. Well, not *all,* she added to herself. Some things were too precious to share.

After the excitement of the past few days, Maggie welcomed the routine of her work. After all, she'd come to Denver to set up the photographic gallery, not to have a love affair. Her heart beat double time at the memory of Wex and what they had shared. But she was pragmatic enough to realize it couldn't last. Too soon he would be on his way to England—without her.

In the week that she'd been gone, Olivia had booked a number of sittings. She was certain that Miranda and Harry had been partially responsible for the interest in the new studio. For that she was grateful.

While Olivia greeted the clients in the reception room downstairs, Maggie posed the subjects and operated the camera. She rubbed her aching back, wishing she'd hired an assistant. Actually Wex was the only helper she wanted.

"Maggie, this is Mr. and Mrs. Roberts," Olivia called from the doorway of the studio. "They would like a portrait to send back east to their parents."

With a smile Maggie turned to the young couple, the woman obviously expecting a baby. Maggie stretched out her hand. "Welcome. I'm sure we can get something of which you'll all be proud."

Olivia whispered on her way out, "Your last sitting for the day."

Glad to see the end of a hard morning's work, Maggie smiled. At last she was on the way to achieving her goal. If business kept up at this pace, her name would be known all over the city.

Maggie ushered the couple to a straight-backed chair. The woman was seated with the man standing at her side. Wishing for an assistant, Maggie pulled out several scenic panels, looking for the proper one for the photograph's background.

"I like the one of the mountains," Mr. Roberts said. "Reminds me of where I made my strike. Want my folks to see what Colorado looks like."

"We'll try it. Then how about this one of the meadow with the flowers? It makes a very attractive portrait." Maggie tugged at the canvas painting, thinking how false and flat the scene looked, not at all like the Rockies she loved. Yet the Robertses were paying customers, and if they were pleased, they would bring their friends to Callahan's for their own portraits, not to mention pictures of the baby when it came.

When everything was in position, Maggie loaded the glass plate into the camera. Only then did she actually pose the couple. The young man placed his hand on his wife's shoulder, and wearing a solemn expression, he glared at the camera.

"It's all right to smile, Mr. Roberts. Simply take a deep breath, and when I tell you ready, both of you think about the baby you'll soon be holding in your arms."

Mr. Roberts's expression softened, and his wife flashed a broad grin. While she had their attention Maggie pressed the spring release on the shutter and counted the seconds. After a few more exposures, the couple relaxed, and Maggie was certain they would be pleased with their pictures. She promised to have copies for them in a few days.

Finally alone in the studio, Maggie entered the darkroom to develop the negatives she'd made during the morning. Although she was tired, she welcomed the diversion from her other problems. Yet everything she did reminded her of the days Wex had worked at her side.

He and Jeremy had left very late the previous evening, and Maggie remembered the sleepless night she'd spent thinking about the man she loved. Common sense warred with her emotions until she questioned her decisions.

Jeremy had made it clear that he and Wex would have to leave within the week to meet their ship in New York. When he'd mentioned leaving, a strange expression had crossed her aunt's face. Maggie suspected there would be two lonely females left behind when the Englishmen crossed the Atlantic.

With the back of her hand, she wiped the drop of moisture from her eyes. It couldn't be tears, she told herself. The acidic fumes of the chemicals always made her eyes water.

Using the techniques her father had taught her, Maggie carefully set the glass plates in the trays, each filled with a different mixture to bring out the image of the subjects. Under the yellow safe light, she watched the light and shadows come into view. At the last stage, she opened the door of the darkroom for a welcome breath of fresh air.

"These are very good, Mary Margaret." The unexpected voice came from over her right shoulder. Lost in her thoughts, she'd neither seen nor heard Wex approach.

The tongs slipped from her fingers. Reaching around her, Wex retrieved the instrument from the large tray.

Maggie took a deep breath to control her emotions. He moved behind her, his wide chest pressed to her back. His closeness rekindled the fires she'd spent the better part of a day trying to bank. She dropped her gaze to his hands as he shifted the glass plate back and forth in the solution. Breathing became difficult as Maggie remembered the feel of those strong hands on her bare flesh. Not one inch of her body had escaped his sensuous exploration. Her nipples hardened, and her knees weakened.

"Your clients should be very pleased with your work," he said, his lips close to her ears.

"Thank you." She whispered the words through the tightening in her throat. Powerless to resist, Maggie allowed herself the pleasure of his presence. His subdued male scent filled her with a longing she couldn't deny. Pressed against the tabletop, she relaxed against his strength.

Wex grazed his freshly shaved jaw across her cheek. "You are a true artist, Maggie."

Her heart pounded out of control at the sound of her name on his lips. It was the same tone he'd used when they had made love in the darkness of the night, when she'd given herself completely and without reserve.

At the touch of his lips to her ear, she gasped. All thought deserted her in the wake of his touch. Needs surged through her, making her want to throw caution to the wind. "Wex, please don't."

He dropped the tongs onto the table and circled her with his arms. His hands rested below her breasts. "Why, love? This is the first moment we've had alone in more than a week." While brushing tiny kisses down her neck, he stroked his thumbs across her nipples, teasing them into tight buds.

She clutched the edge of the table to keep from sagging to the floor. Sensations fluttered in her stomach like the attack of a thousand butterflies. "We aren't alone. My aunt is downstairs."

Somehow he managed to loosen the tiny buttons on the front of her gown. "Appleton will keep her busy for a time. He asked to be alone with her." Wex nuzzled the stiff lace collar aside with his chin. His abrasive jaw brought sensuous delights to her delicate skin.

"Oh," Maggie managed on a long sigh. His fingertips burned a path across the tops of her breasts. The inside of the darkroom grew steamy.

He grazed his damp tongue along her nape. The exquisite feeling was pure heaven. "Appleton wants to take her to England with him."

Maggie stilled at his revelation. "As his mistress?" she asked in a husky gasp.

"I believe as his wife." His hands grew bolder, slipping inside her chemise to caress her breasts. "It will be perfect for all of us. You'll have no excuse not to come to England with her."

Tears burned behind her eyes. Appleton was willing to marry Olivia, but all Wex wanted of Maggie was a mistress. She caught his wrists and shoved his hands aside. "No." The sound formed around the lump in her throat. "I can't, I won't."

He caught her shoulders and spun her to face him. "I love you, Maggie. I've never felt like this before. After my twin died, I felt as if half my heart was dead. Since I met you, I've become whole again. I need you with me."

Shocked by his unexpected confession, she opened her mouth, but nothing came out. Her heart lodged in her throat.

The words she'd been longing to hear brought only a new surge of sadness.

"I want you to come to England with me. I know you care for me. You wouldn't have made love with so much fire and passion if you didn't."

Unable to deny the truth, Maggie nodded. "I do love you, Wex. But my feelings don't matter. Too much is standing in our way. What about your marriage? You're pledged to another."

Silver flecks glittered in his blue eyes. Moisture glistened behind the black lashes. "I don't love some woman I've never met. I love *you*. I need *you*. We can work something out, I'm sure of it."

Afraid of her own emotions, she shook off his hands. "No, Wex. You have obligations to your family, and I have responsibilities to mine. I won't be a rich man's fancy piece. I want more than that. I deserve more than that."

For a long moment he gazed at her. The pale glow from the tiny gas flame glittered in his eyes. He drew his dark brows together. "You're right, Mary Margaret. You deserve far more than I'm able to give you." With a slump to his wide shoulders, he turned on his heel and left the room.

Maggie bit her lip to keep from calling him back. *Yes, I'll go with you to the ends of the earth* formed in her heart, but the words died before they reached her mouth. She loved him too much to settle for a small part of his life. And if he loved her half as much as she loved him, he would understand and not ask her to do something that was totally against her morals and upbringing.

"When are you leaving?" she asked as she walked from the darkroom.

He shoved both hands through his thick black hair. "In a day or two. The sooner I leave, the better off we will both be."

"Wex." She took one step toward him and caught herself before she ran into his arms. "I . . . I hope you'll be happy."

He let out a bark of derisive laughter. His eyes slid slowly up and down her, touching like a hot poker. Heat surged through Maggie. Her bodice was still open, leaving the dusky nipples visible under the thin undergarment. She made no effort to cover herself.

"Happiness was never a consideration with my father, Maggie. I can't be happy without you. I have to accept the responsibility that's been thrust upon me." His mouth thinned to a narrow line. "But I'm afraid I haven't been very responsible with you. I hadn't considered you could even now be carrying my child."

Maggie's legs threatened to buckle under her. She'd thought of little else in the past week. "No need to concern yourself on my account. I started my monthly—there is no child." As she locked her gaze on him she prayed the lie wouldn't show in her eyes. She was late, but she'd been late before. Two nights together couldn't possibly produce a child.

No relief shone on his face. Sadness darkened his eyes. Shoving a hand into his coat pocket, he retrieved an envelope and held it toward her. "I have other news for you. I received word from my agent. He sold all your negatives, and the publisher is asking for more of your work."

Stunned, Maggie opened the envelope and studied the bank draft. "I can't believe it."

"I can. You're very talented. It looks as if you've gotten what you wanted. The photographs are attributed to Mary Margaret Callahan."

Without another word he opened the door and disappeared from her sight and out of her life.

Her legs too weak to hold her, Maggie slumped onto the settee. She crumbled the bank draft and the letter in her fist. His last words echoed in her ears. *He* was what she wanted. *He* was what she needed. She'd reached her goal, but lost the one man who would make it all worth having. She buried her face in her hands and let the tears flow.

An hour later Olivia found her gazing unseeing at the letter in her hand. The success she'd worked so hard to achieve faded in the face of losing the man she loved. The crying had long since ceased, but the pain in Maggie's heart was beyond healing.

She sat up and buttoned her gown, not wanting her aunt to know her distress. "Has Mr. Appleton gone?" she asked.

Olivia sat beside her, her own eyes misty and red-rimmed. "Yes. He asked me to marry him."

"What did you answer?"

On a long sigh, Olivia slumped like a sail on a calm sea. Maggie had never seen her aunt look so defeated. "I told him no."

Maggie covered her aunt's hands with her own. "You don't love him?"

A wry smile curved the older woman's lips. "I'm not sure of my feelings. But I am sure that I can't leave my home, my business, and my family."

How familiar the words sounded. Only Appleton's intentions were much more honorable than Wex's. "But if you love him . . ."

Olivia patted Maggie's hands. "Maggie, I'm forty-five years old, and if you repeat my age, I'll never speak to you again. I've run my own life for too many years to turn the reins over to a man. Besides, I have many responsibilities in St. Louis."

The weight of obligation weighed heavily on Olivia. "You mean the bank?" Maggie removed her hands and slid her arm along the low back of the settee.

"The bank . . . and other things." Olivia ran a long delicate finger along a gray stripe on her skirt.

"What other things? You don't have to worry about me, or Tim or Sarah. We're doing fine."

Olivia's pale eyes locked on Maggie. "Have you spoken to Tim and Sarah about their schools?"

"I enrolled them in the finest schools in Denver. They're doing very well."

"Academically, yes. But I'm afraid neither Tim nor Sarah is happy."

Her words took Maggie by surprise. "They never mentioned it to me."

"They didn't want to upset you, since you are so determined to make Denver your home. I overheard them talking. Tim has been labeled a half-breed by the other boys, and the 'refined' young ladies at the academy snub Sarah."

A band tightened around Maggie's chest. She'd been so involved with Wex and her own needs that she hadn't known the pain her siblings were suffering. "Because they're Indian?"

"There's a great deal of prejudice against the Indians." Olivia brushed a stray tendril of hair from Maggie's cheek. "I think it would be best if all of you return to St. Louis with me. You can reopen the studio, and Tim and Sarah can return to school. We'll be together as a family."

Maggie stood and paced to the far end of the studio. Above her the sun streaked through the glass skylight. From the third-floor window she viewed the Rockies proudly displaying their winter garb like a woman draped in ermine. She loved the mountains, and returning to the confines of St. Louis held little appeal. And she was just now making a name for herself as a landscape photographer. Torn between her love for her siblings and her own needs, Maggie felt her stomach tie into knots.

"Are you sure it's what you want, Aunt Olivia? You won't reconsider Mr. Appleton's proposal?"

"He understands I can't leave everything and follow him to England. We'll communicate by letter, and perhaps sometime in the future . . ."

The future . . . The future that loomed so bleak for Maggie held a glimmer of hope for Olivia. "When are you planning to return to St. Louis?"

"In a few weeks. I'll give you time to close up the gallery, and then we can go home."

Her aunt spoke as if the decision had been made. "I'm not sure I want to go back to St. Louis." She handed the agent's letter to Olivia. "They want more pictures. Maybe I'll go further west, to San Francisco." She'd fallen in love with Wex in Colorado. A change of scenery would do her good. "We'll let Tim and Sarah make their own decision."

Olivia rose and came to stand behind Maggie. "You love him, don't you?" Without mentioning the name, Maggie knew exactly who she meant.

Never able to lie to her aunt, Maggie nodded. "Yes, and he claims he loves me, but there's no place for me in his life. He's planning to marry another woman."

Olivia slipped her arm around her niece's waist. "Appleton explained the situation to me. Wex is caught in something not of his making, and he doesn't know how to get out."

"I understand, but I don't have to like it."

"You're young, Maggie. You'll meet someone else."

Maggie smiled. She didn't want someone else. "Time and distance, that's what I need. I'll talk to Tim and Sarah when they come home."

Olivia glanced at the watch pinned to the lapel of her suit jacket. "By the way, our two Englishmen want to take us to dinner. Get yourself all prettied up, and let's show them what they'll be missing."

"I think not. I want to work on the portraits. You go on, and take Tim and Sarah with you."

With a shake of her head, Olivia moved to the door. "I'll make excuses. But if you change your mind, we'll be at the Windsor."

"Thank you, Aunt Olivia. Thank you for everything."

Wex waited on the crowded platform at the Denver Pacific depot, impatience growing with every passing minute. He pulled his watch from his vest pocket. For a brief second he studied the picture in the lid. He'd lost his brother, and now he was losing the woman he loved. His heart ached as if a knife had been plunged in and twisted.

According to the gold timepiece, the train was scheduled to leave in half an hour. They should be boarding, yet Appleton hadn't arrived. Where the hell was the man? he wondered, snapping the cover and shoving the watch back into his pocket.

While Wex had brought the luggage to the station, the solicitor had gone to the studio to pick up Olivia. Of all the things he'd never expected, Jeremy had fallen in love with Maggie's aunt.

And like him, Appleton was leaving his heart behind.

As each hansom cab drew to a stop Wex studied the passengers. Finally his vigilance was rewarded when Appleton stepped to the wooden platform. Wex's heart began to pound. He hoped—no, he prayed—Maggie had come to see him off. He needed one last glimpse of her to last the rest of his life.

He hadn't seen her in the past few days. She'd steadfastly

refused the dinner invitations, and Wex had too much pride to chase her down.

Appleton reached into the coach and helped a lady to the ground—Olivia. Holding his breath, he waited while she shook out her skirts and Appleton held out his hand for the next occupant. Sarah appeared, then Tim.

When the driver slammed the door shut, Wex's spirits sagged. Maggie had chosen not to come. His last memory would be of her in the studio, disheveled from his attempted lovemaking and her eyes shining with moisture. He'd hurt her, but he, too, was in pain. Falling in love had been the last thing on his mind when he'd come to Colorado. Now it was the only thing he could think of.

He folded the memory of that love into a tiny corner of his heart to cherish for all time.

Shaking off his melancholy, he moved forward, his hands outstretched. Sarah ran into his arms and kissed his cheek.

"Wex, I'm going to miss you terribly."

Both Tim and Sarah had become precious to him, as special as if they were his own flesh and blood. His heart lurched. "I'm going to miss you, too, love."

"Me, too, Wex." Squaring his slender shoulders, his dark eyes serious beyond his years, Tim stuck out his hand.

One arm around Sarah's shoulders, Wex caught the boy's palm in his. "You're going to grow into a fine man, Tim."

After shaking hands, Tim shoved his fingers back into his pockets and shifted from foot to foot. "Maggie said I should thank you for giving Starlight to me. I promise I'm going to take good care of my horse, even when we go back to St. Louis."

The revelation of their returning to St. Louis caught Wex by surprise. "Is Maggie going to open another studio?"

A frown tugged the youngster's mouth. "She's not going with us. We're going to live with Aunt Olivia. Maggie's going to California."

Wex felt as if he'd been kicked in the stomach. Not only would they have an ocean separating them, but an entire continent to boot. "Where in California?"

Sarah spoke up. "San Francisco. But next summer she may go to Alaska."

"I don't know why she don't want me to go with her,"

Tim said. "Since she can't have you, she needs me as her assistant."

Wex swallowed the lump in his throat. "I'm sure Mary Margaret will be fine."

"Tim . . ." Olivia's voice rang out over the din of the crowd. "Come tell Mr. Appleton good-bye. You, too, Sarah."

"Just a minute, Sarah," Wex said. "I have something for your sister." He pulled his gold watch from his pocket and unhooked the heavy chain from the buttonhole. With one last look at the picture in the lid, he pressed it into Sarah's palm.

The girl's eyes widened. "Your watch. But it has your brother's picture."

Gently he folded her fingers over the timepiece. "Tell Maggie I want her to have this to remember me by."

"Oh, Wex," Sarah said, a tear trickling down her cheek. "She'll cherish it always. And I'll never take off the cross you gave me." Standing on tiptoe, she kissed him again.

Emotion threatened to choke him. He glanced at Appleton and Olivia and found them staring awkwardly at each other. The lonesome whistle of the train pulled them out of their stupor. For the next few minutes he continued the farewells, then moved toward the train.

The conductor shouted, "All aboard," as Wex climbed up to the rear platform. He waved to Olivia, Sarah, and Tim. As the train pulled from the station he caught a glimpse of a familiar figure hiding behind a post—Maggie.

It took every bit of his willpower not to jump from the moving coach and sweep her up in his arms. But he had no right. As she'd said, he'd made his bed, and now he must sleep in it.

But he knew it would be a long, lonely night.

Maggie closed the book and set it aside. She'd tried but couldn't concentrate on the story. Since that afternoon when she'd watched the train pull away with Wex standing on the rear platform, she hadn't been able to think of anything except him.

She'd known men couldn't be trusted—she'd known Wex wouldn't stay. So why was she so upset with him? It was her own fault that she'd ignored all the warning signs and fallen in love.

How could she blame Wex? He'd never made any promises. From the start she'd known his intentions were less than honorable. Even if he loved her as he said, he had nothing to offer but an affair.

Telling herself all this didn't change a thing. Maggie loved Wex, and no amount of self-castigation could change it.

Although she hadn't planned to go to the depot, she'd found herself wanting one last look at the man who was taking her heart away to England. He'd looked so lonely, standing on the rear of the train, his black hair catching the wind. She'd barely managed to keep from running after him and begging him to take her with him. But the man in the elegant dark suit was Lord Geoffrey. He'd left Wex somewhere in the mountains, never to be found again.

Alone in her room, she began to open the row of buttons on the front of her gingham dress. A soft knock on the door stopped her progress. "Come in," she called.

Sarah stuck her head around the partially open door. "May I talk to you for a minute, Maggie?"

"Certainly, sweetie. I could use the company." Maggie sat on the bed and patted a place for her sister. "I'm going to miss our girl-to-girl talks when I go to California."

"I wish you would come home with us. We're a family." Tears misted in Sarah's eyes.

Touched by the poignant sound of Sarah's voice, Maggie wrapped her arms around her sister and hugged her close. "We'll still be a family. And after this school term, you and Tim can come visit me in San Francisco. We'll go into the mountains and take more photographs for the publisher. Then maybe I'll go back to St. Louis with you."

"I hope so." She was quiet for a moment, then she dug into the pocket of her apron. "Maggie, Wex asked me to give you something."

Her heart beating like a kettledrum at the mere mention of his name, Maggie looked at her sister in surprise. Sarah pulled her hand out and opened her palm. Maggie couldn't believe her eyes. "It's his watch," she said. "His most prized possession."

Holding the watch by the gold fob, Sarah dangled it in front of Maggie. "He wants you to remember him."

"I'll never forget him." A single tear slipped from her eye. Her fingers tangled with Sarah's as she reached for the watch. She couldn't imagine Wex parting with the watch that meant so much to him.

Sarah tightened her fingers on Maggie's hand. Her eyes darkened, and a strange expression crossed her face. "Maggie," she moaned.

"Sarah, what's wrong?"

"I'm not sure. I had the strangest feeling about you and . . ." She paused. "You and Wex."

"What about us?" Maggie bit her lip, afraid of what her sister had sensed. Sarah's premonitions were rarely wrong.

"Please don't think I'm prying, but did you and Wex become lovers while you were gone?"

Not waiting for a reply, Sarah covered Maggie's stomach with her hand. "You're going to have his baby. No . . ." A look of wonder crossed her face. "Maggie, you're going to have twins."

Chapter
Twenty-six

Two weeks later Maggie had reason to believe Sarah's prediction. At least the part about having a child. Twins were also a possibility since the father was himself a twin.

Maggie stood in the center of the empty studio and looked toward the mountains. The sight of the Rockies in their winter garb sent a chill of longing to her heart. She stuffed her hands into the pockets of her velvet cloak. In one pocket she carried the derringer, and in the other her fingers closed on the gold watch. Both were gifts from the man she loved.

As was the child she carried.

"Maggie." Sarah entered slowly, her handkerchief twisted in her fingers ready for more of the tears she'd shed since she and Tim decided to go to St. Louis instead of going to San Francisco with Maggie. "The cab is here."

"I'm ready," she answered. Earlier the baggage wagon had picked up her trunks, cameras, and studio equipment. All that remained was her small valise holding the necessities for the train trip.

"I wish you would let me go with you." Sarah slipped her arm through Maggie's. "You'll need me, especially when . . . you know."

"If you're going to be a doctor, you need to finish school and get into college. I promise I'll write every day, and if I really am"—she swallowed to get the word out around the egg-sized lump in her throat—"expecting, I'll join you in St. Louis long before the baby comes."

"*Babies*. I know it's twins." Sarah was so sure that Maggie was beginning to believe it, too.

"Please don't dare tell Aunt Olivia. Not yet. I'll tell her when it's time."

"I promise. But what about Wex? Shouldn't he know?"

Maggie stopped and squeezed her eyes shut. When she opened them, she let out a long sigh. "He's getting married, and there's no reason he should know." Besides, she didn't want to go to him like this. It was too much like begging.

A tiny smile teased at Sarah's mouth, and her eyes darkened to jade. "I wouldn't make any bets on that, Mary Margaret. You never know what could happen."

Maggie eyed her sister with suspicion. "Sarah, have you seen something you haven't told me about?"

Sarah waved her hand in dismissal. "Let's go. You don't want to miss your train."

After one last look at the studio Papa had set up, Maggie shut the door on that part of her life. The new owner would move in after Olivia and the youngsters left for St. Louis in two days. They had tickets on the Atchinson, Topeka, and Santa Fe Railroad. Maggie had a compartment on the Denver Pacific; in Cheyenne, she would change to the Union Pacific.

With a heavy heart, she headed downstairs. At the first floor, she entered the parlor and found two unexpected guests. Harry and Miranda stood as she entered. The couple wore identical smiles, like two contented cats having just finished off a juicy mouse.

"Maggie," Harry said, dragging Miranda along by the hand. "We wanted you to be the first to know." He shoved the girl's fingers toward Maggie to show off the plain gold band she wore. "We eloped."

For a moment Maggie could only stare at the pair. Both were handsomely attired, Miranda's blond curls touching the collar of her fur coat. Maggie glanced at Olivia, who lifted her eyebrows and shrugged. Recovering her lost voice, Maggie said, "I'm happy for you both. What did your father say?"

Miranda giggled and wrapped both hands tightly around her husband's arm. Harry's coat, obviously new, boasted a large fur collar and lapels. "He was surprised at first, then he offered Harry a job in his company."

This time Maggie's eyebrows shot up. "Congratulations. Then I suppose you'll be staying in Denver."

Harry puffed out his chest like a rooster strutting around a chicken coop full of contented hens. "We'll have to travel a lot. New York, Europe, on business, of course. Miss Olivia tells me you're leaving today."

Maggie nodded, certain her surprise showed on her face. "Yes, I've decided to try California for a while."

Miranda reached into her handbag. "Then I'm glad we caught you. Daddy loved the portraits, and I wanted to pay you for them."

"Don't worry about that." Maggie covered the girl's hand with her own. "Consider them a wedding present. I hope you'll both be happy." She slanted a glance at Harry. He finally had what he'd always wanted—a rich wife who adored him.

A momentary twinge of envy coursed through her. The man Maggie adored had left her for another woman.

"I hope you will excuse us." Olivia stepped forward and pulled on her fleece-lined gloves. "Maggie has a train to catch. We don't want her to miss it, do we?"

After a few brief farewells, Maggie climbed into the waiting cab for her last ride through Denver. The street was muddy with a foot of snow piled along the boardwalks. Tim and Olivia wore solemn expressions, while Sarah wore a mysterious smile. Maggie studied the passing scene.

The driver of the carriage urged his team into a trot as a horse-drawn streetcar lumbered by. Tears threatened as they passed the drugstore, the bank, and the dozen other establishments she'd patronized in the past month. As usual, the Tabor building was bustling with activity as was the Windsor Hotel. Maggie's heart lurched as she watched the elegant hotel fade from her sight.

In a short time Wex would be attending functions at Windsor Castle as well as at Buckingham Palace, while Maggie would be trudging the hills of San Francisco with her camera.

Not wanting to give in to the wave of melancholy, she turned to her aunt. Caught up in her own misery, she hadn't noticed the listlessness of her usually vibrant aunt. Olivia loved Appleton, and his farewell had left her as depressed as Wex's departure had left Maggie. But there was nothing she could do or say to ease their pain.

The clip-clop of the horses slowed. They had arrived at the depot, and Maggie would be on her way within minutes.

They entered the ticket office filled with passengers and the people seeing them off. Ladies in elegant traveling suits mingled with drummers carrying their large suitcases. Maggie was glad Olivia had arranged a private compartment on a new Pullman car. She wasn't in any mood for company on the long journey.

Several men turned and tipped their hats as she passed through the high-ceilinged building. Maggie averted her eyes, but she secretly appreciated their admiring glances. Her new blue wool suit was trimmed with black velvet, matching her cloak. The stylish bonnet brought out the color in her hair and made her feel quite sophisticated and refined—a welcome boost to her sagging morale.

Excitement sizzled in the air, and even Maggie's heartbeat quickened at the prospect of the journey. A new life with new adventures lay ahead. One thing not in her future was a new man. She wasn't about to risk her heart again.

Maggie's low-heeled boots clicked on the marble floor as she approached the ticket counter. Behind the barred window, the harried clerk shoved his wire-rim eyeglasses up his nose. He checked Maggie's reservation and handed her the ticket to Cheyenne.

"Train's on time, ma'am," he said. "Through the rear door to track four."

With a nod, Maggie accepted the ticket and shoved it into her handbag. Tim carried her satchel, and Olivia led the way toward the loading platform. As they passed through the heavy wooden doors a uniformed conductor announced the arrival of the incoming train from the east. Sarah lingered a few feet behind as if looking for someone or something.

"Sarah," Maggie called. "Why are you dallying?"

The girl shoved her hands into her rabbit fur muff. "I

was . . . looking for a vendor to buy you a newspaper to read."

"Don't bother. I have a book if I get bored." A large man tugging a wife and two children stepped between them. When he moved aside, Maggie lost sight of Sarah. Where could she have run off to? Maggie thought, her brow furrowed with concern.

"Come along, Maggie," Olivia ordered. "You'll be boarding soon." The wind through the open platform whipped the feathers on her wide-brimmed hat. She caught it and retied the bow under her chin.

"I can't find Sarah."

"Don't worry, she'll return before the train leaves." Facing her, Olivia began to recite a litany of instructions, most of which she'd already told Maggie a dozen times. Don't speak to strangers, beware of drummers, keep a tight grip on your handbag—on and on. Maggie nodded, but her mind was on her sister. Whatever possessed Sarah to wander away?"

The voice of the conductor broke into her thoughts. "Denver Pacific headed for Cheyenne connecting with parts east and west, now loading on track four."

"That's me," she said, her eyes scanning the crowd. "Tim, go find Sarah. I want to see her before the train pulls out."

Shoving the satchel into Maggie's hands, he took off at a trot in the direction Sarah had gone.

"I wish you were coming home with us, Maggie. Your papa would be very upset if he knew you were going off on your own." Olivia dabbed her eyes with her linen and lace handkerchief.

Maggie forced a smile she didn't feel. "If things don't work out, I'll be on the first train east, I promise." And if I'm having a baby—or two—I'll be home sooner, she added to herself.

"If you need anything, send me a telegram. I'll wire any amount of money you need."

Maggie half listened while her gaze shifted from the left to the right. She caught a glimpse of Sarah's dark head, her long hair swaying under her bonnet. Tim spoke to her, and both turned on their heels and returned to Maggie and Olivia.

After a long round of hugs, kisses, and good-byes, Maggie climbed on board the train. At the rear door, a conductor took her bag and escorted her down the narrow aisle and opened the door to her compartment. The leather seats were much more comfortable than the benches in the coach on her last trip with Wex. Damn, here she was thinking about him again.

The train lurched as the wheels began to turn. She pressed her face to the window for one last glimpse of her family and of Denver. Sarah and Tim stood on the platform, waving furiously, while tears streamed down their faces. But where was her aunt?

Puzzled, Maggie studied the platform. A few feet behind the youngsters, a couple was locked in an intimate embrace. Maggie's mouth gaped. It was her aunt—with Appleton.

She wiped the moisture that formed on the inside of the window from her breath. That scene couldn't be real. Appleton was halfway to England by now. With Wex.

The train swayed, and the locomotive spewed a blast of black smoke. With loud chug-chugs and the sharp shrill of the whistle, the train picked up speed. Her gaze remained on her aunt. It wasn't at all like Miss Olivia Stanton to put on such an exhibit in public—or in private.

Her face still pressed to the dirty window, she watched until she'd left the station and her family behind. Maggie was confused at what she'd seen, and her thoughts spun in a thousand directions at once. She bit her thumbnail, struggling to make sense of the strange turn of events. If Appleton returned to Denver, where was Wex?

The door to the compartment opened and shut with a click. A shadow darkened the small area. With a long sigh, she turned slowly toward the intruder. "This is a private compart—" Her gaze dropped to the shiny black Wellington boots. She swallowed the lump in her throat.

"I'm grateful for your foresight, Mary Margaret. We'll be much more comfortable here than in an open coach."

There was no mistaking that soft voice or the crisp British accent. Words escaped her. Her gaze continued up his black canvas trousers to the Colt at his hips and over the buckskin jacket. This man was as dark and dangerous as the one who'd stepped out of the shadows months ago. He invaded her private space the way he'd done the fateful night that had changed her life forever.

Then he'd walked out and left her for another woman. Whatever made him think he could simply waltz into the compartment and into her life as if nothing had ever happened between them? Well, a lot had happened, and she wasn't sure she wanted him back in her life.

"I've paid for this space. If you don't leave, I'll call the conductor."

With a warm smile, he removed his wide-brimmed Stetson and tossed it on the empty seat across from them. Then as casually as if he'd been invited, he sat beside her and propped his feet on the opposite seat.

"Love, I was afraid you would be upset with me, so I took the precaution of bribing the conductor to make sure we aren't disturbed."

Upset didn't begin to describe Maggie's emotions. Fury roiled up in her. She shoved her hand into her pocket and closed her fingers on the derringer. "I don't know what you're doing here, or what you want, but unless you want a hole in your stomach, you'll leave this compartment immediately."

He folded his arms across his chest and made no attempt to leave. "Mary Margaret, I'm getting a little tired of your threats—sorry, your promises. You've saved my life too many times to do me in now."

Frustrated at her inability to intimidate him, she jerked her hand from her pocket. He was right—again.

"What are you doing here? You should be halfway across the Atlantic by now."

"There's been a change in plans. I'm not returning to England until you agree to go with me."

The train swayed from side to side, and Maggie was afraid she was going to be sick. "I told you I'm not going to be your mistress."

"Calm down, Maggie," he said. "Let me finish. I couldn't leave because I love you. I need you in my life."

"You told me that before, then you told me you were marrying another woman. I won't be your mistress." She met his gaze. His eyes were dark and compelling, completely honest and warm. For the first time Maggie felt as if she were viewing the real man behind the handsome facade.

"This time my intentions are completely honorable. I'm asking you to marry me."

She heard the words, yet she didn't quite comprehend the meaning. "What about Miss Ferguson? She's your betrothed."

He cupped her cold face in his warm hands. "You're the woman I love. I can't marry anyone except you."

Tears burned behind her eyes. It couldn't be true. "But you have responsibilities to your father and your family."

"My first responsibility is to myself and to you. Appleton and I spent the entire trip to New York studying the situation. It appears all my father wanted was money. Well, he can have mine—all of it. Nothing is as important to me, love, as you are."

Her insides fluttered like a flag in a stiff wind. "I don't understand."

He brushed his thumbs across her lips, firing the needs hidden deep in her. It seemed like years rather than weeks since she'd felt his touch.

"All my life I've struggled to win my father's approval, but I never could live up to his expectations. Since I've found you, I realize I don't need his approval. It's time for me to stand up as a man and take responsibility for my own actions and for my own life.

"I love you, I love this country, I love the freedom to make my own way and my own mistakes without interference from my father, his title, or who I am by accident of birth."

"What about Grace?"

"I've written her a letter of apology and enclosed an expensive piece of jewelry. That should satisfy my obligation to a woman I've never met."

Maggie's gaze dropped to his mouth, full and firm, waiting for her kisses. "What about your father's indebtedness to Mr. Ferguson?"

"Appleton arranged a courier from his New York associate's office to go to London and handle matters until he returns to England. I'll pay off all my father's debts and give him a job managing some of the estates, with Appleton overseeing it, of course. That was another problem. Appleton wouldn't return without your aunt."

"My aunt?"

"He's determined to marry her."

"They deserve to be happy," she said.

His fingers dropped to her shoulders. "What about us, Maggie? Don't we deserve to be happy?"

"It's too late. I'm going to California."

"You aren't going anywhere without me. We'll get married as soon as we locate a minister or a priest."

"I'm not going to marry you." She shoved against his chest to no avail. "After the hell you put me through, telling me you had to marry another woman and leaving me, you think you can simply stroll in and announce that I have to marry you?"

Ignoring her protests, he wrapped his arms around her and pulled her hard against his chest. "I don't care if you don't marry me. But our children will wonder why we have different names."

"Children?" Maggie gasped. Her stomach churned and revolted. He didn't know, he couldn't know. He'd come to her because he wanted her. "Do you mean what you said? You love me and want to marry me?"

"More than I'd ever dreamed I could love a woman." He kissed her gently, brushing his lips across hers. "You've given me love, love and hope that I can be the man you want, the man you need."

Being angry with him was useless. "Then I suppose I'd better marry you. Who else can keep you out of trouble?"

He laughed and cradled her against his chest. "And who else could chase away the shadows from my heart and welcome me into the sunshine of love?"

"I do love you, Wex, and I love Lord Geoffrey, too."

His lips hovered above hers. "Not bad for a lily-livered Brit, wouldn't you say?"

Looping her hands around his neck, she fitted her body to his. "Not bad at all."

*If you enjoyed this book, take advantage
of this special offer. Subscribe now and...*

Get a Historical

No Obligation

If you enjoy reading the very best in historical romantic fiction...romances that set back the hands of time to those bygone days with strong virile heros and passionate heroines ...then you'll want to subscribe to the True Value Historical Romance Home Subscription Service. Now that you have read one of the best historical romances around today, we're sure you'll want more of the same fiery passion, intimate romance and historical settings that set these books apart from all others.

Each month the editors of True Value select the four *very best* novels from America's leading publishers of romantic fiction. We have made arrangements for you to preview them in your home *Free* for 10 days. And with the first four books you

receive, we'll send you a FREE book as our introductory gift. No Obligation!

FREE HOME DELIVERY

We will send you the four best and newest historical romances as soon as they are published to preview FREE for 10 days (in many cases you may even get them before they arrive in the book stores). If for any reason you decide not to keep them, just return them and owe nothing. But if you like them as much as we think you will, you'll pay just $4.00 each and save at *least* $.50 each off the cover price. (Your savings are *guaranteed* to be at least $2.00 each month.) There is NO postage and handling—or other hidden charges. There are no minimum number of books to buy and you may cancel at any time.

FREE
Romance
(a $4.50 value)

Send in the Coupon Below

To get your FREE historical romance and start saving, fill out the coupon below and mail it today. As soon as we receive it we'll send you your FREE Book along with your first month's selections.

Mail To: **True Value Home Subscription Services, Inc. P.O. Box 5235**
120 Brighton Road, Clifton, New Jersey 07015-5235

YES! I want to start previewing the very best historical romances being published today. Send me my FREE book along with the first month's selections. I understand that I may look them over FREE for 10 days. If I'm not absolutely delighted I may return them and owe nothing. Otherwise I will pay the low price of just $4.00 each, a total $16.00 (at *least* an $18.00 value) and save at least $2.00. Then each month I will receive four brand new novels to preview as soon as they are published for the same low price. I can always return a shipment and I may cancel this subscription at any time with no obligation to buy even a single book. In any event the FREE book is mine to keep regardless.

Name _____

Street Address _____ Apt. No _____

City _____ State _____ Zip Code _____

Telephone _____

Signature _____
(if under 18 parent or guardian must sign)

Terms and prices subject to change. Orders subject
to acceptance by True Value Home Subscription
Services Inc.   0024-7